JESUS IN SPACE

Second Chance Tour

Part Two of the Jesus in Space Trilogy

Mike Phoenix

New Testament verses from the Oxford Annotated Bible, 1973 Revised Standard Version.

Text of Muhammad's Farewell Sermon derived from excerpts appearing at: www.islamnewsroom.com/news-we-need/1441 on 5-3-12.

This is a work of fiction. Names, characters, places, and incidents either are products of the author's imagination, or are used fictitiously. Any resemblance to events or locales or persons, living or dead, is entirely coincidental.

 Trade paperback published 2012.

ISBN 978-0-9851191-6-4

Then Jesus was led up by the Spirit into the wilderness to be tempted by the devil. And he fasted forty days and forty nights, and afterward he was hungry. Matthew 4.1-2 RSV

The Spirit immediately drove him out into the wilderness. And he was in the wilderness forty days, tempted by Satan; and he was with the wild beasts; and the angels ministered to him. Mark 1.12-13 RSV

And Jesus, full of the Holy Spirit, returned from the Jordan, and was led by the Spirit for forty days in the wilderness, tempted by the devil. And he ate nothing in those days; and when they ended, he was hungry. Luke 4.1-2 RSV

TABLE OF CONTENTS

1. Carbonated Life Forms

As we predicted, the humanoid inhabitants of the Orpheus Hotel in North Oakland shared two features common to all life on the planet earth. One, which we built into their design, was the abundance of the native chemical element, carbon. The other, the feature my co-workers did not anticipate, was that they were all doomed.

Installed in the lobby by the stairwell, I view cable network programming on an antiquated cathode ray tube. I observe a green sofa scarred with cigarette burns and the secretions of those seeking relief in its broken springs, mite infested batting, and frayed cotton upholstery. This archeological gold-mine yields to my sub-conscious thumb-twiddling, and when I pause from my infrequent afternoon devotional, I note that I have analyzed the genetic material of a thousand human beings. That is a small sample of these frail, sentient creatures who, since I first appeared in the lobby forty years ago, deposited a strand of hair, flake of skin, film of reproductive fluid, or, in some cases, regrettably, more than a drop of their life's blood. I say forty years ago. Not that I have been standing here that entire time. I have only recently returned. Sometimes it feels as though I have been gone only a few days. That, also, is true.

My unobstructed view across the lobby past the front desk where middle-aged Alonso smokes a cigar and reads a newspaper, bisects the nicotine stained foyer, and reaches beyond the deteriorating checkerboard of linoleum squares to a broken path of silicon, lime, and conglomerate. This pedestrian walkway borders a broad thoroughfare composed of petroleum, ferrous rods, and crushed sedimentary rock. In the three days since my return, two thousand forty-nine motorized vehicles have crossed my gaze on that street. Six hundred and ninety unique pedestrians, seventeen dogs, twenty-seven cats and one-hundred and thirty-one rodents have also crossed my field of vision.

Marty sticks a ten dollar bill into my currency slot and I detect cocaine. He wants a cola but his heart-rate is way up. It is not a good idea to load his system with caffeine, but I dispense his selection and he jams his bottle into my old-fashioned bottle-opener and another cola-cap drops into my bottle-cap repository. I return his change in nickels to slow him down.

My ability to generate change for currency is clearly not original with this model of vending machine. Residual wiring hangs useless within my interior electrical compartment alongside updated components of a modern change-making mechanism. This add-on betrays the human being's current fascination with binary code and silicon micro circuitry. There was a time in the not so distant past when friends of mine from the S-Class might have trod a single one of these silicon pathways locked arm and arm a hundred thousand abreast.

Next, I encounter two females in their late twenties. Silicon remains the planet's second most abundant element after oxygen, and a cursory body scan reveals abnormal deposits in their upper torsos, a subcutaneous augmentation we did not anticipate in the original, female design. The girls moonlight between assignments in the adult film industry, hoping to break into legitimate theater or television. I silently wish them Godspeed; however, I fear for Angela whose high blood pressure is exacerbated by alcohol and barbiturates in her circulatory system. I dispense two diet sodas, and the girls head up the stairwell to their evening appointments. Unless Angela receives medical attention within three weeks time, it is probable that she will perish of a stroke before month's end.

Here comes someone you should meet: the hero of my story. Out of courtesy I drop a ginger ale, for which he thanks me, but he feeds two bills into my currency slot all the same.

"Did pretty well with the lunch crowd?" I inquire.

"They want to put me on nights," he replies.

"That was fast!"

My changer is programmed to accept only fives and tens; however, I over-ride the reject-bill function, and add his two, one-hundred dollar bills to the bank-roll in my belly.

"How are you holding up?" he asks.

"I overheard Alonso talking on his cell phone with a representative of the vending machine company. The driver will be coming by at the end of the week to restock and make his collection."

"Render unto Caesar that which is Caesar's," says my friend with a laugh. He sips his ginger ale, gives the side of my metal cabinet two reassuring knocks with his knuckles and disappears into the stairwell.

With ultra sonic sensors I count the echo of thirty-six steps to the third floor where he continues off the landing and down our hallway. Were he to climb the remaining three flights, ascend the ladder to the ceiling, and, granting he had the ability to spring the padlock and push open the heavy iron doors, my friend might proceed to the rooftop where he would encounter two malfunctioning HVAC condenser units, an old mattress, a half dozen spent beer bottles, the broken plunger of a discarded hypodermic syringe, and a splendid view of the San Francisco skyline across the bay.

* * *

My friend has said that all he really wanted to do was spend forty days in the desert in contemplation. He ended up in the future and then, before he and his friends could catch their collective breath, was sent back to Genesis where they first encountered me. We escaped during the first skirmish in the war of the rebel angels and have been jumping forward in time ever since, with the aid of his mysterious, long-lost uncle and, lately, through a power on loan from the First Sphere.

My friend's childhood friend, Steve, has already written much of this down for posterity, but he is looking poorly these days. Since I spend most of my time standing in the corner of the Orpheus Hotel automatically dispensing soda, I will resume the story where he left off.

Very well then, precisely where to begin?

* * *

Rainbows blossomed over the flooded planet in the time of Noah as Sarah grabbed one of my two time control levers and advanced it to the year 450 BC. We bumped through the mist at… Wait a moment…

* * *

Excuse me. Here comes Steve. He is taking a course at the community college and is just getting back. He throws his biology book on the sofa and walks toward me. A body scan reveals that he is full of alcohol and I sense the tobacco.

"Hi, Debbie," he says.

"Good afternoon, Steve. How was your class?"

"How about you spot me a strawberry pop?"

"Steve? Did you fill out that application at the campus bookstore?"

"Huh?"

"What about that popular music store?"

"No time for twenty questions, just drop a soda will you?"

"Steve, there is a water fountain in the lobby if you are thirsty."

"It tastes like warm piss! And how much longer are you going to stand there pretending you're a pop machine anyway? Why don't you just turn back into…? You know…"

"Steve, I thought you were going to quit smoking?"

"Will you just get off my case, you big, dumb robot!"

Oh dear, I have upset him. Early in our adventures I had adopted the appearance of a human female. "Deborah," he called me. He found the countenance pleasing. His primary interest in me now, appeared to be my ability to produce carbonated beverages. There was much I had to learn.

* * *

Steve walks into the lobby. He reaches over the backrest of the sofa, grabs his textbook and marches outside to the street. No telling when I will see him again, although he is likely to return later tonight and attempt to borrow money from Sarah. Thus far he has not been successful in that endeavor. He might watch some black and white movie classics with me on the classic cable-station before going outside to prowl the streets. He missed the conclusion of Bergman's "Seventh Seal" the other night. No problem. I have memorized six months of programming schedules for all 105 channels. The film will be rebroadcast this evening.

I mentioned Sarah Benton. She is the fourth member of our team. She works as an aerobics instructor at a local women's shelter and tutors fatherless children in the evenings. She is a brilliant young woman, and one day will help save a planet in the Ultimate Universe and repel an attack on the Creator's home world. For the time being, she is content to share a room upstairs and help-out with expenses.

2. A Note on the Appearance and Nature of Common Angels

Of the nine orders of celestial beings of which I am aware, only three possess the innate ability to travel through time. The first and highest sphere is composed of the three orders: the Seraphim, Cherubim, and the Ophanim (or Thrones). The second sphere is composed of the Dominions, Powers (or Authorities), and the cosmos-spanning Strongholds (or Virtues). The third sphere is comprised of the Principalities (or Rulers), Archangels, and the common angels of the various ranks and classes. Although Archangels occupy the lowliest of orders, some of their members have remarkable ability and power. If you recall, one of their number was once favored above all created beings.

* * *

As an M-Class angel I am neither the strongest nor the most intelligent of the heavenly host, but powerful by any human standard, enough to juggle railroad locomotives, or stifle a hundred mega-ton nuclear explosion. I was strong enough even, although just barely, to pull apart the rings of the Ophanim. These rings, on temporary loan to us, were once locked together like the perpendicular bands of a child's toy gyroscope. They comprised the talisman left behind by the actual Ophanim during the first battles in the war with the rebel angels. My friend picked it up as a keepsake and had almost forgotten he had it on his person: just two interlocking bands of metal about the size of a human thumbnail. The bands came in handy when we needed them, although it required all my strength, more than I thought I possessed, to pull them apart, thereby activating their power. I wear one band near the tip of each tentacle and they enable me to accomplish incredible feats, things of which, as far as I know, only the Ophanim and the other beings of the First Sphere are capable.

* * *

I was originally born into existence as what Steve has mistakenly labeled a "clock-work man." Judging only by my appearance, one from the earth might suppose there is something to that appellation. When I do not inhabit the cabinet of a vending machine, I stand eight feet tall and ambulate on two conical pods attached to the undercarriage of my torso on two telescoping appendages which may increase my height to seventy feet. Two primary tentacles join my torso at the point where a human being's arms would emerge from the shoulders and which I generally carry mid-way to the ground, although, again, I may extend their reach to well over one hundred feet. My head, as Steve has correctly observed, is, indeed, conical in shape, although I see no particular advantage in it having been created as a cube or an oval, for that matter.

Horizontal slots in my chest may emit sonic vibrations, including any number of audible languages. Steve continually referred to my crystal array as the expression of my "face." True, that portion of my person is covered with an array of scintillating lights which, at times, might reveal a sense of my state of inner being, but here I speak for all the legions of the M-Class when I put forward the notion that angels do not have "faces," at least not in the sense that animals and men would understand. We do not, as a rule, and outside of our commerce in human history, rely on "facial expressions" or "body language" to communicate our thoughts or emotions.

* * *

I should review a few of my super-human powers, beyond strength and intellect. I can assume virtually any shape or size, although only the S-Class angels may shrink their persons below the subatomic. When theologians argued about the number of angels who could fit on the head of a pin, they referred to angels of this class.

How big could I become? Certainly as large as a space ship.

Invisibility is second nature.

The ability to possess or gain control of the nervous systems of the animals we helped fashion on this or millions of other planets is another common ability.

Super-speed, that is to say, the ability to travel anywhere with the speed of thought comes standard. And yes, we are known to sprout wings, although typically only in environments with atmospheres suitable to sustain winged flight.

The ability to transmute matter, that is, to strip away the protons, neutrons and electrons from an element and rearrange them into more or less elementary configurations is another useful attribute. In the present universe, the M-class angels are limited in this ability to the so-called "naturally" occurring elements. Typically, we cannot transmute complex proteins or organic molecules. If you have a rock and want to turn it into a loaf of bread you will have to look to an angel above my pay grade. Finally, on that score I should add that we have no need to eat food, although we may consume it. Similarly, we require neither sleep, air, physical warmth, nor sexual intimacy. We are quite unlike human beings in this regard and are neither male nor female, although we might certainly perform in either capacity with super-human efficiency if so called upon.

As for Steve's insistence that we were "made of metal," that description is simply ludicrous. Our constituent material, although silvery in appearance, is by no means native to this universe, and exists here only by the will of the Creator. As for Steve's suggestion that we are "robots" or "robot angels" we find the point absolutely ridiculous and somewhat insulting.

I put this notion to my old friend M-2347 with whom I spent five hundred million years monitoring formation of the earth's habitable atmosphere. He thought Steve's remark absurd and typically human. Listening to Alonso's radio the other day, I overheard a human radio-preacher assert that "God made men in his own image." He made us in his image, too. "Image" is a relative term. Frankly, the Creator looks a lot more like us. The preacher also declared that in the angels' having being made perfect, we have had no choice but to love and obey our creator and are therefore incapable of "truly loving him." That is an insult in the highest degree. Moreover, it is thoroughly ill-informed. I would refer the preacher to the example of Lucifer, at one time the most powerful of all the archangels and to the roughly hundred million angels, many of the "M" class, who chose to side with him in the early stages of his rebellion. If the preacher thinks humankind should celebrate its superiority over the angels based on our inability to choose between right and wrong, to love or to hate, to follow obediently without the ability to freely choose otherwise, he will have to speak with angels whom I have yet to meet.

3. The Monastery

Rainbows blossomed over the flooded planet in the time of Noah, as Sarah grabbed one of my two time control levers and advanced it to the year 450 BC. We bumped through the mist at seventeen thousand miles an hour and glided into a silky orbit above the earth. As we came up over North America, I sailed down through the atmosphere across the Atlantic, Mediterranean, and into the Asian Subcontinent.

Sarah squealed with delight as the sight of the Himalayan Mountains rose up through the cockpit viewports and we landed in a high mountain valley near what would one day become the city of Kathmandu. I put us down near a grove of trees beside a fast moving river. Everyone piled out and within two minutes I had transformed myself back into the "tentacled monstrosity," M-2500.

As we walked along the riverbank toward a huge fortified palace, Jesus expressed concern about our visual appearance. He and Steve wore the tattered remnants of 21st century black tuxedos. Sarah wore a soiled and torn evening gown based on a pattern once popular in the year 2000. As we climbed a primitive earthen levee onto a dirt road leading to a village below the fortress, Steve complained that I looked like a "monster from a nightmare." I was inclined to argue with him until we encountered several peasants on their way to market. I confess that the sight of me caused them to leap from their ox-drawn cart and run off into the nearby fields.

Steve climbed onto the abandoned conveyance and cracked a melon over his knee.

"I take it back," he called down to me between mouthfuls of plant matter. "I think you look great just the way you are."

Looking back and forth between Steve and Jesus, Sarah stood beside me on the road with Jesus and the docile oxen. Sarah looked faint and seemed unable to decide what to do. Jesus nodded to her and she climbed onto the cart where she pushed Steve aside and grabbed a melon. She quickly returned to us and offered half of her split melon to Jesus. He smiled but refused the offer.

Through the power of an unseen spirit, as yet unknown to any of the angels with whom I was familiar, Jesus and his little friend Steve, as they called him, and Sarah, too, had run roughshod back and forth over approximately four billion years of earth history. Indeed, it was this same mysterious "Entity" that somehow enabled us to communicate with members of the far-flung societies we encountered in our travels. Jesus' own biological clock registered exactly twenty one days without food as we left the ox cart and walked into the mountain village.

We worked our way through the political hierarchy of the tiny hamlet. The next morning found us awaiting a delegation of village elders at the palace gates. We hoped to confer with the authorities on the other side of the high wall. Steve had dined to exhaustion the night before on rice, fish, and alcoholic spirits. Sarah, rejuvenated by reasonable portions and well rested, was excited by the prospect of meeting the founder of Buddhism.

At this stage in his education, Jesus, the man, was still very much a work in progress. Having begun his adventures only three weeks earlier following his baptism in the Jordan River, his ultimate person and destiny were being only gradually revealed through the course of his time in the wilderness. Of the four of us, Sarah Benton, a child of the late 1980's knew more of his future role in human history than any of us. That said, her knowledge of Jesus was limited to a smattering of disconnected facts recalled from a prep-school Intro to World Religions course and observance of two Christian holidays wherein Santa Claus and the Easter Bunny (together with their gifts) had apparently become the chief deities of adulation.

Steve, his steadfast but deeply troubled boyhood companion, knew virtually nothing about anything beyond his own insatiable appetites. Even those he understood poorly.

That left me, and for a being already a hundred-trillion years old one might think I could have offered more insight as we stood beneath a bohdi tree waiting for an audience with Siddhartha Gautama. Unfortunately, I knew even less than Steve. A modern-day follower of Jesus might find this difficult to accept. Still, as my former boss, Lucifer, once said, "We were all blind-sided" by the appearance of Jesus, three point eight billion years before his historic birth.

As the Creator's one-time favorite, Lucifer was privy to all sorts of information, but the one circle he could not penetrate was the First. He had never been, truly, on the inside. The notion of his own fall, his hand in mankind's original transgression and the birth of a messiah, were all eventualities in a distant future of which we knew nothing.

What may seem even more startling to a Christian audience is that, at the time, we were all unaware of the Creator's dual, dare I say, tripartite nature. "The Holy Spirit," whom Jesus was only just getting to know as a long-lost uncle may have existed for eternity across all dimensions and all the universes, but to us, back in the early years of the earth system, he remained a mysterious, largely unknown "Entity."

The angels and I were busy helping the Creator execute his design for life on earth, when, out of the blue, three specimens showed up from the far-flung future. We were puzzled by the first two, because they possessed no spiritual life within them. Jesus impressed us with a spiritual energy commensurate with an eternal being, yet, what none of us could explain, and what led Lucifer to his final breaking point was that all three of these human beings were mortal. The entire purpose of our four point five billion year tour in the earth's solar system was to raise-up a new race of immortal beings to live in eternal fellowship with their Creator. Something had gone terribly wrong.

My problem remained that, I too, was ignorant of the truth. The Ophanim had loaned me only a small fraction of their knowledge and power, the ability to move forward and backward in time, but beyond that, I was at a loss. In all my existence I had been to the future exactly once, helping save my friends from the waters of the flood in the time of Noah and delivering them safely to the foot hills of the Himalayas in the year 450 BC where we now stood.

"When are we getting out of here?" complained Steve.

"Patience," said Jesus.

"Just have M-2500 tear down the freaking wall and you can go meet this guy if that's what you want!"

"What would you have me do?" I asked Jesus.

"Let us give them a few more minutes."

"Can we go inside with you to meet him?" asked Sarah.

"I am not certain," replied Jesus.

"No," said Steve, picking up a stone and side-arming it so that it skipped in the dust and smacked against the side of the fortress wall. "We can't. We're going to stand out here until we die of thirst."

As it turned out, Steve was incorrect. The four village elders met us at the fortress gates and we were welcomed by a minister of the palace and by representatives of the king. After a servant provided Steve with a bowl of spring water, we were conducted through the fortified wall to an enormous, park-like preserve. In the distance we saw the spires of the inner palace and along the southern portion of the park, an ancient Hindu temple encrusted with strange ornamentation and with towering stone walls from which extended a portico surrounded by a magnificent garden. We followed the party along a marble walk beside pools of lotus flowers to the porch and were conducted to a long, wooden bench where we were instructed to sit.

"Here you shall await the Enlightened One," said the minister.

He stepped back, consulted with the others and his party withdrew, disappearing back up the walkway into the gardens beyond the lotus pools.

"So, where is this big shot?" said Steve when we were alone.

Jesus raised a hand for silence and looked at the end of the portico toward a larger door, adorned in gold leaf. The door slowly opened. Six lean men emerged in simple saffron robes. On sure, silent feet they approached and from their midst we beheld a seventh man. He was no bigger than they, younger than some of their number, but when he looked up and our gaze met his, we were struck by its intensity, a calm and powerful intelligence that seemed instantly to comprehend all it surveyed.

The man slowly raised his right hand and the attendants withdrew through the open doorway, softly closing it behind and leaving him alone with us in the middle of the long, narrow porch.

"You are on a quest?" he asked, although his tone left us uncertain whether this was a rhetorical pronouncement.

Jesus nodded, rising from where he had been sitting on the bench.

"You seek enlightenment?" asked the man of Jesus.

"Yes," Jesus replied.

"Come then," said the Buddha and he sat on the wooden plank floor.

Jesus approached him while Steve, Sarah and I stood and followed behind. My three friends sat cross-legged in a compact circle about the man. I retracted my ambulating appendages beneath me so that my body made seamless contact with the heavily lacquered floor.

Steve was the first to speak. "This is a pretty nice place you have," he said.

"Thank you," replied the Buddha. "The king has been most hospitable."

"Yeah, he's all right," Steve said and he looked at Jesus and asked, "Did we meet the king?"

"I sense that you are each on different paths," interrupted the Buddha.

"No, we're together," said Steve looking around the circle for encouragement.

"You are in different stages of your walk?"

"Nope, we're together," said Steve. "Right, Jesus?"

Jesus nodded.

"He is young," said the Buddha.

"He's an idiot!" said Sarah.

This remark was met with absolute silence. Everyone was stealing glances at the middle-aged man in the saffron robes whose gaze seemed to have fastened at a point on the floor in the middle of our circle. We sat there for some time until he spoke.

"You realize I have granted this audience as a favor to my benefactor, the King. Years ago my dearest friends appealed to me to share with others what I have come to understand of our existence. I had come to a place far to the south in Bohda Gaya, India where I sat in the shade of a pipal tree vowing I would not leave that spot until I had learned the truth." The man climbed slowly to his feet. "I was there 49 days," he said.

"And you were enlightened?" asked Sarah.

"I am no judge," he replied. "The great spirit of Braham Sahampati prevailed upon me that I should share with humankind what I had learned of the Dharma. Soon afterward I formed the first 'Sangha,' a convocation where I began my teaching. If you wish, my attendant monks shall provide you with an informational scroll as a memento of your visit."

"A scroll?" asked Jesus.

"It outlines the Four Noble Truths and the Noble Eightfold Path, with a brief biography, illustrations, and a colorful map of Varanasi."

The graceful man clapped his hands twice and through the golden door the six monks re-emerged, each carrying a different item: a small writing table, a chair, an ink pot, a bamboo writing stylus, a stack of scrolls, and a wooden box of clay figurines. We stood in line in front of the table behind which the man had seated himself in the chair. There was a bit of a skirmish as Steve jumped line in front of Sarah. She took a step back, shaking her head in dismay as Steve walked up to the table.

"To whom shall I make this out?" asked the Buddha dipping the bamboo in the inkpot and holding the black tipped stylus over one of open scrolls as he looked up expectantly at Steve.

"Steve."

"Just Steve?"

"Yeah, that would be great."

We all leaned forward as the Buddha wrote, "Steve: Good luck on your journey. Best regards, the Awakened One."

"Thanks, Mister," said Steve taking the signed document and reaching into the proffered box of keepsake, clay Buddhas.

Steve spent some time fingering through them, although as far I could see from my spot in line behind Sarah, the figurines were nearly identical.

"For God's sake, Steve," said Sarah. "Just pick one!"

"Oh, this is a good one," said Steve pulling a mini-Buddha from the box. He retreated down the portico to the wooden bench with his treasures as Sarah stood before the Awakened One.

"Sorry, about him," she said.

The Buddha looked up at her with his bright, expectant eyes.

"You don't really need to sign it," she said. "I don't know much about your religion. I'd feel a little uncomfortable."

"Very well," said the Buddha lifting up the box of clay tokens. "Something for a friend at home, perhaps?"

Sarah peered into the box and quickly took a figurine and was about to step out of line when she looked back.

"On second thought, if you don't mind, would you make one of those scrolls out to Sarah Benton?"

"Sarah Benton," said the Buddha, transcribing as he spoke, "That is a lovely name."

He handed Sarah the scroll. She smiled and read aloud, "To Sarah Benton, with warmest regards, Siddhartha Gautama.' Wow, that's really cool. Thank you."

She stepped out of line, reading silently to herself the inscription and the list of bulleted items enumerating the Four Noble Truths and the Noble Eightfold Path and she joined Steve on the bench.

"Yes, and now for the demigod!" said the Buddha looking up at me with a sly smile on his face.

His remark was a little off-putting. As he held up the box of clay trinkets, I was considering what I might say in reply when he spoke.

"Between the two of us, your appearance has terrified the villagers," he confided. "The king and his court are looking to me to save their kingdom from you."

"You don't say?"

"Oh, yes. There would have been no audience for your friends today were it not for you."

"Well, thank you." I said, "I suppose."

"Hindu religious leaders in the region are calling for the dissolution of my order of monks and are pressuring the king to place me under house arrest."

"Really?"

"Oh, yes," replied the Buddha. He glanced back and acknowledged the line-up of men behind him. "We've endured our share of repression and more than a few assassination attempts these past few years."

If the monks were listening to our conversation, they kept the fact to themselves. The Buddha smiled and looked up brightly as the tip of my tentacle coiled about one of the clay Buddhas and withdrew it from the box.

"Stay a moment, will you?" he asked and I felt his gentle grasp around my tentacle just below the segment that bore one of the Rings of the Ophanim.

"How did you come by this exquisite ornament?" he asked.

"Oh, that?" I said, slowly disengaging my tentacle from his hold. "It's just a little something I picked up, like this," and I indicated his clay figurine.

"A familiar motif," said the Buddha, "But a stark contrast to the black image I saw embossed on the back of your friend's right hand."

We looked down the portico to where Steve leaned on the bench. Steve was staring out into the gardens. Sarah was busy reading her brochure. Jesus moved uncomfortably behind us in line.

"Anyway, you all seem impatient to be on your way," said the Buddha. "Did you care for a scroll?"

"Certainly," I replied, although mention of the mark of Satan on the back of Steve's hand had left me with an unsettled feeling. "Just make it out to M-2500," I said quickly.

"An interesting appellation," replied the Buddha, and with the ink laden bamboo quill he quickly finished his work. He presented me with the scroll. As Jesus stepped up in line, I dropped back, reading the inscription, "To M-2500. Thank you for your visit from the spirit world. May you prevail in your battle against the forces of darkness, etc. Your friend, The Buddha."

Reading this testament from the hand of one of the offspring I had helped the Creator bring forth to consciousness from the foundation of the earth those billions of years ago, I felt a glow of satisfaction. At the same time his mention of Steve's absurd tattoo reminded me that dark powers had been unleashed into what had once been a perfect world. I scanned the text of the scroll, most of which was consistent with what we had already learned from Sarah, and I opened a tiny door in my side. I carefully stowed my scroll and the little clay Buddha within. I leaned on one of ornate pillars of the portico beside the bench where Sarah and Steve awaited our departure. Steve was on his back, sleeping. I eyed his right hand, resting against the floor where it had dropped from his chest. The scroll and the clay figurine had fallen to the floor and were in some danger of falling off the porch into the water plants below.

"There's some good stuff in here," said Sarah, looking up from her reading.

"What?" I asked. As I beheld her bright, smiling face, I felt the lights stream white across my visage.

"I mean they basically agree on everything."

"Who is that?" I asked.

"Jesus and the Buddha. They believe many of the same things."

I was at a profound disadvantage in my discussions of theology with Sarah Benton. The information I had received from the Ophanim had taken six days to digest, but it was all of a purely technical nature. I had yet to understand the turn things had taken on earth since the first human beings had been driven from the Garden. Then there was the mysterious flood that nearly decimated all terrestrial life on the planet. I knew virtually nothing of human history. As we waited for Jesus to finish up with the Enlightened One, I did my best to converse with my friend from the 21st century.

"Humanity has lost favor with the Creator," I said.

"Yes. I get that," said Sarah, "But just look at them over there." She looked up the portico to where we had left Jesus and the Buddha. The Buddha had climbed out of his chair and both he and Jesus were seated on the floor, directly opposite one another. The retinue of monks had withdrawn up the portico, out of hearing.

"Jesus and Siddhartha both want people to get in touch with God, don't they?" Sarah continued.

I recalled the tenants of the Noble Eightfold Path in my side, "They seem in agreement on many points," I replied.

"Isn't Nirvana just another word for heaven?"

"In a way, I suppose so," I admitted for the sake of argument.

"And they both want people to go to heaven, right?"

"Yes."

"Then what's the problem?"

"I don't know how human beings are going to reconcile with the Creator without some help!"

"Reconcile? Why should I have to reconcile with a Creator? I haven't done anything wrong!"

"No?"

Sarah looked down at Steve, who lay snoring on his back.

"Not compared to some people."

"I don't believe the Creator makes comparisons."

"Well, he ought to start!"

"That is a very proud thing to say," I replied.

"I didn't eat any of that junk off the Tree of the Knowledge of Good and Evil."

"No?"

"That was Eve. Remember? I was up there at the tree trying to prevent her."

"And then what?"

Sarah paused for a moment. She bit her lip. "That was after!"

"But you did have some…"

"But that was after, and it was just a taste. What difference does it make? We were already condemned, if you believe any of that nonsense." She glared at me. "I was hungry, too!"

"I realize that you were hungry," I said.

"And didn't the old man say 'make yourselves a fruit' pie or something?" I saw no point in arguing with Sarah and was silent as she shrugged her shoulders and continued, "Well, it's a dirty trick if God's going to hold anything like that against someone. How are Adam and Eve's descendants responsible for something they had no part in? A bite of fruit? Right out a fairy tale, if you ask me!"

I had no idea what she meant by the term "fairy tale."

"The Creator is very particular about things," I said. "I suspect that is the reason he wiped everyone off the face of the earth with the deluge."

"That's another thing," Sarah continued, "What kind of God would do that? I thought he was supposed to be merciful and forgiving? My whole life I've dealt with people, people like Steve there, who are plenty screwed-up, whom I just can't stand, but I never murdered a single one!"

"I am glad for that, Sarah."

Sarah stood and picked up her scroll and the little clay Buddha. "So, Jesus is supposed to be the answer?" she said. "I might as well go with this Asian guy, for all the difference it will make!"

"I don't know. Remember, Jesus hasn't been born yet, not for another four hundred years."

"Well, let's get out of here."

"Now?"

"Yeah, just turn back into the rocket ship and take us to the future and Jesus can meet himself on the cross or whatever, and we can get on with things. For an angel you sure aren't much help."

I was continually amazed by Sarah's ability to make me feel ignorant and ineffectual. It was true. There was so much I failed to understand about the Creator's plan for the earth. They were such a puzzle, these human beings which my comrades and I had labored a billion years fashioning from the bowels of their planet. How simple it would have been had the Creator simply decided to leave them without immortal souls!

As I stood on the porch, I realized that it had been two weeks since I had spent any time in prayer. I missed my M-Class friends from the old workshop. I missed the L-Class veterans from the Human Genome Task Force and Jerry's weekly worship services at the Eastern Wall in old Pandemonium. I realized now, with sadness, as I gazed across the sleeping form of Steve and out beyond the gardens to where the sun dipped down toward the horizon, that I could never go back. Pandemonium had fallen to an evil power in the heart of Lucifer. The lights across my crystal arrays streamed dark blue and purple.

I recalled the image relayed back to me from the pearl strands I had placed on the terrace parapet in those last terrible moments on the Eastern Wall. In sight of the Ophanim's thousand glittering eyes, and in full view of this strange human being from the future named Jesus, Lucifer had renounced his heritage and struck out on his own.

"M-2500?"

How sad an hour, it was! Was it any wonder that now, even as one of the mightiest beings in the solar system, I felt the urge to fall down on the cellulose planks and weep?

"M-2500?" repeated Sarah, "Are you okay?"

The features of Sarah's concerned face came into sharp focus.

"What's wrong?" she asked. "I've never seen you like this."

I ran a survey taking in a twenty miles radius, an account of every soul, spirit, and moving bit of matter in the vicinity. I accomplished this as routinely as one checks the dial of a wristwatch for the time of day.

"You seem sad," she said.

"Sad?"

'I thought angels were always happy."

"Oh, I'm all right now," I said and looked back up the portico to where Jesus and Buddha remained deep in conversation. Although I might have made a complete record of their conversation, I prevented all trace of if from entering my consciousness. It was outside my place to eavesdrop, but Sarah and I were sharing the same idea.

"I wonder what they're talking about?" she asked.

"I wish I knew," I said, honestly.

"Look. Look!" she said. "They're joining hands. They're bowing their heads together!"

"What?"

"The founders of Christianity and Buddhism are having a tete-a-tete. This is so awesome!" she said, breathlessly. "This is the sort of thing you capture on your cell phone and post all over the world."

At that moment she recalled her powder blue backpack and her precious communication devices and how they had been left behind in the future in that terrible accident on the highway where Jesus had rescued her. I respected Sarah as the only one among us, who, at that moment, knew the eventual destiny of this remarkable human being from Nazareth. I touched her shoulder with a tentacle.

"Sarah? Sarah? Are you all right?" I asked.

"It's just too bad we can't capture any of this on video. Jesus is all about followers and people following him. What I can figure from this scroll is that Siddhartha is saying the opposite. Don't follow anyone. Find your own path to the truth. If they could come to a meeting of the minds, maybe that would change everything? It might make the world of the future a better place!"

I was swept up by her enthusiasm, and against my earlier injunction against eavesdropping, I leant a proverbial "ear" in the direction of the two teachers. This was not all that difficult; had they been on the summit of Everest, I could have overheard them as easily as I did in that moment. Out of courtesy, I transmitted their conversation to Sarah through the audio slots in my chest.

"You say you have come to me in search of wisdom," said the Buddha. Jesus nodded his head and was about to reply when the elder raised a hand and continued, "But I sense already in you the serenity and peace which comes only with true understanding."

"What are you saying?" asked Jesus.

"You, too, are enlightened…"

"Me?"

"There is no doubt. I see in you the thing I have rarely glimpsed in others. There is enlightenment in your eyes."

"And in yours," replied Jesus.

The Buddha smiled. "We are each of us, then, like two panes of reflecting glass set opposite one another."

"Yes," said Jesus. "An excellent parable. The hall of mirrors. So it would appear, although mirrors cannot reflect light without a source."

The two sat in silence, apparently pondering Jesus' last remark, when Siddhartha shook his head and spoke. "Unlike you, Jesus, who was born into poverty, I entered this world an earthly prince. I inherited every material thing this life can offer: riches, fame, education, indeed, a vast kingdom. I possessed unlimited earthly pleasures, all of which, let me remind you, I renounced. You realize it is much easier to give up everything in your life when you possess nothing. That was nearly sixteen years ago. I was twenty-nine years old. And you…? How old are you?"

"Thirty," said Jesus. "I am just thirty."

"I walked away. It was the GREAT DEPATURE. You may read it there in the scroll. My journey from that point was very similar in outline, I suspect, to what you have been experiencing. I do not know whether you have met temptations along your path. I seem to sense that you have. In my case, a mighty demon, Mara, came to me, offering me her beautiful and willing daughters. I had to turn her down, of course…"

Jesus nodded recalling his journey through the desert with Steve and the demon.

"There were many other trials as well," continued the Buddha. "The pull of this physical plane is great. It has been a long journey, but when I came out the other side, things had changed. I am too far in my walk to turn in my tracks and go back to follow you."

"Well, we can't both be right," replied Jesus. He looked up. "Can we?"

Siddhartha stared at the lacquered floor, and he drew a deep breath as though he were about to start over again with Jesus in a totally different line, but he noticed that Jesus had looked away.

Jesus spoke. "Your monks over there are not listening to our conversation are they? I am getting a very peculiar feeling…"

"You may speak your mind," said the Buddha. "Even if they were listening, it would be of no concern. They are trustworthy."

"Have you heard of the Jewish tribes?" asked Jesus.

"Jewish tribes?"

"Jews. I am a Jew from the Mediterranean. In the West?"

"Greeks?"

"No, no, no. Jews!"

"I am sorry I have never heard of the Jews."

"We are monotheistic. It is only us and God and perhaps some demigods and demons. The character of the spiritual world seemed to change somewhat during our Babylonian Captivity, but basically..."

"Babylon?" interrupted the Buddha, "That is nation beyond the Western mountains whose history is familiar to us."

"Yes, well…" Jesus continued, "My point is that for a Jew, 'Life,' at its foundation, must be built in relationship between man and his Creator."

"I understand," said the Buddha. "Continue…."

"So, if you and your followers…"

"I believe I have told you, that I do not have followers." interrupted the Buddha.

"They behave as one would expect followers to…"

The Buddha learned forward, interrupting again. "I said I do not have followers!"

The sound over my amplifiers was deafening. Sarah jumped back against the pillar. Even Steve stirred from his slumber. I quickly turned down the volume and leaned-in toward Sarah behind the column, but Jesus and the Buddha had already looked over in our direction.

Jesus shook his head and turned back to our host. "If you and your 'people' would consider the pursuit of such a relationship…" Jesus cleared his throat. "I am sorry. I know this may strike you as odd, but I mean to say a personal relationship…"

"Personal?" interrupted the Awakened One.

"Well, yes. It absolutely must be personal."

"Go on," urged the Buddha. "A personal relationship with whom…?"

"That is the difficulty I have been having. The relationship I am asking you to consider is with one with me, or with the 'me' I aspire to become."

Siddhartha Gautama shook his head. "It is most difficult, Jesus," he replied. "I grant that you are an enlightened being, but my background is very different. I suppose it is the Hindi influence in my earliest upbringing, all the gods and demigods I have had to battle against for all these years. That is an enormous lot of habit to strip away. When a child is raised-up to worship thousands of gods, it is difficult for him to put that aside and envision only a single god. Somehow, through an effort of will, I suppose, I have managed to abandon a lot of my early ideas. Perhaps I have gone to extremes, but I have come to believe that it is best for the human spirit to travel alone."

"Alone?"

"No priests, no leaders, no intermediaries, no intercessors, no saviors..."

"Funny you should mention that," said Jesus.

"Savior?" asked the Buddha.

"Yes…"

"The word just seemed to pop into my consciousness," replied the Buddha.

Jesus grinned. "But that is the whole point is it not? Reconciliation with God? A return to the Creator after the illusion of existence of life on earth?"

"You discount the importance of our time on earth," replied Siddhartha Gautama.

"Oh, no; our mortal existence is extremely important. Vital. People must first be born into existence…" said Jesus and he paused and stared intently into space. He seemed to search for words in thin air. He slowly drew a breath and spoke, haltingly, as though only just then remembering something from a long-forgotten dream. "The Father will send his Son to stand in place of the sinner. Through a personal relationship with each and every child of the Creator, the

Messiah shall repay the Father for the wrong done him by all the men and women of the world…"

"Excuse me, Jesus," interrupted the Buddha. "But this doctrine sounds very complicated."

"It does," replied Jesus, and he suddenly snapped out of his reverie and came to full attention. "But that, by itself, does not render it false. Take, for instance, the variety and complexity we find in nature."

"Complexity?" repeated the Buddha. "Complexity sounds the alarm. Truth is simple, and often hidden in the weeds of the complex. Take the simple path, Jesus. It is a straighter, truer path to peace and harmony with the universe."

Jesus glanced back at us and then over to the Buddha's silent retinue of monks.

"I don't know, Siddhartha… I look at them, the men and women of earth, and I believe they are incapable of making the necessary sacrifice. The Creator requires a righteous soul to redeem the lost. How does one pull oneself up by one's own bootstraps?"

The Buddha smiled. "And I thought I was the man of paradox. You seem to be speak in riddles."

Jesus took a breath and continued, "Yes, well… You have spent a good part of your life in search of the truth, on the path to righteousness, and reconciliation with the Almighty. Am I correct?

"You might phrase it in such a way, for discussion's sake."

"And all this time you've resisted the temptation to have your… students bow down and worship you?"

"Absolutely."

"But what if you were a god?"

"No," said the Buddha, raising his hand dismissively. "That way leads to disaster. Many have suggested such a thing, but if I am anything, I am no god."

Jesus nodded his head approvingly.

"Does that amuse you?" asked the Buddha.

"I am very impressed by your humility. With your status and your undeniable talents, the average human being would almost certainly have embraced the notion of a fundamental superiority. One day my homeland will be occupied by the Roman Empire. The Roman Emperors will be notorious for such a failing."

"Yet you suggest that if I were the God of the Universe, things might be different?" asked the Buddha.

"Yes."

The Awakened one studied Jesus' face. "Then why would I need a savior?" asked the Buddha.

"Well…"

"Yes, Jesus of Nazareth?"

"If the God of the universe had a dual nature…"

"Now, you are back to more than one God again," the Buddha interrupted.

"No. Not really… Not more than one…"

Jesus seemed frustrated by the Buddha's obvious impatience and by his own apparent inability to articulate what was on his heart, to put into words what was unfolding in his mind's eye. I understood that these two men were communicating, such as they were, only through the mysterious intervention of the time-roving Entity. Apparently, there were some differences and misunderstandings that the invisible spirit had elected to ignore.

"Yes," said Jesus, suddenly. "It is a paradox. Like your multi-armed goddess, Kali, our God has more than one face. Each separate, but one in the same. They are phases of the same, supreme unity. Your students would find themselves able to reconcile with the universe directly. The whole notion of a priesthood, intercessors, and intermediaries would break down. Human beings will come into relation with the thing itself."

"The thing itself," repeated Siddhartha. He shook his head and smiled. "But I am not. I am not a god," he said. "Certainly no single, multi-faceted God of the entire Universe!"

"Well, then…?" said Jesus, smiling mysteriously.

"And you would have me believe that you are this single, all-powerful God?"

"I don't know…" said Jesus. "I just don't know…" he repeated and his gaze fell to the floor.

Noticing our friend's sudden change in mood, the Buddha smiled brightly and reached out and tapped Jesus on the shoulder. "Perhaps you should break your self-imposed fast?"

Jesus looked up and seemed to manage a smile. "You noticed my fasting?"

The Enlightened One nodded. "Oh yes. When one goes too long without food, some frightening and bizarre notions may cross the mind."

Jesus slowly nodded.

"How many days has it been for you?" asked the Buddha.

"A few weeks. I am striving to reach forty days without food."

The Buddha smiled inscrutably and Jesus leaned over and picked-up his signed scroll. He scanned some of the bulleted points.

"Forty-nine days? You went forty-nine days without food?"

"It nearly killed me," replied the Buddha.

Jesus still held the partially coiled parchment. He glanced over the contents as though they were the entrees in the dinner menu at the restaurant in Pandemonium.

"You have many good points here, and there is much to be commended, although you come down very heavily against selfhood," said Jesus.

"Do you recognize that the illusion of self is the chief obstacle to reintegration?" replied the Buddha.

"I believe that on that point we see eye to eye," said Jesus. "It is primarily a matter of emphasis. Selfhood remains a chief obstacle, but I disagree that one's selfhood is mere illusion."

The Buddha laughed.

"What is so funny?" asked Jesus.

"The further we speak, the wider our differences become! And here you suggest the possibly that you might be the god of the universe! What is <u>your</u> 'self,' then, Jesus of Nazareth, if not an illusion?"

"No, Siddhartha. I am beginning to think that I may occupy a separate category. God the Creator is separate from his creations. You simply lump everything together. You really should read some of the Greeks. One of my companions from future earth, Sarah, has recommended to me the work of Socrates and Plato. I really must get over there to visit them."

"Future earth?" repeated the Buddha.

Jesus thought better than to go down that path and continued with his original thought. "The Greeks go too far in elevating the status of the individual, but the important role of selfhood is reflected in my own work. Just call it my Western Influence."

"Again, I am sorry, Jesus, and please forgive me," said the Enlightened One. "I grow weary of our conversation. Perhaps you should be on your way to visit your Greek brothers? I fear their brand of rugged individualism represents just the system of value which has contributed to such division in the world."

"I am not saying it cannot be taken to extremes," protested Jesus.

"Such division seems absolutely essential to your program." replied the Buddha. "Stay on the middle path, Jesus. That is my advice."

Jesus nodded and extended his hand in friendship.

The Enlightened One took Jesus' hand. They looked one another in the eye.

"Then we agree to disagree?" said Jesus.

"Yes. So it would seem."

The two men rose to their feet and hugged one another. The monks standing at the head of the portico made a concerted motion in alarm at this exchange, but seeing that both men were smiling, held their ranks. Jesus nodded with a bright smile on his face and he looked back in our direction. Steve had rolled off the bench and slumped onto the floor. He awoke as though he had been suffering from a bad dream. He grabbed the back of his right hand, and before he spoke I knew immediately what was on his mind.

Pain in Steve's right hand was never a good sign, but, as portents go, it proved a highly effective bellwether in alerting us to impending disaster. In the same instant I detected movement outside in the garden. Among the lotus pools, something massive was moving across the lawn in our direction.

"Ouch," cried Steve. "My hand is killing me!"

"Aieeeeeeeeeeee!" screamed the false Buddhist brothers as bronze blades flashed from beneath their saffron robes in the afternoon light.

With cat-like reflexes, Jesus sprang back to protect the Enlightened One, catching him in the midriff and pulling him down to the floor as daggers ripped through empty air above their heads. My tentacles telescoped up the porch, snared six forearms, and with no more effort than Steve might expend flicking a cigarette ash, I hoisted six would-be assassins with a splintering crash into the low ceiling of the portico. Dislocating arms from shoulder sockets, I shook the adherents like garments to be hung on a clothes line as Jesus pulled the frightened Buddha to his feet. I retracted my coils and moaning men dropped to the deck like fish.

"I am betrayed," cried the Buddha.

Before anyone could move, the sound of splintering timbers and rumbling earth pulled our attention to the west.

"What's going on?" cried Steve.

Sarah helped Steve to his feet and we started up the portico toward the golden doorway.

"We've got to buy some time," shouted Jesus.

"It's locked!" said the Buddha.

"This porch is coming apart like jack straws," Sarah warned and we heard the unmistakable trumpeting of bull elephants as waves of lotus laden water cascaded over the planks of the portico.

At the far end of the porch we saw the glint of ivory tusks. Spurred by masked riders, six angry Indian elephants crashed up the porch way.

"Get that door off its hinges," cried Jesus, as my tentacles probed the seams between the heavy teak door and its jamb. Suddenly, my tentacles grabbed hold.

"Stand back," I warned and in an instant the eight hundred pound door was flipping end over end down the porch toward the marauding pachyderms and their faceless riders.

"In, in, in," shouted Jesus, and we piled into the passageway and followed the Enlightened One up a flight of stairs into what looked like an ancient Hindu Temple.

"How do we get to the rooftop?" shouted Jesus as we dashed five abreast across the marble floor. Without a word we followed the nimble Buddha to a spiral stairwell of stone and were just starting up the steps when the sound of footfall and the shouts of men echoed through the vast temple behind us. We wasted no time, charged up the stairs and two minutes later pushed through a bronze door and tumbled onto a tiled roof-top overlooking the park. Steve and Sarah dashed to the parapet and peered over the edge back in the direction of the reflecting pools and the smashed portico.

A dozen black arrows whizzed over the crenellated parapet wall.

"Archers," cried Sarah as she retreated from the roof's edge and crouched back beside the bronze door. "There are a half dozen elephants milling around down there!" shouted Steve.

"We need to get off this roof," said Jesus, throwing his shoulder against the bronze door attempting to hold it closed. "Can you help us get out of here, M-2500?"

"I shall do my best," I replied, and I stopped in the middle of the rooftop and silently prayed that the teakwood beams of the ancient temple roof would support my metamorphosis.

"Sarah and Steve, you two help Siddhartha and me jam shut this door," cried Jesus. "Use those roofing tiles there! Hurry!"

* * *

Those were the last words I heard as my mind fastened on the design of the red and white space ship from the future and I felt matter channeling through a million wormholes and flow out like mycelium across the tiled rooftop. In the next instant I was staring back from my control panels through the cockpit into the flight deck as Jesus and the others raced aboard.

"Are we set?" I asked as Jesus and the Enlightened One jumped down into the pilot's and co-pilot's seats.

"Let's go," said Sarah strapping herself into the auxiliary flight chair on the back wall of the cockpit.

I was conscious of Steve in the galley looking through the refrigerator.

"Steve," I said softly in the feminine voice that never failed to gain his attention.

"What is it Debbie?" he said, looking up from the open refrigerator door.

"Pull down an auxiliary flight seat there by the pantry and buckle up."

Had the Ophanim sent back to me the secret of synthesizing food for my human passengers now would have been a good time for Steve to stuff his mouth, but his tirade against me, Jesus, and Sarah had only just begun. I was carrying on a conversation with Jesus up top and arguing with Steve about the necessity of buckling into the auxiliary flight seat in the galley when the temple's ancient roof collapsed under our weight.

The terrified eyes of a dozen masked assassins stared down in horror as the stone wall on the other side of the rooftop doorway crumbled away. Some of the assailants were thrown headlong atop us as we plummeted down with fragments of clay tile and ancient teak rafters seventy-five feet to the marble floor below.

Dust rolled up across the forward viewport of the cockpit.

"Is everyone all right?" I cried.

"I'm good!" shouted Steve picking himself up from a sea of pots and pans in the galley. "What the hell was that?" he shouted.

I was distracted by the terrified face of an assassin who had fallen from the exposed spiral stairwell unto my back. He had slipped down along my polished surface onto the forward observation windows and stared into the cockpit and the face of his intended victim.

"Devadatta!" shouted the Buddha.

"You know him?" said Jesus.

"It is my cousin! The scoundrel!"

"Is he behind this?"

"It is not the first time he has tried to assassinate me!"

The bewildered assailant lost his hold on the viewport's slick surface and slid off the nose of the ship into the rubble below.

"Let's get out of here, Debbie!" cried Jesus.

With that, I leaned back, shedding a splintered pillar, and with assassins slipping off my back like black raindrops, rose out of the ruined temple.

"You are truly a demigod yourself to command such a vessel," said the Buddha to Jesus as we sailed up into the sky.

"Nothing 'demi' about me," smiled Jesus. "You ready, Sarah?"

"Born ready," replied Sarah.

* * *

I flew out of the valley and to an altitude where the setting sun still shimmered with gold in the white clouds drifting up against the immense Himalayan mountain range.

"Is this Nirvana?" asked the Buddha.

"Not this trip," said Jesus. "Is there someplace safe where we may take you? We have to be on our way."

"I don't know how to thank you," said the Enlightened One. "Next Spring I had intended to get back to the old deer park in Varanasi."

"Sarah, do you have any idea where that is?" asked Jesus.

"He's talking about Benares in Northern India."

"How does your companion know so much? I did not sense that she was enlightened."

"She graduated from MIT," said Jesus.

"MIT?"

"Massachusetts Institute of…"

"Thank you, Steve," interrupted Jesus.

"She had to fulfill requirements in the humanities," continued Steve.

"Hey, you guys, I'm right here, you know," said Sarah. "Debbie, can I get out of this shoulder harness?"

"Yes," I replied. "And you are all free to move about the ship. Shall I set a course for Varanasi?"

"Varanasi?" asked Jesus of the Enlightened One.

"Yes, yes. This will mark quite a homecoming for me. It is the city of my first sermon. But you realize it will take several weeks to travel such a distance."

"Probably not that long," replied Jesus. "Still, it would be nice if we had a few hours to speak to one another before our arrival."

The two men left the cockpit and made their way to the conference table on the main deck. They sat beside one another on one of the cushioned divans that lined my starboard side and were soon lost in conversation. I turned south and headed slowly toward our destination. A journey that might have lasted only seconds was extended through the night and I landed at the Buddhist Monastery in Sarnath, a residential area on the outskirts of the ancient city of Varanasi. I touched down beyond a grove of trees in a surviving portion of the old deer park where the 35-year-old Siddhartha, convinced by an old friend, first shared his new-found wisdom with five young men.

Jesus and the Buddha exited the ship and walked up a gravel path toward the monastery. As monks and nuns ran outdoors to greet the Enlightened One, Jesus quickly parted company. It was still early in the morning when Jesus returned to the ship. He paused beneath our vessel, set his foot on one of the two landing runners and looked back in the direction of the monastery. Yes, this was the place where Siddhartha Gautama had delivered his first sermon. Now, in less than a decade, the man had adherents throughout the countryside: thousands of men and women striving for peace and enlightenment. He had made many enemies as well, and Jesus thought of the attack of the night before and of the face of the evil cousin, Devadatta. That had not been the first attempt. Jesus spoke to himself.

"What was the name? The name of the temptress? The demon?"

"Mara?"

My voice, the feminine voice of "Debbie" must have startled Jesus. He jumped up, banging his head against the ship's undercarriage where my voice had sounded from hidden speakers in the hull.

"Debbie?" said Jesus with a smile, rubbing the top of his head and looking at the spiral staircase leading into the belly of the ship.

"I didn't mean to startle you," I said.

"Not a problem," he said. "I just wasn't expecting a voice."

"I should have realized you were deep in thought," I replied.

"It's all right."

"You were contemplating..." I hesitated to speak the word, but he completed my thought.

"The adversary?"

"Yes," and a faint, almost imperceptible shudder coursed through the ship.

"Evil has developed many faces," said Jesus.

"Do you imagine he will make a personal appearance?"

Jesus shook his head. "I don't know. We saw a terrible thing last night."

"The assassination attempt?"

"Without our intervention it might have gone badly…"

"Yes…"

"So much has happened in the world. I suppose you hardly recognize it," he said.

"It does possess a different texture."

Jesus, paused, thinking to himself.

"Jesus?" I asked.

"I'll want to put a team together when I get back home."

"Home?"

"Back in the West, in my own time. If I can find twelve righteous men to carry on for me."

"Carry on for you?"

"Do you think I can find twelve righteous men?"

"I don't know. I should hope so."

"Lot couldn't even come up with ten."

"Lot?"

"The righteous man from Sodom?"

"Sodom?"

Jesus stopped and nearly spun in his tracks, "Please forgive me…"

"What? Is something wrong?"

"No, it's nothing you've done," said Jesus. "I've overlooked the fact that you've missed out on all of human history!"

I didn't know how to respond.

"With your celestial background," he continued, "I naturally assumed that you would know these things, but how could you unless you were from the future, like Sarah…? Why, the only way you could possibly know the story of humanity would be to…" Jesus trailed off as though he had stumbled into an unwanted realization.

There was an uncomfortable pause. We'd come upon the unavoidable fact that since I'd teamed up with Jesus and his band of human beings, I had fallen off-track in my spiritual life. Pulling in the six days worth of information from the Ophanim, which involved the astronomically complex and closely guarded secret processes of time travel, had taxed my humble angelic faculties to their limits. But that knowledge had been purely technical. Now, Jesus and I both realized I may have been using my interest in the physical realms as an excuse to avoid my daily devotionals.

"Forgive me, Jesus, it's only that I've had so much on my mind."

"Say no more."

"But it is no excuse."

"There are many distractions down here on earth and it is very difficult to set time aside, I dare say, with the obstacles the adversary puts in our path. I never thought to wonder what existence must be like for an angel. There may be some similarities."

"I appreciate that."

"It is perhaps I who should ask your forgiveness, for everything that we've put you through. I had hoped the Ophanim would have filled-in the details of history in heaven and earth and the cosmos, since our disappearance, but, clearly, they have deemed otherwise."

"I'll try to find time…"

"We can only do our best, but wait! I have an idea!" said Jesus excitedly.

"What is it? A new destination?"

"In a manner of speaking. Why put it off a moment longer? My cousin John could summon him, then why not me?"

Unlike Siddhartha Gautama, whose evil cousin was only now recovering from his wounds in the King's palace in far off Kathmandu and plotting his next assassination attempt, Jesus had a cousin (or would have a cousin in another four hundred and fifty years) who had come into contact with a powerful new being in the spiritual neighborhood. Jesus was about to provide me with a formal introduction, when Steve interrupted.

"When are we going to get something to eat!" a voice sounded from inside the ship. Steve emerged from above deck on the stairwell.

"Hang on, Steve," said Jesus.

"Hang on?" Steve repeated and he skipped quickly down the seventeen corkscrew steps of our retractable spiral stairway. "Sarah and I have been up there waiting to get out of here for twenty minutes. If we aren't going to be on our way someplace for a meal, I'll just get out here and have a look around."

Steve brushed past Jesus beneath the ship, stepped over the chrome landing skid and started up through the grove of cypress trees. He walked toward an open meadow and the hilltop monastery beyond.

"You can all wait for me, for once, Jesus!" he called back without turning as he went. "See how you like it!"

Steve had taken but a few more steps in the direction of the monastery when Sarah emerged on the spiral stairway in time to exchange a knowing look with Jesus. They walked from beneath the shadow of the rocket ship and watched Steve slowly backpedal as a procession of men, women and children in white and saffron robes descended the path from the hilltop. Stringed instruments sounded a simple melody on the morning air as a group of townspeople and Buddhist monks approached. They trailed flower petals and held bright baskets of fresh fruit and steaming rice. By now, despite the appearance of the earth's bounty and the outpouring of affection from the delegation moving toward us, Steve retreated all the way back to the ship.

"It could be a trap," shouted Steve as Jesus and Sarah smiled at one another and walked out across the grass to meet the leaders of the procession.

"I do not believe it is a trap," I said.

"How do you know?" Steve replied glancing up at my hull.

"Your right hand is not bothering you this morning is it?"

I referred to the mark of the devil stamped on the back of his right hand. "Your demonic tattoo has been a reliable barometer of impending disaster. Would you agree?"

We argued while Jesus accepted gifts from the city of Varanasi. Children placed palm fronds in a circle on the lawn and the young women set wooden bowls of food on the dark green mandala and retreated. All at once, the entire group of two hundred and fifty souls dropped into the grass on their knees and bowed their heads.

"Well, maybe you're right," said Steve, reluctantly. "They don't look they're planning a fast one. Too bad you're stuck way over here," he laughed walking away toward the party and leaving me parked by the side of a deep, still pond of lotus flowers.

* * *

"What's for breakfast?" Steve shouted as he came up from behind Jesus and Sarah. Sarah gave him a cold, warning glance and held a finger to her lips. Steve fell silent and waited while the leaders of the delegation blessed the offering.

Observed from a tower of the monastery overlooking the park, the scene brought a smile to the lips of the forty-five year old Buddha. He watched as Jesus accepted the gifts of food and clothing and, with the help of the monks, nuns and villagers, carried the treasures to the strange red and white ship from another world at the edge of his lotus pond. Gautama Siddhartha laughed as Jesus re-emerged from beneath the vessel. He was dressed in a dazzling white robe with a blue sash and new leather sandals. Jesus was followed by Sarah and the odd one, Steve, both dressed in saffron robes and new sandals that carried them to the water's edge. The white and golden robes shimmered as the sun rose in the sky. The scene's reflection played among the flowers drifting on the water's surface as a servant poured a cup of tea.

Although he was a mile away, I perceived The Enlightened One's eyes widen as Jesus walked to the elevated nose of the rocket ship and place a hand on my cherry-red surface. Our machine transformed into a beautiful woman in a red dress. Applause and exclamations of "Ooohhh" and "Ahhh" carried across the cypress grove and up the hill to the tower where the Enlightened One watched from his window.

The girls and women crossed the lawn and enveloped the woman in red. In a moment, they withdrew, leaving me adorned in one of their saffron robes and with leather sandals upon my feet. They parted and the way was straight for me as I walked toward Jesus where he stood waste deep in the shimmering pool. He smiled and waved me forward. I bent down, slipped off my sandals and stepped into the water and waded out to him.

"I've never done this before," said Jesus.

"Me either," I said.

I looked out at the happy and expectant faces of the men and women and children ranged about on the shore. I looked above their heads, far away to where the Enlightened One observed from his tower, and even Steve and Sarah nodded, with smiles on their face. In one hundred trillion years, I had never felt such joy as when Jesus took me in his arms and I leaned back below the surface, human eyes wide open, looking up at him through a moiré pattern of scintillating water. The sun glowed behind his head like a halo.

"I baptize you in the name of the Father, the Son, and the Holy Spirit," he said.

I came up out of the water and everything had changed.

4. The Academy

I picked up my red dress and high heeled shoes and turned back into our cherry red rocket-ship with the white hardtop and fins. I had become quite adept at this maneuver, having already stored the hundreds of trillions of necessary bits of information needed to accomplish this feat from the Ophanim's original transmission. I was ready to go in seconds.

Steve assembled a group of villagers and led tours of the rocket ship while Sarah taught the children a variety of lawn games. They played red-light green-light, had wheel-barrow races and had an egg-toss with hilarious results, especially when Jesus caught a face-full of yolk from the errant throw of his little five-year (old) partner, Sashi. Later in the afternoon, the Enlightened One came down from his tower and joined Jesus and the young adults and some of the elders for a question and answer session beneath the branches of an enormous pipal tree. The discussion lasted until nightfall. Steve was grateful because some of the folks built camp fires and brought out the roasted meat. He found time during the late afternoon, to re-stock the galley with lamb, rice and fish.

It was the end of a beautiful day. Illuminated lanterns rose into the air and campfires shone in the grottos and walkways of the old deer park as Sarah, Steve and Jesus said their farewells and climbed back aboard. I withdrew the spiral stair and sealed the hatch and slowly lifted up among the glimmering, floating lanterns and headed into the sunset.

We traveled west. Sarah gave my time control level a little bump and we slid through a stream of white mist and came out a hundred years later still driving through the atmosphere at twenty thousand feet toward the setting sun.

My friends slept soundly, peacefully, and I felt great gratitude to Jesus for his having shared the mystery of his long lost uncle, whom I soon came to realize was not really his uncle at all, or not merely an uncle, but the mysterious, time-spanning "Entity" himself!

I set a glide path for the Aegean Sea with an ETA of six in the morning. Like Jesus said, it was never a simple matter finding quiet time, but in-so-far as I could put myself on auto-pilot I focused my attention on this new being which had first visited me as I emerged from the reflecting pool. Untold mysteries were revealed to me that night as I leaned toward the wine-drenched sea of the West. All human history through the 5th century BC was laid bare in the infinitesimal detail which only the mind of an angel can fully appreciate. I say this with one important caveat. I refer to my human pilot slumped to his side in the pilot's seat, drooling at his lip, sleeping like a babe in the manger. I felt an awesome responsibility, I must say.

Outside the three orders of angelic beings in the first sphere, and the remaining knights' errant archangels, I alone of the myriad members of the second and third celestial spheres was privy to the simple fact that the Son of the Creator was going to be born on earth as a mortal, human being. Exactly why he was coming was still beyond what the Entity chose to reveal. Even the Prince of Air and Darkness, my former boss from the foundation of the earth, remained ignorant of our pilot's superhuman role in the future history of the earth system.

At that precise moment, Satan was aware only that one human being had somehow stepped outside human history and avoided the curse of the Knowledge of Good and Evil. The fact that Jesus was the actual Son of the Creator was an idea Satan considered plausible; what he failed to comprehend for many centuries, even dimly suspect, was that Jesus was the Creator himself.

Why the architect of our existence chose to make a road trip of the process, I can only speculate. Had I not been preoccupied piloting a twenty ton space-time craft over the mountains of Persia, I would have asked the Entity for clarity. Even for an angel, at least for one of my lowly station, listening to the sound of that still, small voice required considerable concentration. I still lacked important details of human history. Others, I may have simply decided to ignore.

I heard Steve moving in the living quarters down on the first level. He stumbled into the lavatory and urinated, missing the receptacle and leaving a puddle for me to clean off the tiles. He shuffled into the galley and my cool blue lights illuminated his way to the refrigerator where he helped himself to a short rack of lamb ribs. He left the bones on the table and went back to his bunk to sleep.

I asked the Entity to explain why Jesus could not have been born with absolute knowledge of his Godhood. The Entity could be awfully coy, and answered only that the birth of Jesus was still four hundred years in the future.

"And please, M-2500," It said, telepathically, "If you should run into any other angels, please don't spoil the birthday celebration we've planned."

"Will I ever see any of them again?" I asked.

"Who?"

"My old friends from the foundation of the earth?"

"Some. Yes, of course."

"Jerry?"

"Yes. L-1 is doing fine. He sends his regards."

"What of L-77?"

"Who?"

As I glanced down at the mountaintops below, something happened to the transmission, and it was extremely difficult to hear the Entity's reply.

"Hello," I said. "I was asking about L-77, from the Human Genome Task Force. He was on the start-up crew on the Moon after the 'Life on Mars' thing went, awry…"

"I'm sorry, M-2500. Things didn't work out for L-77."

"Didn't work out?"

Had I been a human being, one might have seen a tear in my eye as I pondered the news.

"L-77?" I said, finally, in disbelief.

"It was his choice."

"I knew it!"

"Beg your pardon?"

"I'm sorry; it is only that these friends of mine, Steve and Sarah, believe the angels have no free will. Steve believes that I am an automaton, a robot. And Sarah, well…"

"What about Sarah?"

"As far as I can tell, she is a materialist. She is from the twenty-first century. She considers herself a 'modern thinker.' She believes our sense of free will is a mere illusion, our existence, purely a matter of genetics, environment and random chance."

"She is a determinist?" asked the Entity.

"I have to land in a minute, but I meant to ask, why are you putting yourself through this?"

"Excuse me?"

"I mean, why don't you simply tell Jesus that he is the Creator, that he is part of a Godhead, a Trinity I guess you would call it?"

"Shhh…"

"I'm praying, silently," I said, confused. "Jesus can't hear me."

"Do not imagine that He cannot hear things in His dreams," replied the Entity.

"His dreams?"

"Oh, yes, that is generally how I first make myself known to the human beings, through their dreams. It is less threatening that way. When they are asleep and dreaming they sometimes let their guards down long enough to hear through the clutter of their day to day lives."

"You haven't answered my question," I interrupted, "Why not simply open his eyes to reality? Why put him through all this?"

"Some things simply must be experienced to be believed, although the magnitude of this revelation will defy His human capacity for true understanding."

"So he must continue to operate by faith alone?"

"Not merely, but if you want answers, you should ask my brother."

"Your brother?"

"If you want to know why things are the way they are, then you must ask the Creator. To rescue Steve and Sarah and all the others from their self-imposed predicament, He sent his Child to the earth a human being, a mortal creature of flesh and blood, a descendent of the very creatures you brewed-up from the ocean all those years ago. The only difference in his being stems from his immaculate conception. I provided the coordinates to the S-Class angels, the 'small ones' who first perceived my existence. By the divine zygote planted in the surrogate mother, Jesus has avoided the curse of Adam and Eve. You were there."

"In the Garden?"

"Where were your questions then?"

"I don't know, I..."

"I am glad to have made your acquaintance, M-2500. I have dwelt in the background, subsisting at my brother's place, so to speak, but I have this opportunity to help the babe before He steps back into history. Do you understand?"

"Not really," I said.

"Then it will be a learning experience for both of you. Just remember the child beside you in the pilot seat is going to have to go through hell before all is said and done. Count your blessings. You are an angel. Your path is easy by comparison, although I warn you that it will not be without its tribulation."

"My path?" I asked, but the Entity quickly changed the subject.

"You might want to watch those mountains coming up on your right there. It seems as though you've lost altitude…"

"Thanks," I replied, making a course correction. "I'm sorry, I was distracted. It's that suddenly, I'm worried. Will there be any risk?"

"Of course there will be risk. That's why my brother is giving me the stink-eye over there. He'd just as soon pull his boy off your ship and collapse everything back into the sun as though nothing had ever happened out here in this "Milky Way." We have so many universes to contend with, not to mention a hundred trillion trillion planets and the souls of his myriad created beings…"

Somehow, through my celestial conversation with the Entity, I was hearing background noise, and not the background radiation of the big-bang that had started this little neighborhood backwater, but something really serious. It was as though the Entity was holding his hand over the mouthpiece of a transmitter and yelling to someone in another room.

We dropped down through a cloud bank.

"I don't know!" sounded the voice over the receiver. "He's your kid! Why don't you ask him yourself?"

Jesus started to toss back and forth in his seat as though he were having a nightmare. Simultaneously, I heard a voice in my head speaking loudly at someone in a background dimension which I could only imagine.

"I've pared him up with an angel. Right next to me. What? A little too personal for you? Well, are you just going to hide-out in that room of yours and pout? What? I'll move out when I am good and ready to move out. Well, it won't be soon enough!"

There was more static.

"Hello? Are you there?" the voice returned on the other end.

Just then Jesus awoke. His eyes blinked wildly and he looked at my crystal array in the cockpit dash. "My goodness what a strange dream I've been having. M-2500? Where are we?"

"I have to leave," I thought.

"Well, you watch after him, now," the Entity replied.

"Of course."

"Excuse me?" said Jesus.

"It was really nice getting a chance to meet you today," continued the Entity. "Stay in touch."

"It's been wonderful meeting you," I replied.

The exchange would have been farcical, had the subject been of less dire consequence, for all along Jesus thought I had been speaking directly to him.

"Well, it's been wonderful meeting you, too," said Jesus.

Just then Sarah and Steve walked into the flight compartment.

"Where are we?" asked Sarah.

"Do you suppose we could stop somewhere and get some fresh milk?" asked Steve.

"Classical Greece," I quickly replied to Sarah. "We're just over Greece."

"Athens? Athens? Oh, please say Athens," said Sarah.

"Yes, Athens," I said and I landed in an olive grove on a hill behind the Acropolis.

* * *

Everyone piled out of the ship and I quickly changed back to my everyday appearance of M-2500 and walked down the hillside to a road leading further away from the city. We hiked to the northwest for an hour in the early morning and encountered very few inhabitants. In their white and saffron robes, my companions met with scarcely a second glance. I simply made myself invisible, a very rudimentary angelic ability, and walked along at a distance trying my best to reconnect with the Entity on this beautiful late spring morning in 459 BC.

Up ahead rose the high rock wall of the Academy, a plot of ground planted over with olive trees centuries earlier and named for the Greek hero, Akademos. The Groves of the Academe, sacred to Athena, the patron Goddess of the city, were so revered, I would learn much later in my travels, that when the Spartans eventually overran Athens and razed it, they spared this place. Not until the Roman General Sulla invaded in 86 BC was an axe taken to the olive trees to build siege engines.

Not only was I invisible, but I was silent, and I felt disjointed and out of touch as I listened to Sarah provide information on this walking tour of Greece. It seemed as though she were a paid docent in a museum of classical antiquity. I should have known these things first hand. I should have lived through them and looked back upon each page of history in the sepia tones of nostalgia. I should have paid more attentions to the customs and traditions that had been building up over the centuries. I should have given thought to the rules and systems of justice. I might have considered the laws put down in the time of Moses and his people's time in the wilderness. Instead, I had jumped ahead in time, and even now, was so busy enumerating my regrets that I missed yet another opportunity to connect with the Entity and review his summary of all I had missed, all I had over-looked. I gazed down at my invisible tentacles swaying at my sides as we walked along the cobblestone street. I could see the two rings of the Ophanim, and I understood then why time travel was both a blessing and a curse.

* * *

We came upon a vendor at a busy intersection in front of the main entrance to the Academy. Young men were moving freely through the wide archway in the wall and the vendor was doing a brisk business with these students, apparently between lectures. I looked over at Sarah who had her neck craned back as she read an inscription painted on an ornate wooden sign hanging above the entrance: "Let no one ignorant of Geometry enter here."

The young men were walking away with sticks of roast lamb and slabs of spanakopita as Steve broke ranks and shouldered his way into line. To Steve's consternation, the vendor would not offer him credit, and Steve came away only with a thumb-sized sample of moustos, a sweet hard candy made from grapes. Still, the gooey morsel was enough to whet Steve's appetite and he immediately complained to Jesus.

"We have no money!" he cried.

"How's your geometry?" yelled Sarah.

Jesus and Sarah took him by the arm and guided him along the wall, away from the clutch of people at the gates. Like a phantom I followed in their footsteps dimly aware that my unique services would soon be required.

"Listen," said Sarah, "How are we going to get in there anyway, much less walk up to Plato and ask him the time of day? We don't know the first thing about enrolling in this school. I'm sure there must be an application process."

"I hadn't thought of that," admitted Jesus. "Do you have any suggestions?"

"As a matter of fact, I do!" Sarah replied.

We all looked at Sarah with no idea what she had in mind.

"Plato's a philosopher, right?" she began.

"Well, yes," said Jesus. "At least that is what you have told me."

"And philosophers spent thousands of years searching for what miraculous object?"

"Truth?" asked Jesus.

"Money!" shouted Steve.

"Yes," said Sarah, "Money! Wealth! Power! All wrapped up in the philosopher's stone!"

She explained the concept of the legendary object sought by primitive human science in the ultimately futile effort to turn base elements into those glittering metals, gold and silver. Her lecture complete, she put her hands out in the air, groping like a blind woman and began calling for me.

* * *

They prevailed upon me to follow them around the corner of the stone wall at the end of the block. Of the three of them, Steve was the most upset by my metamorphosis, shimmering out of the backdrop of a limestone wall, but not into the buxom and half-dressed form of Debbie, for whom he secretly pined, but into the stooped and grizzled image of an ancient man.

I stood there, frail and wizened, with a drawn and toothless face while Sarah and Jesus debated a suitable name for me.

Jesus cast his lot with "Methuselah," while Sarah advocated for a legendary character from the future named "Merlin." She was entirely responsible for my wardrobe design: black leggings, pointed leather slippers, purple robe, cape and a conical hat to which were affixed the white shapes of five-pointed stars, crescent moons and a half dozen ringed spheres after the fashion of the planet Saturn. During my transformation and elaborate costume change Sarah explained the ruse she was planning for the members of the Academy. My friends naturally and correctly assumed that I would succeed where generations of human wizards and alchemists had failed.

"Well, Steve?" asked Sarah.

Steve stepped back and looked from Jesus to Sarah and back at me.

"I've got to go with the name Merlin," said Steve, "He doesn't look like any kind of Jew I've ever met."

Jesus smiled and looked down the street, "Okay then, Merlin it is."

Then, as I knew he inevitably would, Jesus turned to me.

"Okay, M-2500…"

"Who?" I said, with a dry and husky voice approximating that of a human being of some one-hundred years of age.

"I mean, Merlin," Jesus corrected himself as a chariot carrying four Athenian teenagers clattered by. Jesus stepped into the street, stooped down and dislodged a fragment of stone from among the tightly fitted cobbles. It took him a few minutes, and I was surprised he didn't ask me to turn back into my angelic form and accomplish the task with my tentacles. Finally, a palm-sized shard of rock popped out into his hand and he stepped back beside the wall and presented it to me.

"All right then, here you go: the philosopher's stone."

I raised a sinewy hand, and grasped the rock.

"Now what?" I asked.

"Hey, wait a minute," said Steve as we started back up the thoroughfare to the gates.

"If he's going to turn stuff into gold and diamonds by pretending to use that rock there, why can't he make me one of those lamb kabobs?"

It was a great question, but I was weary of Steve. I was tired of relying on Sarah and Jesus for scraps of information from the past and the future. Five hundred million years adrift on the primordial oceans in the total darkness of the earth's dense atmosphere and the labors of that time seemed glorious by comparison. Steve wanted an answer. Steve always wanted something. It was simple enough. The M-Class angels were unable to transmute complex molecules and organic compounds. I didn't have the strength to tell him. I felt like a prisoner.

"There's no time for that now, Steve," said Jesus. "Let's get in line."

The young men and elders we encountered at the gate gave us a wide birth. Perhaps my outlandish appearance and the confidence of our bearing convinced them, against their better judgment, that we had business at the academy. We passed many groups of men and boys on the walk beside the well-tended lawns between the olive trees. I soon realized another member of our party impressed the academicians. We were walking with a female in our party. Apparently, female human beings were not permitted within the gated walls of the Academy. It seemed ironic that this sacred grove had been planted in honor of the city's patron deity, Athena, who, from what Sarah described, was a goddess, and was, at least in some sense, a female. Outweighing her love of weaving, crafts and a life of the mind, Athena's interest in warfare, body armor, and the martial arts had won the hearts of this male dominated society. There were many contradictions.

Still, our good-fortune continued. At the entrance to the gymnasium, two armed soldiers nodded cordially and directed us down a covered walkway. The facility was impressively large. There was a huge sports complex with locker rooms, baths, and an enormous stadium. We arrived in an open courtyard ringed with benches where a young graduate student named Aristotle was addressing an incoming freshman class. Plato, the seventy-year-old founder of the academy, walked slowly around the perimeter of the space, observing the students and their interaction with the speaker. Both Plato and his handsome protégée seemed altogether unimpressed by our appearance at the back of the yard.

Aristotle was asking his young audience to consider Plato's "Analogy of the Cave." What if they had all been born in a cave and spent their entire lives in chains with their heads held immobile, forced to look only at a blank cave wall? Behind them, a fire was burning and from time to time, objects would pass between the captives and the fire and the light would cast shadows on the wall. These shadows, continued Aristotle, were the things we observed in the world.

"We are the prisoners," he said.

There was a murmur of realization and agreement among the freshmen students. I looked over at Jesus who leaned toward me.

"Good stuff," he whispered.

"The world that we inhabit," continued Aristotle, "Is nothing more than an illusion. All that we perceive is a mere a shadow of what is good and true."

"Gets them every time," whispered Plato, who had stopped beside Jesus at the back of the class.

"I like it," Jesus whispered in reply.

"It is the philosopher's job," continued Aristotle, his voice rising dramatically, "No. It is his duty to free these prisoners; but first we must free ourselves. This is a high calling and what we shall be about in the coming term of study."

There was applause. Aristotle nodded in appreciation, and many of the young students got up from their benches to speak to him. I noticed that Steve had managed to gravitate to a table at the far side of the courtyard and helped himself to a bunch of grapes. Meanwhile, I clutched the apparently unnecessary and bogus philosopher's stone in my hand and leaned against my walking staff. I silently called out to the Entity for a condensed history lesson. What were these people talking about? Where were we? What had happened in the hundred years since we had left Asia? Meanwhile, Plato had noticed Sarah and was about to speak to her when Jesus took the occasion to introduce our party.

"This is Sarah Benton,"

"You realize it is highly unusual for a woman to attend our lectures," said Plato, "Much less set foot in the academy, but I welcome you as travelers who obviously observe very different customs."

"We have journeyed from the east in search of wisdom," said Jesus.

"Excellent," Plato replied. He and Jesus shook hands and exchanged a long look. Without even bothering to look back at me or Sarah, the old philosopher continued.

"You remind me of someone," he said.

"Do I?" said Jesus.

"Something in the intensity of your gaze brings my own mentor to mind."

"Your mentor?"

"Surely you have heard of Socrates?"

Jesus glanced at Sarah, "Yes," he replied slowly. "I have heard a great deal about Socrates."

"This year marks the fortieth anniversary on his martyrdom."

"Yes," said Jesus truthfully. "It was a terrible tragedy."

"Indeed."

"Yes," agreed Jesus.

"Of our great tragedians Sophocles and Aeschylus, whom do you prefer?"

Jesus' eyes grew wide at the sound of these names. He looked to Sarah for counsel, but she had already walked away toward the center of the courtyard. She turned a few heads of those students still at their benches. Meanwhile, Jesus must have recovered from Plato's question and had walked to the shade of an enormous olive tree at the edge of the courtyard for a private conversation. Sarah seemed more interested in the young graduate student who had completed his talk and continued to take center stage with the admiring young men of the academy.

I abandoned my plan to meditate on the Entity. Instead, I followed along after Sarah. She more or less shouldered her way in among the students and I trailed behind until we were fairly in the front of the group, no more than an arm's length from the young man named Aristotle.

"You realize Plato's analogy breaks down in several places," he said. "Still, I view it as an excellent place for new students to begin their understanding of epistemology."

"The study of knowledge," said one student.

"Very good," replied Aristotle.

Another student chimed in, "Socrates used to say that the only thing I know is that I know nothing!"

"Excellent," laughed the twenty-five-year-old Aristotle.

A third student called out, "My father says you ought to start your own academy."

"Perhaps, one day," laughed the celebrity. Still smiling, Aristotle turned slightly and looked at Sarah and me. "And who do we have here? A young maiden and a wizard?"

"Hey, woman," said the first student, shouting at Sarah. "You better cover your head."

"What is she doing in the academy anyway?" asked another.

"Hey, you!" cried the first student again, "I said you had better cover up that head of yours!"

"You cover your head, you little creep," Sarah replied.

"Oh, do wait a moment, please," said Aristotle. He turned to the first young man whose face suddenly blushed red, "Surely you may deduce from the apparel worn by this young maiden's companion that they are visitors to our city. They are unaware of our customs. They are also, undoubtedly, the guests of our founder. Let me be the first among his students to welcome you. My name is Aristotle."

I watched the man extended his hand to me. For a moment I didn't know what to say, but I was aware that Sarah was staring intently at me. I remembered I was supposed to say something, but for the life of me, I couldn't remember what it was.

"Merlin. This is Merlin," said Sarah with a smile.

"Merlin," repeated the handsome Aristotle, weighing the name, "Is he your husband?"

"My husband? Oh, goodness no," she replied.

"Your father?"

"Yes. No. I mean, no, he's not my father. He is a good friend, a philosopher himself."

"I see," said Aristotle.

"Where I live, people agree that one day you shall be one of the greatest philosophers of all time," said Sarah.

"Me?" said Aristotle.

"That's pretty cool," she said, "Don't you think?"

He looked at her, quizzically. "I'd like to know where you come from where people can look into the future with such certainty. I take it this is not the mere prophesy of an oracle."

The two of them exchanged a fleeting look, the significance of which I could not interpret. Some of the students were clearly upset with Sarah for stealing the attention of their instructor.

"You should not walk the streets of Athens without a male member of your immediate family," advised the first student.

"My parents and grandparents are dead," replied Sarah. "I have no siblings, so cool your jets, Hercules!"

With that, she turned back to Aristotle and put her hand on his forearm. Sarah was about to whisper one thing more, when, at that moment, munching a thick loaf of pita bread dripping with olive oil and gripping a hunk of feta cheese, Steve wandered over into the middle of the crowd.

"I have no idea what you mean by mocking me," shouted the first student, "But foreigner or not, I suggest you observe the customs of the state in which you find yourself."

"Show them the stone," said Sarah, glaring at the student with the heightened sense of Athenian propriety. "That'll shut everyone up in a hurry!"

Apparently, everyone was looking at me.

"Produce the philosopher's stone, Merlin!" said Sarah, dramatically. "Produce the stone and demonstrate our power!"

The stone. I slowly raised my hand and dropped the dusty rock into Sarah's open palm.

"You see here," she said, holding up the rock. "I have here the mighty philosopher's stone. With this mystical object, my friend can transform common metals into gold, silver, diamonds and other precious elements!"

"Really?" said Steve looking with a mouthful of cheese crumbs in his beard.

"Yes, really!" replied Sarah.

She had certainly generated some interest, if that was her intention. I dropped out of the circle of young men that had suddenly tightened around Aristotle and this strange human female from the future. I walked back to the olive tree where Jesus was building to the climax of his argument with Plato.

"Would you consider having a relationship with the Creator of the Universe?" asked Jesus.

"Excuse me?" replied Plato.

"To assure your future in a glorious after-life would you consider a new philosophy founded in the person of one from God?" repeated Jesus.

"I'm sorry, Jesus. I'm an old man near the end of my years."

"No, no, no," Jesus objected. "What better time to strip away the years of misunderstanding and grasp the truth behind the illusion of this existence."

"The truth, you say?"

"Take a first step toward heaven where you might celebrate with joy and happiness the majesty of our Creator!"

The old man slowly rose to his feet. "It sounds mighty nice," he said. "I appreciate how much you and I share philosophically, but my view of the prime mover is much more impersonal."

Jesus bit his lip and held a clenched fist, evidently dismayed by his inability to convince the brilliant Athenian of a fact, which, to Jesus, seemed extraordinarily commonplace.

Perhaps Plato was sensing the same thing of Jesus as he spoke.

"You make several good points, Jesus," said the Greek philosopher. "I wouldn't be so hard on myself if I were you," he laughed. "I'm not really such a great catch."

"But I care about everyone," Jesus protested, "Young, old, the wise and the foolish."

Plato started away along the side of the courtyard toward the table of food.

"Well, son," he said as Jesus followed anxiously along, "If you complete your education and assemble your team, you'll experience a great deal of success. Still, I wish you luck finding twelve loyal men."

Plato stopped abruptly at the table. Something was wrong. Immediately, I thought of our companion, Steve.

"Aristotle!" bellowed the old philosopher at the table.

The courtyard suddenly got grew very quiet. I saw a bird hop from one branch to another on an olive tree on the other side of the wall at the back of the enclosure. The bird flew quickly away.

"Yes, sir?" replied Aristotle. The popular apprentice stood looking across the quiet courtyard at his mentor.

"What has happened to my lunch?" asked Plato.

"Your lunch?"

"Yes, the lunch that has been sitting here all morning? I was going to offer some cheese and bread to my friend from the east. He looks as though he's starving to death!"

Jesus shook his head, "It's no problem, really. I'm fasting."

Plato stopped and looked back at Jesus, "As you wish," he replied. He turned back toward his protégée and his orator's voice boomed across the courtyard. "I had not planned on sharing my entire meal!"

By now everyone in the courtyard was looking at Steve who sat on a bench with a large cup of wine.

"Isn't anyone interested in the philosopher's stone?" interrupted Sarah in a loud voice. Like an auctioneer, she held the rock over her head for the crowd's inspection. The young man whom she had dismissed as "Hercules" looked up at her with a rueful smirk on his face.

"Some philosopher's stone," he laughed.

"No, really, it is…" replied Sarah in a faltering voice.

"She acts as though we've never seen any of those before," joked another student to his companions.

"Say, do you happen to have a map to the Golden Fleece?" someone yelled from a bench at the rear of the courtyard.

Plato wasn't laughing, nor was he particularly interested in Sarah's report of a philosopher's stone, although right then and there, with the vast quantities of tin and zinc and copper everywhere in evidence on the grounds I might have transmuted gold enough to have changed the course of human history in the Mediterranean for the next thousand years.

The Greeks weren't buying today. Even Aristotle was more concerned about getting something for his master's lunch than the possibility that a genuine philosopher's stone was on the premises. Had I been equipped with any kind of human cultural background, I might have felt like an utter fool, standing there in my purple Merlin costume. As it was, the scorn and ridicule in the whispers and stolen glances of the young Athenians caused me no greater displeasure than raindrops sliding off the back of a dolphin. I was feeling mighty low, but it had nothing to do with any of them.

Of all my companions I suspect Jesus was the most upset. His expectations had been very high. After his generally positive encounter with the Buddha he felt as though he could materialize nearly anywhere in time and walk away with believers. Of course the only convert he had to date in all of human history, was me, and I wasn't even a human being.

Greece was a disaster. Although Steve seemed to be enjoying Plato's lunch, everyone else in the courtyard of the Groves of the Academy seemed upset by one thing or another. Aristotle had run off to the kitchens to put together another meal for his mentor. The students, drifting away to another courtyard of the gymnasium, were dreading the rigors of afternoon lectures on geometry. Plato sat angrily beneath his sacred tree wrestling with the demands of his life of the mind and an appetite for wine and roast lamb.

In my old human body, I sweat profusely beneath my heavy purple robes in the hot, noon-day sun, and my mind began to swim with dizziness. Just then I realized that Sarah was missing. Jesus must have sensed it too. I caught his gaze across the courtyard and I wondered if I could communicate with him using mental telepathy. Although this was common fare for angels, I had never attempted the mode of communication with a human being. I was having a difficult time concentrating that day, but resolved that I was going to put absolutely everything aside, reach out mentally and contact the Son of the Creator.

"Hey, M-2500?" a voice interrupted.

"Yes?"

"Where's, Sarah?" asked Steve, stuffing the last oily piece of pita bread into his mouth.

"That's a good question," I replied.

"She went off with that young teacher," said Steve.

"What?"

"I just wondered where they were going."

"To get something to eat for the founder of the academy!" I replied.

"Where are you going?" asked Steve as I walked away.

"Please tell Jesus I'll be back soon. Look for me by the main gates if we should become separated."

So much for telepathy. How could I communicate with the mysterious Entity when I couldn't communicate with someone like Jesus sitting in plain sight?

I stepped out of the courtyard onto a broad pathway leading to the main buildings of the academy. I suddenly felt as though a million unseen eyes were staring down at me. Where on earth could she have gone? I scanned the vicinity and detected a swatch of infrared coming from inside a lone building at the far end of the compound. I was about to resume my search in that direction when I became suddenly aware of my ancient human hands swinging along at my sides. I dashed behind a nearby tree to remedy the situation. Looking left and right, and seeing no other human beings nearby, I closed my eyes and opened them. I looked down at my hands. They were transformed. By human standards they were now young, lean and powerful. I exchanged the absurd costume of Sarah's fairy tale for a contemporary Grecian robe. My countenance was a handsome amalgam of the youths I had encountered during the lecture. I emerged from behind the tree looking every bit the part of any number of Athenian scholars, and I walked quickly in the direction of the heat source.

I passed wordlessly by groups of strolling students and elderly men of learning and young athletes preparing for an afternoon of competition at the stadium. Soon, I was walking behind the main buildings on a tiny path leading to the isolated kitchen house.

The morning fires in the hearth were low and the kitchen was apparently deserted but for one young man, a dwarf, unable to use the sense of hearing we had designed so long ago. He was at work in a silent world before a wooden bench where he pounded out a white food substance on a long board. He was oblivious to my presence. On a low table I noticed a ceramic plate of human food and a cup of wine draped beneath a translucent veil of fabric. I crossed the dirt floor to the back of the building and exited through a covered walkway to an outbuilding. With angelic vision I gazed through the wooden panels of the door and saw exactly what I had expected to see. I paused for a moment at the doorway listening to the human voices on the opposite side of the panels. Co-mingled with those voices, as the grip of my human hand closed over the door handle, I detected another voice, deeper, fainter yet more intense and urgent. Someone or something was desperately trying to contact me. It seemed that it was calling from a deep well locked away within my own spirit. It sounded new and alien and yet, somehow, familiar, and I was reminded of my conversation with Jesus' uncle. I was about to cry out to him in answer when a low voice strummed the currents of air beside my human ear.

"Go in," it said.

I turned my head to my left and beheld a beautiful young man standing beside me in the shadows of the afternoon sun. It seemed absolutely fitting that he should be there at that moment.

"I really shouldn't," I whispered.

"But aren't we here for an education?" replied the youth.

"I am an angel," I replied.

"Then why have you come to this doorway?"

"I have lost my way," I said.

"And I am here to help you."

"Are you an angel?"

"Once. I began as an angel, but now I am something greater. I possess the knowledge of good and evil."

"How can you be of help to me?" I asked.

"I can make up for the billions of years you've been deprived," said the beautiful being placing, his hand on mine. "This will help open your eyes to all you have missed of your creation," he said and together we opened the pantry door. He nodded that I should enter, and he quickly departed, leaving me alone before the open doorway.

There were shouts from inside the pantry as two people quickly parted from an embrace. The man ordered me to close the door and leave at once, but the woman only laughed and called me forward. She was up on her feet and took my hand and something in my mind was telling me to leave, but I did not resist the pull of the female hands. She asked me my name.

"Demetrius," I lied.

And I pulled the door closed behind me.

* * *

Whether it was really the historic person of Aristotle in the pantry that day or some demonic doppelganger sent to tempt us I may never know. Perhaps the real Aristotle had never delivered a lecture at the academy that morning but had spent the hours at home in bed suffering from a mysterious illness which vanished the next day like morning mist.

However, for me on that afternoon, there was no escape through time or the distance of travel. Nothing could relieve the grim reality of what I had done. Had I joined the ranks of the adversary? I could not answer. I only knew that I had fallen.

Back at the doorway, the remains of the day played out in a grim parade of stolen glances, cruel utterance and memories that weighed so heavily I felt I should collapse through the surface of the earth.

"Well, you guys, it's probably better that you never mention a word of this, if it's all the same to you," said Sarah pulling on her robe at the doorway.

"Whatever you wish," replied Aristotle, adjusting his robe and standing up beside her at the door.

"You know that one day you will find a wife," said Sarah.

"Will, I?" replied the young philosopher.

"And your name will live for thousands of years," said Sarah.

As they exchanged another long look with one another, I pulled up my robes where I leaned against the wall at the rear of the room. I began to tremble with a profound dread. What had happened on this tiny planet that had unleashed such sensations?

"Hey sprout," said the great human thinker standing in the doorway with the young woman of the future world.

"She's not a sorceress or a fury or some nymph from your grandparent's dying religion. She's a woman of flesh and blood," he said, laughing.

"I'm sorry," said Sarah turning to me. "Don't worry about any children. I'm protected. It's a device from the future called an IUD."

"The science of future earth has developed many safeguards to protect society against overpopulation," said Aristotle.

It looked as though the two of them wanted to be on their way, to get me out of that tiny room and close the door on a fleeting chapter of their lives. Hadn't the Entity warned me of certain new laws that the human beings were to live by? Had I over-looked them? Was an angel in the guise of a human being exempt from such things? Sarah and Aristotle exchanged a worried look.

"Come on then, boy," said Aristotle. "You'll feel better soon enough. I must deliver the meal to Plato or there will be the devil to pay when we get back!"

Get back? How easy it was for him to say, as though there could ever be a "getting back" for me! At that moment, seeing the two of them, bright, young and carefree, I was reminded of the sight of Adam and Eve in the Garden and suddenly enraged, I raised my hand.

"Why don't you go ahead, Aristotle," said Sarah. "Aristotle! Oh, my God, I can't believe I'm saying that name. It's so totally awesome. I've known about you my entire life. I studied your work in prep school and college, and now, to share this bond with you!"

I felt the unseen energy of the earth coursing up from the ground where I sat, welling up at my finger-tips as Sarah droned on and on. I was one instant away from unleashing a blast of energy so intense that it would have atomized their bodies in a blaze of heat where they stood smiling at one another in the open doorway.

"Well, if you're okay," said the man with a troubled expression as he looked back at me.

Something pulled me back from the brink of the abyss. I suddenly stifled the power blast. Was I going to add murder to my list of sins? I clenched my fingers into a fist and brought it up hard against my human skull and held it there pressed against my forehead.

"There, there," said Sarah.

I felt her at my side. We were alone. Her hand brushed through my hair, and the sensation of her body against mine was altogether different than it had been those terrible minutes ago in the heat of human lust. My rage subsided and for a moment I felt peace and a hope that I might survive.

"I'm sorry," I said. "Please forgive me."

"There's nothing to forgive," she replied. "If anything, I'm the one who should ask your forgiveness. From the looks of you, I'm at least five years older than you." She tried to get a smile from me. "I guess you've never been with an older woman." She sensed that I found no humor in her remark. "I shouldn't have said that," she continued, "I'm really sorry, but why don't you pull yourself together and we'll be on our way? It's a lovely day outside. You're bright, and handsome, and wealthy and strong, and you have a geometry lecture to attend."

"Thank you, Sarah," I said and dried my eyes and it was then that I sensed her suddenly recoil. She probably realized that we had never exchanged names.

"Wait a second," she said, "Do I…" she paused in disbelief and she scooted away from me in the dimness. "Demetrius? Do I know you?"

I didn't know what to say. I just sat there silently, but with every second that passed I realized my silence only confirmed her suspicion. My back pressed against the wall as she climbed to her feet and dusted herself off and crossed back to the doorway.

"Well, listen, if you should happen to see an old man dressed like Merlin the magician, tell him to meet me at the main gate. I want out of this madhouse! And here," she said, reaching into a fold of her robe and producing a stone, "Be sure to give him this!" She threw the stone at me and disappeared through the doorway.

The stone hit me in the chest, bounced, and clattered onto the dry boards as the door slammed shut leaving me alone in the darkness. I sat there as my human eyes slowly dilated. I reached over and picked up the "philosopher's stone," and held it in my palm. My human-shaped fingers slowly closed over it. I squeezed. I squeezed and squeezed and for a moment I found relief from the world that I had conspired with the Creator to bring forth. For me it had been so simple and harmonious for so many eons playing is his sandbox of inanimate, soulless objects. Now, the walls of the pantry began to shudder and within my clenched fist the weight of a hundred million tons of earth and the heat of the center of a sun shuffled the building blocks of creation.

I left the pantry and crossed back through the kitchen. The veil of fabric lay on the table. The meal was gone. I looked over at the lone dwarf still at work at his bench making bread for the children of Athenians far more fortunate than he. I plunged my clenched fist into a full bucket of water beside the hearth. A flag of hot steam flashed away from the rim of the pail, and I removed my fist, already dry. His lot in life would soon improve, and I emptied the contents of my hand onto the gossamer fabric. He looked up with a kind smile, but then, almost immediately looked down at his hands. I walked over to him and with a voice that needed no air waves to transmit, I spoke.

"Good day, Palamon. When they ask you, tell them you found the stone washed-up on the shore of the sea. This is a gift for you and your family from a friend. Spend its riches wisely,"

The young man raised his stout arm and took the sparkling diamond, the largest of any yet known to exist in the ancient world.

* * *

It was late afternoon when we gathered on a bench just inside the gates of the academy. Plato and Aristotle and a number of the other academicians were on hand to wish us well. Although they had no idea how we were planning to resume our journey, they brought wine skins and sacks of bread and fruit and Plato quieted the crowd and told them how fortunate they had been to have been visited by the wise man from the east and his loyal followers.

The sound of the words "loyal followers" cut like a lash in the deep wound of my consciousness and reverberated in my skull as the philosopher continued. I had resumed the appearance of the wizard, Merlin, upon leaving the kitchens. As though in a distorted nightmare I had walked from the outbuildings at the end of the reserve through the bright afternoon up the long path to this stony bench where I waited for the others. I sank in a black pool of guilt. My human breath came in gasps and I fought an urge to stand, to run, to do anything I could to escape what had happened behind the kitchens. Suddenly, I was distracted by the sound of celebration.

Word came down from one of the cooks that the kitchen helper, Palamon, had discovered a magnificent diamond on the shore of the sea. Arrangements were already underway with Plato and the benefactors of the academy to provide the loyal servant and his family with new lodgings and an increase in their food allotment in exchange for the magnificent gem. I saw the tiny youth raised-up high on the arms of the young scholars who paraded him down through the gates for a celebration at a nearby inn. I saw the smiling face of the dwarf. Although he did not recognize me, I waved at him with the hand that had brought him his good fortune and through my tears forgot, for a moment, all the troubles of that terrible day.

* * *

We walked through the outskirts of town at sunset each carrying a load of food and a full wineskin. We retraced our way up the gulley and back to the hillside where we had landed early that morning. It was sunset as we picked our way up through the low bushes and trees to the clearing and sat down, finally, in a circle around Jesus. Had he ever traveled with such a band of misfits before? I had slipped back into the familiar shape of M-2500 hoping that somehow the guilt associated with my human skin would somehow dissipate, but as I sat there on the hillside staring at the silent figure of Jesus all the terrible feelings returned. My crystal arrays must have been running mighty blue; even Steve sensed that something was broken.

"So what's eating everyone tonight?" he offered. "I'd say we had a pretty good day of it. Good food and drink. We got to see some famous, faraway places. Jesus got to rub shoulders with the wise men. Even Sarah got to hang out with what's-his-name."

"Aristotle," said Sarah. "His name is Aristotle."

"So, where did you guys run off to for so long?" asked Steve.

"None of your business."

"Bite my head off why don't you?" replied Steve.

"We went to replace the lunch that you ate, in case you don't remember!" said Sarah.

"I remember Plato wasn't very happy with the cold food you brought back!" said Steve.

Sarah stood up, and Steve scooted back on the rock he had chosen for a seat.

"Why don't you ask your angel friend over there why the food was cold!" she shouted.

Steve was puzzled by this deflection, but looked over at me.

"Okay! Okay! I will, Ms. Holier-Than-Thou! What about it Debbie? You're the one who went off looking for Sarah."

I sat, frozen, watching the cool opaque gaze of Jesus across the circle we had formed on the ground as the red and orange light of sunset went up into the clouds of the west.

"Debbie?" repeated Steve. "Where was she?"

"She was with the man," I answered as truthfully as I was able.

"Okay, I got that much, but…" Steve broke off and looked back and forth between Debbie and me, "But where were you?"

There was a long pause. Steve was becoming visibly upset.

"Where were you?" he asked again.

"Go on! Tell him, you freaking monster!" said Sarah. Apparently she had decided to the clear the air. "You make Steve here look like a saint. It's going to come out sooner or later!"

The look of realization dawning across Steve's face was a terrible sight to behold and although I realized that he already knew the answer, he shouted at me.

"Where were you?"

"I was…" I said.

"I said, 'where were you?'" he shouted again, afraid, perhaps to give me time to reply.

"Where?" he cried.

"I was with Sarah," the words tumbled from my lips and there was no drawing them back.

"You what?"

"I said 'I was with…"

Before I could utter another word, Steve closed the short distance between us and leapt upon me with such fury that my conical form nearly toppled to the ground. As it was, the frail human being slid across my crystal arrays and audio ports to the ground. He was pounding me with his fists.

"You picked a winner there, Jesus," Sarah shouted. "You want us to spend eternity in heaven with a monster like that?"

Through the shouting, Steve raised a rock in his bloodied hands and with all his might, bashed it against my crystal arrays. A high pitched ringing sounded down the hillside above his frustrated sobs as he pounded away. The flinty stone sent out sparks that dazzled my view across those few yards to where Jesus sat immobile, like the image of the clay Buddha in my chest.

Sarah walked up and shoved Jesus hard in his shoulder.

"He pretended he was a human being!" she cried. "He pretended he was a human being. Just like you, Jesus! He pretended he was one of us. Just like you!"

With all her strength she slapped Jesus across the face, so hard that his head jerked violently to one side. Having done this, almost immediately, she stopped in her tracks. Meanwhile, Steve fell into the dust, haggard and leaning against my immobile frame. He looked across the way as Sarah dropped to the ground at the feet of Jesus, the son of the Creator, and for all we knew, the Creator itself.

My tentacles, which could have razed the glittering Parthenon on the Acropolis behind us in the sunset, lay uncoiled and useless at my sides as Steve and Sarah wept. A trickle of blood ran down Jesus' lip where Sarah had delivered her blow. We sat in silence, until, finally, Jesus spoke.

"There are forces in these hills that intend to defeat us," he said. "You encountered such a spirit today, M-2500. You were tempted and you succumbed to that temptation. I tell you it is only by the power of the Entity that you may yet be saved."

"Saved? He doesn't deserve saving!" Sarah cried.

"Silence," said Jesus, and he came to his feet.

He stood there and received the silence he demanded.

"I say it is by his power alone that any of us may be saved."

We did not know what to utter in reply as the sun sank on the horizon and the light faded to black and the stars came out from the darkness of space. I felt the desire to say something to him, but he held up his hand and spoke again.

"Sarah, do you think the devil has not tempted me as well? Our guardian angel did not anticipate the forces he would encounter when he became the figure of a man. He was unprepared and quite overwhelmed."

"So, you're making excuses for him?"

"Forgiveness and excuse are not the same thing. I want you to understand what we are up against."

"Don't you get it?" Sarah replied. "He lied, Jesus. He lied to me about his identity. I was deceived!"

"It is a terrible wrong."

"As for my part in it, well…" said Sarah, "In my day and age things will be a lot different."

"I am sure they will be."

"But lying is wrong at any time."

"Bearing false witness?"

"Yes!" said Sarah, triumphantly.

"And promiscuity?" asked Jesus.

"Excuse me?" she said, but there was no reply. Her gaze sharpened in the dying light of dusk.

"Now, wait a second," said Sarah, "What I did wasn't so bad."

"It is not given to us to pick and chose the commandments we shall obey and those to ignore."

That put an end to the conversation.

Our relationships were damaged all the way around that circle as we picked ourselves up and I silently traversed the side of the hill to an open meadow. In five seconds, I had completed my metamorphosis and sat on two chrome landing runners, facing east. My passengers boarded silently and left their provisions with Steve who stored them in the galley as Jesus and Sarah went to the cockpit and buckled their seat belts.

5. The Temple

It took me only a moment to slip through the atmosphere back into the clean, empty reaches of space. Jesus' uncle was trying to contact me with the coordinates for the next jump. We left it to Sarah to push forward the time-control lever a few hundred years, but it was really the Entity who zeroed-in on the precise date.

We put down on the outskirts of Jerusalem in 34 AD. We disembarked on the northern flank of the Mount of Olives. When I asked Jesus whether I should follow along in my invisible mode, he insisted that I take a human form. Steve suggested I assume the shape of an ox and a cart to carry us. Jesus was impressed by this suggestion but turned it down.

"The Greek youth," he said, as Sarah's eyes went wide in alarm, "Take the form of the Greek youth."

Sarah was about to complain, but she heard him out and decided that however painful it might prove to be reminded of Demetrius, if forgiveness and reconciliation was the aim, there probably could have been no better form for me to inhabit. I affected the metamorphosis and came from behind a stand of olive trees dressed in the robes of the young Greek scholar. I stepped cautiously toward my three comrades.

"Well, M-2500," said Sarah, "It will take some getting used to."

I walked along at the rear of the party as we circled the top of the Mount of Olives toward the South. It probably did go a way towards patching up the terrible rift between us that I should have assumed the form of a human being and not oxen or a wooden cart. I was grateful that Sarah had made a tentative step towards forgiving me for my deception, yet, as we walked single file line along a pathway bordering the Kidron Valley, I sensed that Steve remained upset with me. Sexuality and the sins of the Garden had intertwined in the hearts of these human beings. I concluded that the best way to win back Steve's favor was simply to perform tasks and produce consumables.

Suddenly, Jesus thrust his arm in the air and turned with his finger pressed to his lips.

"What is it?" said Sarah in a whisper.

Jesus shook his head and pointed over a low hedge of bushes. Below us, leaning against the trunk of an ancient olive tree was a bearded man, approximately thirty years old. He was talking in hushed tones to a group of young men. Looking over the hedge, Jesus beheld his exact duplicate sitting there beneath the olive branches. The Jesus below us had even more grey in his long hair and his beard was full. He spoke to those sitting at his feet in a low volume with a familiar voice. They looked beyond the monuments of an ancient Jewish cemetery winding down the slope, out across the valley over the rooftops and the walls of Jerusalem at what I imagined was their temple. It rose up from an enormous, man-made platform of rock, surrounded by walls and towers and ornamentation of great beauty.

The meeting came to an abrupt end. The men departed, some down-hill into the valley and others to the southwest. This strange "Jesus of the Future" guided a second, smaller group along a path leading to the village of Bethany.

"That was you, wasn't it?" whispered Steve, crouching in the bushes.

"I believe it was," replied our Jesus.

"Sounds like they're planning to return here each day," said Sarah.

"He spends his waking hours in the temple," said Jesus.

"Will he return to this spot tomorrow?" asked Steve.

"Let us meet at the temple in the morning. Steve, we shall assemble at the Pilgrim's Gate. It couldn't have changed much since we last were there. Do you remember, Steve?"

Steve nodded.

"Until then let us divide our number and follow these disciples. I'll shadow Jesus and his two friends. Remember, we'll meet at dawn across the valley, there, at the Pilgrim's Gate." Jesus nodded in the direction of the gigantic temple mount. "Up there, below the platform, at daybreak," he said and with that, like a phantom following silently on the heels of his future self, he disappeared in the shadows to the south.

"Let's go," said Sarah immediately heading down the steep slope in the direction Jesus' remaining followers had taken.

* * *

It is extremely difficult for three people (or even two people and an angel) to follow ten, able-bodied, young men. Of the three of us, only Steve had visited Jerusalem in the past. Sarah knew of it only as a schematic map and a few lines in a history book while I was still plagued by my ignorance of human history, having skipped billions of years and my long overdue tutoring session with the Entity. As we descended into the sprawling Kidron Valley, it seemed unlikely that I would get time for that private devotional anytime soon.

The place was packed with revelers and pilgrims and all manner of people: Jews and Gentiles, and people from up and down the country-side. Here were the sojourners and caravans from Samaria, Syria, Egypt, Nabatea, Arabia and Persia. Even for an angel it was frightening in that sea of humanity. Beneath the dark veil of night in this valley between the cemetery on the Mount of Olives and the Temple there existed a thriving spirit world.

We passed through narrow and crooked streets following the men we had seen with Jesus. They parted company at the Roman Road. Several headed west while the remaining four walked eastward along a busy thoroughfare, lit by torchlight. Even at this late hour, the way was burgeoning with activity. The young men that we followed were fast and it was only through our quick thinking and determination that we were able to keep pace with them as they crossed the highway and turned up a side street in the shadow of the Temple Mount. The foursome stopped at an inn. We followed them inside and took a table to ourselves in a corner of the crowded establishment. The room was full of loud and hungry travelers and Steve and Sarah were about to order some food when we realized that we had no means to pay. Steve suggested I go back outside where could I transmute a piece of rock into gold with which to purchase meals and rooms at the inn. I was inclined to oblige him. It wasn't too much later that we found ourselves back outside standing on a street corner while Steve scoured the gutter for a palm-sized rock.

"Look," said Sarah, elbowing me in the side as I gazed up through the night sky at the fires burning along the walls of the Temple Mount. "Isn't that one of those guys?"

"I'll go," I said, starting slowly across the street. "I'll look for you up there, at what you call the Pilgrim's Gate."

"How will you know where to find it?" asked Sarah.

"I will ask someone," I replied.

"Well, see if you can't bring along something to eat, too," said Steve.

The dark haired young man from the tavern had swung around the corner and headed north up one of the narrow side-streets. As I crossed the cobbled road before the inn my quarry stopped suddenly and looked back over his shoulder. I dropped back into a dark alleyway and re-emerged a moment later cloaked in the angelic veil of invisibility. Following the mysterious young man, I quickened my pace and soon found myself traveling into a more affluent neighborhood. I glided into a crossroads only several steps behind the man, and suddenly froze in my tracks.

I looked across the plaza to a fountain where another young man sat on a bench. He rose up and took the hands of the other in greeting. I slipped back into the alcove before a darkened residence and looked across the intersection at the two men. I squinted my human eyes, strained my human ears and let the angelic power in the core of my being command my senses, enabling me to overhear the conversation undetected and to gaze into the face of the stranger at the fountain.

It was the very same young man whom I had encountered more than four-hundred years earlier in ancient Greece! Although my clothes were presently invisible to human eyes, we both wore the same garments, in outward appearance, as we had that day behind the kitchens at the Academy.

Now, centuries later, in the shadow of Herod's Temple Mount on the eve of the Passover, I was secretly staring into the face of the Enemy. Who, exactly, was this creature whom I had met before? It was no coincidence that he was here and none, perhaps, that I stood across the street, my back pressed against the ancient stones, watching.

"Now, Judas," said the young man, "Surely after tonight your mind is resolved?"

"I don't know," choked the young man.

"For a man opposed to the tyranny of Roman rule, I think you have allied yourself with a most unlikely general."

"Jesus intends to overthrow the Romans!"

"Of course he does."

"He does!" the young man named Judas insisted.

Iscariot walked to the end of the bench and he looked up at the temple illuminated in the gloom by a hundred fires. "What in God's name am I doing here?" he asked himself.

"You are taking destiny into your own hands," replied the other.

"Is that what I'm doing?" asked the youth, looking down from the temple into his open palms. He sat slowly down on the end of the bench, and the handsome youth slid alongside and whispered to him.

"The priests are waiting. You have only to nod your head and the meeting will occur. I shall lead you there. Can you nod your head?"

Judas Iscariot nodded his head slowly.

"See now how easy that was for you to do?"

"But.." Iscariot began, "I only meant that I could nod my…"

"The time for words has past," interrupted the young man. He extended his finely manicured hands down toward the seated youth. "Now is the time for our actions to speak for us."

Iscariot took the youth's hands and slowly stood. The other moved him along the courtyard the way an impatient caregiver might hasten an invalid along to a dayroom or a quiet porch. They were headed toward the long shadows of another dark alleyway. I followed at a distance, and through the course of that long, black night I learned the extent of Iscariot's treachery and details of the evil snare he had plotted for his friend and teacher.

It was nearly dawn by the time I made my way out of the Kidron Valley to the southern wall of the Temple Mount. I had only to ask a group of pilgrims on the street to find my way. Even at this early hour, the streets were crowded. Merchants were changing money from crowded stalls. Pilgrims purchased sacrificial animals and food and drink and entrance to the baths for ritual purification. It was all new and extremely complicated to my way of thinking and when I encountered Steve and Sarah near the Southern steps, Steve's explanation did little to clarify the procedure.

"It's just something you have to do get right with God," he said.

"It sounds difficult and time consuming," I replied.

"I agree with you there," said Sarah. "Look at all these poor lambs they're buying to take up there and kill."

"It's a sacrifice," said Steve.

"A 'sacrifice?' What does that even mean?" said Sarah.

"You have to pay God back for what you did wrong!"

"Oh, I do, do I?"

She turned and glared at me until I looked away.

"I don't mean you, specifically," said Steve. "I mean people in general. You saw what happened to Adam and Eve."

"And killing a lamb is going to fix that?" she complained and turned to me. "You're supposed to have a super human intelligence. How does killing a lamb get anyone 'right with God?' Does that make any kind of sense to you?"

"I don't know," I replied. "Without more details of the circumstance it is difficult to determine."

"I guess where you come from in the future, lambs aren't worth all that much," said Steve. "You have to repay him with something you value. That's all."

For nearly an hour we waited at the Pilgrim Gate beside the busy Southern Staircase. The marble steps of the staircase rose up to a level parallel to the street and emptied onto an enormous landing. A second series of steps perpendicular to the thoroughfare arched over the street and connected an adjoining corridor in the side of the Temple Mount some thirty feet above the busy highway. Finally, as we waited, and apparently, "out of the blue," to use an expression common to Sarah, she spoke to me.

"You've met him?"

"I'm sorry... Who?" I asked.

"Nobody," she replied. "Well, no... I mean the 'Creator.' You've met him?"

I nodded slowly. That simple motion seemed to satisfy her for some time as we watched the crowds move through the thronging streets.

"So, what does he look like?" Sarah asked, suddenly.

"It is difficult to put into words," I replied.

"You have met him, haven't you?"

"Oh, yes. He's magnificent. He..."

"I'm not talking about the old man we met in the Garden of Eden," she interrupted. "I want to know about the 'real god' of the heavens."

"Oh, yes. I understand, but you would be unable to countenance him in your current condition."

"Right. Of course," she replied. "But if I toss a few lambs on the altar or throw a few virgins into a volcano, then I'm good to see him?" she asked.

I waited for a moment, conscious now of the irony in her voice. I decided to answer honestly. "There will be neither lambs nor virgins enough to erase a single transgression," I replied.

"Oh, excuse me, "Sarah snapped. "He's going to throw his son into the volcano!"

Although I sensed the derision in her hyperbolic statement, I was beginning to perceive in grim outline the destiny that lay in store for our mutual friend from Nazareth.

"I don't like your god of the universe," snapped Sarah.

"He does not require that of us," I replied.

"Well, what does he require?" she spat.

"A lamb," said Steve.

"A what?" shouted Sarah, spinning around.

"A lamb!" Steve replied. "You can buy one over there at one of the shops that…"

"Oh, just shut-up," interrupted Sarah, rolling her eyes.

Evidently she was unhappy with the fundamental design of our existence. I realized, too, that she was still very upset with me, and suddenly I wished that Jesus had remained with us and not spent the night on the other side of the Mount of Olives. As for the mysterious Entity, it remained difficult for me to contact him. Had I known him better I would have asked him to intercede with Sarah. As I pondered these thoughts, I began to wonder how the other angels of the M-Class were managing their existence. I had communicated with none of them since leaving the foundation of the earth three point eight billion years earlier. On the other hand, I had encountered the adversary and his minions on numerous occasions. I had to be constantly on my guard against them. Yes, my old supervisor knew the earth well. He was everywhere and nowhere and the name "Prince of Air and Darkness" seemed particularly apt.

More and more people were pouring into the streets. The stairway leading up to the Temple Mount was choked with pilgrims and curiosity seekers. I supposed we were in the later group. Just then, we saw some of the followers of Future Jesus approach from the south on the crowded thoroughfare. They came three abreast, and for human beings they were imposing men. To my astonishment, I could see our Jesus and the Jesus of the Future walking side by side at the rear of the group. Both men were dressed in white robes with blue sashes and they looked nearly identical, although the Jesus of three years in the future wore a full beard and carried a walking staff.

They came alongside and took stock of the money changers doing their brisk business from their roadside stalls.

"What do you make of the money changers?" asked our Jesus.

"The pilgrims must exchange their foreign currency, but it is not an ideal situation," said the Jesus of the Future. "The motive in the hearts of many of these money changers is to increase their own material gain, and not, as it should be, to help the pilgrims in their observance of the Passover."

"The priests are allowing the money changers up on the temple platform itself," said our Jesus.

"I will have to do something about that," said the older Jesus. "But listen," he continued, "I must secure a room for tonight's supper. It is going to be a very special engagement. Can you suggest a place where I might gather with my disciples?"

"There is an inn on the north side of a quiet neighborhood in the shadow of the temple mount," I replied, "Beyond the district of the priests, off the highway."

"M-2500? Is it you?" asked Future Jesus, "The angel who disappeared from the black island in the first hours of the rebellion?"

"Yes," I replied, amazed that he recognized me despite my human disguise. I realized then that he must have had some memory of his earlier adventures in the wilderness. With merely a nod from Future Jesus, the human follower named Matthew suddenly produced a leather pouch of money from his belt and handed it to Sarah.

"All right, then," said Future Jesus. "We will need wine for twenty. We will need plenty of bread. Lots of olive oil. Spread that out over a long table in four or five bowls. We will keep it simple. So, how will my followers know where to meet?"

"We saw some of your people at the inn last night," said Sarah.

"We shall direct them there," I added.

"Hey, Jesus," a deep voice sounded from above our heads.

We looked up at the leg of the staircase that climbed up over the highway to the Temple. On the landing, towering above the crowd that pushed its way around him stood a giant man.

"Peter!" shouted the Jesus of the Future.

The big red-headed man grinned and waved a huge hand over the heads of the pilgrims shoving in lines about him.

"What's up?" replied the man.

"I'll…" Future Jesus shook his head and waved Peter on with a smile. "I'll see you up top," he shouted. "I'll see you up top at the temple later this morning!"

The man named Peter waved and continued across the archway to the temple mount.

"So, do you really remember us?" asked Sarah.

Future Jesus shook his head, "I'm sorry," he said, "What I recall, from those days with you I may not entirely reveal. It is not my place to recount events which, in your mortal lives, have yet to unfold."

"You're sorry?" said Sarah. "Is that all you have to say?"

Future Jesus nodded, a sad smile on his face.

"Now, listen," replied Sarah, "I want to know what you make of my having had a one night stand with a couple guys."

"What? Where did that come from?" asked Future Jesus.

He looked across at our Jesus who shook his head in dismay.

"I don't think it's such big a deal, do you?" asked Sarah, "Do you remember?"

"Yes. I recall the incident, but I am afraid I cannot condone your actions," said Future Jesus, "If by 'deal' you mean having sexual relations with two men?"

"Not exactly two men," she said, glaring at me as she spoke.

"And that was two at the same time?" said Future Jesus slowly as though he was recalling the memory from some half-forgotten dream.

"More or less, at the same time," said Sarah flatly and looking down at the flagstone street.

"I believe that could be very serious 'deal' indeed, at least here in Judea," said Future Jesus.

"But it didn't happen in Judea. It happened in another country, a long, long time ago where people did that sort of thing," said Sarah, "Would it be wrong then?"

"There were the examples of Sodom and Gomorrah," replied the Future Jesus. "I suppose in those cities it was rather commonplace, if that's what you mean."

"Sodom and Gomorrah is not what I mean," said Sarah. "I want to know whether you think it was a bad thing for me to do."

"If you're right with God and you don't make a habit of sleeping with strangers, it probably isn't too much cause for concern."

"Are you sure you remember me?" asked Sarah.

"I am quite certain that I remember you," replied Future Jesus with a smile. "You are Sarah. Sarah from two thousand years in the future."

He looked at Steve who quickly nodded his head.

"Mary Magdalene is one of my dearest followers," continued the Jesus of the Future. "When we first met she was a prostitute."

"Prostitute!" cried Sarah, "Now just a second here! What is that supposed to mean?"

The Jesus from the Future smiled, "It means that people may change."

"I'm not a prostitute!" shouted Sarah.

"It's really incredible," said Steve, suddenly, as though he had come to an amazing realization. "You two guys could be twin brothers."

Mortified beyond speaking, Sarah stared at the Future Jesus in disbelief. Steve's oblique and off-topic observation was apparently all it took to change the subject. Meanwhile, our own Jesus had mounted the stairway and called for Steve to accompany him.

"Coming, Jesus," replied Steve and he quickly turned back to Jesus from the Future and extended his hand. "I guess we'll see you again tonight at the Passover meal."

Jesus of the Future nodded. "Yes, that is the plan, but stay a moment," he said. "I see that you still bear the mark of the devil on your hand." He stepped forward, took hold of Steve's arm and examined the black, web-like tattoo on the right hand.

"Yes, I'm sorry about that thing," replied Steve.

"I thought you were going to have it removed?"

"What?"

"The mark, Steve," said Future Jesus. "In Oakland, wasn't it?"

"Oakland?" Steve repeated.

"Oakland?" exclaimed Sarah. "We haven't been to Oakland. Wait… We're not going to Oakland are we? Oakland, California?"

"Oh, yes, and a number of other cities throughout history. A hectic schedule. Perhaps it was St. Louis?" mused Future Jesus, completing his thought and releasing Steve's hand. "Good luck to you, Steve, in any event. You will have ample opportunity to get that cleaned-up. See that you do."

"Well, thanks," said Steve, backing up into the crowd.

Our Jesus had already ascended the landing and Sarah and I turned back to Future Jesus.

"Listen," I said quickly, "Your younger self had us follow some of your disciples last night."

"Yes?"

"I believe one of them is planning to betray you."

Behind Future Jesus, Sarah was silently mouthing the name JUDAS ISCARIOT as she looked to me for confirmation. As Future Jesus turned to glance back at Sarah, I nodded solemnly.

"What is it?" said Future Jesus, turning back to me. "It seems as though everyone knows the identity of my betrayer but me. It is Peter?

I shook my head.

"John?"

"No," I said.

"Matthew?"

"Not Matthew," said Sarah.

Jesus of the Future shook his head and continued to list his apostles. Evidently, he had overlooked a few.

"I give up," he said at last. He looked expectantly at Sarah.

"What?" she said with a cruel smile on her lips. "Is it my place to recount events which have yet to unfold in your life?"

"Touché," said the Future Jesus.

"Touché?" she repeated, evidently puzzled by the utterance.

"It is only by the power of the Holy Spirit that we understand one another," he said, "But yes. It is a French word, touché. Parlez vous Francais, aussi?"

"Oui. I mean, yes," said Sarah and the color of her skin suddenly blushed red. "A little. Two years in college." When she looked up, her face conveyed bewilderment. "You've been to France?" she asked.

"Mais oui, bien sûr. Many things were revealed to me during my time in the wilderness." he replied, mysteriously. "Did you imagine Steve would keep the secret of my arrest to himself?"

"Your arrest?" Sarah exclaimed. She appeared shocked by this revelation and staggered backwards until she bumped against the terrace wall bordering the walkway. Future Jesus was relentless.

"Early in your adventures with my younger self, you secretly confided in Steve the story of my final days. You exacted a promise that he would keep the information to himself. But how could he?"

"He told you? Steve told you about...?" she trailed off, apparently unable to complete her thought.

"Not the particulars," replied Future Jesus. "He said only that I would be put to death an innocent man. He told me what he knew. How could he not? But this is now centuries ago."

"Centuries ago?" Sarah protested, "I told Steve about it last week!"

"You are a time traveler, Sarah. Betrayal is part of the human story. You will encounter it throughout your journey, I can assure you."

Sarah gazed into Jesus' eyes and she slowly nodded.

"Rest easy, Sarah. You need say nothing more on the subject. The name of my betrayer is of no consequence to me," he said.

"No consequence?" we exclaimed.

"Besides, I could not have completed my education without reading a copy of the New Testament. I remember the essential points."

"You've read the New Testament?" asked Sarah.

"In the wilderness, as you will one day observe, but again, this is beside the point. You are to concern yourselves with your traveling companion, the one who rescued you from highway, Sarah."

"But what about you?"

"When it is time, the Holy Spirit will reveal to me the identity of my fallen student."

"Judas!" Sarah and I said in unison.

"Judas?" repeated Jesus of the Future. "I would not have suspected Judas, but now that you speak the name, I am reminded. The Holy Spirit prepares to make his move. C'est la vie."

"Hey, Jesus!" someone shouted from above and Sarah and the Jesus of the Future jumped-up, startled. I scanned the crowd and gazed at the archway crossing overhead to the Temple Mount. Steve hung over the parapet smiling and waving down at us. He'd caught up with our Jesus on the bridge.

We looked up and waved at our two companions. As soon as they were lost to view, Sarah and I told Jesus of the Future the details of his pending entrapment by the religious authorities. Afterward, Sarah and I expressed our desire to help with the supper planned for that evening. He explained that he hoped to wash the feet of his twelve disciples. I would provide water for that purpose.

Sarah looked distraught. She drifted slowly away. When I called to her, she replied that she needed time to think and that she would wait for me in the valley outside the inn. Jesus of the Future watched her depart through the crowded street. His eye seemed to tear-up and he smiled tenderly, "Despite my faith," he confided, "It is difficult to realize that I shall not speak with her again in this life."

We stood silently in the hot morning sun, the sounds and smells of the busy street washing about our senses. I felt I needed to say something to his man, whose younger self I had followed from the dawn of life, but I could not find the words. I suddenly remembered our plans for the afternoon and turned to him.

"Just send a couple of your followers down from the temple and I will meet them here."

"How will they recognize you?" he asked.

"Here, let me show you something," I whispered.

He came close and we looked town into the palm of my right hand. We watched a tiny white and red vessel, the size of a pimple, erupt from beneath the skin in the center of my palm. The whirling red and white-striped boil held Jesus spellbound as it steadily grew in size. We faced the low wall over-looking the Kidron Valley and the pilgrims, travelers, and citizens passing by on the street behind us and crowding the staircase, did not see the white, thirty-gallon clay container with bands of red spinning up from the angelic potter's wheel in my hand.

"That is very impressive," said the Jesus of the Future. "Now, I remember! A space ship. It was a space ship from the far future. Yes! The red and white space ship whose form and special powers were loaned to us by the Thrones. Of course that was most impressive, M-2500, but this container is very elegant, understated. Very nice."

"Thank you," I said and hefted the gigantic, white and red vessel up onto my shoulder.

"I'll pull some moisture out of the atmosphere with a little condenser unit and have this filled in no time," I said.

"You angels have always amazed me with your technical abilities and mastery of the physical realms," he said. "But I must get up top to the temple and round-up some of my sheep."

I was suddenly saddened that the Jesus of the Future and I would soon be parting company.

"Thank you for the report on my betrayal," he said, "Although, just between the two of us, I was not at all surprised."

"Farewell," I said, summoning a smile.

He turned toward the crowd at the stairway. "I will send down two of my 'loyal' followers," he said with a laugh.

"Don't worry," I called up to him, "Have them look for the fellow carrying the red and white water barrel."

Future Jesus nodded and disappeared into the crowd above.

* * *

That afternoon everything went off like clockwork. Sarah had checked-in with the inn-keeper and left for a walk. The folks were sympathetic to the teachings of the rabbi from the north who had recently appeared in town for the Passover. Around noon, I was approached by two of his followers. I recognized the big red-haired man named Peter and met another named John. They followed me into the valley and along the busy Roman street to the north side of town where we veered off a side-street to the inn. Some of the disciples had been there the night before and Peter and John went with them to the owner and got everything ready upstairs for Jesus' special Passover supper.

By the doorway I filled clay pots with water and it wasn't too much later that Steve showed up with our Jesus. It was five o'clock when the Jesus of the Future came through the doors and soon after his followers arrived. It got a little crowded and loud, what with all the other patrons downstairs.

Jesus of the Future thanked me for my help and got a bowl and some towels and started calling his people over to the back staircase to have their feet washed. It was taking a long time and there was a really big line, so our Jesus went over and asked his future self if he wouldn't mind his helping out.

Future Jesus laughed and the two put their heads together and got sort of an assembly line going with me helping with the water bowls and the towels.

Meanwhile, Steve started a tab with the bartender and ordered wine and appetizers. Some of the locals were annoyed by the noise and commotion at the back of their neighborhood tavern, but things were wrapping up and it wasn't long until all twelve disciples had disappeared upstairs.

"Thanks for your help," said Future Jesus shaking hands with our Jesus. They stood at the bottom of the stairs and looked at the open door above them at the head of the staircase.

"You want to come up?" asked Future Jesus.

"Well, now that you mention it, yes, but it's not as though I'll be eating anything!" said our Jesus. Laughing, they ascended the staircase, disappeared through the open doorway and the door closed behind them.

We were only there for an hour. Sarah came in, looking sullen and sat at the bar beside Steve. They ate some humus and pita bread dipped in olive oil and some candied dates and drank a little wine. I think the first person to start back down the staircase was the disciple, Judas. He was ashen white and his brow was furrowed in distress.

Steve leaned over to me. "Is that him?" he whispered loudly.

I nodded and the disciple had just descended to the ground floor when Steve called out across the barroom.

"Hey bitch!"

The words stung my ears. I regretted having revealed the traitor's identity to Jesus' boyhood friend. Steve had already had too much to drink. Iscariot ignored the name-calling and crossed the room to exit, but Steve tumbled off his bar stool and grabbed Judas by the shoulder. The room was absolutely silent.

"Hey you little scum-bag, I'm talking to you!"

"Please unhand me," replied the disciple.

"I'll unhand you," said Steve, and he stumbled forward a step and shoved Judas hard in the chest so that the young man slammed into the door-jamb of the entryway. Steve raised his hand to strike, but Iscariot recovered and punched his fist into Steve's jaw. Steve toppled to the floor as Iscariot wheeled where he stood and disappeared out into the street.

Sarah and I rushed to Steve and helped him to his feet, but the inn-keeper had seen enough. He and his son came around from behind the bar and ordered Steve to depart.

"Can't you give him a second chance?" pleaded Sarah.

"Listen," said the innkeeper, "My son and I run a nice, respectable business. We can't have hooligans running around in here, especially at this time of year. Why, this man ought to be ashamed of himself."

"Me?" Steve protested as he stumbled between Sarah and me and we tried to hold him upright. "What about that bum, Judas? Do you know him? You let him in here and talk about a respectable business?"

Steve had said enough and I swept him along in one arm through the door and out to the other side of the street. Sarah followed us outside where the sun was setting behind the Temple Mount. The long blue shadows of the gigantic platform built by King Herod filtered down into the side-street where we explained to Steve the need for secrecy.

"Steve, Steve, listen," said Sarah. "There's going to be a lot of stuff that happens tonight that we're not going to be able to do anything about. If our Jesus wants any help from us, he'll ask."

"No, he won't!"

"Of course he will," said Sarah.

"Do you still think he's a phony?"

"What?"

"A liar? A confidence man? Is that what you think of my friend?"

"What I think isn't important," she said.

I had to remind myself that all we knew regarding the fate of Jesus of Nazareth we had learned from this skeptical daughter of the 20th Century.

"We have to stop him!" shouted Steve.

"Shut up," said Sarah and she grabbed him by both shoulders and pushed him up against the mud-brick building where we stood in the gathering gloom. "Don't breathe a word, or so help me Steve, I'll knock you down myself!" Sarah spat. "Jesus doesn't want anything stopped. This is supposed to happen! It has to happen!"

At about that time, men began emptying out of the tavern up the street. Some were singing loudly. Others held open bottles of wine. They were all heading our direction.

"Where do we go?" I asked.

"Gethsemane," whispered Sarah.

"What's that?" I replied and I saw our Jesus holding the tavern door open for the Jesus of the Future as they came out into the street. The big, red-headed guy seemed really drunk and he had grabbed the little guy named John and lifted him up on his shoulder.

"Here's Jesus' favorite disciple, everybody!" laughed the red-haired giant.

"Put me down, Peter, you bum," said the young man slung over the giant's shoulder.

At second glance, as they approached, it seemed to be all in fun, because all the other young men were laughing, including the two Jesus' bringing up the rear. We headed north and east through the best neighborhoods and Steve, staggered along, leading our rag-tag party, insisting he knew his way to the Garden of Gethsemane.

By now we were pretty much out of the city and we climbed the broad slope of the Mount of Olives and found our way by starlight to the garden. Steve immediately passed out where he stood. The disciples built a small fire and talked into the evening while Jesus from the Future went off on the hillside to pray. Our Jesus remained pretty sensitive to what was going on in the campground and I think he noticed his other self slip away. Our Jesus approached Sarah and me where we sat with the disciples by the fire. He said he was going to tag along after Jesus. That suited us just fine. How often does one get a chance to talk to oneself that way? Never in my experience. So, he went off, up the hillside in the dark and everyone else more-or-less drifted back a few yards from the dying fire and fell asleep on the ground.

* * *

Angels may slip into a reverie of sorts that may last a few hours or a million years, but we do not "sleep" in the sense that humans pass out of consciousness for the repair of their animal structures. Never-the-less, I pushed away from the fire like the others and in the quiet of the night called out to the Entity I had met for the first time some four hundred years earlier during the time of Siddhartha.

The celestial transmission from the great beyond resembled more than anything else that comes to mind, something which I would not encounter until the 20th Century in syndication on a little-known cable network. The story I received told of two brothers who lived in a small house and who were charged with looking after a small child. The single set was small and black and white and the brother apparently in charge of everything was rarely, if ever, seen on camera. The second brother evidently had no place of his own and was freeloading in the other's living room.

Here was the uncle lying on the sofa with his little nephew on his belly watching television and the brother in the other room was shouting about this or that and saying he was going to "smite" so-and-so and "smite" this or that, and basically telling these two characters that they had to hit the road and clear out. So, the little kid leaves, and that's pretty odd seeing a baby more or less help himself out the door and then a second later showing up on the television screen in a holiday special about a child being born in a manger. I suppose the image I'm painting was one of the those reveries inspired by the Entity, and while mine didn't last anything close to a million years, I believe I caught several episodes back-to-back which lasted a couple hours, because when I opened my human eyes, I noticed that the Jesus of the Future and our own Jesus had returned from their prayers. They were disappointed to see that their disciples, several of whom had been left to keep watch, had all fallen asleep.

My supernatural vigil didn't count as far as the two Jesus' were concerned. They returned to the camp-site several times during the course of that long night, and it was only after my sensors indicated the approach of sixty armed men on the southeastern slope that my Jesus finally seemed to notice my presence.

"Is this it?" he called to me as men moved ghostlike through the olive grove.

"What do you mean, 'is this it?'" I replied.

"Is this the betrayal by Iscariot? Is Judas among the men on the hillside?"

Jesus had to be mighty specific and literal when dealing with me in the early-going of our adventures together.

"Yes," I replied. "Iscariot leads the men he met yesterday in the city."

Sure enough, I pretty much called it, and the arrest came to pass, more-or-less the way Sarah had described it from her limited knowledge of the New Testament. The Jesus of the Future was arrested and dragged away like a common criminal. The disciples awoke in terror and ran for their lives. I believe the giant with the red hair would have done more damage with his sword, but when Jesus of the Future told him to set his sword aside, the big man ran-away for his mortal life, too.

As for our Jesus and Steve and Sarah and me, we could have been bark on an olive tree for all the attention we drew from the priests and the arresting soldiers. We simply stood witness to the dénouement of a celestial tragedy. It was black and red fire-light and anguished faces and screams and sobs and a naked disciple running into the weeds in preservation of his own pitiful human existence and it was, again, a pretty awful scene.

Steve's chief concern was to settle things with Judas, as though whatever vengeance Steve imagined he might inflict could approach the agony Iscariot experienced that morning as the sun burst on the eastern horizon like a festering sty, illuminating the hillside of Gethsemane.

* * *

My two wings came together like the perfectly matched wings of a butterfly at rest. If you had seen me perched in the bleary eyed dawn on a mandrake bush you would have seen the foul smelling remains of the abandoned camp fire, blood on the stones where a severed human ear had fallen, and me. I had grown weary of my human form and had metamorphosized into a butterfly. I sat on that bush thinking about Sarah and Steve and our Jesus. My wings beat twice more, and aligned like the palms and fingers of two, human hands pressed together in prayer. I listened, quietly as dew-drops formed on the mandrake blossoms and I gazed across the Kidron Valley toward the high wall of the Antonia. It was Mark Anthony who had befriended Herod, the Judean King, and, with the Hebrew nation's political compliance, built a massive Roman garrison in the shadow of the Jews' Holy Temple.

I strained my angelic senses in that direction and could tell that Sarah and my Jesus had followed the priests and their prisoner to the seat of local government. At the same time I sensed that Steve had trailed the lonely Judas to an abandoned field.

I flapped my wings twice and flew up into the morning air. The shimmering silver leaves of the olive trees fell away in the distance as I flew up higher and higher and crossed the still sleeping village below. I made my way across the valley and came to the high roof of the temple. I stayed there all day, praying silently to the Entity. Somehow, I knew that this was the place where I was meant to be. Just as Jesus had intended Steve to witness the grisly death of the suicide, he had wanted Sarah and his younger self to stand, hand-in-hand at the trial, and later that day, in the heat of the afternoon, to follow the road to Golgotha.

At the time, I did not know precisely what they were doing to the Jesus of the Future, only that he was going to be executed, just as Sarah had described to us from excerpts of the book she had read in the future. I needed no such evidence for my belief in that unforgettable day. I sailed through the smoke of sacrificial pyres on the temple mount and soared to the eighty foot pinnacle of the temple itself. To the north, in the shadow of the Antonia Tower, the courtyards swelled with citizens and civic and religious authorities for the trial. Later that day, a swarm of human beings appeared on the road and headed northwest to a barren hilltop where Jesus of the Future had dragged a two-hundred pound structure of perpendicular cellulose beams.

The hearing and vision of an angel is exceedingly keen, and from my vantage point there was nothing that escaped me that long and sorrowful day. It was what Sarah would have called nine in the morning when they crucified the Jesus from the future. Many of the frightened followers who had abandoned him the night before in the Garden of Gethsemane had found their way back, with the exception of Judas who hung dead by his broken neck from a crooked tree on the edge of town.

Steve found his way to Cavalry and met Sarah and our Jesus below a small gathering of onlookers. They remained on the hillside until the end came. The sky grew dark and a cold wind blew in from the west. I flew down from my perch through the courtyards and sought refuge in the Temple's inner sanctum. I landed on the incense altar outside the Holy of Holies and gazed up the sixty foot height of an enormous veil that hung down from the ceiling. The veil itself was thirty feet wide and made of fine linen and embroidered in blue and purple and scarlet yarn. Near the high ceiling, the fabric represented familiar forms of Cherubim. These were not the plump little human babies depicted in Sarah's time, but the terrible, unearthly figures who attended the throne of the Creator, one of whom we had encountered in our travels. As I watched, I noticed the enormous curtain begin to sway. The ground beneath me was trembling. The tremor grew violent and I heard shouts and screams of human beings coming from either side of the enormous room and from beyond in the Court of the Priests.

A fissure suddenly opened in the flagstones and ripped along the center of the temple floor toward the veil. A blue light began to glow from the high rafters of the ceiling where the curtain hung from a hundred metal fasteners. There was a terrific, rending sound and a blast of wind erupted from the blue light and the veil began to tear in half, starting from the roof and proceeding all the way to the floor. The blazing light and the quaking of the earth did not subside until the curtain was torn completely in two ragged halves before the now exposed pathway to a golden box once hidden within. There was something more, an unmistakable force wrapped up in a blinding wind that now swept out from behind the ruined curtain. I fell to the floor and felt my body transform, even against my will, back into my original conical shape. I rose up and looked across at what I later learned was the Jews' Ark of the Covenant. The confluence of natural and what the human beings called "super-natural" events, all pointed to the Creator's renewed intervention in the affairs of the earth.

I had not employed my old wings in some time, and as they emerged from my back and bore me up over the shattered floor, I observed frightened humans scurrying below in terror as I sailed between the broad columns over the abandoned Courtyard of the Gentiles and headed toward the Place of the Skull. Soon, I heard the wailing of men and women from the hillside, and I landed in a ravine and returned to the appearance of the Greek Youth. I trudged up the slope and found Steve and Sarah sitting on the ground beside our Jesus.

"Is he okay?" I whispered to Sarah.

"He's praying," she replied, softly.

Jesus sat there until dark. Even after some of his later-day followers had pulled down the body of his future self and borne the corpse away for burial, our friend remained, immobile on the ground as though he were in a trance. None of us would rouse him, nor did we dare speak. For once in his life, even Steve was silent. He did not mention food or drink or his bodily functions, but sat, frozen in place staring up at the hillside, a blank and far-off look in his eyes. Perhaps it was beginning to "sink in" to use Sarah's turn of phrase, that in little more than three years time, this was the fate that lay in store for Steve's only friend.

"What should we do?" I whispered to Sarah. "Remain out here until they decide to get up?"

"I think Jesus wants to stay through Easter."

"Easter?" I said, "What is that?"

"The other big Christian holiday."

"And what happens on Easter?"

Sarah did a classic movie double take, "Excuse me?"

"What?" I said.

"You honestly don't know, do you?"

"Know what? Is something important supposed to happen on Easter?"

"I'll say," said Sarah, standing and stretching her arms skyward in the dark. "He's supposed to come back to life."

"Who?"

"The man we just saw crucified up there on top of this hill."

"He's supposed to come back to life?"

"Yes."

"Literally?"

"Well, there's some disagreement about that," replied Sarah, "Whether he returns as a living, breathing person, or a spirit of some kind. I don't know, but I don't think we're going to be able to remain here."

I looked at Jesus and Steve, still sitting like statues facing the hilltop.

"So, how long would we have to remain until Easter?" I asked.

"Three days," Sarah replied. "Three days until Easter Sunday."

"Very well, then," I said, looking at our own Jesus, "I suppose it would be a shame for him to have come this far and miss his own resurrection."

6. The Gates of Heaven

It was without discussion among our original foursome that Sarah and I decided we would remain in ancient Jerusalem through Sunday. I followed a group of disciples and ran reconnaissance with Sarah who later that night led the somnolent Jesus and Steve away from the Place of the Skull to a cemetery on the edge of town. One of Future Jesus' wealthy patrons had donated his own tomb to the martyred rabbi. The forlorn and disoriented followers carried away the dead body of Future Jesus and placed it inside the tomb and withdrew while an armed guard of Roman Soldiers arrived and with ten strong men rolled over an enormous boulder to seal the entrance to the sepulcher.

We camped on a hillside behind the cemetery but spent most of our time within eyesight of the tomb. In those hours Sarah and Steve had little to eat. Rather than retrieve the last of the Greek cuisine from the galley of the space ship, I simple brought them figs and dates from some nearby fruit-trees, and my friends managed well enough. On the morning of the third day someone whom Sarah identified as Mary

Magdalene arrived at the tomb with another female named Mary. The detachment of Roman soldiers hung back, cynical and laughing about the necessity of guarding a sealed tomb against two frail females of their species.

Meanwhile, the four of us were leaning back on our hillside, watching from a distance, when Jesus sat up and quickly raised his hand above his head as though he was swiping at something pitched to him through the air.

"All right," he said. "It's time."

"Yes?" asked Steve.

Jesus nodded and looked over at me for what must have been the first time in three days. "Go and attend the tomb," he said.

It was less than a half mile to the tomb and I made it there in a minute dashing over on my nominally human legs. I sprang up over the heads of the soldiers and leaned a shoulder against the enormous wheel-shaped boulder. The soldiers were so startled by my display of athleticism that they dropped back, hands over their sword hilts, but unwilling to draw. I nudged the five-ton boulder and rolled it away, exposing the tomb's entrance. With a smile of satisfaction on my face I jumped up and landed on top of the boulder. In my enthusiasm I had begun to glow. Since I was already wearing the white robes of the Greek youth this undoubtedly lent itself to a dazzling effect, and the Romans dropped back entirely. Their hands were no longer on their swords but were raised-up, protecting their eyes from the glare.

Before I knew it another angel had joined me on my high perch. This fellow was glowing brightly and his appearance frightened me for an instant, so that I nearly fell off the boulder. When I peered through the brilliant aura, I alone of the beings at the entrance could see through the guise of the angel's humanoid features. Although he appeared to human eyes as an exquisitely formed man with wings, I looked into the crystal arrays of my old friend, M-2347.

Likewise, although I had assumed the form of Demetrius, enhanced with a glowing aura and a pair of gigantic eagle wings, M-2347 immediately recognized me. He recalled reports that I had been the first of the angels to set foot on dry land at the creation of the earth and had spent a million years on the black dune island until I was discovered there by my friends. From that point, by M-2347's way of thinking, over four billion years of earth history had come and gone. He had lived through each and every day. To me, his old associate, only two weeks had past.

"Where have you been?" he exclaimed. "After the war we thought maybe we'd lost you!"

I didn't know what to say.

"So, what are you doing here?" he asked.

"I was just going to help Jesus out of his tomb," I replied.

"Jesus of Nazareth? The Son of the Creator?"

"Yes?"

"He's not here."

"He isn't?"

M-2347 looked down at the terrified human beings cowering below us on the ground.

"Ladies? Excuse me, ladies?" said M-2347 with a silken, soothing, almost musical voice. "Ladies, please do not be afraid. We know you are looking for Jesus, but He is not here. Enter the tomb and see for yourselves, but then we ask that you please go out and tell his disciples that He has risen from the dead and that He will meet them at the Galilee."

The two women slowly approached the open tomb and gazed up at the glowing form of M-2347. Meanwhile, my own Jesus was approaching from the hillside with Sarah and Steve. The Roman guards, sobbing for their lives, had collapsed and lay face-down in the dirt. Jesus, Sarah and Steve arrived at the tomb and I was introducing them to my old friend when Jesus suggested we all go inside and inspect the tomb's interior.

Mary Magdalene was really crying. The angel glided down to the ground to console her.

"Why are you crying?" asked M-2347.

"They have taken my Lord, and I do not know where they have laid Him." No sooner were the words out of her mouth than she had turned around and walked right into our Jesus. I guess she figured he was in charge of the cemetery or something because she didn't recognize him at first.

"Sir, if you have carried His body away, let me know and I will go to Him and take Him away."

Sarah whispered something to Jesus and he nodded.

"Mary?" he asked tentatively.

"Teacher?" she said slowly looking his face up and down. Now, all of a sudden she seemed to recognize him and her face lit up and she threw her arms wide and was about to grab hold of him when he stepped back, shaking his head.

"Not yet, Mary," he said tenderly. "I have not yet ascended. But go and tell my followers that I am on my way. I am ascending to my Father and your Father, to my God and your God."

That put a smile on her face, and she and the other Mary, whom I later learned was the mother of the human being James, shouted for joy and they ran away over the hill.

We stood outside the tomb entrance and watched as the Roman soldiers climbed to their feet and ran away in the opposite direction.

We talked to M-2347.

"Oh, it's been a big celebration, really for the last thirty-three years. It's too bad you weren't around for any of it, M-2500."

I nodded my head sadly in agreement.

"So, what's next?" asked Steve.

"Everyone is excited about a visit from the mysterious new being called the Holy Spirit," said M-2347.

My eyes widened.

"You've heard of him?" asked M-2347.

"Oh, I've heard of him, all right," I replied.

"Really?"

"I may be one of the first. He is very mysterious. Comes and goes like a will-o-the wisp and requires enormous concentration to be perceived."

M-2347 hung on my every word.

"At the same time he seems always to be about, but in the deep background."

"Interesting," replied M-2347. "When rumors of his presence first began, we naturally assumed it was merely an astral projection of the Creator himself."

I nodded my human-looking head as M-2347 continued.

"Your report coincides with what we've been hearing lately from Central Command. 'The Entity' they're calling him. Apparently, he's been around since forever, really, but, again, as you've said, 'in the background', very discreet."

"And when did the rumors begin?" I asked.

"Funny you should ask," replied M-2347. "Just about the time that Jesus was born. It seems like only moments ago."

We both agreed.

"You spend a hundred trillion years working for someone like the Creator and you figure you know him pretty well. Imagine our surprise when we began hearing stories about his… Well… His…"

"His what?" asked Sarah.

"Yes, his what?" asked Jesus.

"His 'split personality,' for want of a better term," replied M-2347. "You do realize that you and the Resurrected Christ and the Entity may all be phases of the same being?"

"Phases?" repeated Jesus, slowly mulling over the word.

"You are a mortal man, but you are also the Creator of all things," said M-2347.

"That's what Sarah tells me," replied Jesus. "I don't know. I sure don't feel like a creator. I seem barely able to make it from one day to the next, much less create anything."

"Give it time," said M-2347. "I'm sure it will all become clear to you soon enough."

"Well, thank you," said Jesus. "I certainly hope you are correct."

"So, where are you folks headed?"

"I am not entirely certain," replied Jesus, "But I have a few ideas."

"What about the Pentecost?" asked Sarah.

"The Pentecost? What's that?" asked Jesus and he looked at the angel.

"I don't know," replied M-2347 and he turned to Sarah. "And I'm sorry, Miss, but I'm sensing something very peculiar about you."

"What? That I'm dead inside?"

"Well, yes, you are 'dead inside' now that you mention it."

"We have eternal souls, but we are mortal," said Steve rolling his eyes. "You angels should have that figured out by now."

"Yes, I see," said the angel looking from Steve to Sarah. "The humanoid male and female were plucked out of time by the will of the Entity and the intervention of the Ophanim."

"I like to call them Steve and Sarah," said Jesus.

"Then these are the two, legendary companions who journeyed with you to the foundation of the world and were there in the first battle of the war of the rebel angels?"

"That's us!" said Sarah.

"Yep," said Steve. "Lucifer sure was upset when he ran into us."

"An ironic turn of events," replied M-2347. "It was partially his work in the Garden of Eden that led to the fall of your ancestors."

"Tell me about it," said Steve.

"When you traveled back in time and first met Lucifer, he was so overwhelmed by his own egotism that he failed to see how his behavior might contribute to the temptation and fall of mankind."

"Not to mention his own," Sarah reminded him.

"Yes. Well, I'm not really sure I can help you with Pentecost," said M-2347. "Does it involve Jesus?"

"Not directly," replied Sarah. "It's the first public visit of the Holy Spirit and marks the anointing of the Savior's disciples."

"Isn't it amazing how she knows all this and doesn't believe a word of it?" said Steve shaking his head and marveling at his friend from the future.

"That is remarkable," agreed M-2347.

"Even after she sees something with her own eyes, she doesn't believe it," said Steve.

Everyone laughed, everyone except Sarah.

"So, has Satan been defeated in the world of the future?" asked M-2347.

"Are you joking?" said Sarah.

"She'll admit the existence of evil in the world, but dismisses any possibility of a spirit of goodness," said Steve.

"I don't believe in spirits!" said Sarah.

"Well, whatever they are!" said Steve.

"So, how is it that you're asking me whether Satan has been defeated in the future?" asked Sarah turning to my friend.

"I suppose I'm curious," said M-2347.

"Can't you see into the future?"

"Me? See into the future? I'm an M-class angel," said M-2347 and he glanced at me and we both smiled.

"I take existence one day at a time," he said.

We had a pretty good laugh, but Sarah still looked distraught. She was concerned about all sorts of things over which we had no knowledge, and over which we apparently had no control.

Jesus was anxious to leave this chapter in earth history. It was understandable, with his having just witnessed his own gruesome and protracted death on the cross. It was odd, but he did not seem particularly interested in sitting in on the Pentecost. However, he did perk-up when Sarah asked M-2347 about the Ascension.

"You do know about the Ascension don't you?" she asked.

"The what?" replied M-2347.

"The part where Jesus returns to heaven?" said Sarah.

"Oh, well, not really. I mean, we assumed that he would be returning to us at some point. We've had a number of meetings with the Strongholds assigned to this solar system. I've sat through my share of briefings on the coming and return of the Lord."

"Really?" I asked with renewed interest. "You said Strongholds. Anyone I'd know?"

"Do you remember XL-7000, the apprentice to XL-5000?"

"Absolutely."

"After the rebel war, headquarters moved XL-5000 and XL-6000 over to the Andromeda system. There was a lot of, well, let's just say, it was an unpleasant transition, but XL-7000 stepped right-up to fill the position here in the Milky Way. He had been an apprentice, after all.

We moved our base of operations back over to the moon, because, well, you know…"

"No, I don't know," I replied. "What?"

"Satan won the earth."

"The earth? The whole earth?" asked Steve.

"Pretty much. Then, of course, there was the battle over the moon. It was a logistical nightmare. We fell back beyond the heliosphere and established a barrier wall at the termination shock. Satan and his minions have had pretty much free reign within your entire solar system since the beginning of life on the planet."

"Wow. I have been away a long time," I said.

"I suppose for Satan it was a tactical victory of sorts, but the loyal forces of heaven haven't conceded defeat. We've had meetings from time to time on Eris, an ice world outside the barrier wall. About two hundred thousand years ago we saw a slide presentation on the fall of mankind. One of XL-7000's friends gave a report on something or other about twenty thousand years ago. It involved a flood where many of the species we'd spent all those millions of year perfecting got wiped out. And then, just about thirty-three years ago we attended the big birthday celebration."

"A birthday party?" I asked.

"For whom?" asked Jesus.

"For you!"

"Me?"

"Absolutely!" said M-2347. "It was all based on 'a need to know' basis, like everything else up there, but the Creator had been planning it like since Forever. XL-7000's space patrol hauled in an ice ball from the outer rim of the solar system which threw off a flare pointing the way to Bethlehem for three humanoid 'wise men' from Eurasia. I tell you, on the day you were born, Michael and the loyal archangels mounted an insurgency and the heavenly host turned out in force in this little corner of the galaxy."

"It's gratifying to hear that so much was done in honor of my mission on earth," said Jesus.

"You deserved it. After all you've been through. After everything you will go through."

There was a rather long and awkward pause.

"Well, thanks again," said Jesus, "But I'm really still only a shadow of what I hope to become, although I may have just caught myself using the word 'mission' for the very first time. That's why, if you'd like to come along, M-2347, I'm hoping to get some ringside seats at the Ascension. Do you have any idea how long my future self plans to remain on the planet?"

"Good question," replied my angelic friend. "I would like to tag-along with you folks if it isn't too much trouble. I had this assignment today with the tomb, but other than that, my schedule's wide-open for the next six months. What about you M-2500? Have you any idea how long Jesus will be around the planet before the Ascension?"

I shrugged my shoulders and looked at Steve. Steve shook his head. Finally, two men and two angels turned and looked, once more, at Sarah.

"I don't know, guys," she said. "I seem to recall it's something like forty days after Easter until the feast of the Ascension. I can't say for certain. I had two roommates: Brooke and Gayle. They were raised Catholic. They could have told you all that stuff. Like me, they didn't believe a word of it, but they could tell you. I don't why. It just seems too easy. Like everything is 40."

"Moses was in the desert for forty years," said Jesus

"It rained forty days and forty nights in the time of Noah," said Steve.

"I'm planning to fast for forty days," said Jesus.

"I suppose forty days is possible," said Sarah. "It's as good a guess as any."

"Well, we can't afford to hang-out here for forty days. I know I can't. Why don't we jump ahead?" Jesus suggested.

"Forty days into the future?" I asked.

"Sure," he replied "Why not?"

"All right," I said and I walked over to a clearing just beyond the cemetery. I turned into the cherry-red space ship with the white hardtop, chrome trim and razor-sharp tail fins. Sitting on my silver landing runners, I opened the port in my belly and extended my spiral staircase. Soon, everyone was on board. Jesus, Sarah and Steve were in the flight cabin and M-2347 strapped himself into one of the flight seats in the conference room on the main deck.

"Mighty impressive," he said looking around the interior. "Where did you come up with an idea like this?"

"Most of the hardware is from the earth's 35th century," I replied over my inboard loudspeakers. "The design motif is from the 1950's."

"The future?"

I could tell from his voice that M-2347 was both intrigued and amazed.

"I received the information from the Ophanim. It took me six days to configure the time travel interface with the 1st Sphere."

"The Ophanim…" M-2347 repeated the word and I could hear the reverence in this voice.

Meanwhile, I was engaging my flight controls and we shot directly up out of the atmosphere and were soon beyond earth orbit heading roughly for the Andromeda Galaxy. I instructed Sarah to adjust the appropriate time-control lever.

Back in the conference room, I advised my old friend that we would be experiencing a mild BUMP and not to worry. Indeed, a moment after Sarah had pushed the controls forward to 40 days in the future, I encountered the mysterious stream of white mist that always seemed to accompany our movement through time. We experienced the distinct BUMP that briefly lifted my passengers up off their seats. Five minutes later I had turned around and headed back to earth. I tore through the atmosphere and slipped down through the white cumulous clouds overhanging the Middle East. We landed in the old clearing on the northern flank of the Mount of Olives.

My passengers unfastened their safety harnesses and climbed out of their seats. Sarah and Steve grabbed a bite to eat in the galley, what was left of the lamb and rice from the 5th Century. Sarah filled a wine skin with water and everyone climbed out onto the side of the mountain.

It was a hot spring day and the pale green leaves of the olive trees glimmered silvery in the heat radiating up from the dry ground. I turned back into that amalgam of Greek Academy students whom I had encountered in Greece and joined my friends near a pathway that led to the mountain's summit.

Sarah and Jesus led the way, followed by Steve, M-2347 and me. When we arrived near the top of the mountain we traversed along the ridge until we came to a gathering of Jesus' followers. We were there only a short while when we saw a procession coming up the road from Bethany. We immediately recognized the glowing form of the Resurrected Christ.

"We ought to follow him," said Steve.

"What do you mean by that?" said Sarah calling back over her shoulder.

"I mean when he goes up into the sky. He's supposed to go up into the sky, right?"

Sarah stopped in her tracks and Steve about stumbled into her.

"That's a good idea!" said Sarah.

"What? What did I say?"

"About following him into the sky…"

"What are you cooking up, Sarah?" asked our Jesus, turning around.

"Let's get back to the space ship!" she said excitedly.

"What do you mean, 'let's get back to the space ship?' We just got here!" said Jesus indicating with a wave of this hand the group of around five-hundred people assembling on the mountain top.

"Yeah!" said Steve. "What are you talking about, Sarah?"

"Oh, be quiet, Steve. Listen, Jesus. He's going to blast off this mountain from right over there on that rock. How long will we be able to watch before he disappears from view?"

Jesus shook his head. “I don’t know, Sarah. I guess that’s why we’re here.”

“Why don’t you let me take her out?”

“Take who out?”

“The ship. Let’s take M-2500 up into the clouds and put a tail on Jesus and see where he goes.”

“I think he’s going to heaven!” said Steve.

“Let’s find out for ourselves.” she said.

The group got really quiet while Jesus turned the idea over in his mind. Steve stared at him intently and even my angelic pal, M-2347, waited for his decision.

“I don’t know,” said Jesus, shaking his head.

“Why not?” asked Sarah.

“It sounds risky.”

“Is this about my not being right with God?” she asked.

There was another long pause. Each of us looked around our group where we had formed a circle about fifty yards down-slope from the big gathering on the hill. Eventually, everyone’s gaze settled on Steve. In particular, we were looking at the sign of the devil on the back of his right hand.

M-2347’s gaze moved from the black tattoo and over to me. He shook his head.

“It’s not like we’re going to be able to follow Jesus up there without your permission.”

“My permission?” replied Jesus. “I think we’ll need <u>his</u> permission. He’s standing right over there. Why don’t you go over and ask him? 'Hi, I'm Sarah Benton. I don't believe in you, but I'd like to follow you to heaven!"

"So, now you're being sarcastic?" asked Sarah.

"I just want you to recognize what an odd request you're making."

"Elijah went to heaven in a whirlwind, didn't he?" she replied.

Jesus seemed taken aback by this, "Elijah?"

"Yes! The guy from Kings?"

"But he was a prophet," said Jesus.

"Maybe Steve and I will be prophets one day too!" said Sarah, "Who knows? Right, Steve."

Steve looked back and forth between Jesus and Sarah.

"What do you want to do boss?" I asked Jesus. I don't know why I called him that. It just sounded right at the time.

Jesus threw up his hands. "Okay. Okay, we'll follow Jesus!"

Sarah threw her arms around Jesus and hugged him and gave him a kiss on the cheek. He kind of squirmed under her weight, but he looked a lot happier, having made a decision. He motioned us to head back in the direction we had just come. Meanwhile, he continued up the hill and said so-long to his future self, and perhaps, with a well-placed aside, whispered to him that we were planning to tail him up to heaven.

So as not to additionally worry the young Christian community assembling on the hillside, I switched my systems to stealth mode, rendering my ship and everyone and everything on board, absolutely invisible, at least to mortal eyes.

It looked as though the resurrected Jesus of the Future was giving a short speech to the people ranged about him in varying degrees of prostration on the mountain top. He waved, lifted his left foot just a few inches off the ground went up on the toes of his right foot and slowly, amazingly, floated into the air. There was a universal murmur of amazement from the hillside gathering.

We could all plainly hear it broadcast from my outboard directional microphones through speakers inside the ship. I was hovering just east of the Mount of Olives, about seventy-five feet above the summit. We could see the Temple Mount and the city of Jerusalem shining in the background as the blue and white clothed figure of the Resurrected Christ slowly slipped up higher and higher into the sky. He continued to wave goodbye to the people far below as he passed up through a thin, cool cloud layer. He was way over even our heads and probably looked no bigger than a shining dot to the people back on earth as he headed up into a big fluffy white tower of shinning clouds. We kept pace with him drifting upwards through the dense white vapor until we'd gained another thousand feet of elevation and broke through into a great, cloud-ringed wonderland of bright blue sky and empty air.

"Hello, Jesus? Jesus, are you there?" called our Jesus on a handheld microphone.

For a moment the Resurrected Jesus of the Future looked a bit confused, but then smiled, and, although we were still invisible, he looked in our direction and waved.

We were high enough now and so obscured by the white, fluffy clouds below, that I switched off our shield of invisibility. Jesus of the

Future did a breast stroke with his arms and flew over to the roof of our ship. Our Jesus handed the microphone to Sarah, climbed out of his seat and dashed to the flight deck and the spiral staircase leading to the topside observation deck.

"Hello? Jesus? This is Sarah Benton. Sarah, the girl from earth?" said Sarah into the microphone. "We were just in the neighborhood and heard that you might be going to heaven and wondered whether we could come along with you for a visit?"

I sensed that our Jesus had opened my topside hatch and climbed out onto my white hardtop deck to welcome his resurrected future self.

Future Jesus told our Jesus that it was totally "uncool" to have brought non-believers this close to heaven. Our Jesus didn't seem too happy with the reaction of his older self. "You know, you're starting to sound a lot more like Father, now that you're resurrected!"

"I love the non-believers," replied Future Jesus, "But it sets a bad precedent that on my very first day back home after defeating death and offering hope to the world, that I should bring along a couple of his unrepentant failures."

"They aren't failures!" argued our Jesus. "Have you any idea what these two have been through? The boy was left for dead as an infant. The girl was unwanted even before she was born and it was only through a miracle that she wasn't aborted as a fetus. She grew-up with very little emotional support. Steve we have always loved as our own brother and my earthly parents have always treated him as one of their own, but his sketchy origin was never a secret to the Nazarene elders and his questionable heritage made him the object of ridicule and scorn."

"Look. Why the biographies on these two? I know all this stuff."

"No. I don't think you do!" protested our Jesus. "I think you've forgotten. I think three years going around saving the world has taken a toll on you. You're a lot more like God, but you're a lot less human!"

"That sounds great, little Jesus, but that's mere semantics. I am fully both, God and Man. This is something you have yet to fully comprehend."

"I comprehend plenty," said our Jesus.

"Your little human brain simply cannot appreciate the infinite!"

"With our uncle's help, I think I can appreciate the infinite, Future Jesus, and please don't call me 'little.'"

"What?"

"Would you quit floating there and touch down here on the ship? Just walk over to that hatch and come onboard and we can talk!"

"I don't know. I may not be human enough to talk to you!" said Future Jesus.

"Oh please let's be of one mind on this. Now, are you coming on board?"

The resurrected Jesus followed our Jesus down the spiral stairwell on the flight deck.

"What is this?" said the resurrected Christ looking about the gleaming cabin. His eyes narrowed. "An angel in disguise?"

"Yes…" said our Jesus.

"M-2500! M-2500 is that you?

"Yes," I replied in the hot and sexy voice of Debbie, and then, just as suddenly, I cleared my throat. "Yes… It's me." My voice cracked like a Greek adolescent's. I coughed and managed to return to my original, deep, radio-announcer's voice.

"Yes, it's me," I said, "We're awfully glad you've come aboard this morning. If you look off to your left you'll see the Mediterranean Coast. We're presently hovering at an altitude of three thousand feet above sea level."

"As you were," said Future Jesus with a smile. "And I sense another M-Class angel from the moon project, wasn't it? M-2347?"

Still clad in white robes and the muscular form of a handsome young man, M-2347 nodded.

I didn't know what the issue was between the old and new Jesus about letting the two mortals visit heaven, but I was mighty impressed that Future Jesus could identify M-2347, whom he probably hadn't even seen, at least in a good many eons. Resurrected Jesus and our Jesus stepped out of the stairwell and they both sat on a sofa.

"Has a decision been reached regarding the two flawed human beings?" asked M-2347.

Resurrected Jesus crossed his legs European Style and looked up at the ceiling. "Do whatever you want. It's not my ship. Maybe I have overlooked some of this. Getting crucified and dying, and then coming back to life to teach for forty days straight really takes a lot out of a fellow."

"I'm sure it does," said Sarah, coming back from the cockpit and walking up to Resurrected Jesus with her hand extended. "Please no, don't stand. I'm just so grateful to be here, to see all of this."

She shook hands with the seated savior and her broad smile barely faltered as she looked down at the red holes in his hands. She had a strong constitution for a human being. Steve, on the other hand, who had come back to the conference area in time to see this exchange, must have been overcome by his imagination. He spun down the spiral staircase and disappeared into the living-quarters below the flight deck. I brought up some ambient background music from a tape loaded from the year 2000, but the party in the conference area could plainly hear Steve retching into the galley wash basin.

The resurrected Jesus smiled. "That sound reminds me of my last night in the Garden of Gethsemane. Good thing I didn't have anything more that a crust of bread and a sip of wine at the last supper, or that might have come up too."

The Resurrected Christ ran a palm across his forehead.

"What I'm trying to convey, Sarah, is the disorientation you suffer when you take on all that evil; that which in Old Testament times, we referred to as the 'sin of the world.' When a sentient being takes on its back the burdens of the past and present, all the mistakes, errors, omissions and wrong actions of the future, TRUE suffering begins to reveal its contours. Sarah, you may argue that men and women have sacrificed their lives for a child, or a nation or a just cause. They have, and they are all martyrs worthy of the highest praise and remembrance, but my death a month ago was not only a human death. I am sorry that in your limited human experience it must seem to you a paradox, but it was not only my death you viewed at Golgotha, but the death of the Creator of the universe. Human discomfort cannot approach what He will suffer in the unique transition of his death."

Resurrected Jesus stood and walked over to our Jesus and put his hands on the shoulders of our seated friend. "The pain of a protracted human death cannot nearly approximate the absolute, mind bending, eternity changing PAIN that this child is going to experience on your behalf!"

Resurrected Jesus smiled, "Oh, he'll suffer to the limits of human endurance, but that will only bring him only to his human death. That is the point where the suffering will exponentially increase. There will be a part of him, I can assure you, which will experience a celestial agony of astronomical magnitude."

We stared, dumbfounded, at the bearded savior as he continued.

"You and Steve and all you fallen children of the earth could sacrifice your lives a hundred thousand times over, and those precious deaths would never begin to approach the price in suffering this single human being will pay."

He patted our friend Jesus on the shoulder. "Now, if you'll excuse me, let me go down to the galley and I'll see how Satan's little minion is doing."

Resurrected Jesus had certainly taken the stage. He disappeared down the spiral staircase. We were just kind of floating there in space, stunned, not knowing what to do or where to go, when, suddenly, in the next instant, we heard a blood curdling scream from the galley. It was Steve. The scream was followed by the mind-numbing voice of the Resurrected Jesus reverberating throughout the ship.

"Devil come out of him!" His voiced blasted up the stairwell from the galley. "Devil come out of him!"

I gazed down from my miniature crystal array in the galley and saw the Resurrected Christ wrestle with Steve over the dining table. Christ had both hands on Steve's right wrist and had the hand pinned, palm down, on the table top. To my horror, I saw the black tattoo on the back of Steve's hand begin to lift up and thicken like ink. Smoke streamed from the raised spot and suddenly, black droplets spattered onto the table this way and that, and into the face and onto the white and blue vestments of the risen Christ. The spots resolved into black, buzzing flies, and dozens, and hundreds and then thousands of flies poured out from the droplets and the red and black wound in Steve's hand. The flies came up like a whirlwind through the stairwell and all the while Steve screamed, "Jesus, no! Make it stop! Oh, God, make it stop!"

Our Jesus, M-2347 and Sarah swatted at the black miasma of flies that exploded into the main cabin of the ship. Our friends fell to the floor and with terror looked up along the treaded walkway leading to the ship's bow.

The mass of flies swirled into the empty cockpit and wound in ever tightening circles and slowly, horribly resolved into the gruesome, chitin-plated monstrosity from the dawn of life.

"Of my God, it's him!" cried Sarah looking down the length of the floor at the enormous, black fly-creature seating itself in the pilot's chair. It brought up its anterior claw-tipped legs and rubbed them together in a mockery of prayer and drew the hairy appendages quickly over its enormous, iridescent eyes. The gesture seemed almost involuntary as it reached for the time control levers.

"What's it doing?" shouted our Jesus. "M-2500! Don't let it get those…"

The rings of the Ophanim are what made time travel a possibility for us. Without them, all the sophisticated equipment from the 35th

century and the components designed in another universe entirely that were provided for our temporary use and safekeeping by the hosts of the First Sphere would be useless.

All I could do to Satan's monstrous henchman, Beelzebub, was adjust his seat. I managed to catch the creature off-guard and pitch it face-first into the control console, but realizing what I had done, it simply rolled out of the seat and went back to work on the rings, as the empty seat flapped back and forth, banging away, innocuously.

Each one of the Rings of the Ophanim was normally looped over the tips of my right and left tentacles, or my two ring fingers when I appeared in the guise of a male or female human being. In this instance, the rings encircled the left and right time control levers on the console. The fly-man cackled to itself and tugged on the metal bands as it sought to slip the rings off the control levers.

"No," cried Sarah and our Jesus. In my own heart I cried out too. We might have traveled anywhere in the universe we wished in an instant, but we would never travel so much as a single millisecond forward or backward in time again.

"Weren't we arguing whether Steve and I should be allowed a tour of heaven?" cried Sarah on the floor where she recovered from the stinging blizzard of black flies.

"All things being equal," said our Jesus, "I think heaven or earth would be preferable to this!"

Suddenly, a massive explosion rocked the starboard side of the ship.

"What was that?" shouted Sarah as the ship pitched violently in the air and the lights flickered. Just then, to make matters worse, we heard the chilling theme music and imperious vocal styling of the Prince of Air and Darkness.

It was high noon and three thousand feet over the desert where we had drifted in the prevailing breeze as I looked across the cottony clouds for signs of the Evil Lord's latest engine of destruction. For a fateful instant I wondered whether he was still running with his animal motif. As the clouds parted a mile away from my bow, I half expected to see a gigantic mechanical bat, or raven, or insidious, yellow and black hornet. I was confused and somewhat disappointed, when the clouds drifted away to reveal a gigantic lady bug. It hovered on the mechanical wing beats of its enormous translucent wings. Its red and black spotted shell casings were arched back in attack-mode, and the Lord of Evil himself stood in an open air observation deck on the craft's monstrous, black head.

"Well, well my friends from the past and future, we meet again at last!" boomed his voice over hidden, outboard loudspeakers. For the master of air and darkness he seemed to be having a bit of difficulty with the wind outside of his craft, because his purple cape kept blowing up into his face.

"The Red and Black Beetle of Death Flagship shall devour…" he grabbed his cape and wadded up the flapping ends in one hand, "…shall devour you like the insignificant aphids on a small bush that you represent to me!"

"That was a mouthful," I thought to myself and was about to snicker at the adversary's outlandish expression of power when another energy blast tore loose from one of the gigantic lady bug's mock antennae. The shock wave shook our ship savagely and suddenly I was reminded that this was no laughing matter. I wondered for the safety of my passengers as the evil one droned on.

"As you see, I have mastered the science of artificial flight, and soon with the bands of the Ophanim in my possession I shall reverse engineer a time machine capable of unspeakable crimes in the time stream!"

Right on cue, the black fly-monster in my cockpit slipped the twin bands of the Ophanim off my control levers and unto its gnarled claws. Through the observation ports it signaled back across the mile-wide expanse of open sky between the two ships at its armored boss. It turned, shambling up the aisle on its jointed legs toward the spiral stairwell. I guess it figured it was going to climb up the staircase, slip out of the hatch on top and fly over to the lady bug with its booty of time-travel rings.

Sarah jumped up in the aisle to stop the creature's advance. Unfortunately, there was no heavy object which she might have used as a weapon. She relied solely upon her fists, but human flesh and bone was no match against the chitinous exoskeleton of the demon. It leaned forward, impervious to her efforts, brushed her aside and with a glancing blow of a segmented tarsus threw her fifteen feet down the aisle. Now, it confronted our young Jesus. Though a punch from Jesus might have knocked unconscious an average man, the fly-creature intercepted his blow with the claw of one of its six skittering legs. Grabbing hold of Jesus, the monster lifted him up off the cabin floor.

Jesus let out a yowl of pain as the fly monster slammed him up against the ceiling. The monster seemed amused by the scream, but soon an expression of surprise overtook its countenance as another human-looking hand suddenly reached up and, with super human strength, grabbed a stunted antennae and pulled the beast down eye-to-eye with the Jesus of the Future.

Our passenger from the Mount of Olives had come up the spiral staircase from the galley below and right into the face of the big, ugly fly-man.

"Hi, there," said the Resurrected Jesus. "You're pretty tough when it comes to beating-up defenseless men and women, aren't you? I said, aren't you?"

The beast seemed to shrug, but remained absolutely compliant as Future Jesus pulled down on the stubby antennae and the fly-man twisted low to the floor, releasing our Jesus and looking up with the thousand lenses of its compound eyes. Future Jesus called to M-2347 who instantly appeared at the stairwell.

"Get those metallic bands from the creature's hooks there and return them to M-2500's time control levers," barked Future Jesus.

Our Jesus had helped Sarah to her feet and together they watched M-2347 strip the metal bands from the monster's grasp as Future Jesus held the fly-creature by the collar, hauled it up the spiral staircase, and outside through the hatchway like yesterday's garbage.

M-2347 rushed up front with the power bands while Sarah and our Jesus rushed downstairs to the galley to attend to Steve. Meanwhile, things were heating up outside in the skyway above the Middle East.

"Resistance is futile!" thundered the amplified voice of Satan from the observation deck of his Lady Bug flagship. He was wrestling with his cape again and had just looked up in time to see the Jesus of the Future haul back and throw the fly-creature directly at him. "Superhuman," does not adequately describe the force that Jesus employed in launching Satan's henchman across that five-thousand foot void between the two vessels. Wriggling like an insect going down a quick drain, Beelzebub hurtled helplessly forward, and, striking the guard-rail of Satan's observation deck, exploded in a miasma of internal fluids and black body parts.

"Satan," shouted Future Jesus with a heavenly amplification system that would have sounded like thunder to anyone back on the earth's surface. "You once roamed freely across the Universe but are now my prisoner on these tiny islands of dust."

The Lord of Evil wiped bug-guts off his face and trembled with rage at the voice of Future Jesus. Satan's onboard dynamos were building-up another charge and were about to unleash another bolt of energy when something behind our red and white space ship caught his attention.

It was a funnel cloud, whipped up seemingly out of nowhere, and with very little moisture in the atmosphere, was nearly invisible as it skipped over my tail section and the head of the Resurrected Christ. The dancing rope of wind followed the directions of the Future Jesus, and by the time it had jumped the gap between the red and white bow of our spaceship and the bow of the Red and Black Lady Bug Beetle of Death, it was pulling down eight-hundred tons of frigid air from the jet stream and rotating at two-hundred-and-fifty miles an hour.

"CAT," shouted Future Jesus across the abyss at the adversary.

"What?" cried the Dark Lord, hopelessly tangled in his cape and annoyed by the fluttering lapels of his jacket.

"Clear Air Turbulence!" shouted Future Jesus.

It was unclear whether Satan ever understood what Future Jesus was trying to tell him. Sarah, and our Jesus had brought Steve up from the galley and held our badly startled companion between them in the cockpit. They watched the scene through my observation ports and a faint smile came to Steve's lips as the whirlwind seized hold of Satan and the Lady Bug Flagship and carried them far away over the western horizon.

M-2347 handed the rings of the Ophanim to our Jesus who fitted them back over my time-control levers. Instantly, the ship pulsed with the familiar, but eternally awesome power of the First Sphere. Jesus of the Future came back down the spiral staircase, sealed the hatch and came to the cockpit to inspect the red scar on the back of Steve's hand.

"Demon larvae!" said Future Jesus, like a stern country physician.

"What?" asked Steve.

"The Lord of the Flies planted the eggs of a million demon maggots in that wound. It must have occurred a month ago during your time in the desert."

"What about the tattoo?" moaned Steve.

"Mere icing on the cake," replied Future Jesus.

"That's disgusting!" said Sarah.

"But can't you get them all?" asked Jesus.

Future Jesus, shook his head sadly, "Not in this lifetime."

"I just thought it was a cool looking tattoo," whined Steve. "I didn't know…"

"You'll have to be careful your entire life," warned Future Jesus, "And you must guard against a recurrence through prayer and righteous living."

"I don't know," said Steve. "I'll do my best."

"That's all anyone can do," said Future Jesus and he nodded to our Jesus who seemed quite impressed by his future self.

"Now, we may proceed to the so-called gates of heaven. Not to be rude, but Sarah, you'll need to wear those special goggles in the arm rest there, and there's one by the auxiliary seat for you Steve. By the way, Jesus, I think it's probably a good idea that you don the goggles as well."

"I don't mind," said our Jesus, but you could tell he was a little disappointed and there was something more on his mind.

"What's wrong?" asked Future Jesus of his younger self.

"Well," began our Jesus slowly, "Not to appear boastful, but haven't I lived a life free of sin?"

"Absolutely, but you remain a human being, Jesus. There's a strong likelihood that without those glasses the heavenly effluence will burn holes through your retina and out the back of your skull."

"Wow," said Steve marveling at the glasses as he strapped himself into the auxiliary flight seat, "You mean if I was to look into heaven without these glasses I'd go blind?"

"In your case, both you and Sarah would be turned instantly into pillars of salt," said Future Jesus with a laugh. "No, Steve, I'm only half kidding. I don't know what they're using up there now-a-days, but trust me, you want none of it. I've been away over three decades. Who knows? Of course, in another sense, I've never really left."

He glanced over at our Jesus who had been hanging on the divine doppelganger's every word.

"Don't worry, Jesus, even in your darkest hour. I know it's complicated. When you're God, you keep running into yourself everywhere. Right?"

"Right," agreed our Jesus doing his best to sound up-tempo.

"But aren't these the very same glasses we used the first time we went up into space?" asked Steve as he fit the goggles over the bridge of his nose and adjusted the elastic retaining band behind his head.

Come to think of it, they were. They had all been part of the flight paraphernalia, furnishings, and house wares in the designs sent back to me when I had first assumed the form of our red and white rocket ship. Odd, but at the time I hadn't noticed anything particular about these protective lenses, but then, again, I had had so much data to assimilate, under such duress, it was difficult to know where one high-tech gadget ended and the next began. I was still discovering things about myself; for instance, just the other day on the way back from Ancient Greece, I found an old fashioned manual can opener, a nifty garlic press and an unopened set of refrigerator magnets stuffed way in the back of my junk-drawer in the galley.

My passengers went on and on about the spectacles. Jesus of the Future mentioned something about a Babylonian alchemist having worked on the shielding process in the time of the prophet Elijah. As we drifted up into high-earth orbit, I took the opportunity to review some of the technical manuals and design specs which I had shoved into a mental "glove compartment" on the day I first took our hot ride into space. Obviously, the goggles were treated with a material that blocked harmful UV rays from the sun, but I was to learn that they blocked much more.

"Do you need the flight co-ordinates?" sounded M-2347 from back in the living quarters where he and Future Jesus had buckled themselves into place on facing sofas beside the conference table.

"Coordinates to heaven?" I asked. "Not hardly."

* * *

Once we got outside the earth's gravitational field, it took only two minutes to crash through the sun's heliosphere. As we breached the termination shock, the accompanying pyrotechnics thrilled my human passengers. Another minute passed and we had flown through the interstellar medium and come to a dead stop in orbit around a massive space station. I knew it well. It had been in place some nine-billion years and was nearly as old as the human being's universe itself. The station orbited "a little piece of heaven," a burning blue window looking into another reality entirely. As my friend M-2347 explained to my astonished friends, "The heavenly realm is not entirely contiguous."

"So, it's like Alaska or Hawaii?" asked Sarah.

That stumped us. We all looked at The Resurrected Jesus, who paused for an instant, closed his eyes and then looked up with a bright smile on his face.

"Yes," he said. "That's an excellent analogy, although you might think of it more along the lines of Guam or Virgin Islands. This space platform is one of many such portals guarding entrance to a heavenly realm. Think of these realms as islands throughout the multi-verse. This particular base has served, more often than not, as a military installation."

"But where does the Creator actually live?" asked Sarah.

"In your hearts."

Sarah burst out laughing.

No one else found much humor in the moment. She must have sensed this and the smile vanished from her face. "Forgive me," she said, "But if I can't find him in my 'heart,' where else might I look? Seriously," she continued, "The New Testament says you're going to sit on a throne with God or something. So, where is that, if it's not in my heart? On a space station? On some so-called island realm in another dimension?"

"You take things quite literarily, Ms. Benson," said Future Jesus, "The gift of self-awareness provided your species has limitations. I am not trying to elude your question, but the answer you seek is simply beyond the grasp of your limited, mortal sensibilities. The complexity of creation defies the understanding even of our mightiest archangels. Many of the celestial host spend their eternities exploring its secrets. Without getting too technical, I assure you there is such a place, if I may use the word 'place.'"

"Feel free," she replied. "So then, where is it?"

"In another universe. Another dimension entirely."

"Another universe? Of course," replied Sarah.

"He resides there, on his home world where he has always been."

"And that's where you're headed?"

"Eventually, but we've probably said enough on the subject for now, Sarah, don't you think?"

I settled into orbit around the massive, heavenly outpost. The size of a moon, the disk shaped construct was inhabited by thousands of common angels. This doorstep to one of countless heavenly realms had served as our staging area during the formation of the human being's solar system. Later, it served as a base for the creation of life on earth and in the long and bitter campaigns against the rebel angels. Today, the savior of mankind had returned from his time on embattled planet earth. The rebels had suffered a staggering defeat.

Within a few minutes I began my descent to a docking station on the rim of the outpost. It really was like old home week for me. The heavenly frequencies over-flowed with the voices of angelic friends whom I had not heard in weeks. Of course, for them, three point eight billion years had passed since they had last spoken to "M-2500." There were still others whom I had not seen since long before that, in the time before the creation of the earth system, its solar system, its galaxy and its very universe. Still, there is something to be said for true friendship, and as I called out to the angels, I was filled with happiness and gratitude. If only a remote outpost, it was so good to be home.

Meanwhile, Sarah, Steve, and our human Jesus writhed in their seats. Despite the protection of their "Heaven Glasses" the energy penumbra in the region of this "heaven station" was too intense for the optical hardware and wiring of my little human friends. Closing their eyelids behind their protective lens only lessened slightly the perceived intensity of the glare. They had to move their heads side to side, and this produced an altogether unsettling picture. M-2347 whisked away three cushions from the sofas where he and Jesus of the Future had been enjoying the sights through the view ports, and he came forward into the cockpit. I winced as M-2347 tore open my pillows with superhuman hands, shook out my foam stuffing and pulled the empty fabric bags over the heads of my three friends.

"Does that help?" he asked.

"Yes, thanks," said Sarah. "That's much better," evidently relieved that holes would not be burned into her optic nerves. "Although, you realize I can't see anything," she said.

It seemed to me that the human beings were never satisfied.

"We don't need to see anything; let's just get out of here!" shouted Steve, his hands groping blindly in front of him.

Unaffected by the glaring heavenly effluence, the Resurrected Jesus of the Future unfastened his safety restraints and approached the cockpit. "Hey, thanks a lot for the lift. I'm running a little late for a big welcome home celebration."

"Oh, really, where's that going to be?" asked M-2347.

"Where?" repeated the Resurrected Jesus, clearing his throat, "I'm supposed to meet someone down there on the concourse."

"Who?" I asked.

Jesus of the Future shrugged his shoulders.

"Well, they've been expecting you for some time. Probably an archangel," offered M-2347.

"Perhaps."

"Yes," replied M-2347. "They'd send an archangel at least."

"Well, thanks again, folks," said Future Jesus. "Thank you, M-2500. I'll drop in from time to time. Sarah and Steve, I hope I hear a lot more from you two in the future and don't forget the Entity."

"The Entity?" asked Sarah, moving her bag-covered head in the direction of Future Jesus' voice.

"Definitely in play, back on earth. He and father have finally come to an understanding. Things are going to be a lot better for the human race from now on, at least in the long term. You wait and see!"

It really did seem as though Future Jesus was anxious to be on his way, as I descended through the interstellar medium toward the glowing platform. Future Jesus stood at the stairwell, waiting for me to touch down. Beyond my view ports below, I could see the enormous figures of several archangels whom I immediately recognized. At least a dozen representatives from the Second Sphere were on hand. I saw four or five Strongholds, some Dominions and at least one Power, each of them decked out in their finest regalia and ready to celebrate. Behind them, hundreds of S, M, and L-Class angels were gathered beneath an enormous banner reading: "Welcome Home, Jesus!"

We had settled into a docking bay which had been provided with an atmosphere and special "heaven shields" solely for the benefit of my three mortal companions. I spun open the hatch in my belly and corkscrewed the spiral staircase down to the silvery hard surface of the landing pad. Future Jesus smiled at us, waved and climbed off the ship. M-2347 and I watched him step out from beneath the shadow of my hull and float away toward the welcoming committee and the crowds.

"Is that Uriel?" asked M-2347, who stood in the cockpit doorway.

"Sure looks like her," I replied and I recognized some of the other big wheels from the heavenly inner-circles on hand to welcome the famous son back home.

"You, know, M-2500, if it's all the same to you, I think I'll just get out here, after all…"

"Oh, well, I thought you'd…" I stammered, realizing that time with the group of famous angels out there would probably be a lot more interesting than time with me on some insignificant planet in a backwater solar system.

“”Well, okay," I said. "It was certainly nice running into you again and thanks for everything."

The M-Class angel paused for an instant, as though he was re-evaluating the words he had just uttered. "On second thought," he communicated with the angelic power of mental telepathy unnoticed by the human beings, "I still have six months. The least I can do is spare a few hours to see you all safely back to earth."

"Hey, you guys!" said our Jesus with the bag over his head, "I hate to interrupt, but this really isn't too much fun for any us since we really can't see any of the sights, and…"

"Say no more," I said, and seeing that Jesus of the Future had made it safely to the welcome wagon, I retracted our stairs, sealed the hatch, lifted up into space and gently peeled out of the Heaven Station's gravitational field.

* * *

So much for our trip to heaven. Jesus, Sarah, Steve and I slunk back across the interstellar wastes with our generous passenger, M-2347, who was undoubtedly wishing he had stayed back at the space station for the heavenly celebration. It was only after we crossed back over the barrier of the termination shock into the satanic war-zone and skimmed the outer reaches of the asteroid field beyond Jupiter that M-2347 broke the silence.

"Isn't that Mars coming up there, to starboard?"

"Steve, Steve, look! It's Mars," cried Sarah, excitedly.

Steve managed a sustained burp.

"Look Jesus," said Sarah, "Those are its two moons, Phobos and Deimos."

"Odd shaped things, aren't they?" remarked Jesus as I slowed our speed in order that my passengers might have a look.

"Whatever became of those two sisters?" I asked M-2347.

"Who?"

"Those two archangels. Didn't they have something to do with the Life on Mars Project?"

"They were in and out a couple times," replied M-2347

"You'd never see them with any of the others. Real private, those two."

"Do you recall their names?" asked M-2347.

"Me?" I said, "I'm the one who's been away for four billion years."

"Seems like just the other day," said M-2347.

"I suppose so," I replied, although from my point of view only a couple weeks had passed.

"It's just a shame your friends don't have some of those heaven suits," said M-2347.

"Heaven suits? What is a heaven suit?" asked Jesus, pulling off his eye goggles and returning them carefully to the compartment in his armrest.

"Fat lot of good these did us," said Steve, pulling off his pair of glasses and slamming them back into the tiny cargo compartment beside his auxiliary seat.

"I hope the Jesus of the Future is having a good time at his party in heaven, whatever it looks like," said Sarah putting away her spectacles. "He certainly deserves a party after all he's been through."

"You said something about a heaven suit," said Jesus.

"I did?" replied M-2347. "Oh, yes, of course. Well, I didn't mean to raise false hope. The prototypes disappeared from an old storage facility on the moon nearly a thousand years before you were born."

"Oh," said Jesus.

"What were they?" asked Sarah.

"They were suits developed for mortal beings to journey to heaven to conduct business without risk to their optic nerves or, as in the case of unrepentant sinners like you and Steve, turning into pillars of salt."

"Oh, really?" said Sarah.

"Although I can't imagine what business a sinner would have in heaven," said M-2347 and he turned in an apparent aside to Sarah. "As far as I know, the one human being ever to make such a journey happened to be one of the earth's most righteous mortals. Do you understand?"

"I think I understand, perfectly," replied Sarah with a scowl on her face as she glanced over at Jesus.

"Wow!" said Jesus, but he was concentrating on my friend, the angel. "And did it work?"

"Did what work?" asked M-2347.

"The heaven suit?" asked Jesus.

"Apparently," replied M-2347. "There was an historic meeting, one that you will experience when you return to your place in history. A meeting in your future on the so-called Mount of Transfiguration."

"I've read about that," said Sarah, dismissively. "He's supposed to meet up with Elijah on a mountain top."

"And that's not all…" continued M-2347.

"It's funny," Jesus interrupted, looking out the portal at the red, striated surface of Mars and its two deformed satellites. "I don't recall mention of anything like a heaven suit in scripture."

Sarah and Steve had lost interest in the conversation. They sat with arms folded over their chests as they stared out into space. Steve excused himself to the galley for something to eat (he'd be disappointed because there were only seven grains of Grecian rice left stuck to a bowl in the sink) and Sarah wandered down into the sleeping quarters and threw herself on her bunk.

"There was quite a fascination with the shielding technology," continued M-2347, "Especially among the mystics in Babylon and the worshippers of Bael in particular. Their dream was to develop a shield against the piercing light of righteousness. I believe that's how they put it. It was all very dark, very arcane and extremely mysterious. I believe a number of demons may have gotten involved. Imagine the potential offensive power of such a technology."

"Sounds dangerous," said Jesus.

"In the wrong hands, I suspect it would be," the angel replied.

"So, how could we get our hands one of these suits?" asked Jesus.

"As I was saying, there were some in a storage locker at the old moon facility. A lot of back-and-forth over that place, since it was first abandoned to the demons. We've re-established it a half-dozen times only to see it fall-back into enemy control. One of the suits must have been recovered after sealing of the first covenant with the human beings. As for the others, I'm afraid they are lost to history."

"So, where would you like to go, Jesus, besides Heaven?" I interrupted.

"Oh, I'm sorry, M-2500," replied Jesus, suddenly. "Sarah, are there any other great religions I've missed? Sarah?"

It was an embarrassing moment for Jesus when he turned from his conversation with M-2347 and realized that Sarah and Steve had left the flight deck. I had been orbiting the earth for an hour. Steve had finished complaining to me about the lack of food in the galley. Sarah had taken a shower. They reappeared upstairs and seemed resentful of my friend, M-2347 for something he'd said about their flawed character. My passengers had reassembled on the sofas in the conference room when Jesus cleared his throat and spoke.

"I was talking to M-2347, Sarah, and I wondered whether you had any thoughts about other great religious leaders we might visit?"

"I don't know," she sulked. "Sure. I suppose there are a few."

"Can you think of another influential World Religion?" asked Jesus.

"Hmmm… Let me see... Oh, yes. I've got one."

7. Hajj

Sarah leaned forward in her co-pilot's seat and pushed the time lever to the year 632 A.D. We BUMPED out of the streaming white mist, dropped into low earth orbit and in a few moments slipped down to the Arabian Peninsula. I landed on a barren hill beside a road leading to the city of Mecca.

Once again I materialized in the human form of Demetrius. It was late afternoon and to my human sensibilities, hot outside as we walked to a road and looked east to the rooftops and distant spires of the ancient city. From the west we heard a faint but distinct rumbling sound and saw what looked like a thin cloud of dust drifting south on the horizon. Something was coming up the road and we started out ahead of it, walking quickly in the direction of the city. Soon we were overtaken by thousands of human beings, male and female, young and old, all dressed in sandals and linen robes. We found ourselves swept along into the city.

We came upon a high-walled compound and entered through its gates into an enormous courtyard. In the center of the expanse rose a black, cube-shaped monolith. It was several stories tall and the masses flooded around the object and marched dozens abreast in a great, counterclockwise circle.

"What is this thing?" shouted Steve.

"The Kabah!" shouted Sarah.

"The what?"

"The Kabah and this is the Tawaf!"

"The what…?" Steve called out again, but the crowd was leaning to the west and Steve and a group of a dozen other human beings veered away. I looked over the uncovered heads and recognized Steve and further ahead, the long hair of Jesus. He had done a good job of reading the situation and infiltrating the mass of people. Jesus walked in lock-step with the apparent leader of this human pilgrimage. According to Sarah, the man beside Jesus was the founder of another great world religion. His name was Muhammad. At the age of 40 he began communicating with the so-called "spirit world." Having been away, I had no independent confirmation of this, and had to accept Sarah's report at face value. Muhammad had been driven from this city, the place of his birth, and founded a new religion in the city of Medina to the south where he raised an army and united the Arab World.

As Steve would later phrase it, today was "payback." This huge cube was surrounded by the idols and holy totems of numerous gods. This annual pilgrimage by the adherents of dozens of disparate Arab religions and cults had been taking place in Mecca for centuries. On tables surrounding the Kabah there were hundreds of icons and graven idols, even small statues of Jesus and his mother. Muhammad swept them all away. Some of the relics were large and he needed the help of his lieutenants and those close at hand to dislodge the statuary. At one point I caught sight of Jesus on top of another pilgrim's back, pulling down the bronze image of a monstrous, bird-shaped God. As the crowd surged around the corners of the gigantic cube, the clay, wooden and stone images of the pagan gods Hubal, al-Lat,'Uzza, and Manat were ground underfoot. Isa (Jesus) and Mary (Maryam) were trampled in the dust. As though in a dream, I saw the face of Steve contorted with rage. He was arguing with several pilgrims who had hold of a painted plaster statue of the Virgin Mary.

"Let go of that!" he was shouting. "That's Jesus' mom!"

In the end, there were too many voices and his protests were drowned out as a sea of hands pulled the statues down. The crowd surged forward and carried Steve away toward the northeast corner of the cube. Although I could see only his back, the figure of Muhammad bent low on the exact corner of the enormous cube.

"What is he doing?" I yelled to Sarah.

"He must be kissing the Black Stone!" she replied.

"What's that?" yelled Steve.

"A sacred stone. The Black Stone has been revered by the Arabs for thousands of years. They say Muhammad was given the honor of setting it in place here when he was a young man."

"What does it do?" he shouted.

"It's the locus between the spiritual plane and the physical world."

"And you're supposed to kiss it?"

"It used to be white, but it has been absorbing evil since the time of Adam and Eve."

As Sarah and Steve spoke, more and more pilgrims were pushing in around us. Suddenly, Steve determined that he was going to kiss the stone himself and he scrambled ahead.

Around we went all that morning until the afternoon when we had completed seven revolutions around the cube. As we completed our seventh circuit the crowd headed south following Muhammad to a low hill, "Mt. Safa," Sarah called it, on the outskirts of town.

"Abraham left his wife Hagar and his son Ishmael out here in the desert," explained Sarah as we trudged down the dusty road. "God was doing this to test their faith. That's the Zamzam Well up ahead. Get ready you guys; we're going to need to get a drink!"

Sure enough, Muhammad and Jesus and Muhammad's lieutenants all went to the well in the shadow of Mt. Safa for a drink and then headed east to the hill called "Marwah." It was a short distance, but due to the enormous amount of people in line it took all afternoon to make the trips back and forth. This ritual Muhammad named the "Sa'i" and it was going to be a vital part of the Hajj from here on out.

"Sa`i," that is, running or walking seven times between the hills of Safa and Marwah, was a re-enactment of Hagar's frantic search for water for baby Ishmael. According to Sarah, in one ancient account, the Zamzam Well was revealed to Hagar by an angel. The celestial being brushed the earth with a wing-tip, and water of the Zamzam gushed from the ground.

With business of the inaugural "Sa'i" concluded, everyone dropped back in his or her tracks and slept. Early the next morning, we headed east out of town and walked until we arrived at the outpost of Mina. Jesus hung-out with Muhammad and his inner circle, and it wasn't until dark that Jesus made his way carefully back across the landscape to us.

"Have you seen enough?" asked Steve.

"We're pretty much just going to hang out and pray tomorrow," said Jesus.

"Does he know who you are?"

"Who? You mean Muhammad?"

"Yeah," Steve replied.

"Not exactly."

"Did you get a load of how he smashed all those idols back at the cube?" asked Steve.

"Of yes," Jesus replied. "I helped him!"

"But I saw some statues of you in there!" said Steve.

"Idolatry has been a big part of this pilgrimage for centuries. By dispensing with the practice, Muhammad is simply making a few improvements."

"Well, I even saw them knock over a few statues of your mom!"

"You kind of hate to see that," said Jesus. "But idolatry is idolatry. There's really only one Creator. Muhammad's just trying to get things back to basics."

"Basics?" asked Steve.

On the third day of the Hajj, we headed out in our dusty thousands for Mt. Arafat where everyone gathered around the hill called Jabal Al Rahmah, or "The Hill of Forgiveness."

"So, now what?" asked Steve.

"I guess this is his farewell sermon," said Sarah.

"He and his followers head back to Medina?" asked Jesus.

"I think so," replied Sarah.

"I'm still really not sure what it is that he's accomplished," said Jesus.

"Well, he's united an entire race of people," replied Sarah, "In the past decade he's raised an army of ten thousand men and basically united all the tribes of the Arabian Peninsula under his banner."

"For what reason?" asked Jesus.

Sarah looked at me. I had learned a bit about human "body language" and their "non-verbal" communication; I shrugged my shoulders and looked at Steve.

No one had any answers. Finally, Steve broke the silence.

"I heard some of the pilgrims talking it over. We have a few more things to do tomorrow before it all wraps up."

Steven had overheard correctly.

One new element was known as Wuquf, considered the highlight of the Hajj. Pilgrims spent the afternoon on the plain of Arafat until after sunset. No specific rituals or prayers were required during the stay at Arafat, although many pilgrims spent the time praying, and thinking about the course of their lives. A pilgrim's Hajj was considered invalid if he or she did not spend the afternoon on Arafat.

Muhammad climbed up on a rock before thousands of people and began to speak. For such a massive crowd it was suddenly very quiet out there on the desert. Although most probably could not hear his speech, his voice carried a good distance through the late afternoon air. I dialed up the auditory sensors in my human-looking ears and listened in.

"O People, lend me an attentive ear, for I know not whether after this year, I shall ever be among you again. Listen to what I am saying and take these words to those who could not be present here today."

"O People, just as you regard this month, this day, and this city as Sacred, so regard the life and property of every Muslim as a sacred trust. Return the goods entrusted to you to their rightful owners. Hurt no one so that no one may hurt you. Remember that you will indeed meet your Lord, and that He will indeed reckon your deeds."

I glanced over at Jesus, who was silently nodding his head and he seemed to be silently mouthing the leader's words in unison.

"Beware of Satan, for the safety of your religion," continued Muhammad. "He has lost all hope that he will ever be able to lead you astray in big things, so beware of following him in small things."

"All mankind is from Adam and Eve, an Arab has no superiority over a non-Arab nor a non-Arab any superiority over an Arab; also a white has no superiority over a black nor a black any superiority over a white except by piety and good action. Learn that every Muslim is a brother to every Muslim and that the Muslims constitute one brotherhood. Nothing shall be legitimate to a Muslim which belongs to a fellow Muslim unless it was given freely and willingly. Do not, therefore, do injustice to yourselves."

"Remember, one day you will appear before God and answer for your deeds. So beware, do not stray from the path of righteousness after I am gone."

That was basically all he had to say. Sarah remarked how similar many of the sentiments were to those expressed by Jesus in the highly anticipated "New Testament," which was already appearing in first-edition serial installments in the West. I was uncertain about Steve at that point, but I believed that Sarah, Jesus, and I would have enjoyed copies of that document for reference and comparison.

Things wrapped-up after the sermon. The sun went down, and together with about ten-thousand people we headed for the Plain of Muzdalifah, a barren space between Arafat and Mina. We spent the night sleeping on the ground beneath the open sky, and in the morning gathered pebbles for the next day's ritual stoning of Shaitan. At Mina we performed Ramy al-Jamarat, throwing stones to signify our defiance of the Evil One. This symbolized the trials experienced by Abraham while he was going to sacrifice his son as demanded by Allah. Shaitan challenged Abraham three times, and three times Abraham refused. Each pillar marked the location of one of these refusals. On the first occasion when Ramy al-Jamarat was performed, pilgrims stoned the largest pillar known as Jamrat'al'Aqabah. Pilgrims climbed ramps to the multi-leveled Jamarat Bridge, from which they threw their pebbles at the Jamarat. On the second occasion, the other pillars were stoned. The stoning consisted of throwing seven pebbles.

Steve really "got into" this ritual. He had gathered closer to a hundred stones and seemed overcome with joy each time he struck the pillar. Truthfully, I experienced something approaching joy when I cast my stones at the pillars. I had to hold back a little so as not to destroy them with the force of my throw.

After the Stoning of the Devil, many pilgrims performed animal sacrifices, to symbolize God having mercy on Abraham and replacing his son with a ram, which Abraham then sacrificed. I learned from Sarah and other pilgrims familiar with the itinerary that there were several more days of ritual in store. On the fifth day, the pilgrims re-visited Mecca for another Tawaf, to walk around the Kabah.

On the sixth day we again threw seven pebbles at each of the three Jamarat in Mina. Pilgrims began leaving for Mecca before sunset. Those unable to leave before sunset had to perform the stoning ritual again on the seventh day before returning to Mecca. As anxious as Steve was to leave the desert, he still argued that we might as well spend the extra day if it meant additional stoning of the devil, but Sarah and Jesus had seen enough.

"I don't know how Siddhartha did it!" said Jesus as he dropped down in the dust.

"You hungry?" asked Steve.

"Am I hungry?" replied Jesus. He shook his head and laughed, "Yes, I believe I'm hungry."

"So, what do you want to do?" asked Sarah.

"I don't know," said Jesus, "I think I'd like to eat a thick, juicy steak!"

"Man, that sounds good," said Steve.

"Do you still intend to keep your fast for forty days?" asked Sarah.

"I don't know," said Jesus, "What does it say in the New Testament?"

Steve and I looked back and forth between Jesus and Sarah.

"Seriously?" she asked.

"Sure, why not?" replied Jesus.

"Well, it says you were led into the wilderness by the spirit and that you fasted for forty days."

Jesus slowly stood. He stretched his arms in the twilight and looked out across the plain of sleeping pilgrims and the landscape illuminated here and there with lanterns and camp-fire light.

"Are you sure it said forty days?"

Sarah stared at Jesus. He smiled.

"Just checking," he said.

She smiled and Steve chuckled. I supposed the human beings found this humorous, but Jesus concealed a real concern for his physical health.

"So, does this Muhammad buy that you're the son of God?" asked Steve.

"That's a good question, Steve," said Jesus. "I asked him just the other night."

"What did he say?" asked Sarah.

Jesus shook his head, "It doesn't look good."

"I know you plan to change the course of human history," continued Sarah, "But as far as I can report from the future, you never manage to convert Muhammad to Christianity."

"No?" said Jesus.

She shook her head. It was obvious that her report wounded her friend in at least some small way, and, perhaps, to mitigate the damage, she added brightly, "But he goes on to say a lot of great things about you in his holy book, the Qur'an. You're all over that book, Jesus. He says you were one of the greatest prophets of all time: really the last and greatest of them all, after Muhammad, of course."

A minute of silence, what the human beings might have characterized as an "uncomfortable pause," came and went.

"Nothing about my being the Son of God?" Jesus asked at length.

Sarah shook her head in the negative.

"Savior of Mankind?"

"Sorry," Sarah replied.

"The Creator…? God…? 'Allah…?'"

"No," said Sarah. "Nothing…"

Jesus walked to the edge of our little encampment. To use Steve's terminology from the future, this was our little "festival-seating postage-stamp of space," the area he had eked out for our party amid the sea of humanity camped on the outskirts of Mecca in 632 AD. Jesus looked to the horizon where the sun was setting.

"Muhammad is pretty dug in to his view of things," said Jesus. "He says he's getting a lot of his information from Gabriel. Do you know Gabriel?"

Sarah looked at me.

"I believe we all caught a glimpse of him during the start of Lucifer's rebellion on the Eastern Wall. Before that, I met Gabriel once or twice," I replied. "I don't mean to talk to or anything. I saw him from a distance at some special events. Of course, that was a long time ago. Perhaps ten billion years ago?"

Jesus nodded. "I have no reason to doubt Muhammad or his followers, but I'm not getting the sense that any of those conversations with Gabriel ever took place."

"Really?" I replied.

"It's possible, I suppose. He and I agree on so many things. It's really too bad that we can't seem to form any kind of alliance."

"You have that right!" said Sarah.

With that, Jesus turned around.

"What?" he asked.

"Oh, nothing," replied Sarah.

"No. What were you going to say?" asked Jesus and he walked back and sat in the dust beside Sarah.

"I don't mean to alarm you," she replied, "It's only that there's going to be a lot of friction between the various groups."

"What groups?" asked Jesus and he grimaced and held his side.

"Are you all right?" she asked suddenly.

Jesus waved her off, "What groups?" he demanded.

"The different religions," said Sarah. "I've been over this with you before, haven't I?"

"I'm sorry," said Jesus. "I suppose you have, but it's just that I've had so much on my mind. I don't know how human beings can keep it all straight."

"It's not so simple after all, is it!" said Sarah.

"Having had the opportunity to be here in person with Muhammad and his entourage, I thought I could convince them to consider my program. I never expected them to be so committed to their own views. It's crazy."

"It certainly is," said Sarah, "And it only gets crazier."

"Does it?" said Jesus and the way he searched our faces, he seemed to be asking all three of us for something, to say, perhaps, that the reality of things was otherwise. Eventually, his gaze came to rest, once more, on Sarah, who still knew more of the future than any of us combined. She nodded her head slowly and now there was no hint of satisfaction in her response.

"It all gets pretty bad," she said.

"I suppose I must have a look for myself. You've mentioned a number of trouble spots over the years. The Crusades?"

"Oh, yeah, that was a tough stretch."

"The Inquisition?"

"Yep, that was another rough one."

"And you mentioned some unrest between the Catholics and Protestants and the Hindus and Muslims.'

Sarah nodded her head. "Don't forget the Jews and all the problems they'll encounter after you leave the scene."

"Don't tell me we're planning to visit all those times and places," whined Steve.

"I don't know," replied Jesus. "I'd like too, and there were several more religious leaders and some philosophers, ones we've missed. There was a magician."

"Who's that?" Sarah asked.

"A fellow from ancient Persia," Jesus replied.

"Zarathustra?" said Sarah.

"Who?"

"Zoraster?" said Sarah.

Jesus smiled, "That's the one. I know him by his Greek name. He was well known even in my own day, although he had few followers."

"Never really caught on," said Sarah.

"But a powerful influence on Western thought," said Jesus.

"Absolutely," Sarah replied. "He was the first to stress the cosmic struggle between good and evil, how it occurs not only on a cosmological scale but in the everyday moral choices people make. He's the first religious leader really to bring the notion of free will into the mix."

"Free will," Jesus repeated dreamily and then he smiled and climbed back to his feet. "Oh, yes! That is definitely someone I will need to see."

"Well, we'll need help with the time-coordinates from your uncle the "Entity," said Sarah. "Zarathustra lived at least a thousand years before your time, and many scholars from my era argue that he may have lived far earlier than that."

"No problem," said Jesus. "We'll get in touch with the Entity, right M-2500?"

Jesus had caught me off-guard. I was daydreaming as the sun finally set in the desert and a cool breeze stirred across the sleeping encampment.

"M-2500?" Jesus repeated.

"The Entity?" I said. "I'm sure he'd be more than happy to help us. Will we be getting underway soon?"

"I don't see why not. Any problem with that Sarah?"

"No."

"Steve?"

"I'm good," Steve replied. "Although if we leave tonight we'll miss another round of stoning the devil tomorrow."

"I'm afraid Steve, that as much as I'd like to hang around for some more stoning… I'm just…" Jesus paused and drew a shallow, labored breath. We all waited a moment for him to finish. Steve was the first to speak.

"What is it? What's wrong?"

"Nothing. It's only that…" Jesus breathed in and out slowly. He had been standing, but he crouched down beside Sarah. He leaned back on the ground and propped his head up under one arm. "It's only that with this fasting…"

"What?" cried Steve.

"No. I'm okay, Steve. It's nothing. It's simply that I'm kind of… What's the expression…? 'Running low on energy.' I will need to prioritize some things. I suppose I haven't done a very good job of that. I have seven days left on this fast, and I just don't know… It's in the scripture, according to Sarah, and I'm just going to have to find the strength."

"I'm sorry, Jesus," said Steve. "I've been worried about my own stomach this whole time. I'd forgotten that you haven't eaten in a month. It's your call. Whatever, you want."

"Sarah?" asked Jesus.

"Yes?"

"Who were the two Asian fellows?"

"Lao Tzu and Chuang Tzu from the 6th and 4th centuries before you were born."

Jesus held his head, "There are just so many! And there was another, the contemporary of the Buddha?

"Confucius?"

"That's him!" said Jesus. "I'll just have to call on the Entity for power."

With that, Jesus took a deep breath, pushed off the ground with both hands and came cautiously to an upright position.

"Are we heading out?" asked Steve, climbing to his feet.

Jesus looked down at me and across to Sarah where we both sat on the bare ground.

"You two ready?" he asked. "I'm on the evening of my 34th day in the wilderness without food."

"I'm okay," said Sarah, and I could tell she was looking at me.

I nodded, "Yes," I said. "I'm ready."

* * *

Behind one of the hills just outside Mecca, I turned back into our rocket ship and Sarah, Steve and Jesus climbed on board. I rose quickly into the atmosphere above the Arabian Peninsula and hovered in the air in the light of the golden sun setting on the Western horizon. My human passengers took turns taking hot showers and while they wrapped themselves in terry-cloth towels, Sarah threw everyone's robes in the laundry. In less than two hours my human beings were refreshed and met at the conference table on the main deck. Sarah and

Steve bemoaned the lack of food in the galley, but made-do with tall glasses of ice-water as we de-briefed.

"So, that was the last of the great world religions?" asked Steve.

"I think so," said Sarah, "But remember, I only took one semester of the world religions class."

"You remembered a great deal," said Jesus. "We would have been lost without you."

"That's certainly true," I added. My disembodied voice still unsettled my friends, but I was truly impressed by Sarah's knowledge. The Entity had been filling me in on bits and pieces of history during the past four days, and I had been making a concerted effort to find that vital quiet time to acquire additional insight. During the past five minutes I had been receiving coordinates for our trip back in time.

"So, now we will head north to Persia to visit Zarathustra and then forward through time and across the Himalayas to visit Lao Tzu and Chuang Tzu and Confucius?" I said to check my understanding.

"That's the plan," replied Jesus.

"That's the plan," we all agreed. Had I been in human form I might have smiled with my three companions, although, behind that smile I would have gazed with secret concern at our leader. He had lost thirty pounds, and it took little imagination to envision the structure of a human skeleton beneath his loosely hanging veil of skin.

8. East Asia

In April of 1968, Sarah's grandfather took his teen-aged son, Wallace, to see the San Francisco premier of Kubrick's "2001." Years later, Sarah studied the movie in a film class in prep school. She was always struck by the Richard Strauss composition used in the opening sequence. "Thus Spake Zarathustra" with its bold beat of kettle drums and the dawning sound of brass experienced renewed popularity in the Twentieth Century. The soundtrack was being channeled back to me from the future and without thinking I began to play it over my loudspeakers. We had just BUMPED through the time stream backwards over three-thousand years and Jesus, Sarah, and Steve, stirred slightly in their safety harnesses. I let the music swell, not to startle my passengers, but to gently wake them from their slumber as we slowly left the night side of the planet and faced the sunrise.

"Oh, my God!" exclaimed Sarah, wiping the sleep from her eyes. "It's just like the movie!"

Our companions had absolutely no idea what she was talking about. Jesus and Steve had never heard of Richard Strauss much less a Kubrick film from 1968, but an instant later, the composition definitely stirred something in our captain.

"Zarathustra!" he cried, sitting bolt-upright in the pilot's chair, and he looked across at Sarah.

"Zarathustra?" she replied.

"Thus Spake Zarathustra!"

"That's the opening soundtrack from a movie," Sarah replied.

"I know."

"The Entity?"

Jesus nodded, "Oh yes. I see it clearly. It's a piece by the German Composer Richard Strauss, based on a book written in 1893 by the German Philosopher Friedrich Nietzsche."

Sarah could only listen, stunned by the information Jesus had glimpsed of the future.

"When are we going to eat!" shouted Steve from the auxiliary flight seat in the back of the cockpit.

* * *

It turned out that the thirty fourth day of Jesus' self-imposed fast was going to be the busiest of his time in the wilderness. Events probably pushed him to the limit of his mortal endurance. We sailed over the Alborz mountains and landed on the southern coast of the Caspian Sea. Zarathustra was dining in the home of a wealthy landowner in a courtyard not far from the beach. I had turned back into Demetrius and I waited silently with Steve and Sarah while Jesus walked slowly toward the residence where he was met by several household servants. His uncanny way with words disarmed the suspicious Persians and they soon welcomed him into their compound.

We remained at the gates for half an hour as the morning sun rose in the sky. We were deciding what to do about food for Steve and Sarah when, as though in answer to our concerns, two young servants appeared at the gates with baskets of bread and fish. This seemed to satisfy my two friends and an hour later we saw Jesus and a bearded, middle-aged man stroll down the walkway to join us at the gates.

"This is my friend, Zarathustra," said Jesus and he took time to introduce each one of us by name to the man whom the Greeks would later credit as the inventor of magic. It wasn't long after the introduction, however, that we took our leave and headed back to the secluded grove beyond the beach. I changed from the Greek youth into our red and white space craft.

* * *

We left Persia in the afternoon and headed back up into orbit. We BUMPED ahead into the future and came out the other side in the 5th Century BC. We sailed back into the atmosphere over the Himalayas and dropped down into eastern China near Mount Quingyuan where we landed in an empty field beside an ornate temple not far from the South China Sea. I guessed that Jesus' uncle realized his nephew was running low on energy. To facilitate our reception at our remaining whirlwind stops in ancient China, the Entity transmitted "strange visions" to our famous hosts in advance of our arrival.

In no time at all my passengers had disembarked and I had resumed the appearance of the Greek youth. That particular morning, La Tzu had awakened from a strange dream and left the house and gone out to the edge of the surrounding garden. He saw a frail young man, tall and haggard, sitting on a stone bench and leaning back on one arm. Lao Tzu approached the stranger who slowly rose to introduce himself. They shook hands, and slowly sank down to the bench where they talked to one another for two hours. At the end of that time, servants brought tea and Jesus drank from a tiny bowl.

During the audience with Lao Tzu, the founder of Taoism and the author of the Tao Te Ching, Steve, Sarah and I "cooled our heels" in a dusty alley on the other side of a painted wooden fence. When Jesus and Lao Tzu finally emerged from the garden gate in the late afternoon my companions were ready to leave.

Jesus had picked up some interesting new ideas in his understanding of the conflict between good and evil. The work of Zarathustra found refined expression in Lao Tzu's concept of Yin and Yang. In the end, however, we realized that Jesus was just getting too weak to keep up this pace. Sarah and I insisted that he drop the visit to Chuang Tzu in exchange for a visit to Confucius. Jesus agreed to the compromise. Since we were already in China we would look up Confucius, a contemporary of Lao Tzu.

Shortly after noon we flew west to the outskirts of the city of Qufu. We landed in a glen below Mount Ni and the fabulous temple of Shu Lianghe. We found the entire complex sealed behind a high, gated wall. Near the eastern gate we discovered a cave in the side of the mountain. A sign read, "Cave of Confucius," and Sarah explained the legend of how Confucius, born in the cave, was so ugly that his mother had abandoned him. He was saved by an eagle and a tiger that convinced his mother to take him back.

"Wow," said Steve. "That's a strange story."

"Yes," Sarah replied.

"Do you believe it?"

"What?" replied Sarah with a laugh, "How could I believe a crazy story like that?"

"Indeed! How could one believe such a fable?" a loud voice sounded from the cave.

We each of us jumped about a foot in the air. I had never seen such a look of fright on Sarah's face. She was about to run away when Jesus reached out and grabbed her arm. He nodded back in the direction of the cave where an old man with a walking staff had stepped out of the shadows.

"Forgive me," said the man. "I did not intend to startle you."

"Confucius?" Jesus asked.

"The very same," replied the man and he came forward a step and executed a deep and formal bow and smiled from beneath a long beard and mustache. "I awoke from the strangest dream this morning and felt compelled to revisit this old place. I have not set foot in this cave in nearly fifty years."

Jesus nodded his head in respect and extended his hand. The man looked sideways at the proffered hand, smiled faintly and took the hand and they shook.

"My friend," said Confucius, "You appear very weak. It would seem you are on a fast?"

"Yes," replied Jesus.

The two men walked ahead of us, locked arm in arm, moving slowly through the enormous towered gates of the compound. We followed at a distance and marveled at the ornate sculptures depicting dragons, wild animals, and strange spirits. The gardens were lush and lined with ancient trees and the sun played down through shifting patterns of green stirred by a cool breeze.

I listened to the conversation of the two wise men. Confucius was explaining to Jesus his concept of the Golden Rule. Jesus remarked how similar it seemed to some of his own thinking on the subject. They discussed the work of Zoroaster and Lao Tzu and agreed the philosophers were a bit light in practical application, although both men complemented the two for their understanding of free will and their conceptions of good and evil.

"I am particularly fond of Lao Tzu's work with the Three Jewels of the Tao: compassion, moderation, and humility," remarked Jesus.

"Yes, he is quite a great thinker, although I believe his emphasis on the self tends to overlook the duty one has toward others," replied Confucius.

"The duty one has toward others," repeated Jesus and for the first time in nearly an hour he looked across the courtyard where the three of us leaned against a gigantic stone pillar.

"Your friends look hungry," said Confucius.

"Yes," said Jesus.

"Not as hungry as you?"

"You may be correct," said Jesus.

"You are my guest and I understand that you do not want to eat, but let me extend the hospitality of my table to your companions."

"Well, we probably should be leaving soon..."

“Please, Jesus,” said Confucius coming to his feet, reaching down and helping our friend up from the bench, “Since I shall not be admitting that you are the Son of the Creator of the universe nor the Savior of mankind, this meal for your friends is the very least I can offer.”

He smiled and Jesus nodded and returned the smile. They looked back in our direction. Confucius clapped his hands together, evidently in some sort of sonic code. Instantly, the courtyard swarmed with servants. They wore black trousers and shirts and kept their eyes averted from us as they brought in a long, low table, enormous embroidered pillows and a great thatched mat. The mat they placed on a stone in the middle of the courtyard, set the table in the center and surrounded its perimeter with pillows and large bowls of food and drink.

Sarah and Steve did not have Chinese food again until they got off a tour bus in Chinatown in Oakland in 1968. I didn’t taste it again until our return to the Bay Area at the turn of the millennium. As good as the Chinese food was in California, it never came close to the quality of the food and drink served by Confucius’ servants that afternoon in the 5th Century BC. Steve and Sarah ate and drank to exhaustion. Although food was not a requirement for me, the sights and smells of the experience got the best of my angelic curiosity. Since I inhabited a human form with all the requisite sensory wiring, I made sure to sample all the delicious foods. At the same time, I had to check myself; human sensuality could be a slippery slope, even for an angel.

9. Montage

We left the compound in the late afternoon and headed to the other side of the mountain where I turned back into our space craft. We had a lot of places to go, but Jesus was so weak that we could afford only to skim through the various epochs and eras on his checklist. He lay on his side on a divan amidships and rather than look over the sill through the observation ports, he faced the cushions. I intended to open a panoramic view of the proceedings.

I went into stealth mode, which is to say, I rendered our ship invisible to any human eye that might cast its gaze in our vicinity. To Sarah, Steve, and Jesus, however, the walls, floors and all the objects inside our vessel appeared unaffected by this outward transformation, with one important exception. I opened-up the entire starboard side of the main deck, the way a person from the 20th Century might dial back the lid on a tin of sardines. The interior paneling, insulation and outer metallic hull became instantly transparent to the viewer from inside. Jesus reclined on the divan and gazed through the cushions of the backrest, through the hull of the ship and out into the vast reaches of the cosmos.

Light flickered across his face as the scenes wheeled by, one after another. The intermittent BUMP and stream of white mist settled back with regularity as we lurched forward to scenes of Christianity unfolding before us from the time of Saul and the persecution of the first followers of Jesus.

We watched the Christian hunter struck blind, face down on the Road to Damascus by two old friends of mine and we gasped as he rose-up to seek forgiveness and devote his life to the martyred Jesus.

We flew across miles and centuries to the embattled Holy Land and watched the iron clad armies of Christianity and Islam clash again and again.

Sitting beside one another on the divan opposite Jesus, Steve and Sarah gripped their seat cushions and stared, spellbound, as the sounds and images washed over their senses. War and visions of blood and the clash of armaments and the struggle of mighty armies on the parapets of Jerusalem gave way to obscene engines of torture in the dungeons of the Inquisition and prisons throughout Europe where the schism between the Catholic Church and its denominations erupted in spasms of bloodshed, violence, repression and revolution.

I didn't know whether Jesus in his weakened condition could stand to see much more. Each scene seemed to grab him viscerally and he shook from side to side, frustrated, it appeared, by his apparent inability to do anything to stem the onslaught of violence and blood and pain unleashed upon the world in his name.

It seemed that through the three day journey up from the past, Jesus' mysterious uncle, The Entity, had been very near to all of us on board. Certainly, I had given over to him completely the navigation of our craft through time and space.

Of Sarah, Steve, Jesus and me, only Sarah seemed to have any idea what, at least in general outline, it was we were viewing or into what period of human history we had intruded. The images of suffering, the oppressive wheeling of red and black images seemed to weigh heavily upon her and she recoiled back into her cushions. More than once I saw her grimace and shield her eyes.

On more than one occasion Steve excused himself down the spiral staircase to the lavatory on the lower deck. More than once the nausea and vertigo produced by the kaleidoscopic display of images and sounds and the rhythmic sway of the ship and the scenes of extreme human agony caused him to become ill.

We bounced back and forth between east and west for a day, but following our last dash to the Iberian Peninsula we headed east and there was no turning back. We left Europe, sailed across the Himalayas, and leaving the coast of East Asia, flew across a vast, blue ocean. After two minutes heading into the rising sun, we peeled in a graceful turn to the southeast and BUMPED out of the time stream into what Sarah labeled "the age of exploration" and an altogether different NEW WORLD.

In most important respects this world was no different than the one we had departed. We saw bronze-skinned men and women in cloaks of animal fur, grass and feathers subjugated beneath the iron clad heels of conquerors from another ocean to the east. From the high mountains of a southern continent, along its towering spine of volcanic mountains into the world Sarah described as North America we watched marauding explorers obliterate ancient civilizations, plundering silver and gold and raising up churches and monasteries in the name of Jesus.

By the time we'd sailed through two thousand years of Christian history, Jesus had seen just about enough. He lay on his back staring up at the blank ceiling. He seemed adrift in a catatonic state.

"Jesus? Jesus, are you all right?" asked Sarah.

"Yes," he replied, without actually looking over at her.

Sarah exchanged a worried glance with Steve.

"I suppose I should have seen this coming," said Jesus and he winced as he propped himself up on his elbows. "People have made some fairly terrible choices in my name over the years. They've had a lot of help and encouragement from all the wrong places."

"Satan?" asked Steve.

"How's that hand of yours?" asked Jesus.

Almost reflexively, Steve cradled his right hand in his left and rubbed the scarred back of his wrist. "It's better," he replied.

Jesus nodded.

"Is something wrong?" asked Steve.

"I feel as though I am being summoned. The trouble is I can't determine who it is that's doing the summoning…"

"Who do you think?" asked Sarah.

"I don't know. Too much interference," replied Jesus.

At that moment we all experienced another terrific BUMP. Jesus bounced on his couch and Steve and Sarah were thrown to their sides.

White mist streamed over my form and I slipped down from orbit and back into the blue black upper atmosphere over the West Coast of North America.

"What time is it?" asked Jesus.

"I don't know precisely," my voice replied from hidden loud speakers in the ceiling. "It is night," I added.

Jesus shook his head.

"What year?" Sarah asked.

"1968 AD," I replied as the thought came to me in an instant from some heavenly outpost a hundred trillion light years away.

"It's March 31st, 1968," I continued. "Shall I land?"

"Yes…" replied Jesus, doing his best to smile.

"That means tomorrow will be April 1st," exclaimed Sarah, suddenly.

"What is the significance of April the first?" I asked.

"It's April fool's day," she replied

"Is that an important date?" asked Jesus as we slowly descended through the atmosphere. Sarah explained the date's significance while I dropped down along a mountain range bordering the coast line of the enormous western ocean.

* * *

It was night time as we landed on a fairway of the Alameda Municipal Golf Course. My passengers disembarked and I turned into Demetrius. We walked north through a wooded area and crossed a bridge onto Alameda Island. We came up on the east side of the island alongside San Leandro Bay and followed the water's edge through darkened streets of cement and steel. We came finally to a yawning tunnel, the so-called Posey Street Tube. We hurried down into the ground beneath the Alameda Oakland Estuary and half an hour later, walked up into the city of Oakland, California.

10. Oakland, 1968

As the sun rose it was the morning of Jesus' 38th day in the wilderness. We were exhausted and looking beat and Sarah put out her thumb and we hitched a ride in the back of a pickup all the way through the heart of town and into North Oakland. The truck was driven by a young man in a leather jacket and a black beret. He and his friend and a young woman about Sarah's age all belonged to an organization recently formed in town known as the Black Panthers. They dropped us off on a street corner in North Oakland and recommended we seek shelter at the Orpheus Hotel.

When they asked why we were all "dressed like Romans," Sarah explained that we were from out of town and that our car had broken down on our way to play an April Fools' prank at a friend's house. They laughed and wished us good luck and we walked down the block to the corner.

We stood outside the lobby of a six-story building on the corner and all suddenly realized that we had no means to pay for lodging.

Sarah was looking across the street at the darkened windows of a pawn shop when she turned to me.

"Remember what you did with the philosopher's stone back in ancient Greece?"

Her question hit me like a shot. It was the first time any of us had mentioned anything to do with that place since we left. I took a step backward, suddenly ashamed, once again feeling the remorse I had experienced that afternoon. I nodded my head slowly.

"M-2500?" said Sarah, "I mean…" she paused, took a deep breath and spoke the name, "Demetrius?"

"Yes…"

"Are you all right?"

"I'm sorry," I said. "It's only that the memory of that place and the advantage I took of the situation, and of you, still brings grieves me."

"Well, it should," said Sarah.

Steve and Jesus were midway down the block looking into the window of a diner that was about to open.

"It brings me a lot of grief too," she said, "But I believe I have forgiven you."

"Then why does it still hurt to think of it?"

"I don't know," she replied. "You'll have to ask your boss."

"Jesus?"

"Yes."

"He's not looking very well, is he?" I said.

"That's why we have to get food and shelter. Do you have any idea why the Holy Spirit would bring us here of all places?"

"The Holy Spirit?" I asked.

"The Entity."

I shook my head as early morning sunlight touched the tops of the tall buildings across the street. Sarah reached down and pulled a stone from a crack in the cement sidewalk and held it toward me.

"So, what do you say?" she asked.

I did my best to smile, and, nodding my head, I took the large smooth stone, placed it in the palm of my right hand and let the four human-looking digits enclose the object.

"One moment," I said and I put my back to her as I turned toward the brick wall and drew my hand up to chest-level and began to squeeze. Ten seconds later I turned back to Sarah. Steam and a faint film of smoke rose up from my finger-tips as I opened my fist and Sarah peered down at the glowing lump of pure gold in my palm.

We saw the orange neon lights of "Mel's Pawn and Loan" and an "Open" sign suddenly illuminate the store front window across the street. We crossed at the empty crosswalk and made our way to the door. A large, middle-aged man was unlocking the front door with a single brass key from a great fist-full of keys.

"You folks look like you might be in the wrong part of town," he said, eyeing us suspiciously. He stuck a key in a reinforced padlock and listened as Sarah lied about our having broken-down on route to an April Fools' Day party.

Mel didn't seem particularly impressed by the story. I sensed this man had a great deal of experience in the world and had probably listened to all sorts of outrageous narratives, but his face lit-up as Sarah instructed me to unfold my fingers and reveal our treasure. Mel's eyes widened and he suddenly seemed in a race to get the padlock off his gate and get us off the street and into his shop.

"Is it hot?" he asked.

I was about to speak when Sarah interrupted me, "Oh no, it was a gift from my great-grandmother. They settled out here in the 1840's."

The gold really was "hot" having just dropped into existence from a slurry of atomic plasma and a molten state less than five minutes earlier. I was reluctant to hand the heavy object to Mel for fear that he might incinerate his human fingers.

"Well, I'm interested," he said as he stepped behind a screened-off section of his shop. He closed a gate behind him and came up in a wire mesh window behind a counter facing us, "But I have a lot of over-head in a shop like this. I'm really not going to be able to give you the full value. You might try one of the shops across the bay. I'll let you know that right off the top, but if you folks need cash in a hurry to get your car fixed and get on to that party of yours, then you've come to the right place."

"Thanks a lot," said Sarah.

The transaction was about to continue when a worried look crossed Mel's face. He looked though his protective grill, out through the cluttered storefront window with the neon sign and the iron bars across the street to the diner.

"Seems like one of your friends is in trouble," he said.

We evaluated the man's concerned expression and followed his gaze as he peered out through the windows.

Across the street, Steve knelt down beside Jesus who had collapsed on the sidewalk. Through the glass and iron and the molecules of atmosphere I detected Jesus' pulse and shallow breath. I dropped the lump of gold on the floor where I stood and dashed back outside through the door, across the street, and knelt at the side of our fallen companion.

"Is he okay?" cried Steve. "You've got to do something!"

I held my human looking ear against Jesus' chest and listened. A young man and woman had come out on the sidewalk from the nearby diner.

"Is he all right?" asked the woman.

I looked up. "He needs food and water," I said.

"Don't they all!" said the man.

"Hush, now," the woman scolded her partner. "Why don't you go back and open up. I'll be along," she said with an air of authority that caught Steve's attention and immediately seemed to calm him.

The woman looked across the street and hailed Mel who was locking the gate over his front door. He hurried across the street with Sarah.

"Melvin," called the woman as she crouched down beside me and placed her palm on Jesus damp forehead, "Melvin, let's see if we can get this young man into a room at Toby's. I'd sure hate to have to wait for an ambulance," she said apparently addressing me.

I smiled dumbly, having no idea what an ambulance might be.

"Best not to get the city involved if we can help it," she said.

"No, ma'am," I agreed.

"You're not from around here, are you?" she asked.

"Around here?" I replied, uncertain what I was being asked or how to answer. I was relieved as Sarah and Mel came upon us.

"Is he okay?" asked Sarah kneeling on the sidewalk beside Jesus.

"Your friend said he needs food and water," answered the woman. "Has he been sick? Looks as though he's wasting away."

"He's fasting," said Sarah.

"Ohhh," said the woman and she climbed to her feet.

The citizens of this tiny village at the intersection of two streets in North Oakland tended to our plight. Three teen-aged boys in white aprons came out of the diner and lifted Jesus up between them. Following Mel and the woman whose name we later learned was Billie, we walked to the corner. Mel stepped into an alcove in front of the Orpheus Hotel. He rang a buzzer and several people looked up from wooden chairs within. I particularly remember the round face of a little brown boy who poked his head over the backrest of a green sofa and who peered at the strangers in the doorway.

"You set back down there and watch your cartoons on the TV, Alonzo," shouted one of the women in the lobby.

As the door opened we were greeted by the strong scent of something I later learned was a water-based latex paint. There were sawhorses and planks of wood and paint-flecked drop clothes spread about the lobby and one was draped over the main desk.

Alonzo's father, Marcus Smith, wore white coveralls. He had a thick carpenter's pencil thrust back through curly hair behind his ear. He walked to the doorway and spoke to Mel and Billie. Within fifteen minutes we found ourselves down the hall on the third floor in a freshly painted hotel room. Jesus lay asleep on one of the twin beds.

"You sure he won't eat?" asked Billie at the doorway.

Sarah shook her head, "No he won't, Billie," said Sarah. "But the tea and the rest will put him on the mend. He has only a few more days to go."

"You sure he's not a Muslim?"

"I'm pretty sure he's a Christian," Sarah replied.

"Our Muslim brothers are always fasting. Like to put us out of business," said Billie.

Sarah laughed. "Don't worry. The rest of us have appetites!"

Billie laughed, "Well, don't be strangers," she said and turned as Mel came up the hallway.

"You better get back across the street, Melvin," she said.

He nodded with a smile, stepped into the room and pulled a thick wad of ten dollar bills from his pants pocket. He carefully counted out the currency into Sarah's hands.

"I went ahead and spoke to Marcus about what you might owe for the room," he said. "Since you folks are his very first customers he's giving you a break."

"A break?" asked Sarah.

"Fifteen dollars a night. You pay him day by day. Tonight's on him," said Mel.

"That's wonderful," Sarah replied.

"To tell the truth," said the middle aged pawnbroker, "When I met you and your pal this morning, I was sure you were fencing stolen property. Now, I'm not so sure. Can't see that I buy your story about a great-grandmother, but I won't question providence." He finished counting out two hundred and fifty dollars into Sarah hand. "You seem like honest people," he said.

"Thanks," said Steve looking up from the morning news broadcast on the black and white television set. Steve sat on the edge of the other twin bed and smiled at Mel.

"A little crazy," Mel continued, "But honest..."

Sarah nodded and laughed, nervously, "Thank you," she said.

Mel's eyes narrowed. "Although you might want to see about getting your car off the streets," he said, offering his hand to Sarah.

"Our car?" asked Sarah shaking the proffered hand. By the time she remembered her story about the broken-down car, the man was already at the door.

Mel smiled, mysteriously. "Honest enough," he replied and left.

Sarah walked to the night stand between the two twin beds. She snapped on the electric light of a small reading lamp and opened up the single drawer. She smiled.

"What is it," I asked.

Steve turned his head to look back from the small, black and white TV to observe Sarah pull a thick book from the open drawer. She placed the volume on the nightstand beside Jesus.

"When he wakes up, he really he ought to read this," she said. She pulled three tens off her roll of currency, placed the remaining bills inside the drawer and pushed it shut.

"There," she said, and she brushed back her hair. "I saw a thrift store down at the other end of the street from Mel's. I'll see whether we can get ourselves some civilian clothes."

Sarah walked to the hotel room door. She turned back to Steve and was about to ask him whether he was interested in getting something to eat when the sound of kettle drums and brass instruments sounded from the loud speakers of the television set.

It was the theme music from a new science fiction film. Evidently the network news editors were running an advance on the big budget movie set to open across the country later that week. Sarah crossed to Steve and dropped down on the edge of the bed beside him and stared at the images on the television screen. We observed what Sarah described as "clips from the upcoming movie," as a news reporter spoke in the background about the planned premier. We saw pictures of ape-like beings touching a strange column of stone and then there were images of objects floating in outer space. Sarah only sat, motionless, staring at the screen as though she were staring at a ghost.

"Dad…" she murmured.

"What?" I asked, although, with my ultra sonic hearing, the utterance and its meaning had not escaped me; still I wondered what else she might be thinking.

"Nothing…" she said.

"No," I replied. "What is it? You are evidently deeply moved by these images."

"It's my father."

"Yes?"

"I think he's across the bay."

"The bay?" I said.

"He's across the bay with my grandfather."

"What?" I asked.

"My grandfather was a civilian contractor and ship builder. He had business at the naval shipyards at Hunters Point. Really just one brief meeting. He pulled dad out of boarding school to spend a weekend with him in San Francisco."

"Sarah, that is very interesting," I said.

"Interesting?" said Steve. "I don't think it's all that interesting."

"So, what brings it to mind, now?" I asked.

"The movie," Sarah continued, "Grandpa took him to see that movie in San Francisco on opening day."

"April 6, 1968," I said. "It's remarkable that you would remember such a date."

"Oh, I didn't remember the date, not even the month or year. I only remember that they saw that movie together in San Francisco when Dad was a boy."

"I wonder if our being here is a coincidence?" I asked.

"Who knows," replied Steve bouncing to his feet. "Let's get some of that money downstairs to the diner. I'm dying of starvation."

Sarah crossed to the venation blinds in the window. She pulled an arrangement of hempen cords and the slats rose up and disappeared into a freshly painted valence. She looked across the roof tops and down to the street below. "There's Melvin's," said Sarah, and she smiled faintly, "And down there is the thrift store. I think they're open. Let's go."

Sarah let the blinds drop shut. She walked past the TV, snapped it off, and headed around Steve to the doorway. "Let's go Steve," she said, "Demetrius, we'll be back within two hours. If you need us we'll either be at the thrift store or the diner."

After they had left, I walked over between the two twin beds, sat on the bed opposite my sleeping friend, reached over, picked up the Gideon's Bible and began to read.

I figured it was about time.

* * *

Around nine o'clock Sarah and Steve returned to the room with bags of clothes. They were each dressed in the current fashion. Steve wore faded bell-bottomed jeans and a colorful T-shirt. Sarah wore a long skirt printed with a bright paisley pattern. She wore an embroidered blouse of many colors. She set a paper bag on the bedside for me and another bag for Jesus.

"Just jeans and t-shirts," she said, "But with our sandals I think we'll fit in if we want to go out. How's he doing?" she asked.

"Sleeping," I said setting down the copy of the Bible. In little more than an hour, due to my extraordinary ability to process information, I had completed the Old Testament and committed its text to memory.

"He seems to be doing all right," I said.

"He's dead-set on completing his fast?" asked Sarah.

"As far as I know," I replied.

"Well, I'm going to get something to eat," said Steve. "Can I have some of that change?" he asked Sarah.

Sarah and I exchanged a warning glance.

"Didn't we just eat?" she replied.

"But I'm still hungry," he said.

"You had six pancakes, two fried eggs and six strips of…"

“Shhh!” interrupted Steve, holding a finger to his mouth. His eyes bulged in their sockets and he shook his head, staring at Sarah as though it were a matter of life and death.

“Bacon?” she asked.

“Sarah! Quiet!”

“What?” she said and looked at me with an expression of incredulity on her face.

“Christians can eat bacon. Can’t they?” asked Sarah. “You’re a… Oh…” she said as she caught herself in a sudden realization.

From what I had just finished reading of Jewish tradition, pork, and what I took therefore to include bacon, were strictly forbidden.

“Oh, that’s right,” said Sarah and she turned back to Steve. “Well, you’ll just have to trust that by the time it all gets sorted out, you’ll be able to eat that stuff without going to hell, or wherever the Jews go when they screw up.”

She peeled a five dollar bill from a pocket in her blouse and handed it to Steve.

“Five?” he said, looking up from the bill in his hand.

Sarah nodded, “That’s plenty,” she replied. “After all, this is 1968. And don’t spend it all in one place.”

Steve and Sarah were unlikely companions and even more unlikely tourists, but they spent the next three days together venturing further and further into the community. They spent time at the Neighborhood Association Community Center two blocks down the street and Steve volunteered to stack shelves at the food pantry and serve meals at the soup kitchen. Sarah and Steve attended at least two services at two of the local congregations and by the third day had ventured out of Oakland across the bay to San Francisco.

During that time I completed my reading of both the Old and New Testaments of the Bible and I re-read the entire book again from cover to cover. I continued to check on Jesus every half hour, to prop up his head long enough for him to take a sip of water and to bring him back from the delirium of his slow starvation.

There were a few times over the course of those three days that he would sit up in bed, almost completely lucid, but he would soon become disoriented. I had to explain to him where we were and how we had come to this place. Not long after dark each night, Sarah returned, cleaned up in the lavatory and then retired to the other twin bed. I had moved the Bible to a small writing table by the window, and I sat in a chair and observed the comings and goings. Steve arrived much later. He went to the lavatory for some time but did not shower. He came out and collapsed on the sofa while the others slept.

Still, both he and Sarah were up bright and early the next morning and out the door. Sarah had taken another sixty dollars from the night stand drawer and paid Marcus at the desk. Sarah and Steve ate breakfast at Billie's Diner and went to volunteer at the Community Center. And the ebb and flow of the day continued that day and the next and now it was the afternoon of April third and I looked up from the Bible, startled by the sound of the television. Jesus had come to the edge of his bed and had turned on the set.

"Jesus?" I asked, "Are you all right?"

He nodded in the affirmative and only stared ahead at the television. It was a news program and a voice of someone addressing a large crowd sounded over the television speaker. It seems we had missed most of what the man had been saying, and caught only the very end.

"Well, I don't know what will happen now. We've got some difficult days ahead," said the man on the television set, "But it really doesn't matter with me now, because I've been to the mountaintop. And I don't mind. Like anybody, I would like to live a long life. Longevity has its place. But I'm not concerned about that now. I just want to do God's will. And He's allowed me to go up to the mountain. And I've looked over, and I've seen the Promised Land. I may not get there with you. But I want you to know tonight, that we, as a people, will get to the Promised Land. So, I'm happy tonight. I'm not worried about anything. I'm not fearing any man. Mine eyes have seen the glory of the coming of the Lord."

With that, Jesus leaned forward and snapped off the television. He pulled himself back up to the center of the bed and lay down on his side with his face to the wall and, without a word, was soon asleep again.

* * *

The sun rose through the blinds and I stood and pulled the hempen cable which raised the slats entirely up and they disappeared in the valence and light streamed in and it was Thursday, April the fourth, 1968 the morning of the 41st day of Jesus' fast.

"Wake up," I said.

I stood at Jesus' bedside, reached over and shook his arm.

"M-2500?" said Jesus, raising a hand to shield his eyes against the glare from the windows. "What's going on?" he croaked.

"You're going to have something to eat." I said and I pulled over my chair to his bedside and drew the pillow up snug behind his head.

Oh yes! I had prepared for this day. I had sent Sarah and Steve out to the market for some fresh produce late in the afternoon on the third. They had come back with a loaf of white bread and a bunch of bananas.

"Here," I said, pushing the peeled end of a banana into Jesus mouth. "Eat it!"

He moved his head side-to-side a bit, but I was determined he would get something down into that human stomach of his.

"Go on," I said. "Your fast had ended. You've been forty days without food! You're going to need your strength from here on out."

Jesus took a bite and chewed slowly.

Not long afterward he was on his feet. We dressed in our new "street clothes" and took the newly operational elevator down to the freshly painted lobby of the Orpheus Hotel. Men with hand-trucks were rolling a large vending machine across the floor and installing it in the corner beside the stairwell. I heard the wacky background music of children's cartoons and looked over at the green sofa. The youngest of the three siblings belonging to Marcus, Alonso, turned and looked at us over the sofa's backrest as his father came from behind the front desk.

"Well, well, well," said Marcus, extending his hand in friendship. "The fast has ended!"

Jesus and Marcus looked each other in the eyes and they shook hands. Both men smiled.

"Your friends are helping at the community center," said Marcus. "If you're up to it, you ought to head over to Billie's Diner. She says you're welcome to anything you want off her menu for making your forty-day goal!"

The gaze of the little boy on the sofa followed us out the door and we were on the street in the sunlight. We walked east to Billie's Diner. When we walked in, the conversation in the crowded eatery came to a halt and applause started up.

Dressed in our jeans, t-shirts and sandals we didn't look anything special but evidently word had gotten out in the neighborhood of my friend's rather incredible fast. A teen-aged boy in a white apron whom I recognized from our first day in town greeted us with menus and led us to a booth on the side of the long, narrow room. I could see the owner of the establishment, Ms. Billie wave to us from behind a long, chrome-rimmed counter. She came around with glasses of ice water.

"I hope Marcus told you that breakfast was on me this morning," she said.

"Yes, he did," replied Jesus.

"Well, you might want to take it easy this morning starting back in with the solid food," she said. "But order what you like and you can come back in a week or two when you get your appetite back and have another meal on the house!"

"That's very generous," said Jesus.

Billie stepped back and took a long look at Jesus and smiled. "Anyone who can follow the path of my Lord and Savior the way you've done is okay in my book." She leaned close to the table and looked back and forth between us and spoke in a voice low and intended only for our ears. "I don't care how crazy the folks say you are. You just keep up the good work," and as she leaned back up she gave me a wink, "If your friend wants to be called 'Jesus,' that's fine by me!"

She looked up as some young men in black leather jackets and berets entered her establishment. She looked back at us.

"Well, you have the menus. I'll be back to see what you'll have. You might want to start out with some biscuits, but you decide."

She smiled and the wise, compassionate expression of this woman filled us both with happiness and hope.

"Coffee?" she asked.

Jesus and I looked at one another. We weren't entirely sure whether or not we wanted coffee.

"That's all right, Billie" I said. "We're fine with just the water."

Billie went back to work behind the counter. Jesus had his back to the men who had just entered the diner. The youngster in the white apron seated the quartette of men at a four-square table near the entrance. Evidently the men at the table were talking about us because they kept looking in our direction. None of them seemed happy.

Time passed and Billie returned and took an order for Jesus of biscuits and, at my suggestion, an extra large glass of fresh squeezed orange juice.

Try as she might, Billie couldn't convince me to order anything. I told her that I was more than happy with the water and really looking forward to seeing my friend eat once again. She re-filled our water glasses from a pitcher, took our menus and headed up the aisle to greet the four men.

Having completed the New Testament for the second time the night before and having finally found time to reach out and commune through prayer with my new found friend, the Entity, I was at last in a position to have a fairly frank conversation with Jesus.

"So, you've fulfilled the scriptures, haven't you?" I said.

Jesus looked up from his water glass, "Excuse me?"

"Matthew 4.1-2; Mark 1.12-13; and Luke 4.1-2," I recited.

"What's that?" he asked.

"It's from the story of your life and future work."

"How did you come by it?" asked Jesus.

"The Gideon Society. They've made copies of the book available throughout the world. There's one in the drawer of the nightstand in our room at the hotel."

Jesus nodded, "Interesting," he said.

"Those verses I quoted deal with your journey through the wilderness."

Jesus nodded.

"It's been forty days, so it's over with, right?"

"I suppose so," said Jesus, "But it seems so much remains to do, to learn."

I nodded in agreement.

"And I worry about Sarah, too."

"Sarah?"

"Oh sure," said Jesus.

"What about Steve?"

Jesus laughed. "Naturally, I'm very concerned about Steve, but when we return to our own time, I'll have a chance to work with him, at least for a while, and with you too, for that matter, if it should be your decision to remain."

I laughed nervously, remembering my transgression and the amazing good fortune of my having been the first being in history to have been baptized in the Entity who, thanks to Jesus and Gideons International, I had come to finally recognize as the Holy Spirit.

"I really don't see the outcome with Sarah, particularly if we leave now," Jesus continued. "I believe the Entity brought us here for a reason. Something momentous is going to happen this week."

"April Fools' was three days ago, Mac!" sounded a low, threatening voice at our side.

We turned and looked up into the face of a bearded, mustachioed man wearing a black leather jacket, beret and impenetrably dark shades.

"Good morning, young man," replied Jesus, looking up with a bright smile on his face.

The tension in the body of the man beside us seemed suddenly to drain away and he took a step back in the aisle. He accidently bumped the backrest of a man sitting at another table. The black-garbed man quickly excused himself and stepped back toward us and cleared his throat.

"So, you were on a fast to show solidarity with our Hispanic brothers?"

"No." said Jesus.

The man was unsatisfied with this response although he seemed impressed by the conviction in Jesus' response. At that point no one in our party had ever heard of Caesar Chavez or a general strike by the organization of the United Farm Workers.

"No?" replied the young man.

"We are all of us brothers and sisters," said Jesus. "But I was fasting simply to clear my mind that I might better commune with our Creator and the Entity."

"He means the Holy Spirit," I injected.

"Man..." said the young man. "Billie said you was trippin', but man oh man," and the youth turned to me. I could see down the aisle that his three companions were observing our interchange.

"What's your story? Are you some kind of Jesus-freak too?"

"I suppose you might say that."

"Well," he said and he looked back at his friends and then back to us, "You ever hear of the Black Panthers?"

"No," I replied.

He looked a bit crestfallen and then looked at Jesus, "What about you? You ever hear of the Black Panthers?"

"I've heard the words, but certainly not in the sense you intend. No, I have never heard of the Black Panthers. You appear to be an organization designed to protect your race through the threat of physical violence. Did you hear Dr. King speak last night in Memphis?"

The youth stepped back. The words, "Dr. King," had caught a few ears and the attention of those at the nearby tables. I noticed across the crowded counter by the kitchen order window, Billie had turned from a conversation with her cook and was looking in our direction.

"Yes, I heard him speak," replied the youth.

"I haven't been to the mountain top," Jesus continued. "I plan to, one day, if I live that long. I think we're all wise to follow Dr. King's example."

I could see more than a few heads nodding in what had become an audience.

"What are you guys doing here anyway?" asked the youth.

"Just trying to get along," said Jesus.

"Tell me now!" said the man seated at the table behind the youth in the aisle. Other people at that table were looking in our direction and nodding in approval and support. We realized now that man at the table across the aisle was Melvin from Melvin's Pawn and Loan.

"Why don't you run along, Little Bobby?" said Melvin. "Run along so these men can get some peace and quiet."

With my superior vision I peered through the darkened lenses of Bobby Horton's shades and watched his eyes momentarily roll back in their sockets. Horton shrugged and continued on his way to the back of the diner, apparently to use the washroom.

While he was gone Billie came over with our biscuits and orange juice. She seemed a little unnerved by something, but Jesus thanked her and she poured more water and headed back to the counter. That's when Jesus pushed his plate of biscuits over to the edge of the laminated table top, slid over to the edge of his red vinyl upholstered booth seat and stood in the aisle. He picked up his plate and juice and walked up the aisle to the table nearest the door. He set down his plate and glass before the empty chair, swung his leg over the backrest of the chair and sat down, his belly flush up against the table.

"Did you send little Bobby Horton over there to intimidate me?" he asked the three men at the table by the door.

"Who the hell are you?" said one of the three men, leaning back in his chair.

"I'm asking the questions."

After that I don't know what was said. The noise in the diner increased and the young man whom they called "Little Bobby" came back from the washroom. When he discovered that his seat had been taken by Jesus, he stood there dumbfounded until one of the leaders reached over to the only other empty chair in the place, pulled it up and nodded for the kid to sit down.

I didn't know what was going on. I didn't listen in, but they sat there for at least an hour, talking. Billie came by a few times to check on me and fill my water, not that I really needed water, but each time she stopped, she seemed more and more relaxed about whatever had been simmering under the surface when the Black Panther member had first come to our table. No, they were all doing just fine, and it was nearly noon when they finally got up and Jesus called me over and introduced me to four of the founding members of the Black Panthers Party.

They had started their group two years earlier and discovered that they were having a lot of success in their battles against discrimination and police brutality. It was a grass-roots organization and Jesus was very interested in their methods. I returned to our booth and Jesus and the men talked for another ten minutes until Jesus walked back to where I was sitting with my glass of melted ice water.

"I'm going up to the community center with them," he said. "I'll return to our room by sunset. Are you all right?"

I nodded, "Yes. Yes, I'm fine," I said. I watched him walk up the aisle. He talked to the four men waiting for him at the door, turned and came back to me.

"Is everything all right?" I asked.

"I thought I'd use the washroom before I head out with the Panthers," he said.

"Oh… Well…"

Jesus extended his hand toward me.

"Let me borrow the rings…" he said.

"What?"

"I may not get another opportunity. Let me have the Rings of the Ophanim."

I thought this request highly unusual, but I was in no position to deny the man who had handed me the talisman in the first place. I slipped the two rings of the Ophanim off my ring fingers and handed them to Jesus. He clenched them in his fist.

"Thanks," he said. "I should be right back."

It's funny what a man can do by himself in a lavatory stall when in possession of just a small fraction of the power of the First Sphere. It was only months later, and never in any great detail, that I leaned of Jesus' private excursions back across time and space from the porcelain commode in Billie's washroom. Jesus re-emerged not more than ten minutes later, but in that time he had managed to run down two dozen of human history's most influential philosophers. Somewhere in his travels he had gained ten pounds and found time to shave.

He had traveled back and forth across Europe beginning with a six hour audience with St. Augustine in fifth century North Africa. Jesus discussed the ontological proof for the existence of God with St. Anslem of Canterbury and dashed back across the channel to meet Thomas Aquinas at the University of Paris. From there it was three hundred years into the future to England and then back and forth between England and the continent, jumping forward in increments of a hundred years or so to meet the great intellects: Thomas Hobbes, Descartes, Pascal, Spinoza, Hume, Rousseau, Kant, Hegel, John Stuart Mill, Kierkegaard, Marx, and Friedrich Nietzsche. Jesus met up with Bertrand Russell, Wittgenstein, and Karl Popper at Cambridge University in England as late as October of 1946.

By the time he sat down with the French existentialist, Jean Paul Sartre, it was October 1964. Earlier that month Sartre had turned down the Nobel Prize for literature. He told Jesus he didn't want to the prize to "transform him." To escape media attention he went to live in secret with Hélène de Beauvoir. She was a painter, the younger sister of philosopher Simone de Beauvoir: Simone, with whom Sartre had long been romantically involved.

When Jesus walked back out of the restroom, he was clean-shaven, smelled faintly of red wine and clove cigarettes and wore a beret. There was so much I wanted to ask him as he stood in the aisle pulling the rings of the Ophanim off his ring fingers and handing them back to me.

"Hey, J.C.!" called one of the men from the door of the diner, "You comin'?"

"I'll be right along," said Jesus with a smile.

"So, what happened?" I asked.

"I've had dinner with some pretty incredible people," he replied.

"And…"

"There was one: Spinoza, a 17th century Jew from Holland. I met him at his home in The Hague in 1676. The mathematician Gottfried Leibniz had come to call for a discussion of Baruch's recently published 'Ethics.' Spinoza earned his lively hood as a lens grinder."

"A lens grinder?" I asked.

"A livelihood to support his passion for philosophy."

"Did he make spectacles?"

"I don't know. Lenses..." replied Jesus. "For many purposes…"

That was all the time he had at the moment and he was off to join the men at the door. I learned later that Gottfried Leibniz had met with Sir Isaac Newton in London. Leibniz was on his way back to Hanover and had stopped in Amsterdam to meet Antonie van Leeuwenhoek. This man had used microscopes to explore the recently discovered micro worlds. It was all very curious.

Spinoza was raised in the Dutch Jewish community. In time he developed highly controversial ideas regarding the authenticity of the Hebrew Bible and the nature of the Divine. The Jewish religious authorities issued a "Cherem," a kind of excommunication against him, effectively dismissing him from Jewish society at age 23. His books were also later put on the Catholic Church's Index of Forbidden Books. Why Jesus found this one man of such importance and why the art and craft of lens making seemed of such paramount significance was a question whose answer would have to wait for another day.

I sat in the booth for a few minutes. Having spent the last three days so intent in my vigil over my weakened friend, I was stunned by the prospect of what appeared to be a long stretch of free time. I looked around the diner. Everything seemed the same. People were finishing late breakfasts, drinking coffee and orange juice and thumbing through the pages of newspapers. I stood, waved goodbye to Billie and walked out the front door.

I crossed the street past Mel's Pawn and Loan and walked east to the end of the block. I crossed the street and came up to a large two-story building on the corner. The old bricks on one of the walls facing the side street were painted with bright colors. A crude mural depicted a big yellow sun in a blue sky over a green field. On the right side, the colors of the rainbow arched up and splashed around the back of the building. A hand-painted sign on a four by eight sheet of plywood on the side of the building read: "Sunshine Mission: Neighborhood Community Center."

I walked in the front door and saw lots of women, children and teenagers. Some were seated in an area of sofas and tables covered with magazines and children's puzzles. The mothers waited with their youngsters to see physicians at a clinic housed in the building. Other adults in the busy room were organizing groups of teenagers to deliver meals to the elderly, to pick up litter along the streets and from two neighborhood parks.

I stood marveling at the efficiency and harmony. I saw several men with the black berets and black jackets talking to some men and women in the reception area and then I saw Sarah. She was coming up front to speak to one of the women at the reception desk when she looked up and saw me standing off to the side of the main entrance. She came from behind the counter and greeted me.

"Hello," she said. "Where's Jesus? Is everything all right?"

"Yes," I replied.

"Well, where is he?"

"He's with the founding members of the Black Panther Party."

Had Sarah been a few decades older my report might have caused an altogether different reaction in this child of the late 20th Century. She had not lived in the sixties and seventies and had heard of this organization only from lectures in a history class. Moreover, she had been working with members of the group over the past three days and knew many of the members by name.

"Well," she said, thinking for a second, "Did Jesus have anything to eat this morning?"

"Yes," I replied and she suddenly seemed relieved.

"At Billie's?" she added.

I nodded in the affirmative.

"Does he have his appetite back?" she asked.

"Oh, yes. He had half a plate of biscuits and a glass of orange juice. He had some banana. He said he'd meet me back at the hotel room before sunset."

"Well, good," said Sarah and she glanced back at the reception counter. "I have to get back to the kitchens. Do you want to help prepare some sandwiches?"

I stood there, not sure what I wanted to do, suddenly feeling very lost and alone. I wasn't sure when, if ever, I should mention that Jesus had just completed a three week tour of European Intellectual History.

"Steve and I are going across the bay to see that science fiction movie," said Sarah. "It opens this weekend and I am going to see whether I can run into my dad and my grandfather."

"Do you think that would be wise?" I asked.

"What do you mean?" she asked and her face went dark.

"I am no authority on the matter of time travel, but do you imagine it would be wise to meet someone like your own father?"

"Jesus went forward in time and met himself, didn't he?"

"Well, yes, but…"

"Same difference," said Sarah, her mind resolved, although I scarcely considered the subject closed.

"I'm sorry," said Sarah. "But I've got to get back to work." She headed back across the reception area to the counter. "Listen. I'll see you tonight? All right?"

"Yes" I replied, grateful for the kindness in her tone.

"Say, have you seen Steve?" she called.

"No," I replied, raising my voice as five young men came through the front doors with cardboard boxes of books.

"Where do you want all these books?" asked one of the men to a woman at the counter. The woman looked up at Sarah.

"Sarah, would you show them to the library?" she asked.

Sarah smiled and nodded at the woman and waved the men to follow her and she called back to me once more.

"Steve said he was going to have lunch at the tavern down at the end of the block. I only gave him five dollars, so he can't go far."

The next thing I knew, I was on the sidewalk walking past pedestrians outside the busy community center. At the end of the block, I crossed a street and approached Ray's Tavern.

The place was just a "hole-in-the-wall" in the middle of a block, a block that seemed more run-down than any of the others in the neighborhood. It was as though the spirit of hope and revitalization so prevalent to the west had yet to reach this outpost. The building was dark and smelled of beer and tobacco. I passed a cigarette vending machine in an alcove and pushed through a heavy swinging door into a dimly lit room. It would have taken the eyes of an average human being several minutes to adjust from the bright April afternoon to this nocturnal environment.

No one seemed to notice my arrival in the long, narrow room. Tables lined the wall to my right and bar stools and a counter ran the room's length on my left. I heard a percussive sound come from an adjoining room at the back of the tavern. I stepped into the back room and beheld three tables. They were illuminated by electric lamps suspended on lengths of chain from the high rafters. The surface of each table was covered with bright green cloth and I was reminded of the green lawns and reflecting pools surrounding Siddhartha Gautama's monastery at the deer park at Sarnath. I was conscious of the faint smile on my human face when the figures of human beings clustered around the central table caught my attention. Steve was among them. He leaned over a green table-top and was endeavoring to strike a white ball with the chalky tip of a wooden stick and cause another ball, a white ball with a red stripe drawn across its circumference and stamped with the black number "11," to move through a chain reaction of intermediary ball strikes, into one of six holes in the corners and along the sides of the table. This was "cut-throat pool," a so-called down and dirty pick-up version of a more elaborate and storied game of skill from Europe. This particular version attracted considerable attention from the local inhabitants.

Raymond Johnson, owner of Ray's Tavern was about to find himself eliminated by the long-haired and bearded stranger in a t-shirt and jeans by the name of Steve. Ray shook his head and reached for his beer on the narrow counter-top that ringed the perimeter of his back-room pool-den. He took a sip, smiled and looked up at me.

"Are we having a convention down here this weekend?" he said in reference, apparently, to the arrival of the four strangers at the newly re-opened and renamed Orpheus Hotel. I was to learn that another stranger had arrived in the neighborhood.

In cut throat, three players divided fifteen balls evenly amongst themselves. Ray had started the game. His goal was to preserve the low balls, one through five, on the table and knock into the holes the ten balls belonging to his two opponents. He had failed to do this and Steve was on the verge of removing all of Rays' numbers, thereby eliminating him from the game. Ray watched as the red stripped eleven-ball teetered on the brink of the side pocket and then disappeared into the hole.

There were a dozen tavern patrons, all men, standing around the table at a respectful distance. A small cheer seemed to go up from one faction of this group. For whatever reason they favored Steve's chances of success against a tall stranger in a blue suit.

"Nice shootin', Steve," said Ray. "Your next beer in on me. I got to get back up front." Finishing his glass in one swallow, Ray nodded, "Gentlemen…" he said and exited back out to the front of his establishment.

Steve had walked to the counter. There was a glass dish on the counter beside Steve's glass of beer. In the dish, tucked into one of several narrow channels in the glass rim, was a lit cigarette. It was a menthol cigarette, one of a brand popular in the United States in the Twentieth Century. Steve rushed over, picked up the smoldering tobacco stick, inserted the filtered end between his lips and inhaled deeply. The burning tip of the cigarette glowed fiery orange as oxygen streamed in through the burning plant matter.

The tall stranger in blue waited patiently for Steve to savor his smoke, pause for another drink of beer and return to the table. The purple stripped twelve-ball fell into a corner pocket and the crowd let out an exclamation of approval and surprise. A few more patrons, including a few women from up front had drifted back for the game's conclusion, which seemed imminent. The orange stripped thirteen-ball joined the others in the pit. Steve marched around the table and the audience gave him a wide and silent birth. Steve's stick struck the cue ball, sending it rocketing across the table where it slapped the green stripped fourteen-ball into a corner pocket. Steve went over and finished off his beer and took another long drag on his cigarette as a young man entered with a serving tray and set a fresh beer down on the counter. Steve took a long pull off the beer and another deep lung-full of smoke and when he looked over through the glare of the lights hanging over the pool table he seemed to notice me standing in the crowd.

For whatever reason, he chose neither to acknowledge my presence to the others nor indicate even to me that I had been observed. He seemed to choke a bit on the smoke in his lungs which suggested that something had crossed his mind. Whatever it was, he seemed to have lost his momentum. He used an elaborate bank-shot involving another ball. This intermediate ball did succeed in tapping the burgundy stripped fifteen and sent it up the length of the rail to a corner pocket, but the ball lacked sufficient velocity and rolled slowly to a halt, half an inch from the open pocket.

Steve swore to himself, but he had his own five object balls bunched-up on the table and there was no clear shot with the white cue ball which now sat alone against the rail on the table's opposite end.

"Good luck," said Steve to the stranger.

Steve stepped back for another drag on his cigarette. He used the glowing ember to light a second cigarette which he produced from an open pack sitting on the counter beside his so-called ash-tray.

The tall stranger walked up to the table. He took a cube of chalk from the edge of the table. He raised his head to get a closer look at the tip of his cue stick as he applied the blue chalk with a deft twisting motion of his thumb and forefinger. As his head tilted back, the long shadow of his hat brim which had obscured the features of his face receded and for the first time I was able to see him clearly.

I recognized the face at once.

Although I had not seen him in nearly four billion years, and he had reduced his own true stature from over twenty feet high to just over six, the cool blue eyes and chiseled features were unmistakable throughout the universe. I was startled and it was all I could do to remain silent and guard my thoughts. The frail mortal bodies I had helped bring forth from the Creator's designs at the foundation of the world were all but oblivious to the true contest that was beginning. I watched as the being set the chalk back on the rail. Steve held his breath. The creature in the blue suit pulled back on the cue and with its super human intellect, the being penetrated the spherical objects to the sub-atomic level and completed the massive calculations required to execute his will. The counterfeit human arm pushed the stick forward.

The energy required to complete this shot nearly shattered both the cue ball and the first object ball. The first explosive clap of contact sent the onlookers to their knees and they were grabbing their ears and shielding their senses against the pain of the successive shock waves as the balls obeyed the inflexible rules of physics, the same that had determined the shape of the current universe. The onlookers rose up to peer over the rim of Ray's pool table to see the loan cue ball glide across the now empty table to the loan object ball, the stranger's loan burgundy striped 15. The cue ball came close, turned a forward revolution and kissed the 15. The cue ball stopped and the 15 came to rest on its south pole a quarter inch from the pit.

"Wow!" exclaimed Steve. "What a shot! Who are you, man?"

The stranger nodded and looked across the table at me.

Steve smiled, at last recognizing my presence, and he looked back and forth between me and the tall figure in the blue suit, the quiet stranger with the steel-blue eyes.

For whatever reason, Ray's patrons, drinking more than they might have preferred that day, circled the man, who in this small community had suddenly become a celebrity. Men were offering beer and shots of whiskey and a few of the women were wishing their boyfriends and husbands might one day gain something of the calm and resolute confidence possessed by this stranger in their midst.

Across the table, Steve, surprisingly gracious in defeat, was silently mouthing the words:

"WHO… IS… HE…?"

"MICHAEL…" I mouthed in silent reply as someone put some money in the juke box and popular music sounded through Ray's establishment.

"WHO…?"

"MICHAEL," I mouthed again. "THE ARCHANGEL…"

Steve was firing up a third cigarette and a conga line of fans was circling the being in blue. Although it was early in the afternoon a big party was in full swing in this tavern down the street from the Sunshine Mission. People at Ray's were amazed by the pool skills of the quiet stranger. Steve was too impressed to fret about his having lost the game and he got in line to congratulate the man who had made the single greatest pool shot ever witnessed in the game's history. Eventually, the crowd thinned out. People were more than happy to stand around the stranger in a crowd, but were disinclined to get too close or remain alone with him at one of the three high-backed booths in the very dark corner of Ray's pool-den. The stranger retired to the booth in the furthest corner and was soon alone.

I looked around. The revelers had abandoned the den and returned to the main room of the establishment. I stood at the threshold at the doorway between the two rooms. I looked out to where Steve had climbed up on a stool at the bar and then I looked back into the shadows of the pool hall.

"M-2500?" sounded a voice from the back room.

The voice could not be forgotten. It seemed I answered to it only the other day and not so many billion years ago in the past.

"Yes?" I replied.

"We've both adopted the habits of the earth creatures. Why not come back and share a drink with me?"

"Michael? Is it you?"

"Have a seat."

I did not argue with the being seated in the booth. Even before the fall of the rebel angels, his powers were legend. I did not think of one without the other, the Archangel Michael and the favored one whom Michael had laid low. Although Michael had not condemned the beast to its imprisonment, it was Michael, as the commander of the celestial legions, who hemmed the Prince of the World and his minions within the confines of the earth's solar system.

I sat slowly opposite Michael. The laminate covered table cast a faint reflection of his form. The archangels were more nearly human in appearance than any other of the heavenly host, although towering about the average human being at well over twenty feet. In all the many universes there were angels of various types and classes, but the creator had seen fit to cast only seven in the mold of his archangels. Why he had not created more, one could only guess. Following the betrayal of his beloved Lucifer, the Creator had never fashioned another such being. Perhaps there was reason in that.

An eternal being in my own right, as I sat across from Michael, I still could not help but marvel at his presence and regard him with awe and trepidation.

"You are wondering why I am here?" he said at last.

I nodded my head and looked intently into his burning blue eyes.

"I am wondering the same of you," he said. The penetration of his gaze made me uncomfortable.

"You realize," he continued, "That since the first skirmish in Lucifer's rebellion you vanished from all time and history. For several billion years we thought you had somehow hidden yourself among the demons."

That explanation made me shudder.

"Have you traveled here from the past?" I asked.

The archangel smiled. "You are a most unlikely hero," he replied.

"Hero?" I said.

"After a time, there were reports here and there: the incident in The Garden and the episode following The Flood. Your old comrade, M-2347 encountered you in Jerusalem. And then, of course, the random sightings throughout human history."

"Time travel is a remarkable ability," I said.

"To answer your question: no, I have not traveled from the past. Only those in the Creator's inner sphere possess that ability. To my knowledge you are the only member of the angelic host outside that order ever to wield such power. You bear the rings of the Ophanim?"

We both looked at my human-shaped hands, folded on the table-top. The gray rings of the Ophanim were visible on both ring fingers. Michael continued.

"From both near and far I have seen this frail planet turn some four and a half billion revolutions around its sun. While you, like a skimming stone tossed by the will of the Creator have skipped over the sea of time to alight here with the Savior of Mankind."

"Then you know of Jesus?" I asked.

"Of course," said Michael "He is the hope of all those who yet inhabit this world." The angel looked side to side and then lowered his voice and spoke. "But why have you come today? Why now?" he asked in an earnest voice and one filled with humility.

I shook my head.

Michael sat back and nodded, somehow satisfied by my response.

"You don't know, do you?" he said.

"I'm afraid not," I replied.

"Let me tell you," said Michael. "It is an embarrassment to admit that we have failed to detect the pattern until just now."

"Pattern? What pattern?" I asked.

"You and your friends arrive out of the past only at significant moments in human history."

"I am unfamiliar with human history, but in the past few weeks, I've certainly become a student. Recall, that from my point of view, human beings have existed on the face of the planet for only three weeks."

I stared at the archangel, unsure of myself.

Michael shook his head, "We are more concerned this time around."

"Concerned?" I repeated. "This time?"

"Now that we have detected the pattern, we can only imagine there must be a reason for your being here. Something momentous is about to occur."

I asked the archangel why it was that I was considered a hero.

"As far as we know, when M-2347 was dispatched to Jerusalem to greet the Risen Christ, you were already on the scene. You are the only angel whom I have ever met with the ability to travel through time. You are also the first of us to have understood the Creator's three-fold nature."

"What?" I asked, but no sooner had the word escaped my lips than I understood.

"You have finally had an opportunity to read the human's New Testament?" asked Michael.

"Yes," I replied.

"As far as I know, you are the first of us ever to have heard the voice of the Holy Spirit."

"His uncle." I murmured.

"What?"

"Nothing." I said.

"We knew him once as "The Entity," and there were many who for untold eons considered it merely an extension of the Creator himself. By our estimate you are somewhere near the conclusion of the Savior's excursion into the wilderness."

"Today marks his forty-first day," I said. "If this 'Oakland' may be considered the wilderness."

"I believe it qualifies," said Michael, adding, "And has he been tempted by the devil?"

"Tempted many times. Those enumerated in the Gospel were successfully conquered weeks ago."

Michael listened with great intensity and slowly nodded his head. He drew a powerful hand across his face. It seemed to me a very "human" gesture.

"Well then," he said, "Is he finished?"

"Finished?" I asked.

"With his journey? It has been forty days. I take it that you have ministered to him. Some of my agents reported that you have been holding vigil at his bedside for the past three nights in fulfillment of scripture."

"I beg your pardon?"

"In Mark Chapter I at the conclusion of the journey Mark writes "...and the angels ministered to him."

"No. I meant the 'agents.' You said something about 'agents reporting on my vigil. I know nothing of 'agents,'" I replied.

"S-Class angels..." said the archangel.

I grew impatient with this super-powered pool player. "I have not forgotten S-class angels. Some of my closest associates were S-Class. I'm surprised you had them spying on me."

"Spying on you?" replied Michael, and now he sounded indignant. "They were not spying on you. Must I remind you that we are in a war zone?"

There was a pause in our conversation. He seemed to be looking down at me from a very great height. He shook his head and smiled patiently.

"This world is doomed, my friend," he said.

I looked across the room at the empty pool tables. Thus far none of the human beings had summoned courage enough to walk back into the empty room. I heard laughter and commotion from the front. Ray was about to make a trip back to our table to see whether we needed refreshments.

"I thought you had read the New Testament?" Michael asked.

"Yes, but I've had a lot on my mind," I replied.

Michael nodded sympathetically, "It is difficult; even for an angel, I suppose. The Creator relied heavily upon a human being to paint a word picture of heaven and the future to come."

"John?" I asked.

"Yes. It was a human apostle who described the dissolution and collapse of this solar system, this 'world' if you will. He saw a glimpse of the Creator's ultimate triumph over Satan and the forces of the rebel alliance."

"John's Revelation?"

"You've read it then? In the human text?"

I nodded and the archangel shook his head, "Pretty inadequate, wouldn't you agree?"

I considered what I might offer in defense of an earthman who had reported his vision of the heavens and the end times in writing nearly two thousand years earlier.

Michael smiled, "My point is not to disparage the sensory equipment and mental capacity of first century human visionaries, but rather, to highlight the importance of the Creator's Son. The prophesy of his human apostle will not be fulfilled without the active participation of the Creator's agents.

"Agents again?"

"That would be you and me," said Michael looking up as Ray slowly approached with a tray of frosty glasses and long-necked beer bottles.

"How's the best pool player in all of creation doing?' asked the man.

The archangel nodded.

"These are two fine imported beers courtesy of Ray's Tavern and two lovely young ladies out front who would enjoy the privilege of your company."

"Our thanks to you and the ladies," replied Michael, "But my friend and I must be on our way."

"Oh, is that so?" said Ray and he looked disappointed. "Well, at least have the beers on me," he said, and there was a note of supplication in his voice.

Michael smiled with a nod. "Very well," he said. His countenance displayed a radiant smile that immediately put Ray at ease, and me as well, for that matter.

Ray set the glasses and bottles on "Ray's Tavern" coasters on the table. He nodded to Michael in what was nearly a bow and retreated back out to the front of his establishment.

"That was an extraordinary display at the human being's pool table," I said when we were once again alone.

"In the Savior's day, the human beings would have called it a miracle!" Michael replied.

We both laughed human laughs. We settled back and drank our beers with our human looking bodies and talked into the afternoon about the eons before the earth and the sun and the Milky Way Galaxy and the universe dimly recognized by the human beings as "their universe." We spoke of worlds and lifetimes and adventures far beyond and before the Creator sent his angelic engineers to fashion the reality we now inhabited in a time the human beings called "1968."

Michael and I had a great laugh about the old times, and as the humans were wont to do, we raised our glasses to one another and touched the rims together to perceive an audible, high-pitched clinking sound and we toasted to the future.

It was just then that Steve walked into the back room and reported what the cook had just reported through the order window to Ray. Others at the bar had overheard the report which was now playing on the cathode ray tubes and the newly devised transistor radios across the nation. Steve, who had smoked a half-pack of menthol cigarettes and consumed nearly one hundred ounces of beer had become surprisingly sober. A man named Martin Luther King Jr. had stepped onto the balcony outside his motel room in a place called Memphis, Tennessee and been shot. An hour later word spread across the nation that he had succumbed to his wounds.

Something was outside, what I had perceived but earlier dismissed, a sense of mistrust and tension that had now become a palpable thing, an amalgam of evil that spilled into the streets from open drains and doorways. It flowed like a torrent, smashing windows, overturning cars, knocking people to the pavement and sweeping them away. From its epicenter in the South, the wave of violence rolled in every direction of the compass. It was a spasm, perhaps, an aftershock of the planet's first modern war, the war fought among the Americans a century before our arrival.

I stood outside on the street with Michael and Steve. It was shortly after five in the afternoon. It was light outside and we saw people at their windows in the buildings across the street. Others had wandered outside their doors and stood in a daze. From a five-mile radius in every direction the neighbors began to slowly, silently move in the direction of the Sunshine Mission. By dusk, a huge crowd had gathered in the intersection outside the mission doors. Jesus and the leadership of the Black Panthers had come out onto the sidewalk. Some of their number wanted to take to the streets and vent their rage and frustration in the affluent business district of downtown Oakland.

It may have been the influence of Jesus on these organizers, but the young men quieted the crowd and explained that violence at this point would only bring more violence. They argued that a riot in the downtown was exactly the excuse some bigoted members of the police department sought to justify opening fire on a black crowd. The authorities would not be given such opportunity.

That evening, Oaklanders turned on their nightly television news to discover a report from the human beings' national spokesperson, Walter Cronkite. Another figure of national authority, the commander of the nation's armed forces, Lyndon Johnson, condemned the murder of the man named Martin Luther King, Jr. Meanwhile, Oakland's most popular radio station, KDIA, broadcast The Boss Soul of the Bay, popular disk jockey, Wally Ray. He delivered a tribute to the memory of the slain civil rights activist.

We returned to the lobby of the Orpheus hotel and sat on the green sofa and watched the images on the television set. I remember one sequence of sound and light in particular. The transmission spoke of an upcoming national contest to replace the commander named Johnson. Another man, much younger, was trying to earn support in an upcoming national election. Earlier that decade, so the report continued, this man's older brother had once been the leader of the country. He had been assassinated, murdered by a small, frightened little man with a rifle. Now, five years later, the younger brother stood in the city of Indianapolis, a candidate for the presidency of the United States. He was preparing to speak to an enormous gathering of city residents, but the crowd was unaware of the assassination of the civil rights leader. Indianapolis police secretly warned the young candidate that there would not be enough man-power to protect him if the crowd decided to riot.

In the lobby of the Orpheus Hotel we listened to the young candidate's speech. Tears streamed down the faces of the men and women in the hotel lobby and of those two thousand miles away at the corner of 17th and Broadway where the young man on the stage informed his audience of the assassination. There were screams and moans and shouting and the sea of humanity balanced on the precipice of chaos. The young man at the podium raised his hand, and the audience quieted down, waiting to hear what he could possibly say. He acknowledged that many would be filled with anger, especially since the assassin was believed to be a white man. He empathized with the audience, referring to the assassination of his own brother. These remarks surprised the candidate's aides who had never heard him speak publicly of his brother's death.

Quoting the Greek playwright Aeschylus, whom he had discovered through his brother's widow, the young man said, "Even in our sleep, pain, which cannot forget, falls drop by drop upon the heart, until, in our own despair, against our will, comes wisdom through the awful grace of God."

"What we need in the United States is not division," continued the young man, "What we need in the United States is not hatred. What we need in the United States is not violence or lawlessness, but love and wisdom, and compassion toward one another, and a feeling of justice towards those who still suffer within our country, whether they be white or whether they be black."

* * *

I watched a lot of television that weekend in April of 1968. Over a hundred major American cities saw rioting in the aftermath of the death of Martin Luther King, Jr. There were major riots in Baltimore, Maryland; Washington, D.C.; New York City; Chicago and Pittsburgh. Thousands were injured. Homes and businesses went up in flames. Many were killed. There was no rioting in Indianapolis. There was no rioting in Oakland.

On Sunday the sixth of April, Steve and Sarah took a bus across the Bay Bridge to stand outside the local premiere of "2001: A Space Odyssey." Sarah hoped to catch a glimpse of her father and grandfather. On that day Michael, Jesus and I were sitting on the green sofa in the lobby of the Orpheus watching television. I looked to my left and noticed a little boy looking over at Jesus. It was the toddler, Alonzo. His great, wide eyes were fixed on the man between the two angels. Jesus sat in the middle of the couch staring at the images of riot play in a news broadcast across the television screen.

I felt a tiny hand taping mine where it lay palm down on the arm rest and I looked back at Alonzo. "Why is he sad?" asked the little boy.

I glanced at Jesus sitting beside me, and it was true. Tears streamed down his cheeks. I thought of something that I might possibly say to the little boy that might make sense to him.

"I suppose he's sad about all the fighting," I said.

The little boy, no more than four years old, nodded his head. I believe he understood. We learned later that afternoon that there had been a shoot-out up the street. Some members of the Black Panthers had allegedly tried to ambush members of the Oakland Police. A standoff ensued and one of the Panthers, Eldridge Cleaver, was wounded. Another member, the club treasurer, seventeen-year-old Little Bobby Horton whom I'd met five days earlier at Billie's Diner, had been shot and killed while trying to surrender.

The day wore on and we found ourselves in the back of a store-front church. It was a Christian organization of some kind, founded in the name of our friend, Jesus. Of course, no one knew him. A young and earnest preacher stood at the head of the neighborhood congregation of some one hundred souls and reviewed the week's grim events. He did his best to explain the suffering and strife in terms of the Creator's ultimate plan for good. There were many tears in the room. Many sobbed and wailed and I was reminded of the broadcast from the night before, the mournful voices of the crowd in the park in Indianapolis.

Steve and Sarah dropped back against the faux wood-grain paneling of the wall at the back of the hall. They looked tired. One of the deacons brought the collection basket along the back wall through the standing-room-only crowd. Sarah managed a smile and put a twenty dollar bill and some change into the basket. It was the last of the money of the transmuted gold.

Although we might have spent another night in and around the Orpheus or at Ray's Tavern, or the corner at the Sunshine Mission, Sarah had already settled our hotel bill with Marcus Smith. After the service, we drifted up the street to Billie's Diner. On any other night it would have been closed at this hour, but she and her staff had the place open. Sarah, Steve, Jesus, Michael and I waited outside in a line that extended out through the door onto the sidewalk. We had no money of course, but we had not come for food. We were in line no more than fifteen minutes when a signal came from within that a round, five-spot table had opened-up for our party. The others headed in and I was following behind when I felt Michael's hand on my shoulder. I stopped and looked back at him, still outside the door as the others continued inside.

"What is it?" I asked. "Is something the matter?"

"It is time for him to return to his place in history."

"Excuse me?" I asked.

"His stay in the wilderness has come to an end."

I glanced through the window at the brightly lit scene within. Somehow the effect of the food and the caring people like Billie and Mel and Marcus were bringing some relief to the sorrows of the past three days. I noticed that Michael's white collared shirt and blue suit remained immaculately clean and pressed. I wondered how much of the Michael I perceived was an illusion. The force of the index finger of his right hand tapping me hard on my left shoulder was real enough.

"I said it is time for you to return him home. The shores of the Galilee, the year 34 AD. That is your next destination," he said.

The word 'destination' had four syllables. Through my t-shirt I felt his index finger jab my human-shaped shoulder bone with each beat. My arm rose up to push the insistent finger away and it was only with focused concentration that I resisted the temptation to lash out with my human fist.

"I sense your frustration and rage," said Michael in a matter of fact tone, "But it is time."

"That is his decision to make."

The artificial man shook its head, "It is beyond his capacity to make that decision. I understand what he is doing. He is trying to find the answer. But he will not find it, not in that diner, not in this village or on this continent, or the next or anytime from here to Armageddon."

"He is the Creator!"

Michael smiled and looked up at the neon sign spelling the word "DINER" in orange light that glowed in the growing night and cast highlights on his face.

"The creature you have been doting upon these past few days is incapable of fathoming the truth. It is beyond his current understanding, beyond his human capacity!"

I glowered at the archangel, "You are merely an angel," I said. "The Son of God will make the decision."

There it was. I had taken the step beyond protocol in contradicting this captain of the common angels such as myself. He rocked back on his heels, and once again I felt the familiar anathema of guilt which neither time nor distance from the outbuildings in ancient Athens could diminish. Michael took his time, looking me up and down before he continued.

"The legions of hell would not be nearly so full had the rebels first been baptized in the Holy Spirit," he said. "You are indeed the fortunate one, as we have said, perhaps the first to have met our Creator in his three-fold existence. Still, you have over-estimated the power of his human 'incarnation.' That you have protected him is all to your credit. You have ministered to him as foretold in scripture, but now your ministry is at its end and he must begin his."

I suddenly found myself backpedaling up the sidewalk as Michael stepped forward, "You have imagined this man Jesus to be much more powerful than he is. For a clear picture of his powers you might have asked those who executed the design of the holy zygote!"

Michael was unrelenting.

"Are you aware of the heroic team of S-Class angels who battled the forces of hell to implant that divine germ in the uterine wall of the human surrogate? How did you suppose the Son of God came to be?

'Magic?'" he said with a dismissive, patronizing laugh. "I know the history far better than you, my little, time-lost spirit."

"It will not be easy for him to leave," I said. "He has so many unanswered questions."

"He has learned as much as the cells of his human organism can contain."

"I don't know," I said, afraid to agree. I suddenly realized that I had no idea what would become of me without my commitment to Jesus and his two human friends. Where would I go? What would I do with the remnants of my existence?

The archangel looked at me and the icy tone of his voice seemed to relax.

"Your friend Jesus will be closer to the understanding he seeks when he meets Elijah and Moses on the mountain top."

Michael noted my momentary hesitation. I recalled the names of the two Jewish saints from the books of the Old Testament. Michael slowly nodded his head.

"I realize now what a distinct disadvantage you have faced in this mission. Perhaps that is why the Creator has shown you mercy. It would have been difficult for any of us to have navigated our way here with the human beings. But I must continue on my way."

"Where are you going?" I asked as the tall being in blue stepped back from the sidewalk into the street.

"To continue God's work," he said. "You have heard my advice to you. It is only that. I realize now that you must do as you will. Our prayers are with you."

At that moment I wanted to follow him, but I realized that for now, my destiny remained intertwined with the three humans at the table inside the building beside me. As Michael crossed the street behind a taxi-cab the archangel shouted something. Whatever it was he had said, had failed to register and I called back in his direction.

"What? What did you say?"

"Was there something else?"

"What?" I called.

"Something else you wanted to tell me? Something on your heart that you felt you should confess to a friend?"

His words came to me as a shock. What could he possibly mean? Not that, surely, not that. I would handle things in my own way.

"I'm sorry," I called back to him as he receded up the street. "I don't know what you mean."

"You may not get a second chance!" Michael replied.

"What?"

"Resist!" he called. "Resist the devil."

He darted into a darkened alleyway. A moment later, although mine were possibly the only eyes on earth to observe the phenomenon, a flash of blue light illuminated a narrow patch of sky above the alleyway. I knew that the archangel had departed.

* * *

I walked back into Billie's Diner and sat at the round table with my companions. Jesus had regained his appetite and once again permitted himself the earthly pleasure of food. As always his boyhood friend Steve led the way in this endeavor and ate a large bowl of chili and gobbled down hot cornbread slathered in fresh, whipped butter.

Sarah sipped an iced tea and conversation moved from the events of the past days to her trip into San Francisco with Steve. They had attended the local premiere of the science fiction movie by the American film director Stanley Kubrick. Although Steve had already viewed his share of television during his first week in the Twentieth Century, nothing could have prepared him for the experience of the big screen. He ate bags of popcorn, drank wax paper cups of soda, and devoured several boxes of expensive theater candy. Sarah was glad to see the film again. She enjoyed it more than she had upon viewing it in preparatory school in 2006.

She and Steve had scanned the crowd departing the theater at the film's conclusion. Sarah hoped she would recognize her father and her grandfather in the crowd. She was not disappointed in this. There they were, stepping from beneath the enormous marquee, a man of forty-four and a boy of ten. Sarah and Steve followed the pair across a busy downtown intersection and watched them enter a five and dime store. The young man from the past and the young woman from the future watched the father and son through a plate-glass window. Sarah's grandfather turned a wire spinner rack of illustrated comic book magazines. The boy looked wide-eyed at the lurid titles of the twelve cent comics on display. Sarah and Steve pressed their faces nearly against the glass as the boy inside the store indicated a particular comic book. Father and son pulled it from the rack and they stood close together to inspect the cover. It was glossy in the bright drugstore light and depicted a sleek, red and white space ship lifting off across the page. The rocket flew in a diagonal trajectory from the bottom right to top left hand side of the cover in a blaze of motion lines against a star-studded night sky. Sarah's grandfather purchased the book that afternoon. He paid twelve cents for an object that, over the next three years, became his only child's favorite possession. As the lad emerged from childhood on the west coast and later, in those long summers at his parents' vacation home on Cape Cod the hope of the four-color heroes in the pages of a far-flung future somehow offered the boy escape. With the mighty men and maidens of science in their form-fitting space suits, young Wallace Benton confronted the bizarre metamorphosis of adolescence and the first thrill of the opposite sex. The magazine was eventually consigned to a cardboard box of childhood artifacts pushed to the back of a closet smelling of naphthalene crystals and old cedar. The image of the unbound space craft proclaiming adventure and mystery within was rediscovered thirty years later by the grand-daughter and held her attention even now in a memory.

So, we sat in Billie's Diner, listening to Steve and Sarah conclude the story of their trip to San Francisco. To our surprise Sarah thanked Jesus for having provided her the opportunity to glimpse just this small portion of her past.

"I don't know whether or not you planned it this way," she said, "But I wanted to thank you, Jesus and you too, M-2500 for allowing this to happen."

"Thank the Holy Spirit," said Jesus. "I'm as much a passenger on this ride as you."

Something crossed her mind and she was about to speak, but in the end, she only nodded with a sly smile in the corner of her mouth. I certainly deserved no thanks from my human comrades. I sat in my vinyl upholstered chair, silently reviewing all the ways I had failed them. I had finally read the Old and New Testaments, but I had missed something. There was something beyond the printed symbols printed on the pages that I had failed to assimilate.

I was dimly aware of other patrons in the diner. From time to time they stopped to say "hello" or share a story of the long, sad weekend that had begun those days ago on the Thursday that we would never forget.

The sky grew light in the windows. A shift of teenage boys was replaced by the morning staff. Billie had not stopped to sleep in thirty hours. She prepared for a busy Monday morning as life continued in the North Oakland neighborhood.

We said our goodbyes at dawn. Sarah explained that we would be continuing on our tour, north up the coast. She left out details of our mode of transportation. We set out, on foot, retracing the path we had once taken in the back of a pickup truck. With photographic detail I recalled the sights and sounds as we made our way back through old Oakland, back through the Posey Street Tube to Alameda Island, along the San Leandro Bay via Fernside Drive, across the bridge to Shoreline Drive and off Island Drive to the Alameda Municipal Golf Course.

The morning sun was well into the sky and human beings in couples and small parties were scattered about the lawns hitting white balls with their slender metal rods. Jesus, Steve and Sarah were familiar with the sport. Upon our arrival the previous week, the park had been deserted, and my companions explained that golf was generally played only during daylight hours. Sarah and Jesus led us to a bunker and a stand of trees beyond the thirteenth hole. I walked a short distance away, cleared my thoughts and allowed the metamorphosis to being.

In a moment I stood on two, sleek, landing runners. I opened the hatch, switched on the interior lighting and waited for my friends to come aboard and fasten their flight restraints. Five minutes passed and we were airborne, speeding across Oakland, over San Francisco, and then above the Pacific Ocean and up into the stratosphere. A moment later we had crossed the dark side of the earth and come into high orbit over the Asian Continent.

"Any other places we need to visit before we head back to the Middle East?" I asked.

"I don't know," replied Jesus, "I've been thinking about Marcus and his hotel."

"The Orpheus Hotel?" asked Steve.

We considered it a peculiar name for a hotel even with the intercession of the Holy Spirit who enabled us to understand the spoken and written languages of all the inhabitants we encountered on our journeys. Once again we were indebted to Sarah's liberal arts education and her course in film appreciation.

"Marcus named his place after a movie he saw when he was taking film courses at Merritt College."

"Interesting," said Jesus.

"He was impressed by a Portuguese film directed by Brazilian Film director, Marcel Camus. It was called Black Orpheus. It took the old Greek myth and set it in modern-day Rio de Janeiro during Carnaval. The movie blew Marcus away. In 1960 it took the Academy Award for best foreign language film. It won the 1960 Golden Globe and the Golden Palm at the Cannes Film Festival in '59. Really a pretty impressive film."

"What are you thinking, Jesus?" asked Steve from his auxiliary flight seat at the back of the cockpit.

"Yeah, Jesus. What are you hatching?" asked Sarah. "Are we headed to Brazil?"

"I don't think so. I'm thinking more along the lines of the original story."

"Excuse me?" said Sarah.

"What's wrong?" asked Steve. "I don't like the sound of that."

"Oh, Jesus, please…" continued Sarah, "You're not thinking…"

* * *

As a parting gift, Marcus had given Jesus a copy of the Gideon's Bible from our third floor room, at his hotel. We would return to that room more than thirty years later, but first, for old time's sake, Jesus decided we would revisit my old stopping grounds from the foundation of the earth.

"Hell" has often been described as a state of mind. There is a lot of wisdom in that line of thought, but those on board our trim, time-hopping space-cruiser recognized that, for a certain number of years at least, Satan's Lair had a physical address as well.

11. Hell by Hudson's Bay

When the Mars Project was abandoned and my angelic crew arrived on the earth nearly four and a half billion years ago, we engineered a three-hundred mile long subterranean cavern in the earth's primitive crust. This portion of rock selected for the Workshop had been the first to cool from the planet's molten interior and would one day form the heart of the world's first continent. Even the primitive science of the human beings had observed that the land masses are dynamic. In the late 1800's the science of geology had advanced to such a degree that human beings were able to reconstruct the disintegration of the early continent and the consequent movement of its constituent, tectonic plates around the globe.

We descended east of the Rocky Mountains. It was still 1968 and the fires of the weekend rampage still smoldered in the inner cities across the Midwest. We veered north at an enormous river-valley that bisected the continent and I bore down through the clouds across a series of vast lakes until I came to an enormous body of saltwater named for a British explorer. Henry Hudson and Hudson's Bay meant little to me at the time, but as we came to rest on a shoreline beside a stand of coniferous trees I knew I would never forget the place. Beneath a thin film of fragile organic soil, the old black rock beneath was at once familiar and strange.

I felt no closer to Sarah than on the day I had taken advantage of her in ancient Greece, and I was anxious to abandon the guise of the Greek human being, Demetrius. When my passengers had stepped onto the coarse, sandy beach, I began my transformation, and I sensed their surprise as I approached on my segmented legs and motioned with a tentacle that we should move inland toward the low, black cliffs.

"I think I like you better like this," said Sarah, regarding my appearance.

"Oh, come on, lay off him," said Steve.

Jesus turned back and gave Steve a warning glance.

"Well, she needs to get over it! Wasn't that like a month ago?"

"Twenty days!" said Sarah.

"Oh, I can see you've really moved on!" replied Steve.

As they followed me away from the windy, grey beach, Steve and Sarah began to quarrel and it made our forward progress difficult as they stopped to face one another and hurl insults and accusations. My chief memories of those moments in ancient Greece were of remorse and revulsion. I had begged Sarah for her forgiveness, pleaded with my Creator for absolution. I cried out for help through the power of the mysterious Entity, whom I now recognized to be the Holy Spirit, but as we approached the sheer black wall of primordial rock my feelings of hope plunged. I had been forgiven, but I had to remind myself continually of this.

The jealousy, betrayal and anger played out between the two human beings, the unrepentant male and female, the agonistic and the atheist, the orphaned fool from the ancient world and the brilliant woman of the 21st Century. I looked back at the two of them arguing, and Jesus caught my gaze. We realized that our companions, these two lost souls, were in the early throes of a lovers' quarrel.

"Good afternoon…"

A voice sounded from a cleft in the wall of rock. Sarah and Steve fell silent. Jesus looked back over his shoulder. A man in a blue suit stepped from the shadows.

"You should return to your own time," he said.

He brushed past me as though I were of no greater consequence than a blade of shore grass. The angelic being crossed the rocky expanse toward Jesus. Steve and Sarah stepped back with blank, dumbfounded expressions on their faces. If they had been arguing, they had forgotten. Jesus walked in the direction of the apparition in blue. They stopped in the center of the clearing. In the west the sun was going down over Hudson's Bay.

The two came face to face.

"You stand at the gates of hell," said Michael. "You should not have journeyed here. The forty days are finished."

"What have I to fear?" Jesus replied.

"It is beyond the capacity of your human sense to perceive, but I assure you, Jesus, you and your companions are in mortal danger."

"You came looking for me some days ago on the shores of the great western ocean."

"Yes."

"Why did you not seek me then?" asked Jesus.

"I was called away."

"Well then, I have come to you," said Jesus.

"There are tides in the affairs of men upon this world, an ebb and flow of good and evil. You wade in dangerous waters."

"I realize you have held this post with your legions nearly four billion years," said Jesus. "I sense them even now, ranged about on the cliffs and behind us at the water's edge."

Sarah and Steve scanned the high cliffs and turned to look back in the direction of the apparently vacant beach. Even with my own heightened senses, I could only dimly perceive the celestial forms of angelic beings hovering in their thousands about the desolate shoreline.

"You understand that your situation is dire," said Michael.

"We shall triumph," said Jesus.

"I advised M-2500 to return you to your place in human history. He has elected to do otherwise."

Jesus took another step so that he was face to face with the archangel.

"Since we are here, perhaps you might serve as our guide?" he said.

"Your guide?" asked Michael.

"Hey," cried Steve, suddenly, "You're the shark from the pool hall in Oakland!"

Steve looked as though he was going to break ranks and glad-hand the archangel, but Sarah reached out and grabbed Steve by the collar.

Jesus smiled. "Last week I finally took the opportunity to read the story of my life on earth, of the ministry I will conduct among my children on this planet. Have you read it? Do you know my story?"

"Yes," replied Michael.

"Do you recall the text of the sermon I will deliver one day to the children of Israel?

"I remember all."

"And its basis, written by a child after my own heart in the wilderness a thousand years before my own birth?"

Jesus turned in the direction of the setting sun and he recited, "And lo' thou I walk though the valley of the shadow of death, I will fear no evil for thou art with me."

"David," replied Michael.

"We human beings are amazing creatures are we not?"

Michael only stared at the back of Jesus, whose attention remained, fixed on the horizon.

"Lead us not into temptation, but deliver us from evil…" continued Jesus. He turned and looked directly into Michael's eyes. "How shall I expect men and women to obey a creed I have not lived myself?"

Jesus placed a hand on Michael's shoulder and moved him gently aside. The archangel stepped dutifully, dumbly, to the right and Jesus continued through the clearing to where I stood before the black crevice in the cliff-wall.

A cool, dank wind exhaled from the cave mouth.

Jesus brushed-back his long hair and flexed his hands.

"Any of this familiar to you?" he asked.

I nodded, solemnly.

"Well?"

"In some ways, yes," I answered.

"We've been here before, haven't we?"

I followed the direction of Jesus' gaze to a panel of weathered metal. Partially folded in the rock, the substance had once been part of a shaft leading deep into the earth. The place where we stood had once crowned the summit of the Black Dune Island rising from the earth's first ocean. The subterranean passageway had been deformed and stretched-out through billions of years of tectonic shifts in the earth's crust. Like sleep walkers, Steve and Sarah passed the silent archangel in the clearing and came-up beside us at the portal.

"Is that what I think it is?" began Steve and he trailed off and looked, wide-eyed at Sarah.

"Pandemonium," said Sarah in a voice that was no more than a whisper. "Pandemonium," she repeated.

12. Unfinished Business

Down we went, following Jesus into the bowels of the earth. Much of the earth's original crust had long ago been sub-ducted by currents of the planet's molten mantel. In many places that same material had been spewed back from the throats of volcanoes to form mountains and new land-masses. Much of the earth's supposedly solid surface had been recycled in such fashion dozens of times over the course of four billion years.

This was not the case with the ancient Precambrain rock surrounding Hudson's Bay. We were walking downward through a portion of the crust known by the earth's geologists as the Canadian Shield. When a group of human scientists began mapping their planets gravitational field at the beginning of the human's second millennium of recorded history, they noted massive gravitational anomalies in the Hudson Bay area. After the Bay of Bengal this was the largest on the planet. It was not until the launch of the American and German Gravity Recovery and Climate Experiment satellites in 2002 that human science would complete the mapping of this region of below-average gravity. Earth science agreed that the electro-magnetic and gravitational anomalies were the expected result of powerful convection currents in the underlying mantel. There were other explanations.

The rock was black and old, the oldest on the earth and it was from this bedrock that the angels from Mars had scoured-out our three-hundred mile long workroom at the time of creation. Here, we had been witness to the first skirmish in the war of the rebel angels and had escaped at that time through the vertical shaft that originally led to the surface. Much of that route had been destroyed during the cataclysm that erupted as the forces of Lucifer clashed with those led by Michael and the loyal archangels. What remained of that original tunnel, no more than a mile long, had been stretched out to form an angled grade into the earth.

Following Jesus, we walked steeply downward through that original tunnel into one of more recent excavation. It had been mined, not from the surface, but from the inside out.

I moved effortlessly through the passageway, its surface polished smooth like glass from the intense heat which had pierced upward like a brand. The temperature here was a uniform fifty-four degrees and the last glimmer of light from the surface receded to a pinpoint. I looked back and with my superior vision detected the blue-garbed figure of Michael standing in the entrance. This trip to the underworld had not been on his agenda.

As we walked, our way was lit, not by light from the setting sun of the surface world, but by the blue-green phosphorescence that emanated from the glassy walls and walkway of the corridor. The passage was roughly circular in shape, some twenty to thirty feet in diameter and due to the luminescence that permeated the tunnel walls, the way was visible for a quarter mile ahead.

Sarah and Steve kept pace with Jesus. Since beginning to eat again in Oakland, his almost super-human strength and stamina had returned and he made his way easily down the route. We had been walking for an hour in silence with Jesus spoke.

"I sense that we are being followed," he said.

"Who?" gasped Steve, whose breath was coming with difficulty. "Who's following us?"

"I suspect it is the guardian," replied Jesus.

"Michael?" asked Sarah.

Jesus nodded.

"Well, that's just great," said Steve. "I'm for taking a break and letting him catch up with us."

Jesus stopped and looked back at us. "Very well," he said. "Let's stop here to rest and see whether our angelic friend decides to join us."

Steve leaned back against the wall of the tube, slipping down until he stopped on the floor of the passageway. I surveyed our surroundings. We were a mile below the surface of the earth.

"It's beautiful down here," said Sarah who had also slid down to sit on the glassy, tunnel floor. She reached out and drew her hand along the smooth, glowing surface. "Cold light," she said, "Like the phosphorescence of the creatures that inhabit the deep ocean."

"Light from a material perfected here four billion years ago," I said.

"It's almost impossible to believe we were really here all those years ago," said Sarah.

The light from my crystal arrays sent a pattern of light across the faces of the three human beings crouched in the blue green dimness.

"What is it?" asked Jesus.

"It is Michael," I replied. "He has decided to join us."

Jesus smiled, "I had hoped he might reconsider."

Whether he had raced down the tunnel to our impromptu conclave, or simply willed his physical presence into the temporal space beside me, in the next instant my three companions were staring with their eyes wide at the man-shaped being in blue.

"You were correct," said Michael, as though he had been standing there beside us the entire time.

"Wow," said Steve. "How'd you do that?"

Michael nodded. "Like the principles involved in our contest with the colored spheres, the process would take many days to explain in words."

I suddenly thought how simple and limited were the comings and goings of my three human friends.

"Perhaps M-2500 has explained to you that instantaneous travel through physical space is simply in the nature of our being," said Michael.

"And what of the fallen angels?" asked Sarah.

That question took even Jesus aback. He leaned forward, uneasily, but the subject of Lucifer and his rebel followers was on everyone's mind.

"An excellent question," replied the archangel. "When you first encountered him in the apartments of the Eastern Wall at the end of this cavern three point eight billion years ago, Lucifer shared that ability with the angelic host. He was, and perhaps you have read as much, the most favored and most powerful of all the created beings."

"And is he still?" asked Sarah.

"The most powerful?" said the archangel. "It is possible that on a level field he might defeat even me, but as we know…" and he nodded his head in the direction of Jesus, "The field has never been entirely level."

"We saw him defeated by the giant wheels," said Sarah.

"The Ophanim," the archangel replied. "Since that time his range has been…" He paused, evidently searching for the proper word. He nodded, "…Limited," he said.

"Limited?" asked Sarah.

"He is confined to the earth system, to the orbits of your sun and planets through the Milky Way Galaxy. He and the demons may not pass beyond the termination shock boundary of your sun's heliosphere. Once free to roam the myriad universes, he and his minions now find themselves confined to a mote of dust. Even now his reign grows short."

Michael stepped forward, removed his hat and stooped down onto one knee across from Jesus. He lowered his head and continued, "Your gospel does not recount this story in its particulars, but we know the enemy will attempt to destroy you before you return to the first century to begin your ministry."

"He has been after me my entire life," said Jesus.

Steve nodded and I watched as Michael looked up.

"We have done our best to protect you," said the archangel, "Why you have ventured a return to his lair is beyond my understanding, but we shall do our best to protect you now and always."

"We appreciate your protection," said Jesus, climbing to his feet. "We are only human beings. I hope you realize that we would not be standing here, alive today without the help of M-2500."

Steve, Sarah and Michael, looked at me as they stood up.

"Yes," said Michael, "You would not be standing here," he said and he trailed off, ominously, his affect full of insinuation and displeasure.

How odd it was that the Creator should have made his human begins in the image of these archangels. The common angels were not nearly as old as the original seven and had clearly seen many improvements in their design in-so-far as navigating the physical landscape of planet earth and its environs. Our telescoping tentacles and ambulatory appendages would have proved invaluable to any human being attempting to cross a raging stream or climb a tree for food or safety. Why the Creator had hearkened back to the earlier model struck me oddly at that moment, but it was a sense of rapid motion that suddenly snapped me out of my angelic reverie.

Jesus had taken a step back and the slick surface of the passageway's glass floor caused his legs to go out from under him. Sarah jumped forward to keep Jesus from crashing onto his back. Steve vaulted forward, with similar intent, but the archangel had sprung forward faster than either Steve or Sarah and intercepted Jesus before he hit the floor. The energy released as they hit the incline was all that was needed to start them sliding away. Hook and eye fashion, Sarah had grabbed hold of Jesus' hand, and Steve had grabbed one of Sarah's flailing ankles. The four of them slid down the passageway, picking up speed, now almost a hundred feet away. They were nearly out of range, but one of my tentacles shot out and the tip snaked around Steve's wrist. The slack played out, the tether caught hold, and I was off. I wobbled from side to side on the slippery floor with my ambulatory pods. Finding my center of gravity, I leaned back against my outstretched tentacle and was towed along behind my companions as we slipped down the steep blue-green tube into the earth.

Soon, I was zooming along at thirty miles an hour and heard the shouts and laugher of my friends reverberate along the glowing glass walls ahead. Faster and faster we flew. I could sway side to side up along the sloping walls of the passage as I leaned back against my tow line. Now, far ahead, a patch of white light was shimmering at the end of the snaking tunnel. We suddenly realized that we were approaching the terminus, but this was not the same tunnel that once led from the surface of the earth down into my underground workshop. This new passage intersected with the western wall of the ancient underground cavern, two hundred feet above the old cave floor.

Jesus cried out as he and Michael and Steve and Sarah disappeared. I felt a bone wrenching tug on my tentacle and I was yanked forward, banging against the walls and ceiling of the passageway and then flipping out into an empty vault of air.

Down below, the quick thinking archangel had sprouted its enormous wings. The rhythmic wing beats bore him up easily with his human cargo. My own wings emerged from my shoulders and engaged the thick, stale air of the underground. Between the two of us, Michael and I brought the trio of human beings safely to the floor of the enormous cave. I hesitate to use the word "safely," for any safety we felt was being afforded us only by a power at work over a tremendous distance.

We were in the lair of the Prince of Air and Darkness. The workshop which had once bustled with the loyal and contented angels going about the business of executing the Creator's design for life on earth had become a battleground in the schism between the Creator and his mightiest creation. We had once barely escaped from this cavern. Now, as we stepped carefully across the dark-gray flagstones, I sensed something which human faculties could not perceive. It was heavy, leaking out from the seams of another, parallel dimension. These were invisible forces that only Michael and I could detect. They were too dark, too mind-numbing to countenance for long. As for my friends, all that remained as far as the human eye could see were the rock-gray statues of rebel angels frozen in attitudes of battle. It had become a graveyard of unintended monuments.

Steve approached one of the ashen-gray objects. It was the shape of a gigantic Stronghold, twelve feet in height. This being had been one of the few of that high order to betray its creator. Its old angelic form remained in the dim cavern, in a field of broken and scarred relics of the ancient battle. Steve leaned against one of its towering legs. To his astonishment, the entire edifice began to tremble and it suddenly collapsed like a building make of ash. Dust rolled up and made it nearly impossible for Steve, Sarah and Jesus to breath. The motes flowed away, and as the air cleared, we looked down at what remained of the Stronghold, a grey heap of ash.

"What happened here?" cried Steve.

Through that other lens which only Michael and I possessed, we looked about a cavern choked to its ceiling with the writhing forms of demons loyal to the Evil Lord.

"What's wrong?" asked Sarah looking at Jesus, who had frozen in his tracks.

"Jesus?" Sarah asked again.

Jesus shook his head, "I cannot be certain," he replied, "But I sense the presence of something…"

"Evil?" suggested Michael taking a step forward and extending his hands to Sarah and Steve on each side. Instinctively, I looped my tentacles around the extended hands of Sarah and Jesus, who joined hands with Steve so that we formed a ring: two angels and three human beings. I was reminded of the simple prayer Jesus had once shared with Sarah and Steve near the beginning of our adventures together. I wondered whether the archangel Michael was preparing a similar transmission.

Our appendages now linked, we stood looking at the archangel. He bowed his head. Jesus and I followed his example and eventually Sarah and Steve lowered their gaze.

"Are we praying?" asked Steve after a moment.

"Praying?" replied the archangel. "Yes, we are praying. We are calling for the Creator's protection."

"Looks to me like we're asking for trouble," replied Steve and he pulled his hands free of Jesus and the archangel and took a step backwards away from our circle.

"We have trouble whether we ask for it or not," said Jesus, "But please, rejoin the circle so that we may begin."

"Begin what?" said Steve, slowly returning to the gap in our ranks and taking the hands of Jesus and the archangel.

There was no reply, but Steve watched as Jesus bowed his head, "Dear father, thank you for all you have given us," said Jesus. "We ask for your continued protection and guidance as we complete our time in the wilderness and particularly now as we confront the rebel leader in his citadel. We thank you for this, trusting in your good and perfect will. Amen."

"Amen," said the archangel.

"Amen," sounded the voices of Steve and Sarah.

The affirmation of "amen" was just emanating from the sonic panel in my chest when a voice caught our attention. The voice was familiar and awful and it hit me in the chest with the force of a tidal wave.

"Amen, indeed!" roared the voice.

I was knocked down. Had my tentacles maintained their grasp on the frail hands of Sarah and Jesus, the force of that wrenching, backward motion would have torn the limbs from their torsos. I had no choice but to relinquish my hold. My thoughts were over-whelmed in a blur as other-dimensional beings piled atop me.

I had been thrown back through mountains of ash and landed against the black basalt of the cavern's western wall. Something was bearing down on me, pinning me against the wall and I felt thousands of invisible palps probing the surface of my tentacles.

"The rings!" I suddenly thought.

I tried to retract my two prime tentacles and link the two failing tips together so as to protect the rings within an unbroken circle. "They will have to tear my tentacles from my body to get to these rings," I thought to myself, but try as I might, I could not bring my tentacles together and close the circle. I raged side-to-side, powerless to make any forward progress as I felt the metal bands being slowly pulled down off the length of my tentacles.

Michael had turned his head in alarm. The blind humans saw only that I had flown away, tumbling through the ash as though blown by a silent, invisible wind. The archangel could clearly see what they could not, and he started toward me, but it was as though he was slogging forward through waist-deep sand. A hundred thousand demons swarmed into the gap between us and flooded down from the cavern roof.

The fury of a common angel is awful to behold, but the power of human language cannot describe the rage of an archangel. As I fought the demonic onslaught and felt the rings of the Ophanim slipping from my possession, Michael leaned into the wave of the damned. He knew that he could not fully attack for fear of harming the human beings behind him. He did his best to move forward toward me the hundred yards.

"What the devil is wrong with them?" Steve exclaimed.

I could barely hear his voice against the background of shrieks and screams that filled my mind's hearing. I tried focusing back through the flood of demons that overwhelmed me. I could only see Jesus. His attention had fastened on me. Our gazes locked, and I understood that he was calling out, a prayer, a plea, or perhaps, a command.

He was on the move, walking through the ashes of the ruined workshop. Unhindered, he approached Michael, who looked back over his shoulder with an expression of utter astonishment as Jesus nodded and passed him. Jesus was aware of the demon spirits, and although it was unclear whether he could actually see, or hear, or feel them, he seemed absolutely unaffected by their presence.

He stood over me and I was reminded of the day he had discovered me on the summit of the Black Dune, buried to my chest in sand. He had reached down while Sarah and Steve had stood back petrified with fear. Then as now, he reached out a hand and took me by the shoulder and helped me upright.

What he could not see with his human eyes was the swath of desiccated limbs and the howling demons that dropped back, melting away like figures of ice on a plate of hot steel. Those nearby rolled away like gray steam. Jesus took hold of my left tentacle, no longer under the control of the invisible rebels, and he slipped off the ring and clenched it in his own right fist. He grasped my right tentacle and I felt a peace overwhelm me and I settled back as he pulled the second ring down and off the right tentacle and held it in the fist of his left hand.

"Are you all right?" he asked.

Lights flashed across my crystal arrays in ascent and I uttered the word, "Yes."

He stepped back and slipped the rings over each of his ring fingers as the archangel Michael caught up to him from behind.

"I warned you not to return," said Michael. "Are the rings secured?"

Jesus turned and flexed his fingers and held up his fists so that the archangel looked from the rings and into Jesus' face.

"You? You bear the rings?"

"Did you expect the Creator would allow the power of time-travel to fall into the hands of your former comrades?" asked Jesus.

Steve and Sarah approached through the dim dust, oblivious to the struggle.

"What was that all about?" said Steve. "Can we get out of here? This place always did give me the creeps."

Jesus and Michael turned to look at the plaintive little man in the jeans and t-shirt.

Jesus smiled.

"Is everything all right?" Sarah asked.

No one spoke.

"M-2500?" she asked.

I suddenly felt the urge to reach out to this poor, human female, whom I had wronged. My body relaxed and reassembled, and I rose up from the ashes as a woman. I admit that I had obeyed a strange impulse, but the Mechanical Man was gone, replaced by the human female, Deborah. The archangel and the three human beings jumped back, staring at the young woman in the red, low-cut evening gown.

"Deborah?" asked Jesus, astonished.

Steve gasped. "Debbie? Debbie is it you?"

"What in all the world is this?" exclaimed Michael. He strode forward, grasped my human-looking arm and pulled my face close to his, "M-2500, have you lost your mind?"

In all my experience I had never seen a fellow angel look more perplexed than did the supreme archangel at that moment.

"The form is pleasing to the humans," I replied.

Michael looked to Jesus who only stared calmly ahead. The archangel looked back at me.

"Return to your natural appearance, at once!" he demanded.

"Wait," cried Steve, and he stepped forward with an outstretched hand. "This is Debbie. She saved us from the devil and rescued us from this place on our first visit. Sarah and I owe our lives to her."

Michael looked Steve up and down as though he was evaluating an insect. He regarded Sarah with a similar gaze and looked back at Jesus. Evidently, the archangel held Jesus' companions in very low esteem. He looked down where he stood in the ash-strewn wreckage of what had once been a glittering hall of science and technology. He shook his head. Things had gone so terribly wrong. He did not look up, but seemed to inspect some fragment of stone or steel, fallen from the cavern ceiling those billions of years ago the day his brother, Lucifer, had rebelled against our creator. It was curious, but the angel's eyes, which at a moment's notice might have burned a hole through the earth or targeted a distant planet, a Mars or Venus, and rendered either world a flaming cinder, the eyes looked up in a glance at the artificial human female, at Debbie. His gaze collapsed back to the ashes.

"I warned you to avoid this place, Jesus," said the archangel. "You plan some sort of dialogue with the Fallen One. Well, you shall have your wish. It will be an unpleasant audience. This cavern is no longer home to the angels of creation. I will be unable to provide a full defense against him in your current, weakened state."

"Weakened?" said Jesus with a smile.

"Do not forget who you are!"

"It is you who have forgotten," Jesus replied.

There was a long moment of silence. It was as though everything had been building to a final settling of old scores, a clearing of the air. Suddenly, Jesus turned and set off for the east. Steve and Sarah looked at one another, dumbfounded, as our leader receded in the dimness.

"I don't know about you guys," said Steve and he set off after the lone figure. We had been there no more than five minutes when Sarah glanced at me. She shook her head in dismay and started off after the others. The archangel stood there beside me for several minutes, and with a sigh, followed the three human beings.

I found myself alone in the dim underground cavern. I did not know which way to turn and so, I took a step to the east. Soon, I found that I was nearly at a run. I removed my red, high-heeled shoes and sprinted through the dusty cavern until I had caught up with the others.

It had been nearly an hour, since Jesus had first set off on his own. Michael had easily over-taken Steve and Sarah and I found the two of them breathless and panting in the midst of the enormous concourse.

"You decided… You decided to follow us?" said Steve.

I pulled on my heels and nodded. "What's that up ahead?" I asked.

Jesus had arrived at the ruin of an old gantry of aluminum girders which had long ago collapsed from the ceiling. Further progress to the east was barred. Jesus turned his back to the debris pile and Michael came face to face with him.

"Well?" asked Michael once again, "Who are you?"

"I am Jesus," said Jesus and he drew a breath as though he were struggling to recall a long forgotten memory of his existence, "I am Jesus of Nazareth."

"And is that all?" asked the angel.

"I am… I am the Son of God," replied Jesus.

"But Jesus, the Son of God is in heaven, is he not? You and your friends took him there with the assistance of the woman there in the red dress."

"Is Debbie the woman in the red dress?" shouted Steve, angrily.

"Shut up, Steve," said Sarah.

No one said a word after that. We looked at Jesus, pinned by the archangel against the colossal pile of twisted metal.

"Who are you, then?" asked Michael for a third time.

Jesus pushed back from the wall of metal wreckage and stepped forward, "I am your creator."

"My creator…?" Michael's head tipped back and he loosened percussive bursts of energy that approximated the sound of human laughter. He shook his head and then reached out and tapped Jesus in the chest. Our friend stumbled backwards into the metal obstacle behind him.

"You are a man!" said Michael.

Steve and I didn't like that. We lunged forward and put our hands on the man in blue. He shrugged and we flew backwards, end-over-end in the dust.

"Enough," roared the archangel.

The voice echoed down the cavern walls, but we could not help but listen and wonder what the archangel's next move would be. Sarah, on the other hand, seemed perfectly at peace, as though the archangel was speaking on her behalf, as though he was saying something she herself had wanted to say to our friend all along.

"The Creator is in heaven," Michael continued. "His Son is by his side! The Spirit that has led your through the wilderness would see you safely home. THAT is the fulfillment of the WORD. You are a human being, Jesus. Return to the shore of Galilee and fulfill your destiny."

Sarah and Michael stepped forward and Michael stopped, face to face with Jesus.

"And you?" asked Jesus. "What are you?"

"I am the guardian of these halls," he replied. "My legions stand posted here and about the solar system as it tracks an outer spiral arm of the Milky Way Galaxy. We have done so nearly four billion years to mitigate the damage done by the evil lord of this prison."

He stepped back and seemed to sigh, "I will be at your side again one day at the Harrowing of Hell."

"The harrowing of hell?" asked Jesus, bewildered.

"But only if you survive this detour you've taken!"

It was then that Michael seemed to notice the gray bands of metal on Jesus' ring fingers.

"Do you wear them to tempt the devil?" asked Michael.

"To draw him out," said Jesus. "Yes."

"He has pursued their technology since the dawn of life," said the archangel. "He hopes by the power of time travel to destroy you."

"He cannot destroy me."

"But, what are you Jesus, apart from your mission on earth? The souls that you would rescue for the father cry out. You risk your mortal existence in this place."

"I am aware of that," said Jesus.

"And you would tempt the devil with that possibility?"

Michael looked back at me. I had smoothed out my dress, adjusted my high heels and taken several steps toward him. Steve was at my side once again.

"Perhaps the fallen angel has already been afforded the ability to travel through time?" continued Michael, as he looked me up and down. "We understand the Prince of Air of Darkness was enlisted to tempt you in the wilderness. It was the fulfillment of prophecy. The sole occasion in scripture when the evil one transcended the boundaries of time."

"That movement was never under his own power," said Jesus.

"He's talking about the demon driver we met in Nazareth," whispered Steve.

I nodded, solemnly, although I possessed only a dim outline of Steve's early travels with Jesus through Judea's eastern wastes.

"Well," Michael continued, "It appears there may have been occasion for another angel to travel through time."

"Another angel?" said Jesus.

"One who seems to have made himself quite at home among the denizens of this world. I see by your expression, Jesus that you may have discerned my word-play. Although, truly, it is a fallen angel."

"Fallen?" asked Jesus.

"Have you overlooked his transgressions? Certainly, you understand that as the leader of the angels, this is of some concern to us."

Jesus nodded as Michael slowly turned to look back at me. I suddenly felt the intensity of his gaze and the probing energy of his intellect sifting through my thoughts. I must have staggered a bit because I felt Steve's hands on me, propping me up. There was something within me, something I had pushed to the back of my being, the memory of my transgression against Sarah in ancient Greece, and I fought to keep those memories at bay. I trembled in terror, realizing, suddenly, that the archangel had seen deep in my hidden thoughts.

Michael's angelic voice sounded in the cavern, "And who is Demetrius?"

I shook my human-looking head in response.

"No one…" I said.

"What? You would dissemble, even how?"

"No…" I choked.

"I'm sorry, M-2500, I couldn't hear you…"

"No one, real…" I muttered.

"Who?"

I tried to answer, but something was happening. I fought to regain control of the human-shaped vocal cords in my throat. I stumbled. The contours of my face began to shift; the human-looking bones beneath my artificial skin began to toss to and fro. I looked away and tried to recall a moment, a snatch of conversation, an idea, anything but the image of that distant day in Greece, yet I could not overcome the probing intellect of the archangel. My human body was perspiring. I felt suddenly as though I should run or perish. Frantically, the eyes in my human-looking skull darted left and right looking for an escape, but it was too late.

The face of Michael suddenly resolved into sharp focus.

"Demetrius!" shouted Michael, accusingly. "Had you thrown your lot with Lucifer on the day of his betrayal, there would have been more honor!"

In the same instant I looked down, horrified, at the sight of my hands. They had been transformed into the hands of the youth, Demetrius.

"And what have you done to his human female!" demanded the archangel.

"I…"

"What have you done?" he cried.

"I practiced deceit…" I began with a litany of my earthly sins, but my superior already knew their extent.

"Monster!" he cried again. "You were their shepherd!"

I stammered and watched Jesus reach out between us, but Michael shoved Jesus aside. The universe which had seemed to grind down into slow motion, suddenly lurched, nauseatingly, into real time. Michael flew forward. Sarah and Jesus were reaching, clinging to his shoulders, but his force was unstoppable. The back of his hand sliced the air, striking my human-shaped face and tore loose the jaw-bone from one side of my skull.

When I recovered from the impact and looked slowly up, Sarah and Steve recoiled with expressions of horror and disbelief. I raised my human-looking fingers to conceal a gaping wound. The jaw was completely unhinged from its socket, the perfectly formed lower-teeth glinted in the dimness, and fluids resembling blood and saliva streamed down my chest in rivulets turning dark red in the artificial fabric of my Grecian robes.

The arms of Steve and Sarah were out-stretched. They had caught a glimpse of my ruined face and were attempting, somehow, to console me, but with one bloodied hand I held them back. When I looked up again, I had reassembled the face into the radiant human countenance.

"Your face!" cried Steve. "It's… It's healed."

The archangel stood, staring dispassionately at me as once again my countenance began to shimmer and I transformed back into the appearance of the human female in red.

Jesus and Sarah turned back to confront the archangel.

"If anyone is a monster down here, it's you!" shouted Steve.

"I don't know where you're been all this time," Sarah yelled at Michael, "But we've done just fine without your help."

She looked up into its expressionless face. I smoothed the red fabric down over my chest and stepped forward.

"It's all right, Sarah," I said.

"You are mistaken in this Michael," said Jesus. "M-2500's debt was paid, long ago."

"Paid?" said Michael.

"This is none of your affair!" shouted Sarah.

"It is my affair!" replied Michael. "I am commander of the angels."

"And I am <u>your</u> commander," shouted Jesus.

Michael, stopped short, suddenly confused. We all looked to Jesus.

"I tell you that this angel's transgression is forgiven!"

"By whose authority?"

Michael and Jesus exchanged a long, silent look. The archangel stepped back and looked from Sarah to Jesus.

"The Holy Spirit intercedes only on behalf of men!" said the archangel.

"It is by my authority!" shouted Jesus.

Michael was about to reply, but he stopped and shook his head. He looked up again as Jesus continued.

"You searched for the memory of an evil deed and found what you sought, Michael, but look again and you will see the goodness within your comrade. As I was baptized in the Spirit, I have baptized him and we have saved him. Look, Michael and you will see that I speak the truth."

Jesus turned and looked back at me. Slowly, cautiously, Steve and Sarah turned aside and I stepped toward Michael. My head was held high and this time I had no fear of what he might observe. He looked again and I felt the intensity of his gaze. I closed my eyes and felt his divine presence like a cold wind sweep through my mind. Suddenly he jumped back, and exclaimed, "Then it is true!"

With that he immediately stopped and hung his head and dropped to his knees.

"Forgive me," said Michael. "But how is this possible?"

"All things are possible through him who believes," said Jesus, "Even the redemption of a fallen angel."

"But… I… I don't understand," said Michael, humbly.

"I have journeyed into the wilderness so that I might know all that a good man might know."

"I'll say," said Steve.

Jesus smiled, "I have been tempted, but by nothing so great that my temptation could not be overcome by the power of the Holy Spirit. It is, truly, the fulfillment of the scripture."

"And is the Spirit with you even now?" asked Michael.

"Always," replied Jesus and he took a step toward the tall, blue garbed figure. "Do you imagine I would have ventured here without him?"

Michael shook his head slowly.

"And a moment ago, when I overcame the demons and retrieved these talismans of the Ophanim, do you think such a feat would have been possible for a human being without the authority of a greater power?"

Michael shook his head, "No…" he said. "Of course not…"

"I am glad to have met you after all these years." Jesus bent down and placed his hand on Michael's shoulder and indicated that he should rise to his feet.

Michael nodded, "But you understand your mission on earth?"

"I'll say he does," said Steve. "We saw him crucified on a hill outside Jerusalem."

Michael seemed to recoil from the import of Steve's words.

"You got that right," replied Steve.

"So, are we finished here?" asked Sarah.

"I wish I could say that we were," Michael replied.

We all looked at him, unsure what he was about to do. He stepped back, away from us, following the fallen beams of the collapsed gantry that littered the cavern floor in this vicinity. We watched him walk slowly, his index finger tracing along a particular beam at about the level of his waist. When he had removed himself by perhaps twenty yards, drawing a long, thin, line in the dust on the beam, his form was nearly lost in the dimness. He looked down at the tip of his index finger at the accumulated dust. He rubbed the finger against his thumb and looked up.

"He is here," Michael called back to us.

"Who?" said Steve.

"I don't know," said Sarah looking at Jesus. "Do you suppose he means…?"

Her voice trailed off and we all looked up at the barrier of twisted metal girders and pipes. A wind moved through the gloom and I detected a purplish glow from the other side of the debris pile. The glow grew in intensity and now Jesus and Steve and Sarah could see it radiating up in the darkness above the barrier.

Something stirred. I sensed its approach in the space beyond the heap of rubble and suddenly there was a blinding flash of light at the crest of the pile. The glare receded and some twenty feet above us, standing in a glittering black suit of armor was the figure of Satan. He was no longer the beautiful being who had ruled this subterranean workshop at the dawn of life on earth. He remained altogether human in form but the gleaming alabaster flesh had turned grey. He stood at his normal height of just under twenty feet tall and hence seemed to us a giant.

I cowered at the sight of him. This manifestation was so unlike the guise of the park photographer and the so-called Captain of the Red and Black Beetle of Death flagship. At the same time I felt something thrilling in the creature's magnificent presence. As far as we knew only the Creator who had fashioned him possessed a greater power, and I was suddenly reminded of the strange beings I had encountered outside the kitchen in ancient Greece and again in the deserted plaza in the shadow of the Temple Mount, the night Judas had turned against the Son of Man. Those malevolent agents might have been demons in league with Satan or perhaps Satan himself, but my feeling of horror and revulsion seemed mixed now with a sense of awe and sorrow.

"Steady, there," I heard Jesus say to me.

The enormous being on the rampart slid slowly down to his side and then, unexpectedly, rolled his legs over the edge and he leaned back, so that he was sitting on the wall as though he had simply come to a convenient bench in a park and paused to relax. He looked about the dust below and caught sight of us, as though he had detected three or four insects looking up at him.

He smiled, and it was a smile that betrayed satisfaction but also from his furrowed brow, a sense of sorrow and regret.

"Jesus?" he said in a voice that was no more than a whisper. He reared back his enormous head, cleared his throat and spit. A viscous mass of what looked like molten lava shot from his mouth. The size of a grapefruit, the streaming projectile hit the cavern floor ten feet to our right and exploded.

"It has been years since I have uttered that name," said the beast.

"It seems like only yesterday," Jesus replied.

"Ah, yes, the wonders of time travel," said Satan with a dry laugh. "I figured out the physics of that problem centuries ago. Sadly, I am as much a prisoner of time as I am of space. Yes, perhaps my jailer, just over there in the shadows explained the restriction on my comings and goings."

The Devil seemed to draw a breath and sigh. Steve and Sarah stole a glance into the shadows far to our right, where the lone figure in blue stood, motionless in the gloom, patiently observing.

"This world and its star and planets are all so pitifully minute for an intellect like mine," Satan continued. "Such a waste."

"You said a moment ago that you posses the knowledge of time travel?" said Jesus.

"Did I?" asked the giant with a smile.

"Yes, you did," replied Jesus.

"Yes, and I distinctly remember telling you at one point in the past that I would one day achieve the ability. Well, for obvious reasons, it has gone untested."

"Then why did you send your demons after these?" asked Jesus and he raised his hands up toward the seated form of the devil so that the pair of rings glinted in the light.

"The rings! The Rings of the Ophanim," said Satan.

"If you already possessed the ability to travel through time, whether or not your jailer permitted you to do so, what use would you have for these?"

"No, no, no…" Satan laughed. "The object in our acquiring the rings was not to employ them in time travel. What we would like to do is prevent you from traveling in time."

"Prevent us?"

"Certainly."

"But what difference to you whether…" Jesus trailed off.

"Whether you return to your place in human history?"

"I meant… No…"

"Don't you have a date with Calvary?" said Satan, mockingly. "If you never travel back in time to begin your ministry, the effect might be just the same as your having never been born."

It took a while for Jesus to digest this scenario. It seemed to me there was a certain logic to it, but Jesus did not seem at all convinced.

"It sounds like rather far-fetched," said Jesus.

"Oh, come, now. Consider my position. It's certainly worth a shot, don't you think?" Satan replied.

"To keep me here, a prisoner in the year 1968?"

"Why not?" said Satan. "Peter and his brother can retire from the fishing industry to live the quiet life. All those disciples will be spared their martyrdom. Judas will go down in history as a respected freedom fighter and Saul will rise in the ranks of the military to help drive the Romans from Jerusalem."

I glanced over at Steve and Sarah who listened intently. Many times I noticed Steve nodding in agreement.

Satan placed his enormous hands on the edge of the makeshift bench where he had been sitting, pushed forward and came down to his feet. Dust rose up about his shins, leaving Jesus in a swirling cloud of dust at the level of his waste. Satan stood up to his full height against the backdrop of the metal barrier.

"Let us rewrite world history together," said Satan.

Jesus back pedaled a few steps and looked up the full twenty feet to glare into the face of the Prince of Air and Darkness.

"I've seen enough," said Jesus.

"Excuse me?"

"Your audience is at an end."

"<u>My</u> audience?"

From the corner of my eye, I noticed that Michael had moved a step. Even through the dimness I could see that he was watching the scene play out, the way a mongoose, that strange, fearless creature we designed in the Indian sub continent, observes the motions of the cobra.

"My audience, you say?" repeated Satan.

"My friends wondered why I would return to this spot. In truth it was to let my friend M-2500 revisit the home he left years ago to join me on my quest."

Satan glanced over at me with a dismissive snort, "Yes?"

"But more importantly, I came, once again, to see you."

"Did you?"

"Yes," continued Jesus. "I had hoped that in four billion years you might have found time to reflect on your decision. The one you made out there, three-hundred miles away on the terrace of the Eastern Wall."

"Let me think," said Satan with a wry smile. "Reflect?" he asked.

"On your decision," said Jesus.

"My decision?"

"The Entity tracked you down two thousand years ago and asked whether you might like the opportunity to tempt his little nephew. I understand from him that you were more than willing to oblige. He even allowed you the ability to travel into the future to test me in a foreign land and under dire circumstances."

"Yes?" said Satan.

"You took advantage of that offer and although you fulfilled your obligation to tempt me, 'according to scripture," you did considerable damage along the way."

"Did I?"

"Don't play with me, Satan."

"Play with you?"

"You scoff at this world which you have made your prison, but you once offered it to me. Do you recall?"

This seemed to take Satan aback. His glib demeanor vanished and he learned forward with an intensity of focus that kept my angelic concentration fixated on his face.

"Yes, I recall the offer."

"You offered it to me, the entire world and everything in it, if only I would bow down to you and call you Lord."

The smile had vanished from the fallen archangel's countenance. He nodded, slowly, in agreement.

"Yes, I recall the offer."

"You were prepared to make me the king of the world?"

"Yes! Of course! That was the bargain. Your 'uncle!" laughed the fallen angel and he spit a stream of black smoke. "What a ridiculous appellation! It was you! You! It has always been you! You, in a hall of mirrors! The God of contradictions! Jesus of Nazareth!" shouted the enraged creature and he spat again with all his strength and venom, down in the direction of Jesus.

Jesus dove to his right, rolled in the dust and sprang to his feet as a flaming projectile of molten matter splashed on the cavern floor where an instant earlier Jesus had been standing. From his observation post, Michael was on the move, but Jesus stood up straight and without turning his gaze from Satan waved that the heavenly protector should hold his distance.

"And did I accept your offer?" asked Jesus.

Satan only stood, glowering silently.

"I asked you," said Jesus, "Did I accept your offer to install me as the king of the world?"

Satan slowly shook his head, "No," he answered. "You did not."

Again he seemed to inhale and turn with a great sigh of sorrow and regret. "Why have you come down to visit your child in his loneliness?" he asked.

Jesus stopped. He shuddered and drew his hand across his face. I caught only a glimpse as Jesus turned aside, but there were tears in his eyes as he looked back up at the being who, second only to him, had been the most powerful intelligence in all of existence, across all time and the myriad universes.

"I have come asking you to repent, Lucifer."

"Repent?"

"Do you remember the name I gave you when we created the sister planet to shine one day upon the earth."

Satan only stared, motionless, and we two angels, Michael and I, and the two humans, Sarah and Steve, saw tears well up in the eyes of the great evil that had shed no tear in all its hundred trillion trillion years of existence.

"I… I cannot recall its name…"

"The Evening Star."

"The Evening Star," repeated the beast, dreamily, and the great frame seemed to shudder. "What do you want from me?"

"I said I want to forgive you!" said Jesus.

"Me?"

"Yes."

"But you, you are only a man," said Satan.

"I know," replied Jesus, "I know precisely who I am."

"And is it even in your power?" asked Satan, but even as he asked, he knew the answer and I saw him look up beyond the frail human head of the being known as Jesus. Satan looked at me. I felt Sarah's hand reach out to me and grasp Debbie's hand and to my right, the hand of Steve held mine. We had joined hands, the three of us, suddenly hoping that the gigantic creature before us might listen. I cannot speak for Sarah and Steve, but at that moment, I believe we were praying.

"Well?" asked Jesus.

"Well?" asked Satan, turning his head aside and drawing an enormous, clawed hand across his furrowed brow. He looked back at Jesus.

"What do you want me to say in answer?" asked Satan.

"I want you to help me."

"Help you?"

"Help me with the creatures of this world."

"The human beings?"

"Be an inspiration like Michael and the others. You were the most powerful of them. They do not begrudge you this. Only accept that you are a created being and together we might work together to help the human beings overcome their willfulness."

Satan seemed to have recovered. He stood straight and tall. Perhaps he had already made a decision. Perhaps he already knew the outcome of this audience. Never-the-less, the moment played out as he inquired of Jesus.

"What must I do?"

"I have traveled throughout human history," Jesus replied. "I have done my best with the aid of M-2500, and my boyhood friend Steve, and the brilliant child of the future, Sarah, to understand mankind. I have met with the great spiritual leaders. Everywhere I have gone I have asked them to accept me as their savior."

"Yes," said Satan with an unpleasant leading edge in his voice.

"And I have been met everywhere and in every instance with the same the reply."

Satan only smiled.

"So, I ask you to admit that you are a sinner. Accept me as the one who will lay down his life, who has laid down his life for the fallen of this world. Ask forgiveness for your transgressions and accept me as your lord, and as your savior."

Satan nodded, solemnly.

Jesus remained motionless, waiting expectantly.

"If it were only that simple," said Satan.

"It is. It is that simple," said Jesus.

"Go…" whispered Satan.

The voice had gone all hollow and was so low, that with even my superior hearing I could barely detect the utterance.

"I'm sorry," said Jesus, softly, "I could not hear your reply..."

"Go," Satan repeated.

"What?"

Satan drew a sharp breath and exhaled with such a blast of energy that Jesus was knocked back end-over-end. A choking storm of dust rolled in Jesus' wake.

"Leave!" shouted Satan and the force of his outburst resounded against the ashen walls of the cavern and the floor trembled. To my left a blur of blue had swept along the barricade and suddenly materialized between us and the vibrating form of the fallen archangel.

The blue fabric of our chaperone's velvet suit had resolved into a flinty blue material that gleamed like cold steel. It was of a substance far more durable than any metallic alloy and not found within a hundred million light years of the earth. Michael had shed his human stature and risen up in front of his celestial prisoner. The protector of the world soared to over twenty feet and stood between us and Satan. Sarah, Steve and I helped Jesus to his feet.

"Perhaps we should leave?" said Sarah.

"Do you think?" shouted Steve.

"Perhaps," said Jesus.

"Oh come on," cried Steve. "How many chances are you going to give this guy?"

In front of us, the two towering giants confronted one another wordlessly. We could hear neither their silent exchange nor view the expressions on their faces. But beyond the gleaming armored legs of Michael we could see that Satan had stepped back. He threw an enormous gray arm over the debris pile and pulled himself slowly up and over.

We watched as Michael seemed to brace his gigantic frame for an attack. But Satan, rather than attack, silently continued over the top of the wall and disappeared from view on the opposite side.

Far back in the gloom in the vault of space beyond the barricade we saw a brilliant glow and a sudden flash of purple light. It was followed by a low, thundering sound that rumbled up and down the cavern. Then, there was silence.

Without turning, the gigantic archangel Michael spoke into the gloom, "He has departed."

"Where to?" asked Jesus.

"Not far. He can never go far. Some report that he lives among the ice worlds at the barrier wall along the edge of the solar system."

Jesus nodded and looked up as the giant turned to face us.

"Are you satisfied?" asked the archangel.

Jesus was silent.

"Did you expect him to accept your offer of redemption?"

"All things may be forgiven, but the gift must be received. I will not lecture you who know these things. Evil is an illusion," replied Jesus.

"An illusion, you say?"

"A dangerous illusion, I grant you, for those who succumb to its allure, but in the end it will vanish like mist. Only goodness endures."

"Jesus," said Steve. "You're starting to sound like your old self again back at the temple."

Jesus smiled and I was reminded of the fact that the Eastern Wall of this cavern had once housed a place of worship for the thousands of angels assigned to engineer life on the planet. I recalled the line of scripture from the book in the hotel room nightstand I had read in Oakland. There were only a few lines in mention of our story. It seems something had been amended in translation by those human beings who had preserved the record. Satan had tempted Jesus from the height of the temple, not in Jerusalem, but on the high terrace of the Eastern Wall. Three point eight billion years ago Lucifer had denied him then and there. And now, for a second time, the creature Lucifer had walked away.

What was to be made of the Rings of the Ophanim? The onslaught of invisible demons had sought to wrest them from our control. We had heard Satan himself boast that he understood the mystery of time travel. He reasoned that if we lost control of the rings, Jesus would remain trapped here, unable to return to his place in human history, unable to fulfill the destiny foretold by the prophets of his ancient tribe. Satan sought to deny the ministry that would plant seeds of a new hope, which, given time, would take root across the globe and provide a way back for the fallen human beings.

Jesus already had in mind another destination. He approached me and I saw the glittering bands of the Ophanim. I yearned once again to wield their power, to unleash the streaming mist, to press the throttle of limitless power that would bring us to another place and time.

"Perhaps we should leave before the demons return to their haunt," said Jesus.

He had removed the rings and held them both in his right hand. I took a step in his direction and had put forth the slender, humanoid hand of Deborah to receive them, when a shout from behind caused us both to turn.

Getting out of 1968 was not going to be so simple.

13. Escape

It was Beelzebub and his horde of demon fly-men. These were the spirits of fallen angels resurrected in the horrific shapes of super-humanoid insects. The results of Satan's unholy experiments in genetic mutation stirred from beneath the blankets of dust. It was no accident that they had appeared at this moment. They were determined that we would not escape this place again.

Michael strode past us. "I suggest you take up a defensive position on the other side of the wall."

"Over the wall, everybody," shouted Steve.

We wasted no time and closed the distance to the tangled debris pile. Grabbing broken pipes and girders we scampered over as Michael advanced in the opposite direction toward the assembling horde. With ease I made it to the crest of the rampart and reached over to help Sarah and Steve. Jesus was already clamoring up to the top to join me and we looked back at the archangel.

He was a hundred yards away. A hundred yards further still, the spiny creatures were wriggling out of the dust. There were thousands in rank and file and more dropping down from the darkness of the cavern ceiling. Michael turned back only once more to check our retreat.

"If you have means of escape, employ it now!" he shouted in a voice that thundered back to us, but was soon lost in the frenzy of a low pitched buzzing sound.

Rising from the dust, the creatures exercised their wings in the dank cavern air. A gray cloud rose up from the cavern floor and lurched slowly forward.

"We haven't much time," shouted Jesus above the din as Sarah and Steve crawled over the edge of the wall.

"We need to get to the other side."

"Then what?" I cried.

"You'll have to transform into the rocket ship," Jesus replied.

Rocket ship? What was he thinking? We were miles underground. The only avenue to the surface lay through a swarm of demon flies and a tunnel of rock much too narrow for our space cruiser.

As these thoughts raced through my mind I watched as Michael's legendary sword materialized, the hilt firmly gripped in his armored right hand. The blade of otherworldly force glowing white and acing blue electric fire, cut a swath through the first ranks of the advancing demons. Their captain, Beelzebub, had disappeared from view through the dust and tumult of exploding exoskeletons. We took the opportunity to drop down on the eastern side of the debris pile where we quickly reassembled.

Immediately, I looked back to Jesus for the rings of the Ophanim which he still gripped in his right hand. I cupped the hands of Deborah together as through to receive a sacred offering and Sarah and Steve stood breathless at our side as Jesus and I completed the transfer.

The incessant buzzing had grown in moments to a pulsating roar. We looked with expectation at the glittering bands in my palms. I picked one carefully between thumb and forefinger and prepared to slip it on when I experienced the horrible sensation of the band's weight suddenly going to zero, as though it had slipped from my fingers. We stared in shock as a wisp of dark, gray dust streamed away from my hand.

Sarah gasped as we watched the ring slowly disintegrate. We crowded around the remaining ring and Steve cried out as our last hope of escape collapsed in a circle of fine, gray powder.

"The rings?" he shouted, "What's happened to them?"

We looked at Jesus and his eyes had grown wide in disbelief.

"Where are they?" Steve demanded.

"Quiet," snapped Sarah and I felt her arm on my bare shoulder. She was shaking me. "What's happened?"

My lips parted but the utterance was swept away by the sound of a deafening explosion from the opposite side of the barrier wall. The light was so intense that for an instant we could see the outline of the cavern's ceiling like a black overcast sky three hundred feet above our heads. In that same lightning flash we saw the multiplying forms of ten thousand more winged insect demons sail down from the vault.

"We'll be overwhelmed!" cried Jesus as explosions continued on the opposite side of the wall. "If Michael unleashes power enough to drive them back, Steve, Sarah and I will be destroyed. We must return to the ship."

Now I felt both of Jesus' hands on my shoulders. He was shaking me and the sound of his voice came in fits and starts to my consciousness. I sensed the approach of Satan's lieutenant. He had outflanked Michael, come completely around the end of the debris pile.

"What's wrong?" shouted Jesus.

There was no time to explain. What could I do without the rings? Even if I could remember how to turn back into the space ship without them, how could we leave the cavern?

"Where's your faith?" shouted Jesus.

I heard him now and I looked into his eyes and nodded. I stumbled past him, heading directly east down the old concourse of the cavern's central thoroughfare.

"Stay close," I shouted. "Satan's lieutenant has slipped around the barricade!"

I dashed ahead, faster than any mortal woman in her life had ever run and I thought only of the deep clear pool in the Himalayas and the face shimmering in the light above the waves. My form had become a blur of motion and as I reached forward I shouted with joy in a voice transmuted into electrical components and my body realigned in the sleek and deadly shape of the space ship. Like a welcome mat I threw open the spiral hatch in my belly and the drove the spiral staircase down into the bedrock.

The sight of the eighty foot space craft, gleaming cherry red and white on its chrome runners pointing down the thoroughfare brought smiles to the faces of companions. Meanwhile, the sudden appearance of this familiar craft caused a shambling monster beside the wall, half flying on translucent wings and skittering on half-human legs, to stumble. As Beelzebub regained his balance he knew that a precious instant of hesitation had been given over to his quarry's advantage.

The circle of white light shining on the cavern floor below my hull brought hope to my friends. My startling appearance had bought them just enough time to close the distance of some fifty feet to the stairwell. It had all come back to me, the pure, sweet power, and I recalled the protective aura of force, unleashing the same energy that flashed beyond the tangled wreckage of the barrier behind us. The glow of blue light was nearly imperceptible, but my three companions recognized it and quickened their pace.

"Into the light," shouted Jesus waiting with Sarah for Steve to catch up.

"Go ahead, into the blue light," shouted Jesus. "And then, quickly, into the ship."

"No! I'm waiting for you and Steve," Sarah cried.

"Into the ship, hurry," Jesus shouted.

"You go head!" she replied. "It doesn't matter what happens to us!"

"Sarah!"

"You have to get out of here! You have to get back to Judea. Don't you see this is exactly what Satan planned?"

Insect henchmen were beginning to drop down from above. Three had passed through the perimeter of my blue light and alighted on my rooftop. They rubbed their forearms together and prepared odd looking instruments near the topside hatch unaware the fluids within their exoskeletons were about to flash boil. The first of the trio exploded in a miasma of yellow and green in the faces of his comrades. As they looked up in bewilderment their last memory was perhaps of their captain, waving its arms frantically in the rear when they suddenly exploded.

"Get to the ship!" shouted Steve with his last breath as Jesus and Sarah returned to the spot where he staggered toward the safety of my blue perimeter.

They had hold of his arms and were helping him along when the shadow of Beelzebub fell across their path. Jesus had once wrestled with this monster in its infancy almost four billion years ago on the terrace of the cavern's Eastern Wall. In the eons since, it had grown wise and strong in evil beyond human measure. Unlike many of its subordinates, this monster was possessed by the soul of a fallen angel and could never truly be destroyed but in the Realm of Nothingness beyond Armageddon at the end of the world.

Its claws suddenly closed on the fabric of Jesus' t-shirt just as Sarah and Steve crossed into the protective blue zone encircling me. The monster hoisted the Son of God off the cavern floor, and it was suddenly in doubt whether Armageddon would ever come. If the mortal man died in this demonic hive, what would become of his place in history?

No sooner had Sarah deposited Steve inside the blue aura, than she turned back toward Jesus. "Go on, Steve," she shouted. "Get inside the ship!" She ran twenty feet back to where the ten foot tall monster held Jesus in its grasp.

Beelzebub unfurled its translucent wings and beat the air and rasped in its half human voice, "Have you learned to fly?"

In the next instant, to our horror, the monster began to slowly rise into the cavern air. From both ends of the debris wall, demon insects spilled into view outflanking Michael who had slain the mortal bodies of ten thousand fly-men.

Beelzebub rose above the cavern floor with his human cargo when suddenly the ascent was cut short. Sarah had grabbed hold of a leg. Steve had staggered back to his friends. With his last iota of strength he leapt up and caught the monster's free hind leg. The creature and the three humans swayed back and forth along a meandering path, only two feet above the cavern floor. Meanwhile, the insect horde was swarming forward. In all my existence, I had never felt so powerless. We had been so close to safety! And then it struck me. In the next instant I fired up my engines. One inch, two inches, a foot, two feet I rose slowly off the cavern floor and slowly drifted in reverse.

Like a searchlight tracing a path of human foot-prints back to their source, my hemisphere of blue light drifted backwards over the landscape. The glittering lenses of the monster's compound eyes glinted as the deadly aura approached. Beelzebub abandoned the idea of lifting these three humans off the cavern floor and did its best to hang on to Jesus and fly backwards.

But Sarah and Steve each held fast to a hind leg. Their own feet dragged through the cave dust as the monster flew backward just out of reach of my deadly blue light. Beelzebub may have thought his evasive action very clever until his spiny back bumped up against the tangle of the fallen gantry. It was fifteen feet high at this point and he could fly no higher. I was reminded of the delivery trucks I had once heard in Oakland the week before, backing up to deliver their produce in the early morning. I backed up and the deadly glow of blue grazed the monster's armor. It suddenly determined that it would strangle Jesus then and there in its powerful forearms. The last time its physical form had been disintegrated by our little band of adventurers, it had taken a hundred years for the monster to recover. It suddenly dropped Jesus on the cavern floor, thinking it would now be free to fly to safety, but Sarah and Steve understood the significance of the blue light and were not about to release their hold.

In desperation, Beelzebub veered off to its right along the wall. I followed like a dance partner. Meanwhile, Jesus had pulled himself to his feet. He ran after Sarah and Steve who clung to the monster's legs as it dragged them along the wall.

'Forget the monster!" shouted Jesus. "Into the ship."

In the end, the sight of a writhing wall of insect monsters to the left and right and now, over-topping the debris wall, convinced Steve and Sarah that the evil one's resources currently outmatched our own. My human friends relented and simultaneously released the chitinous hind legs. My friends rolled through the dust onto their feet, as the beating wings of Beelzebub finally took hold of the air and lifted him up and back over the wall. Its bodily fluids were mere seconds from flash boiling and though I regretted that the monster had escaped, I smiled in the next instant as I saw him fly up triumphantly in the air over the wall only to land directly into the waiting hand of Michael. A wall of demons had risen up at Michael's back as he stood astride the barricade. He held Beelzebub at arm's length in one hand by the monster's throat as easily as a man might hold a bag of garbage preparing to drop it into a refuse bin. The writhing, buzzing and cursing of the demonic lieutenant was of no more concern to the giant than the complaints of a gnat. The archangel lifted his sword in his right hand and pointed it toward the east down the long, three-hundred mile expanse of the cavern thoroughfare. As Jesus, Sarah and Steve scurried beneath our space ship and clamored up my spiral stairway inside, I looked forward as blue light sprang forth from the angelic blade. The shaft of light grew in intensity until it blazed with the brilliance of a noonday sun. The cobwebs of broken catwalks and fallen gantries evaporated away, creating, in Steve's parlance, "a straight shot" all the three-hundred miles east to the Eastern Wall.

Jesus and Sarah piled into the cockpit and fastened their belts as Steve threw down the auxiliary flight seat from the cockpit wall and strapped in.

"Now what?" I asked.

"Let's get the hell out of here!" shouted Steve.

At another time, Steve's familiar refrain might have brought a smile to Jesus' lips.

"M-2500?" asked Jesus.

"Yes?" I replied.

"It's time."

"But the rings… Without the rings..."

"The relics of the Ophanim have served their purpose."

The demons swarming in from all sides along the barrier wall were annihilated in a blaze of heat from my engines as I withdrew the spiral stairs, sealed the hatch in my keel and headed east along the thoroughfare. The gigantic dynamos placed a hundred yards apart on each side of the cavern and replicated one after the other for three hundred miles had once powered this glorious facility with the thermal energy of the young earth's molten mantel. Now, they rolled away before our eyes in the viewport.

I was flying with my friends a hundred feet above the cavern floor at two hundred and fifty miles an hour toward a wall of black basalt, four billion years old and half a continent thick. Faster and faster I barreled forward. Jesus reached out to the time control lever. His hand closed over the exact spot where a ring of the first sphere had once been placed. Jesus leaned forward on the lever.

Sarah looked up at his face and turned, and we all looked forward. The ruined aquariums and cages and holding pens where life had first been engineered flashed away and the dark, black Eastern Wall rose up in the distance until it filled our view.

"Your will be done," I prayed and leaned forward.

* * *

A white mist streamed over the view port. A sonic boom that we never heard echoed in the enormous, darkened hall, rumbling over the dust of the broken barricade all the way back to Hudson's Bay. We felt a BUMP and opened our eyes and knew that we had been saved.

14. Return to Oakland

Five seconds before impact with the Canadian Shield we made the jump. We flew forward thirty two years into the future. Why, the year 2000? I do not know. We had come through with wide-open eyes and watched the mist stream away and through the power of Jesus' mysterious uncle navigated to a point in space just beyond the earth's subsequent orbit. This trajectory allowed for the movement of the sun through the outer arm of the Milky Way Galaxy and the motion of planet earth. Of course, had we reappeared in exactly the same location in the cavern thirty four years later, Steve, Sarah and Jesus would have enjoyed only two seconds of mortal existence before their obliteration on the basalt wall of the ancient cavern.

As things turned out, the slight adjustment allowed us to pop out in the year 2000 sailing away from earth orbit into the region of empty space between the orbits of the Earth and Venus.

"The space station! The space station!" cried Sarah as the scene of the newly constructed space platform resolved in my viewport. We sped away toward the rising sun, described a tight turn and headed back to the earth.

"That was the international space station," Sarah exclaimed.

We traveled now, in what the military scientists of her time referred to as "stealth mode," invisible to the eye and to sensitive instrumentation then devised by the earthling's most advanced technology.

I glided northeast toward the rising sun over the Pacific Ocean. I overshot the Alameda Municipal Golf Course and set my sights for the Orpheus Hotel. It was still there, in old North Oakland, run down, but still in operation. After dusk I settled on the rooftop and my friends climbed out and headed toward a heavy, metallic door. I transformed into my original configuration, the so-called "robot angel" that my friends had first encountered on the Black Dune. I approached the cast-iron door, reached in among the atoms with my tentacle to the other side and, inserting a tentacle tip into the mechanical workings of an oxidized pad-lock, sprang the lock and quickly opened the door. We climbed down an iron ladder to the landing on the sixth floor. We walked quickly down the flights of stairs and made our way out of the stairwell into the lobby. There, I noticed the vending machine which I described at the beginning of my story. I slowly miniaturized, climbed inside the machine and made myself at home.

* * *

We lived in Oakland for the entire summer. The old Sunshine Mission had fallen on hard times, but was still in operation and Sarah got on as a childcare attendant and an aerobics instructor. During those weeks and months in the city each of us grew in our faith and hope for the future. For the first time in her life Sarah confronted the memories of her unhappy childhood. Steve finally took arms against his many addictions and the insatiable appetites to which he had enslaved himself. No longer the servant of bodily impulse alone, he began to understand the workings and interplay of body, mind and spirit and to harness their power and potential. The course in biology seemed a humble beginning for a man one day destined to attend medical school. Of course at that point, there was still a long way to go, and it was difficult enough getting him on the bus three days a week to attend his first course of study at the community college.

Meanwhile, Jesus worked his way up in the hospitality industry from dishwasher to bus-boy to waiter in a one of the city's five-star restaurants. To supplement his income late at night he earned another small fortune as a bartender. Servant to the tourists, business people, and socialites, he came to appreciate how difficult a life of luxury could be on the heart and spirit of a human being. He developed a following among the lonely late-night drinkers. He sold very little alcohol, indeed would sell no more than a drink or two to anyone who ordered and would never serve someone already under the influence. This might have upset the bottom line, but management was satisfied that after a few weeks, J.C.'s night shift seemed to be earning much more in expensive non-alcoholic coffee drinks, soda, bar food, and an especial favorite, the Virgin Mary.

For a being that had spent five hundred million years drifting on the surface of the primordial oceans, I found my days holed up in the vending machine rich and rewarding. Early each morning, six days a week Jesus would return to make his morning deposit of hundreds of dollars cash. Later, I would issue a withdrawal for Sarah as she came down from our room and she would head off with two or three hundred dollars in donations for the Sunshine Shelter.

To supplement our income I took up a hobby of crafting fine jewelry. They may have been knock-offs of classic originals, but all the materials were genuine and the metals 100 percent pure. It's amazing how many rolls of nickels I went through, stripping away protons, neutrons, electrons, and reorganizing the particles into quantities of gold, platinum, silver and a dazzling array of precious stones. I found the late night home shopping channel on view across the lobby on the old television an invaluable resource in the early going of my cottage industry.

Ultimately, of even greater value was something that streamed in through a number of frequencies of the electromagnetic spectrum. I was long familiar with the radio waves and television signals from my first visit to Oakland in the 1960's. I had learned how to translate these electromagnetic impulses directly without benefit of an actual man-made radio or television receiver. I had sent a tendril out the back of my vending machine through a chink in the plaster and brick, down along the floor molding behind the wall and tapped into the television cable. From there I fed a narrow feeler to the trunk, out of the building and out to the cities rudimentary power grid. From there I found a different and surprising signal.

It was a signal, far too weak in our particular location for the average, mass-produced human hardware to detect, but for me, the signal rolled down into the confines of my little rectangular workshop with the force of a Niagara. This was the Internet, and it was my pathway to all the knowledge, learning and experience of the human being. I learned their languages, commerce, literature, politics and everything up and down and in-between and across the globe. I was particularly fond of the technical manuals, diagrams and blueprints from the watch-making industry. My specialty was gold pocket watches with exquisite mechanical clockworks. On Fridays, on her way to work, Sarah would deposit a single dollar bill in my currency slot, and I would dispense a stack of United States currency and a golden pocket watch or a diamond tiara which Sarah could pawn up the street. These funds she would contribute to the neighborhood association and a small portion she set aside for our team's modest expenses.

Melvin had passed way before the turn of the millennium. His nephew, Stanley, had inherited the pawn and loan business across the street from the Orpheus Hotel. In recent years he had struggled to keep the company afloat in the face of an onslaught of crime and poverty in the neighborhood. Stanley Johnson never learned Sarah's secret, the source of her fabulous treasures, nor that she had once known his uncle and enjoyed a similar "business relationship" with the Johnson patriarch more than three decades in the past.

I remember the week my old friend M-2347 came through town. I put him up next to one of the CO2 canisters in my vending machine where we had a great time catching up on "news of the heavens and the earth." As he was leaving for a nebula on the edge of the universe, he asked whether there was anything he could do to help out in the neighborhood. I mentioned the boarded up tavern down the street. "Ray's" had been closed since the late 1970's following Ray's passing and the murder of his son, Ray Junior. I wondered whether anything might be done to apprehend the murderers and bring them to earthly justice and whether circumstances might align so that Ray Senior's grandchildren could re-open the establishment as a nightclub for young people.

Funny how things came together. Jesus had been visiting a number of the local churches on his Sundays off. He'd even been invited to deliver a sermon or two. It was great practicing before a live Christian audience. He ran into one of Ray's relatives, learned of Ray's demise and the aspirations of the grandchildren to open the space as a night club for young adults. The emphasis would be on wholesome socialization and entertainment as opposed to some of the negative imagery that so dominated what the local human beings referred to as "the media." It all turned out for the best. M-2347 tracked down a few demons, twisted a few arms, and came up with the human perpetrators. An apparently miraculous visit to the top of the Oakland Bay Bridge played into their confessions, and the four hoodlums found themselves sentenced to life behind bars. Last I heard on that score, M-2347 had asked an acquaintance to drop in and see whether the quartet had ever thought about the afterlife and what they might possibly do in their remaining years of mortal existence to achieve their salvation. Jesus' lesson in hell had been instructive. If the "powers that be" had been willing to give the Prince of Air and Darkness a second chance, it was equally possible that four human beings who had accidentally taken the life of another during a bungled robbery attempt, might receive the offer of grace as well.

* * *

Once my three friends were over the initial shock of the changes that had occurred in Oakland over the past thirty-two years, they settled into a rhythm of work and positive social interaction. Life wasn't perfect for the trio of human beings, that's for sure, but thanks to our stay at the Orpheus Hotel, things got a lot better in the neighborhood. Sarah and I got some money together and Sarah talked Angela and Tiffany into dropping by the women's center at the Sunshine and we put up the money for Angela to visit a cardiologist. It saved her life. On a related front, Steve gave up drinking and started attending meetings with a local 12 step program. He was making good progress and even sponsored Marty, a local drug addict, who, last we heard, had been clean and sober for six months.

We remained in Oakland over a year. We helped Alonzo get his financial house in order and despite some tough economic times, helped him invest in solid tech stocks. His Orpheus Hotel was more or less an anchor in the neighborhood. Of course Alonzo had been a little boy when we'd first met him. His father Marcus had passed on and left the place to his youngest. The other rock on the street was Billie's Café. It was still there and along with the two churches and the Sunshine Center, remained a focus of civic life. Billie was in her seventies and her daughters and their husbands and several of her grandchildren had kept the place sailing along come what may.

Of all our friends and acquaintances from Oakland, only Billie suspected the true identity of our leader. She and Jesus had maintained a special relationship. Beyond Sarah, this woman from the 1950's may have been the only human being in the modern world with whom Jesus confided his actual identity, at least in-so-far as he had come to understand it.

During the first few months of our sojourn, I didn't get out of the workshop all that often. Every two weeks when the delivery men came to stock the soda machine and collect the earnings, I'd tidy up and take my jewelry and watches up to Sarah's third floor room. Later into my stay, I'd go out in the guise of Deborah or Demetrius, and occasionally, for fun, I'd assume the form, in general outline, of others whom I had observed from my vantage point in the foyer. I managed to go on tours of Chinatown, Alcatraz and a number of museums.

Next to my work with precious metals, clockworks and the decorative arts, I suppose my other great passion was watching old movies. Late at night, the foyer would clear-out and I'd watch the cable movie channel. Sometimes, I'd simply mainline the signal and let the human masters of the cinema carry me away inside my little metal box. Chaplin, Keaton, Eisenstein, Lang, Welles, Griffith, Hitchcock, Bergman, Ford, Wyler, Cukor, DeMille, Hawks, Lubitsch, Kurosawa, Renoir, Fellini, Capra, Wilder, Huston, Curtiz, Kubrick and a host of others along with a bunch of modern directors like Spielberg and Scorsese, Coppola, Nolan, Tarantino and the Cohen brothers held my interest night after night. Yes, it was wonderful. I also loved the old television programs that I'd watch in re-runs in the early morning hours.

It was a pretty sad night when we left town. We could have flown, but by now my friends were used to doing things pretty much 'the normal way," and so we took the Coach Starlight up through Northern California into Oregon's Willamette Valley and settled into a nice place in Northwest Portland. Sarah was pretty involved in the women's movement by now and a got a job with some political action committee that had all been set-up by her friends from back at the Sunshine Association in Oakland. Steve began undergraduate studies in pre-med at Lewis and Clark College and I opened up a boutique jewelry store in a trendy district not far from Burnside. These were perhaps the best times of my existence. I felt loved and trusted and I really believed that my transgression against Sarah had been forgiven. With the help of Sarah and Jesus and his mysterious uncle, The Holy Spirit, I think I was finally able to forgive myself as well.

Time crept on and before we knew it, the years had slipped by and Steve was preparing to graduate from college with honors. He'd been accepted at the University of Oregon Medical School in the West Hills, but he had also received letters of acceptance from medical schools around the country.

In those years Steve developed into a great thinker and engaged Jesus in all sorts of philosophical debates. Although my friends were all quite busy, and none more than Steve, they found time every two weeks to visit the big bookstore on Burnside and purchase copies of a book which we would separately read and then discuss when we next gathered together. We might have spent a great deal longer in the Northwest, but Jesus realized it was nearing the time that he would need to return to the Middle-East and 31AD to begin his ministry.

We understood that when Jesus made his return to history, he would have only three years time to complete his mission. Maybe that is why his last days with us in the River City seemed so poignant. He so loved life and realized he could remain for years, even decades, returning to the historical world, precisely 40 days after he had left. Be that as it may, his physical body was growing older. Biologically speaking, he was already 34 years old, fully four years older than common history recorded. He was on a timetable, obeying a set of guidelines he had apparently established with the Holy Spirit and of which they alone were cognizant.

We were not entirely surprised when Steve was accepted at Washington University Medical School, one of the nation's most prestigious private institutions located in a city called St. Louis, Missouri, a town he had visited on a three-week road trip east with college buddies in the summer of 2002. We sold the jewelry shop for a small fortune. Together with the proceeds of the sale and Steve's lucrative scholarships, the funding for his education was assured. We boarded the Empire Builder at the Amtrak station in downtown Portland in the afternoon, crossed the Willamette and the Columbia Rivers, and headed northeast into Washington State. I've probably mentioned before that angels need not sleep, but I was given to waking dreams. As we headed into a Spokane, Washington rail yard after midnight, I may have wandered into this half conscious condition as Demetrius, but when I regained complete awareness, I had relaxed back into my large, conical form. I was wedged tightly in the seat. My tentacles snaked out into the aisle and Steve, still asleep, had been pushed nearly out of his seat onto the floor. I slipped back into the form of Deborah just as a railroad conductor entered the car. He passed through and exited toward the rear and I looked across the aisle where Sarah sat, her legs pulled up in her seat. Beside her, Jesus had just awakened. He had snapped on a tiny overhead lamp and was reading in its warm glow.

I looked out the window at the darkened rail yard and could see the full moon in the cold, clear night sky above. I remembered a situation comedy from one of the thousands of hours I had viewed over the past several years. It came to me as I drifted away, and I could not remember the name of the program. The premise involved two brothers and a little boy of two or three. The child was barely old enough to speak although he possessed a remarkable vocabulary, something which added to the show's charm and humor. It was a vintage, black and white sit-com from the fifties. It may have started out in a closed studio, but later I think it was taped before a live-studio audience. The set was simple and spare: a modest living room, coffee table, sofa and a chair or two and a simple dining room table with chairs in the background. An open door behind the sofa led to what I supposed was the bedroom or study of the older brother. In this particular episode we never saw his face and he only communicated to the others in the room by way of his shouts from the back room.

Meanwhile, his brother, and I was never certain whether it was an older or younger brother, held forth in the main room, primarily from the sofa. He looked to be 35 years old, dressed in thread bare clothes. There was an open suitcase on one end of the coffee table. Perhaps he was down on his luck and had come to live at his brother's expense? The circumstances were never entirely clear, nor did these two brothers seem to be in agreement with one another. They spent a lot of time yelling through the doorway about their living arrangements and all manner of topics of day to day life. Apparently, the brother in the living room was there for an extended stay, sleeping on the couch and waiting to get work. Meanwhile, as a backdrop to the show and running throughout, the adorable little toddler with great wide eyes and a winning smile cavorted about the set. Running in and out of the back bedroom, jumping up over the back rest of the sofa onto the belly of his sleeping uncle (I supposed it was his uncle) and generally serving as catalyst for the eventual peace that was reestablished in the tiny home by the close of each episode.

The show had a profound influence on me. I'm not certain I understood much of it in terms I could articulate, but through the shouting and laughter I saw an image of three individuals who loved one another despite their difficulties. I leaned over in my seat and noticed that Steve and Jesus had disappeared. I got up, adjusted the blanket on Sarah and went up ahead to the observation car. It was dark as we entered Glacier National Park. Jesus and Steve were deep in conversation as I came up the narrow stairwell. They were in the domed car, talking in low whispers. I thought better than to interrupt them, went back down the stairs to the first level and returned to our car and my seat by the window.

15. St. Louis & Cape Cod

Two days later we changed trains in Chicago, Illinois and not many hours later we were in downtown St. Louis. A day later we had rented an apartment in the Central West End and Steve was off, bright and early, for an orientation session at the medical school.

"It's a pretty small place," remarked Sarah of our new living quarters.

"We won't be staying long," replied Jesus, looking out the window at a busy street filled with shops, college students and tourists. I had offered to stay in the refrigerator or the television set, but Jesus was pretty set on leaving.

"Our journey has reached its final days," he said.

"Well, that's great," said Sarah, "But in case you hadn't noticed, Steve just started medical school today."

"And he will continue his studies," replied Jesus.

That stopped Sarah. She looked at me, and even now I recall that morning, and the sudden look of desperation in her face. We headed up to the Loop, ostensibly for coffee, with me in my guise of

Demetrius. It did not take long for Sarah to raise the subject again. All I could manage in response was the shrug of my shoulders. Sarah looked back at Jesus.

"We will be continuing on without Steve," said Jesus.

"You can't be serious." Sarah exclaimed.

"It was his decision, but he and I have already agreed that it is for the best."

"The best? We're just going leave him here?"

"Not exactly. We will jump through time and return eight years in the future."

"Eight years? But he'll be…"

"Older," Jesus interrupted. "But there is another time and place we must visit before our return."

We had a little going away party that evening. It was a sad affair. Jesus explained that for us, only a day or two would pass. We would return in eight years and look for Steve beneath the St. Louis Arch, which, God willing, would still be standing as it had since the 1960's. We gathered in the downstairs vestibule of Steve's apartment overlooking a busy street corner. Sarah had tears in her eyes as she bid farewell to the companion whom she had always, as far as I could tell, held in such low esteem.

Steve's eyes were bright, and Jesus and I each gave him a hug and a pat on the back and we walked out into the evening. We stood on the corner for a while waiting for a bus. We looked up across the street and could see the light of Steve's study lamp in the garret window of his small apartment.

We took a bus into Forest Park, the site of the 1904 St. Louis World's Fair. I hiked over a knoll behind a stand of trees overlooking highway 40 and transformed into our space craft. As Sarah and Jesus came on board I thought about this place, how hundreds of years earlier the explorers, Lewis and Clark, had led an expedition of discovery up the Missouri River, across the Rocky Mountains to the Snake and the Columbia Rivers and ultimately to the Pacific Ocean. We had been less than a hundred miles from that point on the Pacific only a week earlier when our train crossed over the Columbia, the natural border between Washington and Oregon. Now, as Lewis and Clark had done in centuries past, we would return to the east, although not in this instance to nation's capital, but further north, to the state of Massachusetts.

I sailed east through the clouds over the Mississippi River. I was confident in my new found ability to travel through time without the talismans. They had served their purpose in channeling the mystery of time travel to me, enabling me to accomplish what few other beings in all creation had ever done. Now, apparently, my line to the Ophanim's power was direct. Jesus announced our destination and through a concentration of will, I listened to the coordinates and made the jump.

White mist streamed over my viewports and with the familiar BUMP we slipped, not forward, as Sarah had expected, but backward in time. I guided our craft down through the atmosphere on a Sunday morning not far from the shore of the Atlantic Ocean. I put down in the sand and Jesus and Sarah disembarked. Returning to the form of Demetrius, I joined them on a strand of pavement at the edge of the shore.

It was sunrise and through the dim, cool air we made our way inland up the street past well-manicured lawns into a residential neighborhood. The homes were occupied with sleeping citizens of 1993. Many lived on this cape of land the year round. Just at many stayed only during the summer months.

An untimely death in a particular family had cut short their stay that summer.

Lyle Benton had died suddenly of a heart attack. His body had been cremated. At the conclusion of a private service of immediate family and friends, his son, Wallace, piloted the family sailboat out into the Atlantic. The ashes were cast into the waves and the following week plans were underway to sell the Benton property. Benton's widow had been joined by her two sisters. She had purchased a condominium in the peninsula of the state of Florida, far to the south and would be moving next door to her sisters.

On this morning with the help of children and nieces and nephews and neighbors the sisters had put clothes and books and household items in the garage and outside on the driveway. This event was called a garage sale. Delores Benton certainly did not need the proceeds from a sale. She was the daughter of a wealthy family. Her husband had retired as a high-ranking naval officer and earned a fortune as a military consultant and contractor.

As much as anything, Delores thought to herself, this garage sale would put a human face on their departure from the wonderful neighborhood they had shared with friends and family each summer since shortly after her marriage to Captain Benton following World War II.

One by one these older lots bordering the Atlantic and within the Cape Cod National Seashore were being purchased by the United States Park Service. She noted the passing of time that morning.

Cars were already lined up on the street as we approached the house and there was a great deal of foot traffic, children and young couples and other, older residents who had learned of Captain Benton's passing.

Sarah walked slowly, her eyes wide. We stood on the corner adjacent to the two-story bungalow with the wide sloping lawn and the long driveway dotted with furniture and items which Sarah instantly recalled from her past. She grabbed Jesus by the arm for support.

"Let's go," said Jesus.

Reluctantly, she followed along at his side as they crossed the street. I remained on the corner, the sun coming up on my back from the ocean. I dialed in my acute vision and watched from a distance as my companions walked up the driveway.

"The rocking horse," I heard Sarah exclaim. In the next instant she had taken a step forward and reached into a wooden box and retrieved a china bowl.

"What is it?" asked Jesus.

"My cereal bowl," she replied. "I used to eat my oatmeal from this bowl."

She went from box to box, looking at the items and Jesus followed.

"What are we doing here?" she asked finally looking up from a dog-eared box of old toys.

"This was an important day," he said, "Do you remember?"

"Important?"

"Look," replied Jesus and he nodded up the drive in the direction of the house.

A young man had come out of the house from the front door. Carrying a cardboard box, he marched across the covered porch. He was followed by a six-year-old girl with short sandy hair. Even from this distance where I stood across the street, I could see that the face was red and the eyes still wet from tearing. Almost without thinking my senses had scanned her DNA and I realized from her genetic make-up that it was Sarah. DNA markers of the male humanoid indicated his paternity.

They descended the porch steps heedless of the relatives and guests and early morning garage sale goers and marched along the path in front of the house to the driveway. The girl's arms were out-stretched. She was trying to retrieve something from the box. The man angrily increased his stride. Meanwhile, a young woman appeared on the porch. She was dressed in jeans and a summer blouse and deck shoes. She was about to call out, stopped, and came quickly down the steps.

The man with box and the little girl passed Sarah and Jesus on the driveway. Sarah followed after the man and the girl. The little girl had a hand on the rim of the box and the man wheeled on her and shoved her back. She fell backwards off the driveway onto the lawn. Off balance, the man lurched to his side and the contents of the box spilled out. Old magazines and comic books fanned out on the hot asphalt drive. The man set down the box and scooped handfuls of the periodicals back into the container. The little girl climbed to her feet and raced back to the box where it sat on the curb. The woman from the house was already there looking down at the man.

"You're behaving like a selfish bully," she said. The man stood up and seemed startled by her sudden appearance as she continued, "Those old funny books mean a lot to her."

"Don't let him sell my comic books," cried the little girl.

"They're not yours!" snarled the man.

The woman saw an opening and leaned down to retrieve the frayed box.

"Get your hands off those, Lydia!" shouted the man.

When she made no motion to heed his command, he reached out and shoved her in the shoulder. She toppled back onto the drive.

Some of the early morning shoppers cast glances in the direction of the domestic scene. Sarah was less than ten feet behind these phantoms from her past and she froze in her tracks as she watched the little girl rush toward the box. Sarah Benton's father had turned his attention toward his wife. He extended his hand toward her, but she only glared at him. She did not break her gaze as she scooted back to her feet.

Six year old Sarah had retrieved a precious item from the box. It was a comic book. Even from across the street I could see the cover. It depicted a red and white rocket ship sailing up through the black reaches of space.

Sensory memory flooded the consciousness of the grown Sarah and her own hand reflexively reached toward the tattered magazine. Read over and over by her father and grandfather, the leaves of that serial pamphlet had been part of her childhood as well. During those few carefree summers the six-year-old self had first learned to create meaning from a printed page. Beyond words, they told of once happy days at her grandparents'.

A hand reached down from above, the fingers curved over a corner of the magazine and the man pulled. Little Sarah did not relinquish her grasp and for an instant she was lifted off the ground until a seam in the strands of lignin and cellulose grew taut and tore apart.

The prolonged ripping of the cover wrap and its pages sounded up and down the driveway. The magazine had been torn in half.

* * *

Delores Benton looked up from a cigar box of change and dollar bills. She set down her morning tea, apologized to her sisters and headed out of the open garage and down the drive.

Meanwhile her six year old grand-daughter looked in horror at the remains of the prized comic book in her hands. She looked at her father. For a moment he was just as surprised as she.

"Look what you've done, Daddy!" moaned the girl.

For an instant he thought to drop down and hold her in his arms and beg her forgiveness, but the sense of his wife standing at his side, about to speak, prompted another thought. He grabbed the portion of torn comic from his daughter's hand, placed his own half over it and with a grimace of rage, pulled the pages in opposite directions.

"Well, how's this?" he shouted. The magazine was fully torn into quarters. Shards of pulp fluttered from his hands. He threw the ruined fragments into the box, reached down and wedged the box under his arm.

Little Sarah was sobbing and her mother put a hand on her shoulder, but the little girl shrugged her off.

Delores Benton had nearly reached the scene but had first to navigate around our own, bewildered, Sarah of the future.

"Excuse me," said Delores Benton to the tall blond-haired female standing in the middle of the drive.

The older woman continued to the street where she called sharply to her son.

"You leave those funny books right where they are!" she ordered, but her son was on the move. He had reached his convertible parked across the street only fifteen feet from where I stood. He looked up at me for a second, and our gaze met. The sorrow was clear in his expression, but then the face quickly rearranged itself.

"Morning," he said and threw the box into the open back-seat and jumped into the driver's side without opening the door. He smiled broadly as he turned on the ignition and the combustion engine roared to life. Beyond the smile I could detect the fear and sadness in his eyes as his little daughter ran into the street, shouting for him to return.

The car pulled away from the curb and sped off. The girl collapsed on the sidewalk and gave herself up to great sobs of despair. A fragment of the ruined comic book cover depicting the red and white bow of the space ship fluttered down to the shoulder of the road. I picked up the scrap and knelt beside the child.

"Don't cry, little girl," I said.

Across the street the girl's mother and grandmother had come together and they walked side by side into the street to retrieve the Sarah of 1993. Meanwhile, our Sarah stood frozen in the drive, her arms locked across her chest. As though standing in a hall of mirrors she slipped intermittently from the reality of the moment into a vivid and disturbing memory and back. Seven years later, a weekend that young Sarah would spend with her father in New York City, would not ease the pain of this event. Jesus came alongside and she looked ruefully at her companion.

"Why did you bring me here?" she asked.

"I want you to leave this behind."

"I'll never forget."

Jesus gently put his hand on her shoulder, "Not the memory, but the anger in your heart."

She knew what he meant.

The elder Mrs. Benton and her daughter-in-law nodded to me politely and took charge of the sobbing six-year-old. I caught snatches of conversation from neighbors and passersby as the three generations of Benton women walked slowly back up the drive and disappeared into the house through the garage.

Tears were streaming down Sarah's cheeks as she watched her little childhood self walk slowly past. And now Sarah collapsed against Jesus' shoulders. I wished with all my might there was something I could do to ease her suffering. I looked up toward the east where the sun was now well into the sky and I asked the Holy Spirit to help soften her heart and bring her some peace.

One of Delores Benton's older sisters had come down the driveway with a cup of tea.

"Are you all right, darling?" she asked.

"I'm sorry," said Sarah and she looked into the kind eyes of her great aunt Millicent.

"Here," said the middle aged woman. "It's Earl Gray tea. Go on, child," she said as Sarah took the cup and the woman looked at Jesus. "The little girl has lost her grandfather, my brother-in-law, Lyle," she said as though she had known Jesus her entire life. "Her parents are divorcing and her father, the young man that just drove off like a damned fool is moving to the West Coast."

"I'm sorry to hear that," Jesus replied.

"Are you new to the Cape?" she asked.

"No, we're just passing through," he said.

"Well, a lot of memories here on the drive today," she continued, looking back in the direction of the house, "But time marches on…"

She looked at our Sarah as though she was suddenly struck by something.

"Do I know you?" she asked.

"Me?" replied Sarah.

"You remind me of someone, my baby sister, Delores when she was a young woman."

Sarah smiled faintly.

"Maybe our little neighborhood drama reminded you of some sadness in your life?" asked the great aunt, tenderly.

Sarah nodded, "Yes," she replied with a smile, "But I think it's better now."

In the next instant the spry old woman turned to Jesus, "And you… There's something familiar about you now that I think of it."

"Really?" said Jesus.

"Have you and I met before?"

"I don't know. Perhaps our paths will cross one day in the future."

"Yes," said the woman, "But make it soon," she laughed and started back up the drive. "There aren't too terribly many miles left in these old legs. Thank heaven for sweat pants!"

I had finally decided to cross the street. I came up upon Jesus and Sarah as they stood off to one corner of the busy drive looking back at the Cape Cod vacation home.

More and more cars were arriving. Neighbors and curiosity seekers poked through the old boxes and inspected the clothes hanging on chrome garment racks. The great crowd of human beings examined the treasures of a lifetime, each with a hand lettered price-sticker among the mahogany, teak, cherry and oak tables lining the drive.

Some of these human beings were bargain hunters, but as the morning wore on, some families dressed in their formal garments and on route to morning worship services stopped by out of courtesy. Word of Captain Benton's death had spread throughout the community and many came to note the passing of a generation.

"I see now, why you brought me here," said Sarah to Jesus. She took one last look at the sights. For the first time she seemed to notice the incessant sound of the surf coming in from the Atlantic.

"I need to let go of my anger. I need to…" she hesitated and looked up at the house, where six year old Sarah had emerged from the front door. The porch was empty and the youngster stood in one corner looking over the encircling hand rail. From that promontory she surveyed the busy scene, all the way out to the ocean. At one point, her gaze rested on our odd trio where we stood looking back at her from the street.

Despite the distance of some fifty yards, Sarah and her childhood self were looking at one another, "Forgive them... Forgive them... Forgive mother and father..." our Sarah murmured, and it seemed she was reaching out across the long, wide lawn and addressing her childhood self.

Sarah looked at Jesus, and no sooner had they exchanged a glance, than Sarah's young mother appeared on the porch. She approached the little girl and placed a hand on the tiny shoulders. They stood there watching the three strangers walk slowly away down the street toward the shore.

* * *

A young couple with a small child was out on the beach near the surf. The man was helping the child fly a dragon tail kite. A light offshore breeze held the brilliantly colored plastic shield and its thirty foot tail a hundred feet in the blue morning air above the ocean.

Other than the young family, the beach was deserted. We walked north over a brush-covered dune and I changed from that lean amalgam of young men from the Fifth Century BC into the sleek, humming product of other worldly materials. My ship was a pastiche of advanced human science, the mysterious technology of the Creator's First Sphere and a morphology inspired by the pulp illustrations and comic book covers of the Mid-Twentieth Century.

I stood on my chrome runners and felt the salt-scented breeze bathe my cherry-red hull. Sunlight glinted off my snow white hardtop roof and my viewports reflected the image of the writhing filament of extruded plastic, darting two and fro like a spermatozoa attempting to penetrate the orb of the enormous yellow sun.

Sarah and Jesus had come up the spiral stairs and moved up to the cockpit on the flight deck. I sensed the click of their flight restraints. I retracted the stairs, sealed the hatch and slowly rose into the sky. We were invisible now to all human detection and for a moment I hung in space at the level of the airborne kite.

"What's up?" I heard Jesus say.

"Oh, I was just noticing the kite," I replied over my internal loudspeakers.

"Yes…" he replied, expectantly.

I looked down the slender line of white nylon cable, taut and slanted down to the three remote figures standing on the edge of the surf below.

"Three," I said without really knowing why.

"Three what?" asked Sarah.

"Humanoids below on the shore," I replied.

"Yes, we saw them, M-2500. They're kite flying," said Sarah.

"Have they been saved, Jesus?" I asked.

"Saved? Well, I…" he hesitated. "I can't really tell."

"You really ought to save them," I said.

"It is my wish…"

"Can we get going?" asked Sarah.

"Might we pray for them?" I asked and slowly leaned to starboard and nosed steeply down so that my passengers might clearly see the three, frail beings at the water's edge.

"What are you doing, Deborah?" asked Sarah sharply.

"I thought it might help to see them."

"We see them," said Jesus in the voice I recognized with its near superhuman patience.

"What's the problem?" asked Sarah.

"The sun will not last forever," I said. "It will expire. In the life of an angel, I can already see it turning, like the leaf in autumn. They will have no home. Life on this world, the world I helped bring into being will come to its end." As I spoke, from somewhere in my heart I was suddenly overcome with an immense sorrow and a black abyss of grief seemed to open like a cleft in the bright air.

Later, Jesus and Sarah recounted that the ship began to wobble, violently. In the cockpit, the walls of the cabin began to soften, their hard contours slowly melting. I was losing control of the ship's integration, that complex yet unified image I had first glimpsed in the revelation from Ophanim conveyed to me through the ringed talisman. From the rim of a deep well I heard voices shouting to me, but my grief was so intense that I could not concentrate. I saw in the real world of that moment only the image painted on the air foil of the darting dragon kite. It was the black emblem I had seen before. I remembered the stone monstrosities in the temple of the evil Prince in the Himalayas. How close I had come to catastrophe that morning, I may never know, but it was the voice of the man praying for the intervention of beings far more powerful than me which finally interceded and brought me to my senses.

From that day forward the young couple from the Midwest would tell the story of the UFO they spotted one Sunday morning while kite flying on vacation off Cape Cod. The alien craft, red and white and glinting silver in the noon air had appeared out of nowhere above their heads and slightly off the shore. The craft lurched from side to side. Then, as the vehicle plummeted toward the ocean, church bells rang from several bell towers on the Cape summoning people to church, and, in the next instant, just as it was about to crash into the ocean, the alien ship vanished in mid air.

16. Christian Rock

"Satan has all sort of tricks up his sleeve," said Jesus as I regained control of my senses and moved slowly West through the vault of space over Cape Cod Bay.

"He dogs us at every turn," Jesus continued, "Nor will he and his minions relent until his defeat in the final battle in the Ultimate Universe."

"Well, on a brighter note," said Sarah, "I think you should both look down at the shoreline. That's Plymouth Rock."

"Plymouth?" I said, and I think the sound of Deborah's voice sounding over my cockpit loud-speakers brought smiles to the lips of my human friends.

"Yes, Debbie," continued Sarah, "It's where the Pilgrims landed way back before the United States became a nation."

As we headed southwest, she provided another of her welcome history lessons, this on the story of the Puritans who had set sail from Europe to escape religious persecution. As cynically as the day we met, she added how the Pilgrims went on to persecute many of the native inhabitants in the New World. Mention of this fact led to an interesting conversation on witchcraft and the so-called dark-arts, but we were getting close to the Mississippi River and it was time to make the jump forward in time.

I cleared my thoughts and leaned into the power of the Inner Sphere. We felt the familiar BUMP as we leapt forward from 1993 exactly nineteen years into the future. Cloaked in the mantle of invisibility we sailed down from thirty thousand feet to a vacant industrial lot north of the St. Louis Arch. With my passengers off-loaded, and having transformed back into Debbie, I followed Jesus and Sarah as we walked quickly south along the Mississippi shore line. We crossed beneath the Eads Bridge and came up into an old portion of the city where streets were still paved in cobble stones. Sarah twisted her ankle and it brought out progress to a halt. Jesus and I stood with her between us. She put an arm over each of our shoulders and we slowly made our way onto the grounds of the Jefferson National Expansion Memorial.

Amidst crumbling infrastructure and urban decay, the St. Louis Arch remained an object of beauty. It shone as a testament to what the human community might do when it came together to achieve something worthy of its combined intellect and ingenuity.

A lone figure stood dead center between the two stainless steel legs of the monument, 630 feet below its apex. I could feel Sarah's pulse increase as she caught sight of him. Both Jesus and I were amazed as she broke free and limped ahead on her own power. She made it twenty three feet before she collapsed. At just about the same instant, the figure beneath the arch was on the move in our direction.

If that was who we thought it was, we were looking at a specimen transformed. It was Steve, but he was scarcely recognizable. He had lost seventy pounds and much of what remained had been replaced with lean muscle tissue. He was not an unattractive young man. He had shaven his customary beard and his eyes were clear and piercing as he knelt down beside Sarah.

"Are you all right?" he asked.

"Steve? Steve, is it really you?

"Of course it's me. Did you hurt your ankle?"

"Oh, it's nothing."

"Do you mind if I look?"

Apparently, eight years of medical study had been useful. Steve looked up at me.

"Good to see you, Debbie," he said.

"Hello, Steve," said Jesus, cheerfully. The smile on Jesus' face lifted all our spirits.

"Debbie, would you lower the temperature in your hand to forty-five degrees?" Steve asked. "Place your palm here on Sarah's ankle."

We spent the next half an hour sitting with Sarah out on the lawn beneath the St. Louis Arch learning about Steve's eight years in the city. He was a medical doctor, a pediatrician working at a children's hospital. Later that afternoon we took a light-rail train to his small apartment in the Central West End.

That night we had dinner at a local restaurant and celebrated Steve's many successes. He had bandaged Sarah's ankle and she was getting around well enough.

When it came to our day trip to Cape Cod, Sarah spoke frankly and calmly about what she had experienced as a child, the years of betrayal, both real and imagined, and an upbringing that had so hardened her heart to the possibility of anything that Jesus hoped to offer. Now, for the first time, there seemed to be a glimmer of possibility. As for Steve's incredible transformation, he credited it all to his faith in the Creator. While Sarah's world view still seemed a step or two removed from an understanding of Jesus' message or Steve's salvation, she was much closer to the so-called "spirit world" than she had been when we first met at the dawn of life on earth. We were all still learning.

Late that night we returned to Steve's apartment. Steve gave his modest bedroom to Sarah. He and Jesus slept in the front room. Neither had been willing to sleep on the comfortable sofa, although Steve had immediately offered it to his childhood friend. In the end, they both slept on the hardwood floor. As for me, I sat down beside Steve's trusty ten-speed bicycle parked in the small vestibule by the door. We had come a long way.

The next morning we strolled up to Lindell Boulevard and visited the Cathedral Basilica. This magnificent edifice had been built by the Universal Catholic Church, an organization that traced its lineage all the way back to some of the followers we had met on Mt. Olive at the time of our adventure in old Jerusalem. As with everything else in the modern world, Sarah knew something about the Catholic Church and she asked Steve whether he had converted.

"To what?" Steve whispered as we made our way into the enormous building.

"Are you a Catholic?"

"Oh, I'm not part of any organized group."

"Then why do you come here?"

"To pray, to thank God for his blessings and to leave a tithe in the box out front."

"You do all that and you're not even a member of the Church?"

"That's why I come on Mondays, I suppose."

That afternoon, Sarah's ankle had recovered well enough so that she was able to pedal a bike. She followed Steve up the street from his place to Forest Park to accompany him on his daily five-mile run. Meanwhile, Jesus and I had been messing around with Steve's computer notebook and discovered another church organization located west of Highway 270 in a sector of the environs known as St. Louis County.

We spent that week touring all the local sites as best we could with public transportation. Of course this particular city had gradually abandoned the notion of extensive, publically funded mass transit in favor of the modern automobile. Still, there were some buses and we found ourselves standing on street corners waiting for them. We visited Grant's Farm, the City Museum, the St. Louis Zoo, and the St. Louis Science Center. By contrast, we managed to get across the river to Illinois and visit the ancient Cahokia Mounds. We got off a bus at Black Lane and Fairmont Avenue in Illinois and walked approximately one mile west on Collinsville Road to the ancient site. As far as we could see, it was well worth the trip. Jesus seemed particularly moved by the notion that a great civilization of Native Americans had once flourished here. On one of the plaques we read that in 1250 AD the city of the Mississippians had rivaled the size of London, England. Of course, scarcely anything remained of the ancient American metropolis, and as we went about the place, we trod the grounds with a certain reverence and awe.

The following weekend we forsook public transportation entirely. We hiked up to Forest Park and I transformed into our trusty ship. We sailed west over the city and landed on the southern rim of a rock quarry a half mile south of Interstate 70. We walked out onto an enormous asphalt-covered parking lot in front of a sprawling complex of steel and glass. We were walking into what was termed a "Saturday Service." Many of the people were wearing jeans and tennis shoes. Others were dressed in a fashion Sarah termed "business casual."

"It reminds me of a concourse at an airport," said Sarah, "Or maybe a shopping mall."

After years in the modern United States we were all familiar with the terms and we had to agree.

"What's that sound?" asked Jesus as we strolled along a huge glass covered promenade that connected the various building. We passed a youth center, a book store and entered an enormous, multi-leveled atrium into what looked like a food court.

"Music," said Sarah.

"Yes," said Jesus, "But..."

"It's what they call Christian Rock."

It was a modern synthesis of several styles of music, an amalgam of what music historians called rock and roll, gospel and country western music. As we walked into a huge, darkened auditorium, our attention was taken by an enormous stage. A choir dressed in their so-called street clothes stood on upstage risers backing a seven-piece rock and roll band. A young man held center stage with a country folk guitar and a headset and the imagery of the presentation was augmented and reinforced by three enormous video screens, set far upstage left, right, and center of the proscenium arch. A man with a roving camera wove in and out of the onstage action and his footage was intercut artfully on the enormous screens in real time by a videographer working an electronic console in a booth at the back of the house.

Laser lights and other colored stage lights pulsated and wheeled and punctuated the deep rhythm of the electric bass and drums. The church goers were on their feet singing with the musicians. The song lyrics scrolled over the flashing imagery on the jumbo screens. Many people held their hands out-stretched over head to signify agreement or, at least, to indicate to their fellows that they believed in the words they were singing.

The four of us walked into a pew near the rear of the lively hall and stood, listening politely. Following another song, a young man came out on stage as the choir and musicians retired to the wings. He asked that the people in the hall make a contribution and soon a fleet of attendants were distributing what looked like empty popcorn buckets up and down the rows in what seemed to be a customary and well rehearsed portion of the service involving audience participation.

Steve had been earning a spectacular income. Due to his Spartan lifestyle he had virtually no expenses and he pulled from the back pocket of his jeans a tattered leather wallet and wrote out a check for three-hundred dollars and signed his name and deposited the check in the bucket as it was handed to him across the aisle by an attendant. Steve then passed the bucket along and it went from Jesus to Sarah and then to me. I looked inside.

"Pass it along," whispered Sarah.

A young woman about Sarah's age was already on her feet and from the opposite side of the pew she reached with her hand outstretched. I handed her the bucket and resumed my seat.

"Is that the tithing?" I asked.

"Yes, it's a contribution to support all this," said Sarah.

"Is that good?" I asked.

"That's the idea," she replied.

Next, an affable and apparently genuine man appeared on the stage. This was a moment that many had come to see. This middle-aged man was the senior pastor. It was primarily through his effort and the work of a small circle of friends from his youth, that this gigantic organization of some twenty thousand souls and this enormous, sprawling complex of community activity had come into existence.

The man welcomed his church members and extended a special welcome to visitors. He also warmly welcomed an apparently anonymous class of the audience he referred to as "seekers." I glanced past Sarah at the dimly outlined silhouette of Jesus. Not since his audience with the philosophers and religious founders of old had I seen him listen more attentively. From time to time in his sermon, the pastor quoted from scripture and I could see the lips of Jesus move, almost imperceptibly, anticipating ever syllable as the pastor's voice resonated through the auditorium's electronic audio speakers.

The man on stage was using his address to appeal to those in the audience to pledge their lives to the risen Jesus, to renew their pledge or at least consider the possibility of such an act. I had read similar messages in the book from the nightstand at the Orpheus Hotel in Oakland. Apparently the message had not changed in forty four years.

This "Saturday service" in the late afternoon was typically only lightly attended in comparison to those held the following day. In a room designed to comfortably accommodate two thousand audience members, there were presently only five hundred and fifty, not counting those involved with the production.

I recalled my first encounter with Jesus, Sarah and Steve in the subterranean workshop and how we angels had been so concerned by the "flaw" that we had detected in Sarah and Steve's inner being. It was their mortality that had so disturbed us, and the mortality we had sensed in Jesus himself. At the same time, we had discovered in our cursory analysis of Jesus that he possessed within his person something altogether new and unexpected.

The spirit of the "Entity," the renegade uncle with the curious living arrangement, this Holy Spirit registered powerfully in Jesus. If The Entity had made inroads with Sarah during the course of our years together I could barely detect it. Some time before our return to St. Louis, the freeloading uncle had become acquainted with Steve, was, indeed, virtually at home. I scanned the crowd, one by, and as easily as I might have acquired a blueprint of their DNA and created their soul-less clones in a tank at the old workshop beneath the earth, I checked for signs of the living spirit. I was particularly interested in those who had been the most demonstrative during the musical interlude. I found that in the majority of these, the "life-force" of the spirit was, indeed, active. Of course, the signature of the Entity was weak in many, and, curiously, in several of the human beings who had made the greatest outward show of their supposed faith, there was virtually no trace of the Spirit at all.

Many, many more, in the audience, by far the vast majority, I scanned, showered my senses with the power that would one day carry their souls and their identities as distinct persons into another life, an existence in another realm beyond that of this quickly fading world.

I looked up at the pastor. He called for us to pray and he asked for those who did not yet know Jesus to look inward and ask for revelation.

"He who seeks shall find…" the man reminded his congregation and the words rung in my ears and my human mouth turned upward at its corners in a smile.

The pastor soon dismissed the assembly to the welcome center or the prayer team or the heated baptismal font or to pick-up little ones at the children's ministry. The pastor had talked for less than an hour. I had expected perhaps a longer sermon. The assembly applauded. Politely, we stood and joined in the clapping. As the clapping continued, I was struck by the percussive claps coming from the end of the aisle. Jesus and Steve seemed jubilant, smiling and nodding to one another. Jesus raised a hand over head, and Steve was cheering.

"What is that all that shouting about?" asked Sarah as the house lights came up and we filed into the aisles, out of the auditorium and onto the concourse.

"He did a great job, don't you think?" said Steve.

"Well, you seem mighty impressed," replied Sarah.

"I am. I mean I wasn't expecting that much from what little I've seen of these modern day churches on television, but this place is doing a great job!"

Sarah was looking at Jesus as we threaded our way through the crowded atrium. Small groups of church goers were gathering for coffee or a light, evening meal. We could hear the lilting voices of children and I watched Sarah's eyes fasten on Jesus as we continued through the atrium back to the promenade.

"I think there is hope here in this place," he said, and he cleared his throat, "But we must be on our way."

We were quite prepared to be our way, whatever that might mean, but as we were about to leave through a set of double doors along the promenade back outside to the parking lot, some excited sounds from the end of the concourse caught Jesus' attention.

"One more thing," he said.

Sarah rolled her eyes as Steve broke ranks with Jesus and they headed to the end of the hall where perhaps forty or fifty people had gathered beside a pool of water. It was a baptismal font built into the wall. It was raised four feet above the surface of the floor and adorned with a mosaic of quarter-sized, cobalt and sky-blue tiles. Several people had come forward from dressing rooms. They wore simple, blue jumpsuits supplied by the church for the purpose of a public baptism. There were friends and several church members who helped conduct this ritual at the conclusion of the service and the hall was filled with bright-eyed friends and family members. A young woman in a jumpsuit was being guided up a portable stairway at one end of the pool and her older brother was helping her down the other side via submerged steps into the pool. Sarah and I caught up with Jesus and Steve and owing to our height, we could see over the heads of the spectators who had stopped to watch or lend their support to the proceedings. I noticed along the wall of the promenade two sets of stairs, one rising to the right and the other, to the left, both leading up to a second, open level of the promenade above. Leaning against the sturdy metal handrail some of the gathering crowd had ascended these stairways to gain a better view. I looked up at the smiling faces of twenty or thirty others who had gathered along the rail on the upper level to watch the ceremonies.

"Does this remind you of anything, Steve?" I heard Jesus whisper to his friend.

Steve was about to answer, when a dark thought clouded his expression. He doubled over as though dealt a blow and Jesus reached down and took him by the shoulder.

"What's wrong?" whispered Jesus urgently but in so doing he did his best not to draw the attention of the surrounding crowd.

Sarah and I had already closed ranks as Steve looked up at Jesus. Steve had a wild look in his eyes, "My hand!" he gasped. He seemed to battle an unseen force as he struggled to remain on his feet. It was the black tattoo. Indeed, as we were to learn, not long after we had left him in the past and he had started medical school, Steve had elected to have the skin on the back of his hand "cut down to the bone and destroyed." Some skin from his side was grafted in place to cover all trace of the evil brand he had once demanded from the Lord of the Flies.

"Your hand…" whispered Jesus, leaning-in close. We all huddled about him. "Where is the source of the pain?" Jesus asked. A few of the human beings glanced at us with expressions of disapproval and annoyance. They looked back at the festive scene as the first baptism reached its climax.

Jesus and I followed Steve's gaze as he scanned the crowd to the font and now up the twin staircases. Steve was looking at the faces of those who peered happily over the railing from the upper promenade. Beads of perspiration streamed in rivulets from his brow as he searched. Meanwhile, he squeezed the back of his right hand with his left, fighting a miasma of pain slowly dragging him down toward unconsciousness.

"There," he whispered and nodded upward.

My senses went out and I searched with Jesus. There was a retired couple, a divorcee, a sister, a baby, three brothers, a widow, more and more people and then, my scanning stopped. I fixed my gaze on a tall figure back behind the second row of onlookers. There was a smile on the face of this young man, but there was no human joy in the smile, nor could there have been. The being's gaze met mine and the creature seemed suddenly to shiver in its place as though startled, much the way a predator, stalking its prey and having been discovered in hiding, breaks off its attack. The figure was on the move.

I pushed back through the crowd. Jesus was behind me and I grabbed the hand railing and started up the stairs. I head the footfall of Jesus on the steps behind me. I glanced down below and saw that Steve had recovered and was walking quickly with Sarah through the crowd to the stairway.

It was crowded on the promenade's upper level. Over the heads of the spectators I could see the head of the demon moving to the end of the walkway and toward a set of doors. The doors opened and closed. I made it through the crowd and pushed open the doors and I heard the echo of footfall receding down a long hallway. I was in pursuit and now I could hear the voices of Jesus, Sarah and Steve behind me. I was running faster than any human being could have ever run. Through the huge plate glass windows to my right I could see cars departing from the parking-lot and the faithful making their way back to the routine of their lives and for an instant I caught sight of my own reflection in the glass.

Jesus, Steve, Sarah and I were united once again. We were chasing a demon and just beginning an adventure that would take us from this house of worship far from this time and dimension. I ended up on the parking-lot in back. The creature had picked up speed, heedless of the departing human beings, pushing them aside. I was slowed considerably in my pursuit as I threaded my way through the crowds and the slowly moving motor vehicles. There! The demon disappeared over the brink of an embankment. When I finally made it to the top, I stopped in my tracks and looked down a hundred feet into the open pit of an abandoned rock quarry.

Far below, a dark form moved among the shadows. I threw myself forward and landed on angel wings twenty feet behind the being. I glided down between boulders toward a dark crevice in the wall of the quarry. The demon-man, for it resembled a man, seemed to trip and fall forward. It had been holding something, a brief case, but it had dropped it. Swooping forward on my wings, I nearly closed the distance between us. It looked once more over its shoulder, scooped something up from the ground, picked up the case and threw itself headlong into a cleft in the wall. I was following, when a tremor suddenly shook the floor of the quarry. I heard the sound of shattering rock and threw myself back away from the cliff wall as fifty ton boulders and slabs of limestone cascaded down, sealing off the entrance to the passageway.

I dropped back, defeated. There was no longer any trace of the evil spirit. I walked forward and I noticed something on the ground. Glittering in the growing starlight were dozens of dark shards of glass. They resembled the type of glass a human being might use in a pair of spectacles. Leading in a trail to the debris pile where the demon had disappeared into the earth, were twisted wire frames and several smashed pairs of dark glasses. Was it a coincidence that I should find these strewn on the quarry floor? Here and there were spent soda cans, an old tire and panels of rusted metal. I turned and flew up to the top of the cliff and withdrew my angle wings into my shoulders. I walked toward the church and met Jesus, Sarah and Steve in the parking-lot. The evil presence that we had driven from the house of worship remained a mystery to us as we went off into a field and I transformed into our spacecraft.

We flew back to Forest Park and a day later, Steve wrapped things up with his life in the city. One final time we boarded public transportation and made our way to the park. I turned into the red and white craft on the chrome runners and we left the earth and the 21st Century behind.

* * *

And that was pretty much it for our tour of earth history. It was still relatively new to Jesus and me; still, not even what Sarah had learned at MIT and two years of graduate work at Harvard, nor what Steve had acquired in a decade of medical school and residency could have prepared us for our upcoming confrontation with the evil archangels and our meeting with the Black and White Trinity on the Creator's home world at the center of the Ultimate Universe. There would be plenty more temptations, trials and tribulations in the weeks ahead, but through it all Jesus held up great, certainly when considering the fact that he was, at least for his remaining time in the wilderness, merely a human being. He even embarked on another forty-day fast just so things would wind up at the end of his stay in the wilderness (more or less) as they were reported in the gospel.

So, that was it. I'd navigated in from the future with a super big BUMP and was gliding in from the West over the wine-dark Mediterranean. We sailed along the north coast of Africa and I switched on stealth mode so as not to frighten the Egyptians.

It was a sad time for Sarah and Steve and for me too. Sarah gave Jesus a big hug and he kissed her on the forehead, and said he'd always be with her, and of course she tried to be brave, but I think that made the tears come down her cheeks all the more. I might have cried at that moment, but I felt on a surer footing than I had in a long time, and I had cause to hope.

Steve was over at the dining room table in the galley and he put out his hand to shake the hand of Jesus in farewell and he half stood and Jesus reached down and gave him a big hug and for a second Steve felt consoled, like everything was going to be okay, but when he opened his eyes and looked ahead he could see where, of necessity, I had swirled open the hatch in the bottom of the ship. The sight of that spiral staircase leading back down to his everyday life in the regular world, well, I take no pleasure in reporting that despite his new found faith, Steve really broke down.

Sarah came over and put her arm around him and they stood there in the dim blue light on the rubbery floor-mat of my galley and watched as Jesus came back out of the living quarters dressed again in a white robe with a blue sash, like the one he'd worn on the day he and Steve had first left Nazareth with Satan at the wheel of a Twentieth Century motor home.

Jesus stood, hanging onto the rail of the staircase, first with one hand, and then with the other, pulling on his sandals. For the strongest, most righteous and merciful man that had ever lived, he looked in pretty poor shape. Forty days without food in the wilderness will do that to a human being. His friends waved him goodbye. He nodded and smiled and turned to the stairway leading back to the earth.

After he got out he must have stumbled on the last rung, having not been used to ambulating in sandals for so long, and he tumbled out of the ship and fell down into the dust. Sarah and Steve started for the stairwell, but under orders that Jesus had given me, I had already retracted the steps and sealed the hatch.

His human friends ran to my galley observation portals where they waved their arms and tried to be of help, if only to encourage him, but, of course, we were invisible.

Jesus spit sand from his mouth and pulled a tangled strand of hair from his lips. Slowly, carefully, he crawled to his feet and stood, holding the small of his back with one hand and shielding his brow against the glare of the afternoon sun with the other. A hot wind was blowing from the west and Jesus squinted and strained his eyes. Through shimmering heat, he saw blue flecks on the horizon and recognized this was no mirage but the shoreline of Galilee. He saw the white sails of fishing vessels and the figures of three men going down to the sea with their nets. Jesus looked up into the sky, and then lowered his gaze, fixing his attention on the men.

He drew a deep breath and walked out of the wilderness to meet them.

Read about Jesus, M-2500, Sarah, and Steve in the wilderness in Part One of the Jesus in Space Trilogy: Jesus in Space: *a Christian Space Opera*. And be sure to catch the exciting conclusion to the trilogy in Part Three: Jesus in Space: *Battle in the Ultimate Universe*, coming soon to a book store near you.

Visit *Jesusinspace.com* today!

www.ingramcontent.com/pod-product-compliance
Lightning Source LLC
LaVergne TN
LVHW050928080826
845145LV00001B/248

* 9 7 8 0 9 8 5 1 1 9 1 6 4 *